Agency and Consequences

Agency and Consequences

A Novel

By

G. Kenneth Cardwell

© G. Kenneth Cardwell 2013, St. Peters, MO

All rights reserved. No part of this book may be reproduced in any form or by any means without permission in writing from the author, Gaylen Kenneth Cardwell, 41 Roland Lane, St. Peters, MO 63376. This work is not an official publication of The Church of Jesus Christ of Latter-day Saints. The views expressed herein are the responsibility of the author and do not necessarily represent the position of the Church.

ISBN-13: 978-1492331865

Dedication

Dedicated to my Beloved
Elizabeth who has taught me so
much of life, patience, love,
forgiveness and charity; and to
our children, Byron, Ivan,
Joseph and Mary, because of
whom has come so much of the
inspiration—even the necessity—
to learn and teach the principles
within these pages.

G. Kenneth Cardwell

Table of Contents

Preface		*v*
Part One: The Man and the Hole		**1**
1.	The Man and The Woman	3
2.	Drunk and Disorderly	6
3.	The Hole	7
4.	Subconscious Memories	9
5.	Secret Life	13
6.	Last Dinner Together	15
7.	Release and Good Bye	19
8.	Questions	22
9.	Light	24
10.	The Search	26
11.	Resolve	27
12.	Judgment and Mercy	29
Part Two: The Strange Treasure		**31**
13.	Rescued	33
14.	George and Sarah	37
15.	Hospital Room	40
16.	A Long Day Ends	42
17.	The Hole's Strange Secrets	44
18.	Picnic	48
19.	No Secrets and Engagement	52
20.	Repentance Begins	60
21.	Starting Life Together	62
22.	Honeymoon	68
23.	Paul's Confession	74
24.	Ruse and Arrest	81
25.	Restitution	86
26.	Doubles	87
27.	Wonderful and Spontaneous	91

G. Kenneth Cardwell

Table of Contents

28.	Revelation	95

Part Three: Better That One Should Perish — **97**
29.	Right For Each Other	99
30.	Parenting	102
31.	Questionable Date	106
32.	Narrow Escape	109
33.	All Safe and Sound	115
34.	A Most Important and Sacred Subject	118
35.	Council and Counsel at Midnight	127
36.	Braiding the Whip	151
37.	The Demonstration	162
38.	Celebrity Status	181

Part Four: And The Last Shall Be First — **185**
39.	Transition	187
40.	The Phone Call	189
41.	Flight to Mountain Home	195
42.	Tragedy	200
43.	New Beginnings	207
44.	Date in Missouri	211
45.	Prepared for the Extemporaneous	218
46.	Obstacles	227
47.	Sharing the Load	241
48.	Youth Conference	254
49.	Agency and Consequences	260
50.	The Fulcrum	263
51.	Ordeal	271
52.	Healing	285

End Notes — **297**

About the Author — **309**

Agency and Consequences

Preface

One of the most fundamental doctrines of The Church of Jesus Christ of Latter-day Saints concerns the gift of agency.[1] A second, equally important, doctrine is consequences are linked inextricably to our use of agency and we cannot choose those consequences.[2]

As it follows, one of the most critical uses of agency is how each of us decides to use or misuse the powers of procreation—how we preserve or abandon our chastity. My observations and experiences, during many years of church service, professional life and generally, have made it clear chastity is no longer considered a virtue to be cherished and prized by large segments of our society. Even within The Church, old, young and between are being deceived. Both my current bishop and stake president report a clear majority of the problems they deal with involve sexual transgression in one form or another.

Consequently, as I wrote this story, while steering clear of being crude or coarse, I deliberately chose to present the subject of chastity and several other fundamental, crucial principles and virtues of a happy life in different, sometimes graphic, even earthy, ways. My greatest hope, for those who read it, is these principles and virtues will stick hard to the walls of their souls. In particular, within the narrative, parents teach carefully and clearly the reasons for chastity and the joy of proper sexual relationships within the bounds of legal and lawful marriage. Nevertheless, as many of us do, the characters struggle in their own, unique ways with these natural and powerful forces within their beings.

All this said, the representations of and interpretations of the principles and doctrines presented herein are mine. Therefore, they should not be taken or understood as either the official position or teaching of The Church of Jesus Christ of Latter-day Saints.

G. Kenneth Cardwell

* * * * *

    This story is about what happens to two characters, The Man and The Woman, and those close to them over the course of nearly thirty years. The Title: *"Agency and Consequences"* is the theme that runs throughout its entire narrative as principles and laws are taught and learned. Choices are presented, principles obeyed and applied and blessings received; or principles are disobeyed and penalties imposed.

    Each character (as are we all) is literally in the palms of the Lord's hands.[3] The kind of person each of them (and us) becomes depends on his or her use of agency, the choices made and the consequences attached to those choices. It is seen the Lord sustains them (and us), offering His grace and mercy, in all things. Or, He leaves them (and us) to the full effects of justice when they (or we) persist in doing evil long enough.

* * * * *

    So, how did this novel come to be?

    In January 1967, six months before beginning my service as a missionary in England for The Church of Jesus Christ of Latter-day Saints, I wrote a short story, I titled *"The Man in the Hole."* That story, much expanded, is now Part One of this novel. It was originally written to depict the images I saw in my mind as I listened to the 3rd movement, "Largo," of Symphony No. 5 by the Russian composer, Dmitri Shostakovich.

    I originally wrote the story in long hand. My mother typed and put it in a scrapbook where it remained for 39 years. I rediscovered it in early 2006, retyped it into my computer, made a second copy and started tinkering with it—updating the language, adding elements and so on. I also refined the principal characters of the story, The Man and The Woman.

    During the Christmas season of 2006, I shared this story, along with several pieces of my poetry, with family and close friends. One of their questions was: "Why didn't you give The Man and The Woman names?"

Agency and Consequences

That's a good question. Primarily, the term "The Man" refers to "the natural man"[4] spoken of in the scriptures. So, I decided, as I updated the story (I was tempted to give the characters names), to leave the reference to The Man as it was. My concern, if I used a more specific name, was each person reading the story might be inclined to associate that name with someone else in their associations, rather than see at least some part of "The Man", that is "the natural man", in him or herself.

As for The Woman, I gave several references to those characters in history and fiction she admired. These seemed to me sufficient in giving her a noble, powerful and singular identity.

During this process, it occurred to me all of us find ourselves in "The Hole" at times. Notably, there are in history, several individuals who have found themselves in "The Hole," who escaped and became what they had the potential to be. These include, from the Bible, Paul, Moses, Joseph of Egypt; from the Book of Mormon, both Alma the Older and Younger, the four sons of Mosiah; and finally, Joseph Smith and the Savior Himself. As did these individuals, when we find ourselves in the pit, we need to find the escape route through faith. We must choose to be rescued through the grace and mercy of Christ's atonement, leave the old person behind and become a new creature.[5]

As we wander through life's journey, like Joseph of Egypt, we will come across "a certain man"[6] (sometimes several) who will show us the way to "Dothan" and our future. The Woman in this story is a "certain man." The Man, however, consumed with his own guilt and the tragedy of his life, cannot recognize fully the help offered. Consequently, because of fear, he rejects what he does recognize.

The Woman, like Alma the Older, is faithful, devout and prayerful.[7] As she prays for The Man, she realizes she may never know the impact she is having in The Man's life; but with complete charity, she acts wholly on faith. It is because of her The Man is shown the vision of his potential. In the end, however, The Man is left alone to use and exercise the agency given him—he has no control of the consequences—only the choices.

Other questions I hoped people would ask in their own minds as they read the story include:

Were The Man's efforts, despite his relapse following his fall back into the hole, sufficient to be reclaimed?

Were The Man's final surrender and crying sincere indications of his acceptance of God's will? Or, were they just deathbed giving in?

Will The Man be found alive? If yes, by whom? And what then? Or, is The Man found dead, drowned in the rising water in the hole?

As it turns out, since the end of the original story is open-ended, these questions, in one way or another, were constantly asked of me. Seeing a need to answer those questions, in January 2008, while on an extended consulting assignment in Nashville, Tennessee, I decided to answer those questions and began work on what has become "Part Two: The Strange Treasure." In this part, The Man and The Woman, as well as the other characters in the original story, are all given names. However, I encourage the reader to not cheat and read Part One as it was originally written and intended to be read.

When I began writing Part Two, I conceived a three-part novel; but as I worked on "Part Three: Better That One Should Perish," its length justified dividing it into two parts. Thus, "Part Four: And the First Shall Be Last," was born.

* * * * *

This is a story for all of us. Do we use our agency wisely? Do we heed the direction of the certain men (and women) in our lives? When we find ourselves in the pit of adversity, will we make good choices? Will we find the ladder half buried in the rubble? And if we do, does the ladder represent the best choice?

If you or I is a certain man, trying with all our heart and mind to help someone in great need, when will you or I give up the quest? At what point do you or I let go and move on and never look back? Or, like The Woman, do you and I let go, bury the remnants of the relationship, move on and still care enough to brave the storm and risk our own safety to seek out the one lost?

Agency and Consequences

I invite you to become acquainted with and come to know The Man and The Woman. Travel this 30-year journey with them, their families, friends and associates as each exercises his/her agency, makes choices and reaps the consequences.

* * * * *

One final note on the characters' names. Except for Brother Richard Oscarson and Sister Linda Oscarson, all the characters' names are fictional. The Oscarsons, long-time friends, were released on the 3 November 2012 as President and Matron of the St. Louis Temple of The Church of Jesus Christ of Latter-day Saints. Their names are used with their permission.

GKC
St. Peters, MO

G. Kenneth Cardwell

Part One

The Man and The Hole

G. Kenneth Cardwell

Agency and Consequences

1. The Man and The Woman

THE rage of the storm had passed. While a heavy, confining drizzle of rain persisted to come down, the sound of sirens and breaking glass was punctuated by arcs of lightening and permeating thunder. In its wake, the storm left catastrophic destruction.

On this night, most of the local residents desperately worked to recover from the storm's devastation. Utilities and services had to be restored; property had to be cleaned up; belongings and other valuables needed to be salvaged.

And while the situation presented itself favorably to such uncivilized behavior, here and there, local thugs added to the chaos and destruction by ransacking and pillaging damaged homes and businesses.

But there was on this night one, who, like on all other nights, aimlessly, pointlessly, staggered from one bar to the next. The differences for The Man this night were, because of the massive damage caused by the storm, not all of his favorite bars were open, he drank alone and often had to demand he be served.

* * * * *

The Man came from a good respectable family and was once considered a respectable person. The down-side, however, while growing up, he had been given all he needed and wanted by his parents without any effort on his part. The result of which, most of the local populace perceived to be the root of his problems. A spoiled, irresponsible, lazy, good-for-nothing, drunken bum was the consensus of him by the town's people.

The Man, despite his life style, is well built, always well dressed. Some said he came right out of GQ Magazine. Haggard and leathery, The Man's face is clean-shaven, with cold, hard, blood-shot eyes that were deep, dark pools of glaring emptiness. These characteristics made The Man look much, much older than his thirty years and a well known figure in town.

The Man lived alone on his family estate and except for an occasional dinner with The Woman at her restaurant and his almost nightly bar hopping, he had no social life. His only outward loves were his alcohol and his pet cocker spaniel dog, a gift from The Woman shortly after losing his parents.

* * * * *

The Woman is an extraordinary person. Trained since her youth in the restaurant business, she now owned and ran the upper-class eatery her parents had founded.

The Woman had long ago taken to modeling herself after the great women of history and fiction she admired. Among these were Ruth and Esther from the Bible, Florence Nightingale and even Cinderella. But her favorite was J. R. R. Tolkien's, Ēowyn, "White Lady of Rohan," "Maiden of the Rohirrim," "...child of kings, slender but as a steel-blade, fair yet terrible."[1]

The Woman kept all this within herself saying nothing. Yet it was all the more evident to everyone because of her bearing, kindness and her charity among the needy. But it was especially evident as she, with genuine elegance and graciousness, her face aglow with youthful radiance, her eyes penetrating and warm, greeted her customers each evening dressed in a shimmering, white gown that always left everything to the imagination.

Despite often unkind, but well intended, suggestions she could do and deserved much better, The Man had been The Woman's Lord Aragorn (at least that is what she saw).

The Woman felt if only she could slay the Lord of the Nazgûl within the heart of The Man, he would come to terms with his potential and become what she knew he could be. Just as Ēowyn had killed the dread, Dark Lord on Pelennor Fields, maybe this was something no man, but only a woman could do.[2]

The Woman tried over and over to explain it all to him, to share her deepest feelings, to help him and to show him by her interest in him, her willingness to be there for him. But, none of it ever appeared to register; it was always just weird, female mush; The Man just didn't seem to get it. Her life style, her restaurant, her grace, her elegance, her charity were all too tame for him.

Nevertheless, despite all the red flags high on their poles and stretched straight in the stiff wind of the facts, for reasons The Woman never understood and in time just accepted, she loved The Man. It was a pure love that just sat there, hovering, floating, never far from her heart or consciousness; a love that

Agency and Consequences

just sat softly within the folds of her soul. Sometimes, it caught her by surprise when doing the most mundane tasks or when watching a sunrise or sunset.

But the love The Woman felt was a double edged sword. It pained her. As she watched The Man, her soul ached. She often cried herself to sleep and wanted him close. She felt trapped; she felt guilty when she looked, even with casual curiosity, at another man.

The Woman also knew her love for The Man was only a seed—freeze dried—waiting to be sowed, warmed, watered and fertilized.

So, for all of The Woman's optimism, hope was fading. Her practical side told her time was running out. She wanted a marriage and children.

The Woman often wondered and worried: "Would there be a Faramir who would understand me, honor me and not be jealous of long-nurtured, hopeful fantasies of a life with The Man?[3] Is there someone who can release me from love's long winter? Can I turn my heart and give it fully, without reservation or regret to another man? Can I ever go to sleep at night and not imagine being married to The Man, having him next to me, having a family together?"

The Woman did not know the answers. And despite her religious faith, business acumen, social graces and her otherwise happy and buoyant spirit, she was uncomfortable with the unknowns posed by those questions.

The Woman just knew, despite every feeling in her soul for The Man, a decision, unalterably final, whether made by herself or forced upon her by unseen forces, was close at hand. Their last meeting was terrible and ugly. The remains of their relationship were buried. She was now, at last, prepared to let go, to move on.

G. Kenneth Cardwell

2. Drunk and Disorderly

THE time had rolled around to the early morning hours. All the local bars, able to open following the storm, had now closed for the night. The Man's driver's license had long ago been suspended and a month ago, in an ugly, drunken display of an authoritative tantrum, he publicly fired his chauffer. So The Man started his drunken, staggering walk to his estate just over a mile away on the edge of town. As was his usual custom, while he made the trek, he rationalized to himself his condition.

Not caring how many he woke up at that hour of the morning and shouting as if the whole town should hear, The Man preached his sermon: "What stupid fools you all are—working and worrying yourselves to death—and for what? What stupid, damn fools. You're out of your minds."

Next, The Man focused on himself: "Why, look at me; I haven't got a care in the world. When mother and dad died, they left me everything—the house, business (which incidentally yielded a big fat price), and their thick, little, bank book—bless their little hearts. I'm living on top of the world—I've got it made."

Once in a while, someone opened a window and yelled at The Man telling him to shut up in a not so kind way. The Man would respond in an even less kind way marked with profanity and vulgarity. And when he really sounded obnoxious, someone might throw a rock or some rotten fruit (saved for just such an occasion) at him. But mostly, he was ignored. The less the town people had to deal with him, the better they liked it.

A short distance from The Man's estate, not recognizing his own dog, a soaked, cocker spaniel came running, happily with tail wagging, up to him. He angrily and quite clumsily, kicked at it while barking: "Who the hell let you out. Get outta' my way. Go home you mangy son of a bitch."

The Man started to laugh—a loud, haughty, sarcastic laugh.

Then, except for the sound of the distant thunder and the patter of the light rain on the ground, it was silent.

Agency and Consequences

3. The Hole

THE man didn't know how long he had been unconscious; but when he awoke, it was day. The sky was still alive and coal black with clouds; but at least for the present, the rain had subsided. Thunder still quaked through the sky now and then; so he reasoned the storm was only in a temporary calm.

As The Man looked about, he surveyed himself to be in one of the new sewer trenches being dug in the area. To be exact, it was a large, circular hole for a manhole.

By some unlucky stroke of fate, the storm had caused the safety barriers around the hole to fall in and the walls of all but one of the connecting trenches to cave-in. By a second stroke of bad luck, he, himself, had caused his only other possible passage of escape, the last connecting trench, to cave-in when he had fallen in. He was fortunate to not have been buried alive. The bad news, he was boxed in all the way around the hole.

But, what really upset The Man was, either during the scare of falling into the hole or during his period of unconsciousness, he had wet himself. The stain and odor were unmistakable and he was embarrassed for himself as he complained: "Damn it to hell, look at my pants; they're ruined. How the hell did that happen?"

At that moment of self-concern, The Man concluded his surveillance of the hole. Consequently, he failed to notice a half-buried ladder lying under the rubble just a few feet up the opposite trench from where he had fallen in.

The Man's first impulse was to yell for help; but, just as he opened his mouth to shout, he looked again at his pissed-in pants and decided against it. So, just as The Woman, out for her morning run, jogged by within ear-shot, he disgustedly flopped down to the ground. He then realized he had to figure a way to get out. As with everything else, however, he couldn't even get serious enough to set about the business of saving his own life.

"What I need is a drink. Then, I'll get out of this hole in no time," The Man said to himself arrogantly.

Reaching into his inside, coat pocket, The Man removed a pint of his favorite whiskey. Looking at the bottle as though it

G. Kenneth Cardwell

contained his very soul, strength and confidence, he opened it. Guzzling almost half the bottle's contents, he was sure he could effortlessly just walk out of this man-made Grand Canyon.

"Why, all I gotta' do is climb—up—and out," The Man said with casual flair as he screwed the lid back on the bottle of whiskey and put it back into his coat pocket.

So, rather pompously and in his usual, nonchalant manner, The Man stood up and strolled over to the side of the hole and began to climb. He clawed and dug, even kicked at the sides, but to no avail.

"Why the hell do they dig these damn—these damn holes where people can fall in'em anyway. The stupid, damn fools;" The Man cursed.

Reaching again into his coat for the bottle of whiskey, The Man lost his balance in the slippery mud. Almost falling on his back, he collapsed in the very muddy, middle of the hole with a slosh.

Horror struck, as he noticed his dirty finger nails and realizing his designer clothes were now not only pissed in but soaked and muddy, The Man cursed again: "The stupid, damn fools. They're idiots—the whole damn lot of 'em."

Thunder rolled across the sky causing dirt to slide down the sides of the hole. At the sound of the thunder and dirt sliding down the sides of the hole, The Man looked anxiously about wishing ... hoping .... But, he was still alone.

Then, as The Man opened the bottle of whiskey and placed it to his mouth, he realized his magic potion had failed him. So, he flung the bottle with mindless anger against the half-buried ladder, smashing the bottle to bits.

Paying no attention to the metallic sound of the bottle hitting the ladder, he threw his head into his hands in anguish and he sulked aloud. Then, wrapping his arms about himself as if embracing an imaginary Teddy Bear, he sobbed and whimpered for his mother. Soon, curling up into the fetal position, he slept.

Agency and Consequences

4. Subconscious Memories

DEEP in The Man's subconscious, memories of the past began to speed through his mind. It seemed his whole life was about to be presented in review, in vivid, haunting detail.

As a young man, The Man really seemed to have it all together, everything anyone could want or need were his. He had been a star athlete, a real jock, during his high school years. He had earned better than average grades in both high school and college. And, he had never had to worry about having a car, money, a new suit of clothes or any of the things his friends had to worry about. His parents had provided him with everything.

During the last quarter of The Man's high school senior year, a friend had lined him up with a wonderful, young woman; a young woman who would fall in love with him. And he fell in love with her too. But, he was too caught up with the game, being a stud, showing off for his friends, to figure out and understand what those early feelings really meant, the seeds they were, what they could become. If only ...?

From The Man's perspective, The Woman was an enigma. She was smart, tough, beautiful, opinionated and thoroughly modern in so many ways. She was practical and innovative with her business. She was positively the most genuinely feminine woman with whom he had ever been associated. But she was also stubborn with what he considered her Victorian views on relationships.

His life in review now led him through a summary of his early conversations with The Woman and what she had said. He wondered why so many of those conversations were still so vivid, why they stuck so hard on the walls of his mind and heart.

The Woman, then in high school, was quite flattered at first when someone of The Man's station in the community took an interest in her. They dated though high school graduation and into the summer.

The Woman soon realized, however, despite The Man's obvious potential and outward persona, he lacked character. He was not ready to handle the responsibility she knew he must in order to live in the world she knew and be the kind of husband

and father she needed, wanted and deserved.

So, when just dating The Man for fun had run its course, The Woman had decided to break it off with him. But then something inside her prompted her to be patient and to work with him. She really didn't want to, then her heart changed as she saw him though a different pair of eyes. A seam path opened just a sliver. She envisioned The Man between the here and now and as he could be. At that moment, she seemed to hear the paraphrased words of a poem by Hafiz she had recently read:

> *"There is a Beautiful Creature*
> *Living in the hole [he has] dug..."*[1]

This was no Wendy falling for Peter Pan syndrome. The Woman really seemed to know (that didn't mean understand) she was crucial to The Man's life and he to hers whatever that all meant and wherever it would lead.

For The Woman, it was no longer an issue of being serious right then; she was looking to the future. And while she didn't see The Man desiring to become, let alone becoming, what was ultimately necessary if they were ever to have a successful relationship and marriage in the near term, she had faith in her vision of him.

The Man in his memory now came to the most difficult issue between him and The Woman: sexuality.

While The Woman was neither prudish nor naïve, she would have nothing to do with The Man's tawdry advances nor his suggestions of going with him to college and living together. To her mind and heart, giving away that which she considered the most precious part of herself, without a full and complete commitment on his part to do the same, was not an option.

Fact of the matter was, and The Woman told The Man many times, she looked forward to and wanted to enjoy all a man and woman were designed to enjoy together. The Woman compared it (though she was sure it was a weak comparison) to anticipating getting a drivers license and learning to drive a car. Once you had a license and a car, as long as you followed the rules of driving, you could go almost anywhere. You could race in certain designated places; you could go mudding; you could go off-roading. In other words, you didn't have to stay in the

Agency and Consequences

neighborhood doing only 20 miles per hour.

So The Woman emphasized she would never give her everything to The Man (or any man) on his (or any man's) flimsy, noncommittal terms.

For The Woman, that most intimate part of real love was for marriage only. That was the way it had been with her parents. She had seen the difference in relationships where abstinence before and or complete fidelity after marriage were missing. Of course she knew there were no guarantees. She only wanted what was, to her mind and heart, the best possible chance for a successful and happy marriage.

Without such commitment, without the sharing of day-to-day life, the ups and downs, the house work, finances, everything, The Woman concluded there were no real intimacy, no trust, no bonding and no soul-to-soul communion that's so much deeper than just physical copulation. Rather, it was nothing more than cheap sex turned into a glorified good night kiss.

But more important than the logic, the sociology, the avoidance of disease, all of it together, she often asked friends and dates: "When did God rescinded the commandment: 'Thou shalt not commit adultery?'"[2]

And if The Man heard The Woman say it once, he heard it a dozen times, and oh how it aggravated him: "If it was good enough for Joseph of Egypt to flee and not offend god, it was good enough for her."[3]

Outwardly, The Man thought and told The Woman she was old fashion in this matter of "sexual intimacy." She supposed by "modern standards" she was, but she made no apology and didn't care about his opinion.

But The Woman hated having to defend her position on sexuality. She simply wanted to be a virtuous woman and often wondered why she wasn't prized like a ruby[4] for trying to be one.

Instead, The Woman was often a target. She even heard of bets between some of the boys she dated as they bragged about who could get her to "do it." Some of her girlfriends suggested she go out and "just get it over with." It sickened her to even think of doing such a thing.

The truth told, in The Man's heart of hearts, he admired

G. Kenneth Cardwell

The Woman then and still. He wondered if she had relented, "to prove her love," if he would have thought of her then or now with the same respect. Or would he have just considered her another trophy, another notch in his pistol grip. He knew the answer and at this moment, even in his dream state, it shamed him that he had ever tried to seduce her.

And so, despite The Woman's every attempt to patiently influence The Man, to kindly nudge him toward a wholesome relationship, there was no working together; no individual or common goals to guide the preparation for and the building of a future together.

For The Man, it always came down to the same things: "I just don't want to get serious yet; I want to play the field and have some fun before I settle down." And the most telling one of all was: "What's in it for me right now?"

Then, when the time came, The Man went off to college. But, for some funny reason (or so he thought), he couldn't get The Woman's memory out of his mind. No matter what he did or who else he was with, his heart longed for her. He just couldn't muster the courage to call or see her.

Meanwhile, The Woman went to work. She built the restaurant her parents had started into the most frequented eating establishment in the region and finished a four-year degree in business administration in three by going summers.

In time, The Woman also matured, and needed no more to defend her principles. They became their own reward.

And all the while, the vision of The Man seemed ever before The Woman. It filled her soul with a love for him she could not comprehend, could not explain and at times she wanted to curse, but could not.

The Man's recollection of The Woman trying to explain it all to him now stabbed him. He felt impaled once again just as he had been that last early evening at her restaurant. At this moment, he was both amazed and frightened by it all and he began to worry about what he had so stupidly and arrogantly rejected.

5. Secret Life

AND then there was that other life The Man had lead while in college, the life among the shadows and in the darkness. The news reel in his mind played on and he saw again the parties, the booze, the drugs, the women, the deals, the seedy characters, the gambling and the in-over-his-head debts, all the secrets or else …. These haunted him.

In the middle of them all, what haunted him most, was his irresponsibility became the catalyst for the automobile accident that took his parents. This guilt was a millstone around his neck. It was a terrible burden; and to be free of it would mean public humiliation and probably ….

During The Man's senior year at college, both of his parents died suddenly in a terrible automobile accident and left him everything. The realization of whom and what he secretly was, his knowledge of the cause of his parents' deaths, certainly arranged by his seedy, shady associates to make sure he solved his financial problems, all contributed to his crushing guilt.

That guilt, combined with the new pressures and expectations associated with the family business, were all too much to deal with for The Man. He quit college with only one semester left to graduate, sold his parents' business and accelerated his long fall into the dark abyss of self-defeat, alcoholism and hopelessness.

To help console The Man in his loss, The Woman gave him a beautiful, cocker spaniel puppy. The Dog became his only source of comfort and he loved it dearly. For hours, he sat on the veranda of his mansion with it on his lap, talking to it as he stroked its long fur.

As the hours of each day moved toward dark, most evenings The Man left his mansion and his dog and he tried to drown his sorrows at one or several of the bars in town.

* * * * *

The years passed and The Man saw himself more and more as a victim and he became progressively more bitter and cynical. He couldn't confront the reality of himself. He couldn't

G. Kenneth Cardwell

make the decision and commitment to conquer the demons within. All of that would have been just too humiliating.

And there were other considerations. These were the real issues. These were the issues with consequences so terrible he could not consider under any circumstance setting them aside.

But through it all, The Man couldn't help but acknowledge at every opportunity, The Woman tried to help him, tried to love him into the man she envisioned he could be. She never criticized. Imbued with love, she only encouraged and suggested. But her love and respect for him only made him more miserable because he knew he could never give any of it back.

Agency and Consequences

6. Last Dinner Together

NOW The Man came in his life's review to that evening—that most eventful evening.

It was only a week ago The Man had a private dinner with The Woman at her restaurant before she opened for the public. She had his favorite meal ready (omitting the alcohol). But, he just had to have some wine, so she relented and had a bottle of his favorite brought to the table.

As The Man and The Woman were finishing the meal, she reached across the table and laid her hand upon his and offered once again to help him. She suggested he go into a recovery program and then learn the restaurant business. She was sure with his native intelligence he could, in time, be an asset to her business—even a partner.

The Man felt The Woman's love and wanted desperately to appropriately respond. But fear and the wine got to him once again. His response was evasive, defensive and accusatory. Finally, he resorted once again to his old litany of standard excuses: "I don't need to recover from anything. I'm doing just fine. Life is great just as it is. What you're suggesting isn't me. Your life style isn't exciting enough."

But, the reality was The Man heard The Woman and felt the truth of what she had said. After all, wasn't that why he kept accepting her invitations to dinner? Tragically, his house-of-cards ego, made brittle by the secret burdens of his past, couldn't let him accept the truth he heard and felt—it never did.

The Man now realized The Woman had gotten too close. He threw his napkin on his plate, stood abruptly tipping over his chair and angrily began striding out of the restaurant, leaving The Woman starring in hopeless pity after him. As he made towards the exit, with a longing, desperate edge in his voice, he muttered through his tightened jaw and mouth: "Why won't that woman just leave me in peace?"

When The Man reached the door, he wheeled towards The Woman trying desperately to restrain the tears that began to flow and the tender swelling in his heart. As he faced her and his eyes met hers, she stood at the table; her eyes, as she gazed back at him, were laser beams, penetrating, glistening, full with

G. Kenneth Cardwell

amazed and tender pity.

At that moment, as The Woman never had before, she saw The Man not as he was, but kingly, heroic and dignified, weeping with great compassion.

The Man felt as if The Woman were looking right through him. Then, he pleaded in a prayerful tone that revealed an underlying gentleness and concern that belied his real need and feelings: "Please—please, you don't understand; just leave me alone. You must leave me alone."

Like Ëowyn on Pelennor Fields, The Woman stood majestic and silent, luminous, a shaft of light in her long, white gown, face grave, fair yet terrible. With longing and tears in her eyes, heart aching, full of yearning and compassion, it was impossible for her to blench.[1] Her hope and caring love, having already forgiven all, stood fast as she sensed the Dark Lord's hold upon The Man's heart was at last weakening.

The Woman moved from behind the table which enabled her to step towards him. As she did, with a voice couched with forgiveness and love, she responded with complete conviction to The Man's plea. Though she recited the poem from Hafiz, she spoke as if the words were her own:

"There is a Beautiful Creature
Living in a hole you have dug.

So at night
I set fruit and grains
And little pots of wine and milk
Beside your soft earthen mounds,

And I often sing.

But still, my dear,
You do not come out.

I have fallen in love with Someone
Who hides inside you.

We should talk about this problem—

Agency and Consequences

*Otherwise,
I will never leave you alone."*[2]

The Woman paused a moment allowing the words of the poem to sink into The Man's heart and mind. And then she said, her voice almost a whisper, trembling: "I am ready to understand. I want to understand. Please, give me a chance. Tell me everything."

The Woman extended her arm, her face inviting The Man to follow her as she said with anticipation: "Let's go into the lounge. We can talk there. You can share everything with me."

In all their years of association, The Man had never seen The Woman thus. He had never felt the full power of her being as it wielded an invisible sword that penetrated his soul between the crown and mantle of his well-fitted armor.

In that instant, The Man felt emotionally naked. The Woman's words were liquid fire searing his heart and mind. She was exposing him, unzipping his inner sanctum, releasing all the imps of his facade; his keep was being breached.

A great and terrible battle now raged in The Man's soul. He wanted to run to The Woman and be loved and to love her. He turned and stepped tentatively toward the lounge were she pointed. And then, it all came crashing in on him. Faces appeared in his mind, their voices screaming he couldn't say anything, that it was all too late. A vision of The Woman murdered in her restaurant, executed by a would-be customer sent by those from his past in retaliation for not being silent, ravaged his conscience. For him, there was no other choice.

The Black Rider upon The Man's heart won. The Man screamed his rebellious defense as one cursing the light, preferring the darkness: "WHY THE HELL WON'T YOU YELL AT ME? DAMN YOU WOMAN! WHY CAN'T YOU JUST MOVE ON **AND LEAVE ME THE HELL ALONE!!!**"

The Man spun around, almost falling to the floor. Hunched over, appearing to shrivel, his soul in a pain and agony that was foul and bitter, he tumbled out the door.

Regaining his feet, The Man made a beeline to the nearest bar a short distance down the street. He threw open the door and swam through the tobacco smoke and bodies in a crazed panic. His only intent: to get thoroughly plastered—to get

G. Kenneth Cardwell

The Woman out of his head and hopefully out of his heart.
    "How many times had this happened before?" In The Man's subconscious, he wondered. He needn't have wondered. He knew the answer: "It must have been nearly every night for years whether he saw The Woman or not. And it never worked."

Agency and Consequences

7. Release and Good Bye

A day or two later, The Man was told by a mutual friend, The Woman's restaurant manager, what happened after he left the restaurant. He now envisioned that scene as it was related to him.

When The Man left and the door closed behind him, The Woman stepped to where The Man had sat at the table, righted his chair and caressed his crumpled napkin. Gently, she picked the napkin up and held it close to her heart.

The Woman stood in elegant, stoic silence looking at the door. She knew that almost she had slain The Man's Lord of the Nazgûl.[1] Almost she had helped him be rid of his chains. Almost she had helped him lower a draw bridge from the gate of his Fortress of Darkness, across the mote of his own fears and cross into the light of love and faith.

Instead, severely wounded by The Woman, The Man had shivered her heart into its tender shards with the mace of his words. Even so, in what was left of her heart, there was no anger or humiliation; she was long since past these. She only felt gut-wrenching disappointment in her failure to really reach him and overwhelming pity for the tragic creature he was.

The Woman now realized and knew, in that same way she knew she loved The Man, she could not reach him. She didn't know why; she just knew. Some words from the Bible came to her mind:
"...Peradventure the woman
will not follow me.
"...thou shalt be clear from my oath."[2]

The words seemed a clear message to The Woman and she knew how they applied to her at that moment. Her mind and heart sensed a bitter-sweet assurance she had done all that was possible, all that was expected; she felt a sense of release. There would be no more attempts to recover The Man. She would do as he had pleaded—she would move on; she would leave him alone. It was time to make herself available, to hope for and look for a Faramir.[3] The decision was now made.

Finally, The Woman, as though she were looking at The

G. Kenneth Cardwell

Man through the door and with the emotion of unrecoverable loss, allowed herself to quietly voice her feelings: "Oh, my dear one, I am sorry I could not love you enough or in the way to which you could respond without embarrassment. I did the best I could, the best I knew; that's all anyone can do. And now, you must go on without me. I must go on without you. Wishing it will or could be otherwise has spent its course. Good by my love; my dearest love, good by."

After gently touching her own tears with the napkin, The Woman laid it back on the table and then meticulously, as she had learned years ago and with a respect like that owed to the dead, she cleared the entire table—the silver, crystal, china and linens.

The Woman carried the linens and the entire setting back to the restaurant's kitchen. Then, with the tenderness of a mortician serving a dear, expired friend, she donned a kitchen apron, folded the linens and after washing and drying each piece of the setting, wrapped each piece with packing tissue and then placed everything carefully within a water-resistant, heavy-duty, tri-wall, fiberboard box. As she packed the box, her plan was finalized. No one but she knew that later, that very night, she would be done with it all forever. When each item was perfectly positioned and protected, she sealed the box with shipping tape.

The Woman then opened the restaurant and greeted each customer as always—with graciousness, warmth and a smile. Occasionally, but discretely, she would excuse herself momentarily, to weep and freshen her face. Except from her close friend, she hid all she felt that evening from everyone. Her complete and utter disappointment, her shattered heart were put almost totally on hold. She kept it all to herself. She revealed nothing of her plan to be carried out following the restaurant's closing shortly after mid-night. Then, she would mourn.

When the restaurant closed, The Woman went to her apartment on the second floor and quickly changed into an old pair of jeans, a sweat shirt and hiking boots. She asked her friend and manager to see the receipts were counted and all the cleaning completed. She took the sealed box, got into her car and drove into the night.

Agency and Consequences

* * * * *

How calloused The Man had tried to be when this report of The Woman's actions after he left the restaurant was rehearsed to him.

"After all, it was The Woman's fault. If she'd just lay off and leave me alone," he defensively said.

"Well," according to the mutual friend, "you won't have to worry about that anymore."

The Man thought that news would make him feel better. It didn't. Now, he really felt alone.

The Man was curious though about what The Woman did with the box. He asked: "What did it mean?" The mutual friend didn't know.

G. Kenneth Cardwell

8. Questions

THE man's tortured reverie continued with the ever-present, relentless, haunting questions and the hidden burdens that, like a coat of heavy, iron mail, had become the fabric of his soul. His mind raced, as it had so many times before, asking and answering his own questions. He knew both the questions and the answers all too well.

The Man always began with the same questions: "Why couldn't he have just accepted The Woman's love? Why couldn't he have trusted her? Why couldn't he have openly loved her in return?"

The Man hadn't been able to love or trust himself for longer than he could remember. And finally, it would have required an admission to all too much. All too much!

Then, there were the consequences: "And what would The Woman (and everybody else) have thought and been forced to do then? What would the law have done? What would The Man's past associates do?"

The Man knew what his past associates had threatened to do. Once before, when they threatened him with his parents' lives he didn't believe them. He wouldn't make that mistake again. But the cost was so dear.

There were so many things, so many skeletons. It would have been just too much. Better to let old dogs lie, better for everyone to just leave well enough alone. Neither The Woman nor anyone else should be stained with the indelible ink of The Man's past. Only he should carry these burdens; they were his and his alone.

Making amends and restitution were impossible given the risks. There were risks, terrible, life and death risks, if The Man were to say anything to anyone.

That last night at the restaurant touched The Man more deeply than he was willing to admit. But it didn't matter. There could be no sharing of everything. Though he had so little, The Woman had so much and he would not risk it. There was too much for her to lose.

Only The Man's dog had heard him speak of these things,

of his sins, indiscretions, crimes, of his guilt, his remorse, of his love for The Woman. To no one else dare he say anything. Even in his drunken stupors, the lock on his dark, deep past, on his feelings, was impenetrable.

G. Kenneth Cardwell

9. Light

"BUT, oh, dear God, if there is a god, they are such a weight, such a crushing, paralyzing weight," The Man said prayerfully in his heart and mind.

Then, at this moment, somehow, for reasons The Man couldn't at all understand, he really sensed what a pathetic, dark, vile creature he had allowed himself to become. Like a red-hot, branding iron, the creature image of his current state seared his soul. The pain was exquisite as it found its way into every cell of his body and spirit.

Then, just as the intensity of the pain and the realization of The Man's current state were about to engulf, swallow and consume him as if he were within the molten lava of a volcano, a faint glimmer of light began to disperse the shadows of fear within his consciousness. He began to feel a softening and tempering, a pushing back of the realization of the creature he was. He felt the hot iron's wound begin to cool. He now started to feel he could face the creature he was and become the man he had the potential to become.

Next, The Man saw himself, as he stood before a refracted image (for it surely was not he as he was) of his soul. The creature he was now looked into the eyes of the man he might have been and maybe—just maybe—could yet become!

At first, the image The Man saw frightened him. He was experiencing the same feeling he had in the presence of The Woman that last night at her restaurant.

Then, at that moment, he felt the fetters, the heavy chains, his armor, the millstone around his neck and the façade of his defenses all fall away. For the first time in his life he could remember, he felt truly free, vulnerable and open, empowered to choose his life path.

And yet, though The Man was uncomfortable, he sensed this man, the one he now faced, was THE MAN he wanted to be. He saw himself sober, joyously, contentedly married to The Woman, running the restaurant with her, with a family, his respectability restored.

The Man could not tell if this was a vision, a dream, low

Agency and Consequences

blood sugar due to his empty stomach or a crazy hang over. Or was it some sort of Dickens-like attempt from some unknown somewhere beyond this earthly dimension to get a message to him? All he knew, whatever it was, it had his full, unencumbered, rapt attention.

Now, as this "could be" image of The Man stood before him, with eyes, penetrating in their gaze and with great seriousness, the image said: "The first choice will soon be yours; the effort connected to that choice will fix the consequences and choices to follow. Do you understand?"

What did this mean about a first choice, effort, consequences and choices to follow? The Man did not know and his only fear was the possible answer if he were to ask. So, with a voice couched with humility and meekness, without pretense or guile that greatly surprised him, The Man heard himself reply simply and affirmatively: "Yes."

The image of The Man smiled and, with a bearing and voice that stabbed and scorched him the same way The Woman's being and voice did that last night at her restaurant, said: "Very good. I'm depending on you."

There was now a grave finality and urgency in the image's countenance. And then, the image was gone.

The Man wondered: "Was this just a clear indictment of the life he'd lived? Was it a prelude to his own, bitter hell—to always have the image of what he might have been, what he might have enjoyed, indelibly pressed into his consciousness?"

In his mind, The Man reasoned: "The image said there would be a choice; so the vision, or whatever it was, must be a possibility."

The Man now struggled to focus, to fix his mind on the positive image, to steel his resolve and commitment. He somehow knew what he had to do. He felt a hope he had never felt before.

G. Kenneth Cardwell

10. The Search

MEANWHILE, back in town, life was beginning to get back to some degree of normalcy when The Woman realized she hadn't seen The Man for quite some time. Other people in the town, whom she asked, hadn't seen him either. The bar tenders in the local bars told her they hadn't seen him since the night of the storm.

Finally, in desperation, The Woman went to The Man's estate and, unknowingly, drove past the very hole into which he had fallen. The gate was unlocked as well as the front door. She found no one in the house. As she exited, she found The Man's shivering, soaked cocker spaniel on the veranda. She tucked the dog inside her coat and raced back to town for help and again drove past the hole.

Everyone in town was now preparing for the worst. The sky was roiling and hellish black. The thunder was drawing nearer and louder while the horizon was periodically and erringly illuminated by bolts of lightning. The weather casters' reports, full of severe storm warnings, were not optimistic.

The Woman finally found her close friend, her restaurant manager, who, after questioning her about the events of the last dinner with The Man (as it was she who related to The Man what happened after he left the restaurant), agreed to help her. She assured her friend the long years of pining were over. She only wanted to find The Man and make sure he was safe. She left The Man's dog with her friend's children and together, they began a systematic search for The Man.

11. Resolve

THE man was violently shaken awake as a clap of thunder crashed above him. It was raining again; but that didn't matter now. He was tired, dirty and hungry. But more than these, the images he saw while lying in the mud returned and seemed as vivid and clear in his mind as if projected on a crisp, HD, TV screen. He had now resolved to make something of himself when (not if) he got out of this hole alive.

The Man wondered about The Woman—would she still have him? After their last dinner together—what he had said, how he behaved, what he had learned about how she now felt, he wondered. And what if she would consider giving him another chance—why? Surely, he wasn't worth it. But, it was all he had to cling to—all he could hope for. He had to go for it, take his chances, tell her everything, let the chips fall where they may.

The Man scanned the hole one last time and tried to determine his best possible route for ascent and escape. But because he was so focused on the wall, he again overlooked and did not recognize the ladder lying half-buried only a few feet away.

The Man was looking face to face with the wall of the hole. He began a careful ascent. Scaling the wall ever so carefully so as not to cause the dirt to slide out from under him, he climbed with new-found determination, strength and vigor; a will to live with the hope of a new life were his magic potions now.

At that instant, everything became sharply, blindingly illuminated as a lightning bolt arched across the hole's watery canopy striking a nearby tree. The Man felt the tingle of electricity dance across his skin as a fraction of an instant later, the most violent thunder clap since falling into the hole crashed through everything and the whole earth about him reeled in commotion. The fragile, rain-soaked soil beneath him began to slip away. The Man was panic stricken as he struggled with the ebbing ground for foot and hand holds. He grabbed a tree root and decided to just stay still until the wall settled.

G. Kenneth Cardwell

* * * * * *

Meanwhile, against all good judgment, The Woman and her friend were frantically braving the renewed fury of the storm. They searched every possible nook and cranny where they thought The Man could have sought refuge. It never occurred to them he might have fallen accidentally into one of the new sewer trenches being dug.

* * * * * *

Back in the hole, it seemed an eternity; The Man's hands were aching and bleeding. When the wall of the hole finally stopped sliding, he again clamored for the rim above.

"I'm gonna' make it. I just have to make it," The Man said, gritting his teeth, in solemn, prayerful desperation.

The rain, up till now, had just drizzled down; but, like it had done the day of the storm, it seemed now to come as a tidal wave, in one massive, unending barrage.

The Man was nearing the top; but as he did, rivers of rain water were eroding his path out from under him. He fought frantically against the torrents of mud and water. The rim of the hole was so near, yet so far, far away.

Soon, The Man was exhausted, battered by the elements and mentally finished. He had nothing left. The Man closed his eyes and let gravity have him. He fell back into the cold, hard, deep, pooling, empty, black depths of the hole. His decision and commitment, made mere minutes ago, seemed but clinkers in the furnace of trial and adversity.

Agency and Consequences

12. Judgment and Mercy

HIS face and body pummeled by the relentless rain, The Man lay there, nearly comatose, on the cold, muddy ground, soaked, muscles twitching from their effort with the wall. He was completely expended. His eyes, fixed straight up, starred lifelessly at the black-robed sky. The thunder rumbled, reverberating in the ground beneath and around him; but The Man heard or felt nothing, not even his hunger. His senses had left him alone to himself.

In the distance, The Woman called The Man.

Quite soon, The Man's alcoholic soul found him. Oh, how he wished for a drink. That's all he wanted—just one, stinkin', lousy drink. He reached, quite by unconscious habit, into his inside, coat pocket for his whiskey, but found nothing.

"The damn stupid fools anyway," The Man cursed hysterically.

Then, The Man laughed his loud, haughty, sarcastic laugh.

Except for the sound of thunder, the gurgling noise of water draining into the hole and the patter of rain falling on the ground, it was silent again. The Man closed his eyes, his twitching body finally stilled and all he could do was helplessly wait.

The hole, now filling with water, became erringly illuminated as another lightning bolt flashed across the sky. Almost simultaneously, the lightning was seconded as the thunder authoritatively gaveled once again through the firmament.

Off in the distance, The Woman and her friend were now also soaked and exhausted. They decided to end their search. The Woman, one last time, called for The Man.

Now, utterly alone, the image of The Man as he could have been came vividly again into his mind and stood before him. The image was kingly, heroic and dignified, weeping with great compassion as he spoke:

> *"There is a Beautiful Creature*
> *Living in a hole you have dug ..."*[1]

G. Kenneth Cardwell

The Man interrupted and screamed in tortured, horrible agony: "WHY THE HELL WON'T YOU YELL AT ME? DAMN YOU MAN! WHY CAN'T YOU JUST MOVE ON **AND LEAVE ME THE HELL ALONE!!!**"

The Man surrendered and cried bitterly.

A few feet away, still only half-buried, the ladder lay half-exposed—waiting.

Near the ladder, exhumed by all the rain washing the earth away, lay a once sealed box. Its contents—china, crystal, silver and linens, were now exposed, soiled by the mud and water.

Part Two

The Strange Treasure

G. Kenneth Cardwell

Agency and Consequences

13. Rescued

THE storm was now finally past. George Kenneth Kindman, owner of Kindman Trenching and Piping, with Crew Chief, Sam Noble and his crew, were inspecting the damage to the new sewer line trenches they had prepared just before the storm hit. The damage was severe. Many lines would have to be completely re-dug before the concrete pipes could be laid.

As they neared the outskirt of town, they came to a main terminus where several lines came together. All the feeder lines to the terminus were completely caved in leaving the large manhole terminus as nothing more than a large hole in the ground about eight feet across and sixteen feet deep. As they came upon it, George, Sam and their crew couldn't believe it. Sam wondered aloud: "How could the walls of the hole have been left so shear when we've seen so much water and erosion everywhere else. It's as if some invisible force put up a form around the entire circular wall of the hole."

As they reached the rim of the hole, George, seeing the body of a man lying in several inches of water at the bottom, not thinking of the distance to the bottom, instinctively leaped to the bottom of the hole. He quickly recognized the man, Paul Tenter, the rich, town drunk; the man, his close friend, Sarah Christensen, had so desperately looked for the previous day during the final rage of the storm.

George quickly examined Paul and determined he was yet alive but suffering from severe dehydration and hypothermia. He called to Sam: "It's Paul Tenter. He's alive. Get the Paramedics here fast. And get one of the big backhoes ready to use as a crane to lift a paramedic and stretcher in and out of the hole with Paul on it."

There was no way to pull Paul out of the water, so George removed his coat and laid himself next to Paul with the coat over them both to help get some warmth into Paul.

At that moment, Sarah Marie Christensen, out for her morning run, just as she had the previous morning, ran right beside the hole. Noticing all the activity, she stopped to see what was going on. Knowing Sam as one of George's employees and a frequent visitor with his wife at her restaurant, she asked: "Sam, what's going on?"

"Oh, hi Sarah," Sam said a bit startled. "We found Paul nearly dead in the bottom of the manhole. George is down there with him and paramedics are on their way," Sam explained.

Sarah quickly moved to the rim of the hole, went to her knees, and peered in. Her mind raced remembering she had run right past this hole the previous morning and, going and coming from the Tenter Estate, had passed the hole. Finally, with her Manager, Alice, they had come near the hole at least twice. How was it in none of those close encounters, she had not thought to look in the hole for Paul? "How could I have not looked into something as obvious as this hole yesterday?" She said aloud weeping.

Sam had now positioned a large backhoe as close to the rim as he dared. If it were any closer to the rim, a machine that large could not be supported by ground so saturated with rainwater.

The sound of sirens indicated the approaching police and ambulance. They arrived very quickly and Sam quickly explained the situation and the proposed plan to lower a paramedic with the stretcher into the hole using the backhoe. The paramedics indicated there may be spinal injury after falling that far and suggested they also send a backboard down with the stretcher. They quickly rigged a sling with chains to attach the backhoe bucket to the stretcher, while a paramedic laid himself on the stretcher. A guide rope was also attached to the stretcher and tossed down to George, who was now on his feet ready to assist the paramedic.

In the cab of the backhoe was Sam's best operator and with the practiced precision of years working together, Sam gave the hand signals that guided the operator as he lifted the stretcher and paramedic out over the rim of the hole. They lowered the stretcher into the hole while George, holding the line, kept the stretcher from spinning.

The plan was to get Paul out of the hole as quickly as possible and examine him. Not knowing if Paul had broken

Agency and Consequences

anything when he fell into the hole, the paramedic took no chances and quickly put a neck brace on him, as George removed the chains from the stretcher and removed the backboard.

The paramedic instructed George on how to rotate Paul's body as he slid the backboard under him. Paul was quickly strapped to the backboard and then they lifted Paul and the backboard onto the stretcher. George reattached the chains to the stretcher and gave the signal to lift Paul out of the hole as he again steadied the stretcher with the attached line.

When the stretcher with Paul reached the rim, the backhoe operator carefully swung them to solid ground where the other paramedic was waiting to examine him. Sarah ran to Paul and tearfully asked the paramedic: "Is he going to be alright?"

"I don't know yet. We need to get him to the emergency room as quickly as we can. We'll know more in an hour or two," the paramedic responded.

As soon as Sam disconnected the stretcher from the chains, the backhoe operator swung it again out over the rim of the hole with just a chain hanging from the bucket. They lowered the bucket and chain back into the hole. George instructed the paramedic on how to put one of his feet safely into the large hook at the end of the chain. While holding onto the chain, the backhoe operator lifted the paramedic from the hole. Then, they lifted George from the hole by repeating the procedure.

As soon as George lighted from the chain onto solid ground, Sarah ran to him. Throwing her arms around him and sobbing uncontrollably, she cried: "Thank you, George, thank you!"

Quickly, the paramedics ascertained Paul's condition, began hydrating him with an IV and were on their way to the hospital emergency room. George instructed Sam to get their equipment secured and to put barriers around the hole and then to send the crew home. Meanwhile, he and Sarah got into his truck and headed for Sarah's Place, her restaurant. When they arrived, he pulled a bag, with an extra set of clothes, from the truck. While he cleaned up and changed in

G. Kenneth Cardwell

the restroom, Sarah went to her upstairs apartment and changed out of her sweat suit. She then quickly scribbled a note for her manager, Alice, explaining Paul had been found and was at the hospital and she may be a little late for the opening that evening. They were then off to the hospital.

Agency and Consequences

14. George and Sarah

GEORGE Kenneth Kindman was a tall, muscular man. He had a smile that was warm and an infectious laugh. These qualities let a person know right away that he was good-natured, kindly and gentle. But he was also a man of presence and authority. He ran his business with a "gentle vice" firmness that gave no doubt who was in charge.

George grew up in a town only a few miles from where Sarah and Paul grew up. Their high schools were rivals on the football field and George and Paul were arch competitors as opposing quarterbacks. But, it was in college, where George and Sarah met, during Sarah's last year, as they took many of the same business classes together and spent many hours doing homework, taking hikes in the nearby mountains and attending church together.

As an Eagle Scout, George loved the outdoors, and shared with the young men of his community that which he had enjoyed so much as a young man himself. He had served a mission for The Church of Jesus Christ of Latter-day Saints in England, loved geology, soils and minerals. Like Sarah, he had grown up in the business he now ran and had a passion for his work and being a positive contributor to his community.

But George's greatest love was Sarah. For years, he had listened as Sarah shared her feelings, frustrations and desperate attempts to reclaim Paul. For George, it was his greatest privilege and honor to be with Sarah. Somehow, despite her feelings for Paul, he felt inspired by her and wanted only to be all he had the potential to be for her. They seemed to have the mutual ability to lift one another, take the tension out of serious situations by finding a way to tease each other and they enjoyed treating each other with old-fashioned courtesy. Like Sarah, he had similar religious convictions; and he sensed a bond between her and him that fueled a hope, if he were patient, in time it would come to fruition.

So, last week, when Sarah told George she had made

her last and final attempt to reach Paul and he had left her restaurant in a rage, he was quietly hopeful their relationship would at last have the opportunity to grow and blossom.

But now, as George and Sarah got into his truck to drive to the hospital, he was unsure how this would all play in Sarah's mind and heart. He couldn't help wondering: "Would she retreat back to her long held hopes for a life with Paul?"

* * * * *

As they began their drive, Sarah just looked at George. In her mind, she went back to that last night in her restaurant with Paul. What she saw in Paul as only future possibilities, she now saw in George. Only in him, it was not a future glance of might-be-possibilities; it was here and now. This man was for real and she knew he loved her and he loved Paul even as she did. He had asked nothing of her and now she understood he was her Faramir. She reached out her hand and stroked the back of his neck as a tear ran down her cheek.

George gently pulled the truck to a stop at a stop sign. He turned and looked at her as she said from the nucleus of every cell within her: "I love you, ya know."

Quickly, George checked his truck mirrors for any vehicles behind them, put the truck in park, and took Sarah in his arms. With his body and voice trembling, he said: "Sarah, I love you too; I have for a very long time."

They looked at each other for what must have seemed an eternity, their eyes, like lasers, communicating gigabytes of all that had been unsaid over past years. Then, they sealed their expressions of love with a kiss. This was not a kiss charged with impatient, inappropriate passion; but it was passion; it was gratitude; it was respectful; it was full of awe and wonder because of the wholeness they now felt; it was a blessing and privilege; it was communion; it was a signal of partnership with each other and with God.

As George and Sarah resumed their drive to the hospital, there was a sense of unity. They each felt all they had waited and prepared for since their youth, the moment they had just shared together, was worth every minute, every hour, every day. There was now anticipation that could hardly be contained. As George drove, Sarah studied, with new eyes, the man whom she believed God had prepared for her, and she for him. But now the time was right, he was right, she was right. The joy she felt was exquisite.

G. Kenneth Cardwell

15. Hospital Room

GEORGE and Sarah arrived at the hospital and quickly rushed into the emergency room. Upon inquiry, they learned Paul was doing well, was conscious and had been moved to a private room. They asked if he could receive visitors and were told he could have a very short visit.

Paul was lying in his bed staring blankly at the ceiling. He was still in the hole and the vision of the Man he could be was there again. He was being reminded of the choices that would yet be presented to him as George and Sarah entered the room holding hands.

Sarah, went immediately to Paul's side, bent over him and kissed him on the cheek. Paul, as he returned to the physical reality, blinked, turned his head and recognized Sarah.

The sight of Sarah standing there startled him. At first, he thought the vision he had seen in the hole of a life with Sarah was about to become true.

But, then Paul saw George. In the next instant, he saw their hands clasped together. He wanted to turn away and ignore them, to retreat into his hole. At that moment, the experience of the hole flashed again in his mind and he realized there was no timetable set for anything. A small flame of hope ignited in his heart. He smiled and said: "Sarah, how are you? Thank you for coming. George, is it true you found me and got me out of the hole I'd fallen into— one of YOUR damned holes?"

"Yes, Paul, we found you in one of MY holes. You're always bellyaching; calling the rest of us idiots. I'm wondering, did it meet your required specifications?" George replied with light-hearted sarcasm.

Paul couldn't help but chuckle. He hadn't laughed it seemed forever and it felt good.

"Touché, George," Paul said. "Ya know, I've been dry now for almost two whole days. That must be some kind of record," Paul said complimenting himself.

"No you haven't. You were soaked to the bone just

Agency and Consequences

this morning," George corrected with a smile as big as the crescent moon.

Paul laughed again and felt a safety with George he hadn't known with any man in a very long time.

Sarah then spoke: "Paul, I'm fine. I'm really sorry we didn't find you sooner. I tried to find you and somehow ..." She hesitated as she started to sob: "Somehow, for some reason, I just never thought to look in that hole. I'm really, really sorry."

"That's OK," Paul said. "I believe there were reasons for me to fall into that hole. I don't yet fully understand those reasons and I'm not sure I can ever measure up to the challenges now before me. But, I'll say more to you both on that at a later time," Paul concluded.

"Oh, by the way, do either of you know what happened to Ruffles ... my dog?" Paul queried with a note of concern in his voice.

"Yes," Sarah responded. "He's at Alice's and her kids are really enjoying him."

"Paul, they told us down stairs to make this short. Sarah needs to get back to open tonight; so, I think we had better get going," George said.

"Yeah, I understand. I think the medication they gave me is making me drowsy anyway. I really thank you for coming," Paul said with a bit of disappointment.

Sarah took Paul's hand and gave him another kiss on the cheek and George gave him a strong handshake as they said: "good by and have a good evening."

As George and Sarah reached the door, Paul looked at them and said with great affection and with a sincerity that surprised him: "Make sure you invite me to the wedding."

George and Sarah looked at each other and then at Paul and the three of them smiled a smile that just knew.

"Alright you wise guy; I'll see you in the morning," Sarah said with a bit of girlish excitement.

G. Kenneth Cardwell

16. A Long Day Ends

WHEN George and Sarah got in the truck, George asked: "After you visit Paul in the morning, how 'bout we go on a picnic?"

"I'd like that a lot," Sarah responded. "I'll fix it all up. What time will you come for me?" Sarah asked.

"Would noon to half-passed be all right?" George suggested. "I have to take care of some things with Sam in the morning," George explained.

"I'll be ready," Sarah said with anticipation.

"Paul was really different today. I haven't seen him like that since high school," Sarah observed.

"He was different. He was sober. I wonder how long it will last. I like Paul. I hope he can pull himself together for the long term," George replied.

"What do you think he meant when he said something about 'measuring up to challenges?'" George wondered aloud.

"I heard that too. I don't know what it meant. Apparently, something happened to him while he was in the hole. He did say he would talk to us later about it," Sarah responded.

"Hey, come on in and have something to eat with me before you leave for home," Sarah invited as they pulled into the parking lot at Sarah's Place.

"You read my mind," George said gratefully.

As George waited for Sarah and their meal, he called Sam on his cell phone and told him Paul was doing fine. He then asked him to get the crew working on re-digging the trenches that had dried out enough to be safe. He wanted no one to get hurt trying to get it done just because of a contract. He'd deal with that. He then asked Sam to bring the soil sample kit and to meet him at the hole where they found Paul at eight the following morning.

Presently, Sarah joined George for dinner. Dressed in her white gown, she was more luminescent than ever. George had seen her dressed like this before to greet her customers, but this evening he saw a woman that startled him, dazzled him. He rose to his feet, helped her with her chair, and couldn't help feeling like the most honored man on the planet.

* * * * *

Meanwhile, at the hospital, the battle was raging within Paul's soul. The challenges, the choices he had to make scared him beyond comprehension. He had been given a chance and he was on the precipice, the knife's edge. His alcoholic soul was at war within him and despite his expression of happiness for George and Sarah's obvious love for one another, he felt betrayed. The vision was a lie. It all seemed overwhelming. He had been here before when his parents were killed and all the responsibility that suddenly became his was all too much. He felt himself shrinking. Wishing for a drink, he cried out: "The damn stupid fools; they're all idiots, every damn one of them."

A nurse quickly came in to Paul's room and injected a sedative into his IV. Soon, Paul Tenter was asleep.

G. Kenneth Cardwell

17. The Hole's Strange Secrets

THE following morning, about half an hour before the time he had agreed to meet Sam, George arrived at the hole where Paul had been found. He unloaded a long extension ladder, set it up against the wall of the hole and climbed down.

George began a careful inspection of the hole. It amazed him how shear the walls were. Then he noticed the ladder that lay half-buried and wondered aloud: "How in the world did Paul not see that ladder?"

George then noticed the broken whiskey bottle that had been shattered against the metal ladder and wondered aloud again: "Didn't he hear the bottle break against the ladder?"

Then George noticed something that really startled him. There, lying in the bottom of a caved-in trench, only two or three feet from the half-buried ladder was a cardboard box; its contents of high quality china, silver, table linens and crystal were strewn by the water from the storm. His mind raced back to the day following Paul's last evening at Sarah's Place, the day Sarah had told him it was over with Paul. When Sarah was not willing to tell him all the details, Alice had taken him aside and gave him a detailed account that included Sarah taking the complete table setting and sealing it all in a cardboard box. After closing the restaurant that night, she changed her clothes, grabbed the box and drove out into the night.

It was now obvious to George what Sarah had done that night and what she had intended by it. She had borrowed one of his ladders (which she apparently couldn't get back out of the hole) and then buried, never to see the light of day again, the table setting, symbolic, as it was tied to Paul, of her yearnings, her feelings and her hopes. But, the storm, the hole, whatever happened to Paul within that hole and even he himself as rescuer had changed all that. The earth had literally given up her dead. He wondered: "What if Sarah was to see this table setting un-earthed? Would she take it as a sign her relationship with Paul really

Agency and Consequences

wasn't over?"

In an instant, George made a decision. Sarah buried the box with the intent it would never be unearthed. He would rebury it himself; but not here in a sewer trench. He took off his windbreaker and quickly, but carefully, wrapped the china and crystal in the napkins and tablecloth. Then fashioning his windbreaker into a makeshift back pack, he placed everything, the table setting, all wrapping tissue and the soaked box, within it. Shouldering his makeshift pack, he ascended the ladder and after quickly making room, placed this Strange Treasure in his truck box behind the cab of his truck.

At that moment, Sam arrived with the soil sample kit. Sam and George gave each other a hearty greeting of "Good Morning." Sam then gave George a succinct and pithy report on the work the crew was doing re-digging the trenches. George went first down the ladder into the hole with Sam down second as each steadied the ladder for the other.

Without George saying a word, it didn't take Sam long to notice the half-buried ladder with the broken bottle fragments lying close by. "Would you look at that! There's one of our ladders half-buried in the mud and a broken whiskey bottle shattered against it. It's amazing. How on earth did Paul not notice the ladder?" Sam said with amazement. Then, answering his own question, he replied: "He must have been really plastered."

"Yeah; I noticed it too, just a few minutes ago," George said.

"You've been down here already?" Sam inquired.

"Yeah; I got here about seven-thirty, unloaded and set up the ladder, then took a look around," George answered.

Sam handed George the soil sample kit and said: "While you take the samples, I'll get my shovel, unbury our ladder and clean up the broken glass. I still don't understand how or why the wall of this hole is so shear?"

"I don't understand it either. That's why I'm going to get some samples of the wall face and have them tested. Until the results of the tests are back, I don't want anyone or anything disturbing this hole," George firmly instructed.

45

G. Kenneth Cardwell

"I'll wait for your direction to clean up the hole and re-dig the connecting trenches," Sam acknowledged.

"Thank you. Before you get your shovel, would you help me take the needed measurements of the hole?" George asked.

Sam nodded affirmatively and he and George made the needed measurements. George then drew a detailed map of the hole while Sam went to retrieve his shovel. As George took his samples of the hole's wall, he carefully documented each sample on his map by location on the wall and height above the bottom of the hole.

By the time Sam had completed uncovering the half-buried ladder, getting it out of the hole and burying the broken glass deep in the bottom of the hole, George was ready to take his remaining samples at heights on the wall that required Sam's help in moving and steadying the ladder. By eleven that morning, they were finished.

As they were securing both ladders on George's truck, George observed, "Sam, I've been studying the soils in this area since I was fifteen when I earned my geology merit badge in the Boy Scouts. None of the samples we've taken today looks any different than what I've seen for fifteen years. Why this hole didn't slough off during that storm is beyond me. There should be no reason, even without that ladder left there by mistake, why Paul should have been trapped in that hole.

"It does seem like a mystery," Sam replied.

"More like some kind of miracle that's still in the process of occurring," George postulated.

"What do you mean," asked Sam.

"I'm not sure I know. But Paul was in that hole for well over a full day. When Sarah and I visited him yesterday afternoon, he was sober and he said some things that lead us to believe something happened to him down there. Maybe God has intervened in that man's life and given him an opportunity to come clean and make his life right," George explained.

"I don't know about that," Sam said with doubt. "For as long as I've known him, Paul has been nothing but the town drunk, unable to do anything but gripe, drink and be

Agency and Consequences

disorderly," Sam said with conviction.

"I know. That's how he's been for the last eight or nine years. Sarah and I have known Paul since high school. Sarah dated him; she liked him a lot and for years has seen in him something worth trying to pull out. She has taken a lot of abuse from him and others, for trying to be his friend. I played against him on the football field; we were opposing quarterbacks. He was tough, smart and a worthy competitor. Yes, he was always the rich, spoiled kid. But, something happened while he was at State University. Sarah and I met at a church-run college so neither of us knows what happened," George recounted.

Pausing briefly and putting his hand on Sam's shoulder, George concluded: "All I know, all Sarah knows is Paul is a man of great potential; and if somehow, he can get control of himself and harness it .... Well, I don't want to get soapy. Let's just see what happens."

Sam smiled and turned toward his truck. "Sam, Sarah and I are having a picnic in about an hour," George said with a grin that belied his plans.

Sam turned back towards George and said with a congratulatory tone: "I hope she says 'yes.' You're both ready and I think you will be a wonderful couple and very happy together."

"So, do I," George replied hopefully as he got into and started his truck. When he put the truck in gear, he remembered the table setting, that Strange Treasure, in his truck box and he felt a slight pang of fear well up in his soul.

G. Kenneth Cardwell

18. Picnic

GEORGE drove to his home, unloaded the ladders into his business garage and then took his makeshift-windbreaker back pack with its Strange Treasure from the truck box into his kitchen. He put all the china, silver and crystal into his dishwasher; and into the sink, he put in the best stain remover he had and filled it with hot water and then added the linens. He quickly showered, shaved and put on a pair of dress slacks, shirt and blazer. From one of his dresser drawers, he retrieved a small box; he opened it, smiled, closed it and tucked it into one of his blazer pockets. He was then off to meet Sarah for their picnic.

When he arrived at Sarah's Place, he entered by the employee entrance and found Sarah in the kitchen, her hair down her back, dressed in a beautiful, flower-print summer dress, hose and loafers, putting the final items for their picnic in the basket. "Look at you," George exclaimed.

"I'm glad you like it. I feel … well, I feel very womanly today. And you look pretty handsome yourself Mr. Kindman," Sarah said affectionately.

George took Sarah in his arms, they kissed and just held each other as they looked into each other's eyes for a few moments. "I've looked forward to this all morning," Sarah whispered as she lightly kissed George's lips again.

"So have I, Sarah. If you're all ready, why don't we get going. I'm really hungry," George said with a humorous lilt in his voice.

"Huh, just when a girl's feeling a little romantic, all a man can think about is his stomach," Sarah teased as she grabbed the picnic basket.

"Here; you carry it," Sarah commanded in her best authoritative tone as she thrust the basket handle into George's hand and put her hand into his other hand. Then they both laughed as they went out and got into George's car.

As they were leaving the parking lot, Sarah couldn't help another little, kind-hearted tease as she said: "Boy, this

Agency and Consequences

is the first time I've ever had the privilege of riding in your car. How come I didn't rate before? I only got to ride in your truck before today. What gives, George?"

"My truck was dirty or I would have brought it instead, Sarah," George replied mater-of-factly. They looked at each other and laughed again. They both sensed this picnic would change the course of their lives forever. The teasing was their way of postponing the more serious conversation that was to follow.

*****

George picked a spot where they had been before. It had become "their spot." Their previous conversations here quite often centered on Paul and the reasons Sarah could not let go of him.

Sarah packed a beautiful picnic. It included ham, chicken, potato salad, coleslaw and Sparkling Cider. She had provided some of her best china, silver, crystal and linens. It was absolutely perfect. George even noticed this setting of china, silver, crystal and linens was different from that in the Strange Treasure he had found that morning. That, he hoped, was a good sign.

*****

As they finished eating, Sarah snuggled against George, slipped her arm through his and took his hand. "This has been perfect," she said. "Thank you for this special time together," she whispered looking at him.

"Sarah," George said a bit pensively. "I have something to ask you," George quietly announced feeling nothing like the authoritative man running a very successful company with a couple dozen employees.

Sarah knew what was coming and her heart began to race like it did when she did sprints most mornings. She knew before she could answer George's question she should explain some things. But she waited for the question.

George reached into his blazer pocket and pulled out the box. He brought it over to the hand Sarah was holding and opened it. There, in the box, was an engagement ring and wedding band. At that moment the sun's rays hit the

G. Kenneth Cardwell

diamond and it sparkled like a thousand rain drops.

"Sarah Marie Christensen, will you marry me?" George asked with a depth of love and respect that penetrated Sarah's heart and mind like nothing she had ever felt before. All the experiences that had so bound her to Paul in years past were nothing compared to what she felt at that instant. But, before she could speak, George continued.

"Sarah, I bought these ring years ago. I carried them to this very spot more than once when we picnicked together; but .... So, while I could afford much more now, I hope they will remind you I've loved you for a very long time and I promise to love and stand by you always, even forever, if God finds me worthy," George promised.

"Oh, my beloved George," Sarah said in a prayerful voice as she looked at the ring set and then at him.

"The rings are magnificent and I will be honored to wear them. But before I say 'Yes' to the most touching proposal of marriage I could ever have dreamed of, I need to share with you some things you already know about and some things you don't know. Before we agree to be partners in marriage, I want you hear it all from me. I want you to hear my voice, look at my face and into my eyes and feel my hand in yours as I tell you what happened last week, yesterday and this morning. I want there to be no secrets about anything regarding what happened between Paul and me.

"I want you to know why I feel about you as I do; so, when I say 'Yes' to you, I say it with no regret or reservation and with all the love and commitment I have within me. When I'm finished, if you wish to withdraw your proposal, please know I'm honored beyond words you would even ask me," Sarah explained as tears trickled down her cheeks and she dabbed them with her napkin.

"Sarah, there's no need to explain anything," George offered.

"George, unless I say what I feel I need to say, I can't say 'Yes' to you," Sarah countered. "Will you please listen and hear what I have to say?" Sarah quietly but earnestly pled.

George had always known Sarah was not a woman to take lightly nor could she be moved from a course her heart

Agency and Consequences

told her was right. At this very moment, he knew she was setting a pattern for their life together—it would be open, honest, respectful and truthful. In his heart and mind, he wanted to hear her side of the story. He just hadn't expected it to be a condition of becoming engaged. "Sarah, I apologize if I sounded disinterested or insensitive to your need to talk about this. Please forgive me; tell me everything." George said apologetically.

Those last words rang like a bell in Sarah's mind taking her back to when she had said the same words to Paul that last night at her restaurant. She wondered if she could get through this. But she loved George and she felt their union must have no hidden wedges left in the tender branches of their new family tree. So, she inched even closer to George (if that were even possible), she placed her free hand on George's as he held hers which prompted George to place his free hand on hers. Then, she began.

G. Kenneth Cardwell

19. No Secrets and Engagement

"GEORGE, I want you to know first of all, I've loved you for a very long time too.

Sometimes, I found myself in a real battle. I often felt guilty loving you and knowing, for reasons I couldn't explain, but in time, just accepted, God wanted me to love Paul. God put that love in my heart and I could no more deny it than I could deny I lived and breathed. So, for years, I did everything I could to reach him except do anything that would compromise my own integrity and virtue. George, I know there have been rumors, but I want you to know I am a virtuous woman. My greatest desire has been to present my husband, whomever he turned out to be, a clean soul on our wedding day and an untouched body on our honeymoon.

"Then last week came. I had invited Paul to the restaurant prior to opening for the public. I had his favorite meal ready. I wanted to try again to persuade him to get some help for his alcoholism and I offered him a position at my restaurant. Well, that all went over like a lead balloon. I was too simple; he didn't need help. Then he stood up, knocked over his chair and almost ran for the door mumbling 'Why won't that woman just leave me alone.' He reached the door and just stood there. I stood up and looked back at him as intently and as lovingly as I could. I seemed to see him as he could be—a sober man; a man of honor and dignity, of positive influence in our community. Paul then said: 'Please—please, you don't understand; just leave me alone. You must leave me alone.' George, there was something in his voice. Something that told me he really did care about me; that he wanted to change; to fix all that was wrong with his life. I responded to his plea to leave him alone by reciting a poem by Hafiz:

> 'There is a Beautiful Creature
> Living in a hole you have dug.
>
> So at night

Agency and Consequences

*I set fruit and grains
And little pots of wine and milk
Beside your soft earthen mounds,*

And I often sing.

*But still, my dear,
You do not come out.*

*I have fallen in love with Someone
Who hides inside you.*

We should talk about this problem—

*Otherwise,
I will never leave you alone.'"*[1]

George couldn't help but notice how everything Sarah was saying, especially the imagery in the poem were all so coincidental (or were they) with what had really happened.

Sarah continued: "I invited Paul to sit in a private place and tell me everything. He turned as if to accept my invitation and then .... Then, it was as if his whole soul collapsed from within and he just simply couldn't ...."

Sarah started sobbing at this point of her story. George took his hand that Sarah was now clutching very tightly and pulled it out of her grasp. He gently put his arm around her shoulder and pulled her reassuringly closer to him. Sarah, quietly, resumed her report.

"Paul then yelled at me; he swore at me saying something about why didn't I yell at him. He told me, in no uncertain terms, to leave him alone and move on. He then stumbled out the door and ran to the nearest bar.

"I stood there shattered. I was disappointed I had gotten so close and then to have it all come down like a house of cards.

"George, then the most remarkable thing happened." Sarah, looked at George, taking hold of his hand that had been placed on hers with both of hers.

"Do you remember the story in the Old Testament

G. Kenneth Cardwell

when Abraham sends his servant to find a wife for Isaac?" Sarah asked.

"Yes, I do; but ..." George responded as Sarah interrupted.

"Well, Abraham's servant makes an oath with Abraham to do all Abraham had asked him with regard to finding a wife for Isaac. But, in the story, the servant inquires of Abraham: '...Peradventure the woman will not follow me?' And Abraham answered: '... thou shalt be clear from my oath.'[2]

"George, at that moment, when that scripture came into my mind, I knew I had done everything required of me with regard to Paul and I was now released from any obligation to him. I stood there next to that table feeling about as bittersweet as any woman could I guess. My biggest fear at that moment was my release might have come too late.

"I don't remember exactly, but I stood there alone and in soliloquy said something about how we each must now move on without the other and ..." Sarah paused to regain her composure: "... I said 'good bye.'

"I, then, gathered up the entire table setting from dinner, took it to my kitchen, cleaned it all up, wrapped it and put it all into a water-resistant cardboard box. I opened for business that evening and did the best I could to hide all that was going on inside. At the close of business that night, I changed into a pair of jeans, sweatshirt and hiking boots. I went out into the night alone. I mourned for Paul; I prayed for healing and the capacity to forgive; finally, I buried that box where it can't be found.

"That brings us to the last couple of days. All l have left to tell you about are the ride to the hospital yesterday and this morning when I visited Paul at the hospital.

"Yesterday, as we drove to the hospital, moments before I told you I loved you, I was looking at you as you drove. It was as if everything I had seen Paul could be I saw in you right now. I saw my friend; I saw a virtuous, godly man; I saw a husband; I saw a father. It was like God parted the veil and I got a glimpse of you as God, Himself, sees you. The darkened glass had been cleaned; I no longer saw through the glass darkly;[3] and the love I've felt for you for years was now unchained, unfettered by other commitments.

Agency and Consequences

So, with all my heart, I said yesterday, as I say now: 'I love you.'"

George gave Sarah a squeeze and said: "I love you too."

As Sarah continued her story, her whole body trembled as she struggled to speak without her voice breaking: "I arrived at Paul's room this morning just as he had finished breakfast. I stepped into his room and said: 'Good morning, Paul; how are you doing?'

"Paul replied: 'I had a pretty rough night until they gave me a sedative. And breakfast, well, hospital food isn't like the food at Sarah's Place.'

"I thanked him for the compliment and asked: 'So, what are the doctors saying? Do you know when you're going to be released?'

"Paul answered: 'They tell me I can go home anytime I want to. But, Sarah, I'm scared. I haven't had a drink since I fell in that damned hole of George's. At some point in that ordeal, I think I broke a bottle of whiskey and haven't had a drink since.'"

George injected at this point saying: "Sarah, Sam and I found his broken bottle this morning. Paul's recollection is correct."

Sarah continued: "Paul then said: 'Sarah, I don't want to be a drunk anymore; but, I can't do it alone.'

"'What do you mean,' I asked Paul.

"'I mean,' Paul said, 'is there any chance you'll be there to help me?'

"George, the only thing I could think to say was: 'Of course I'll be there to help you; but, not the way I think you want me to be.'

"I continued by saying: 'Paul, you told me to leave you alone and to move on. I have; I finally and really have. But, the thing is, Paul, you have to get sober because it's the right thing for you to do, not for me. Paul, I'll support you anyway I can as your friend who loves you as a friend; but, if my guess is right, you have a whole lot more than just an addiction to alcohol to deal with and I, for my own sake, have to move on. Paul, after you left my restaurant that night last week, you left me shattered. For both our sakes, I

G. Kenneth Cardwell

buried everything associated with that night.'

"George, I thought Paul was going to scream and swear at me and tell me to get out. He looked at me and said: 'Sarah, you're right. From the time we dated in high school, you've always been right. Now it's time for me to take your advice for a change. Before you came this morning, I decided to leave this afternoon for the drug and alcohol rehab center in Capital City and have already made the arrangements. Do you think Alice's kids could continue to take care of Ruffles for a while? I'll give you some money for his room and board.'

"I told Paul when Alice and Ben knew the reason for leaving Ruffles with them they would most likely be happy to help especially since you are willing to pay.

"I called Alice as soon as I got back from the hospital and explained the situation. When I told her there was a check for $5,000.00 waiting at the restaurant, she couldn't believe Paul could be so generous. Anyway, while Paul is in rehab, Ruffles will be well taken care of.

"Then Paul asked me about us. I told him we weren't engaged yet; but I felt that wasn't too far off. 'Well,' Paul said, 'as I said last night, you better invite me to the wedding or at least the reception seeing as how I wouldn't be able to attend your wedding.'

"At the end of our visit, Paul again mentioned he wanted to speak to both of us as soon as is practical after he gets out of rehab given what our plans might be."

"So, that's it; all of it," Sarah said with a sigh of relief. "Now you know everything," she reiterated.

*****

Except for the breeze blowing softly through the tree above them, there was silence. George and Sarah just sat there as Sarah's trembling body settled, letting the weight she had been feeling completely dissipate.

Sarah broke the silence with another question: "You know some in town will say I only said 'Yes' because I'm desperate and on the rebound. How would you feel about that?"

George answered in Socratic fashion: "Are you

Agency and Consequences

desperate? Are you on the rebound?"

Sarah straightened up in George's arm, squared herself and looked him as steadily in the eyes as she could and said with a soft, intense firmness that was her own: "George, I don't think so; I don't feel like I am. We've been friends for many years. I know you as well I as I know any one. And you know me in the self same way. I've said the things I've said today so one, our relationship will be completely above board; and two, if there is any hint of desperation or rebound, one or both of us would recognize it. I don't sense it. But if you do, we can wait a little longer. Otherwise, if you don't feel or think I'm rebounding or acting in desperation then, with all of my heart, my answer to your proposal is 'YES.'"

George didn't hesitate, he took the engagement ring from the box and placed it on Sarah's left ring finger and said: "Let the old biddies wag their tongues all they want."

"George, there's only one other thing I'd like you to do for me." Sarah said in the middle of their kiss after putting on the ring.

"What's that? If I can I will," George replied.

"I'd like for us to start having children right away. If we become pregnant on our first time together, on our honeymoon, I would be thrilled," Sarah said with an anticipatory twinkle in her eyes.

"I think I'd like that too. It's a deal .... As long as it's a boy," George said grinning from ear to ear.

Sarah took her napkin and began playfully to bat George on his cheeks with it.

Then George noticed there was still some Sparkling Cider left in the bottle and interrupted Sarah's whipping saying: "Hey, before you hurt me, let's drink a toast to us and our future family."

Sarah took the cider and poured the rest into their glasses. Each took a glass, they hooked their arms together and said simultaneously: "To us, to our children, to our forever family."

George and Sarah drank their toast. It was now official. George Kenneth Kindman and Sarah Marie Christensen were engaged. Sarah then asked: "George, do you have a tuxedo?"

"Huh, ah, yes I do …. Why?" George replied with a question in his voice.

"Is it one of those 'wild' colored ones?" Sarah queried with concern.

Sensing the opportunity to tease, George said with great sincerity: "As a matter of fact, if I remember correctly, it's maroon … or is it chartreuse …? It's something like that anyway."

Noticing the smile that just appeared on George's face and the impish twinkle in his eyes, Sarah jabbed George in the ribs with her fingers and said lightheartedly: "You big tease. You just couldn't resist could you? Now, for real, what color is it?"

Laughing because of his ticklish ribs being jabbed, George pleaded for Sarah to stop the jabbing: "Stop! Stop! It's just a regular, standard black one, with a black bowtie, cumber bun, black studs for the shirt, matching cuff links and I even have a pair of black socks and black dress shoes. Now, what do want to know for anyway?"

"Well," said Sarah, "since we just got engaged, I thought I'd like to show you off at the restaurant tonight by having you stand next to me as the customers come in. Would you be willing to do that with me?"

"Sounds like you want to get the brush fire called the rumor mill started quickly," George said with some concern.

"I can't control that; but if people are going to gossip, they may as well get it over with," Sarah responded with resignation.

"Actually, George, I want all your old girl friends to know I won; that you're mine," Sarah said with a fake snobbish tone.

"So, you want to brag; you want to gloat," George accused, as he picked up on Sarah's new line of teasing. "What if I don't want to be shown off like a trophy?" George protested.

"George, seriously, I really want you to be with me tonight. Tomorrow is Saturday and you don't have to be up early," Sarah said with a persuading smile.

"Of course I will; I wouldn't miss it. It was just fun to

Agency and Consequences

laugh with you for a few moments," George confessed.

"But, we better get going," George observed as he looked at his watch.

George and Sarah quickly picked up the picnic stuff and were on their way back to Sarah's Place. As they drove, George queried: "When do you think a good day to get married would be?"

"Well, there isn't much to arrange. I own one of the best places for a reception and the food and cake won't be anything out of the ordinary to take care of. All we need to do is to have our interviews with Church leaders, make arrangements for the ceremony, have our picture taken, send out the announcements and arrange for a wedding photographer. And, oh, get the license," Sarah enumerated as though she had thought about this a thousand times.

"OK …. So, how long do you think it will take to get that all done and still take care of the day-to-day things we still have to do?" George said quietly pressing.

"I'm comfortable with eight weeks from today, George. How does that feel to you? If we divide these tasks up, we can have them all done within just a couple of weeks …. Don't you think?" Sarah responded with excitement.

"I'm good. Let's announce the date as eight weeks from today and Sunday, after Church, we can plan it all out," George suggested.

Sarah looked at George as he drove; then she leaned over, kissed him on the cheek and whispered: "That's perfect."

Now, she looked at her left hand as they approached town. The sun caught the diamond on her ring and its light refracted in a dozen directions, the flash of brilliance surprised her causing her heart to feel as though it skipped a beat. Sarah never felt more womanly in her life than she did at that moment, sitting next to George with that ring on her finger.

20. Repentance Begins

MEANWHILE, Paul was riding in a transfer van on his way to the drug and rehab center in Capital City.

After Sarah had left that morning, all the anxieties, doubts and fears he had experienced for years returned. The images of his seedy, old friends making their threats against Sarah as they had his parents with their deadly follow through played again in his mind.

What made it worse, during the night, his alcoholic soul had surfaced again and it tried desperately to take control. As he had the night before, he became agitated, thrashing around in his bed and began to curse. But, as the nurse came in to give him a sedative, he somehow checked himself and asked her to give him only enough to calm him. He wanted to stay alert. She agreed indicating if he needed more, he could have it.

Paul thanked the nurse as she left his room with a warm gentility, which genuinely surprised her. After all, wasn't this the notorious, infamous Paul Tenter, the obnoxious, loud, disrespectful, spoiled and rich town drunk that had publicly fired his chauffer one early evening only a month or so ago? Was he not the same man who would walk to his estate at three or four in the morning, after drinking all night, swearing and cursing, belittling everybody and everything, waking everyone from their sleep on his path home? The nurse turned, looked back at Paul, noticed his expression of sincerity and said: "You are most welcome." With an exchange of friendly smiles, the nurse again turned and walked back to the nurses' station feeling something she had not experienced before so profoundly and certainly never expected to feel from this man—real appreciation and gratitude—that was warm, even cozy, in her heart.

Paul's resolve was strengthening. The visions, he had experienced in the hole, were seared indelibly into his heart and mind. They seemed to be catalytic in helping him to map the course he sensed lay before him. Sarah was right. There was more than just the alcoholism. That was only the

Agency and Consequences

beginning.

He would get himself clean and sober.

He would reveal everything to Sarah and George regarding his past.

He would make appropriate arrangements to notify the proper authorities and reveal all he knew about ....

He would submit himself for prosecution.

He would do his time and would make restitution as much as possible.

Presently, the van arrived at the drug and rehab center. Now the real work would begin as he realized Sarah would soon be planning her wedding, it was unlikely anyone would come to visit him. This would be hell on earth and he would face it alone.

G. Kenneth Cardwell

21. Starting Life Together

GEORGE and Sarah arrived at the restaurant, they kissed as George let Sarah out of the car and they said their "See ya laters." Just as he started to get back into his car, he heard a scream from inside as Alice was obviously being shown the ring on Sarah's hand. He couldn't help but laugh a little and be amazed by why women would make such a big deal of an engagement ring. After all, it was only a little gold and highly compressed carbon; just a little yellow metal and a piece of highly refined coal. But, he was sure grateful Sarah was so happy to be engaged to him.

George got to his home and quickly checked on the Strange Treasure. The dishes, silver and crystal came out wonderfully in the dishwasher. Then he looked at the linens that had been soaking in the sink. He was amazed. All the soil stains were gone. He drained the water from the sink and just to make sure, he put the whole lot into the washing machine with some other white clothes that needed washing and turned on the machine.

By the time George got dressed in his tux, the clothes washer had finished. He put the cleaned clothes and the linens into the dryer and was out the door and on his way back to Sarah's Place.

It was Friday night and it seemed every couple within a fifty-mile radius had decided to come to Sarah's Place for supper. Sarah had picked an especially beautiful gown for the evening that featured a collar that closed mid-high around her neck and with long sleeves ending snuggly around her wrists and featured the point of a triangle on the back of her hand, which seemed to say, pointing to her diamond ring: "Look what I've got."

Sarah simply could not restrain her exuberance. She was full of all her womanly self. George simply was delighted to be with her. While many tried to tell him how lucky he was, he already knew it and he became even more determined to make sure Sarah always had reason to be just as thrilled about him as she was that night.

Agency and Consequences

* * * * *

When George got home early Saturday morning, he pulled all the linens from the clothes dryer and again was amazed all the soil stains had come out. He found some large, plastic, zip-lock-type bags and carefully wrapped the china, silver and crystal in paper towels and packed them into the bags. He folded the linens and placed them into a bag as well. He then locked The Strange Treasure into an empty drawer of a file cabinet in his office.

* * * * *

The eight weeks Sarah and George had to plan their wedding and reception just seemed to fly by. The day of their wedding was a beautiful, mid-summer Friday. With a few of their closest friends and relatives in attendance, they were married for Time and all Eternity in a special sealing ceremony presided over by Sarah's Uncle Abraham who had the unique and special authority from God to do so.

"With this kind of marriage ceremony, only performed in specially dedicated buildings called temples, there is no pomp and ceremony. And for most people in the world, that's what it's all about—a big show, a lot of expense—all in an effort to give the appearance of something important. But in the Temple, it's the most joyful, solemn, happy and serious of occasions. The rooms in which couples are married are small with only the closest, worthy friends and family in attendance."[1] For George and Sarah, it was the most profound experience of their lives. Sarah felt overcome with feelings of gratitude to God, for her deceased parents who had taught her to prepare. But most of all she felt as though every cell in her soul was grateful for and committed to George, the man God had prepared to walk beside her from this day on and forever as her friend, confidant, lover, husband, father to their children and protector. As the ceremony ended and they kissed across the alter, she could not restrain her tears of joy as she felt an overwhelming peace and approval from God Himself.

G. Kenneth Cardwell

* * * * *

The reception was an absolute success. Alice, after the wedding ceremony, left with her husband, Ben, and made a beeline back to the restaurant and made sure everything was perfect. The cake was magnificent, the food was, as it always was at Sarah's Place, Five-Star.

Around Sarah's neck and on her ears she wore a matching necklace and earrings of beautifully set diamonds in the 'S' shaped forever setting. Since George decided to give her the engagement and wedding rings he had bought years ago, the necklace and earrings were his wedding gift to her.

* * * * *

About half way through the evening, the whole place went deathly silent as all eyes, like a flock of birds swirling together, looked toward the main entrance. Paul Tenter stood magnificently in the doorway, dressed in an Armani business suit and looking almost like the thirty-year-old man he was instead of the haggard, hard, crusty sixty-year-old people were used to seeing. As Paul walked towards the reception line, he paused briefly but often to shake hands and greet those he knew. The Paul everyone was meeting was a renewed version. And George and Sarah could not help showing how pleased they were with their smiles.

Rather than going to the line to greet George and Sarah, Paul found a table where some old friends were sitting and asked if he might join them. They agreed and were soon complimenting Paul on his appearance and asking about the changes in his life. Paul began his reply by sincerely apologizing for anything he might have said or done to offend his old friends. After giving a brief answer to his friends' question, he excused himself, went to another table and did the whole thing over again. This he did until he was the only one left except for George, Sarah and Sarah's staff.

"I hope you don't feel I crashed your party," Paul said to George and Sarah.

"Not at all," George said as he took Paul by the hand, pulled him in to himself and gave him a big bear hug. "I am so proud of you," George said with tender emotion.

Agency and Consequences

Sarah looked at her new husband and Paul. She couldn't help but weep. Then Paul took Sarah in his arms gave her a kiss and said: "Sarah, I love you. I've never been able to say that before; but ...."

"Can you tell me where you're going on your honeymoon?" Paul asked mischievously while clearing his throat.

"No," George said tersely in a playful abrupt fashion.

Paul looked at Sarah as if to ask the same question and she said: "I don't know where we're going. George is surprising me."

"Well, I have something for you anyway," Paul said as he reached into his inside coat pocket and drew out a rolled piece of paper. The rolled paper was held together with a strange looking piece of metal and a white ribbon bow.

Paul handed the roll to Sarah and said: "I'm sure you remember the night when we were last in this room together and you recited a poem to me. Well, I found this poem recently by a poet named Cardwell and thought it would be appropriate on this occasion. Why don't you remove the roll from the ring and ribbon and read it."

Sarah's hands trembled as she began to remove the metal ring from the roll. George suddenly recognized the ring and said: "That's a prairie diamond. It's a ring made from a horseshoe nail."

"That's right," said Paul as Sarah finally got the roll out of the ring, unwound it and began to read aloud.

Prairie Diamond

Nauvoo, at the edge
Of western frontier—
A couple fall in love
And their relationship
They desire to seal,
To the blacksmith they go
Where a horseshoe nail
He forms into a ring,
A prairie diamond,
To serve as wedding band.

G. Kenneth Cardwell

Traditionally,
Wedding bands
A complete circle form—
They have no beginning;
They have no end;
And, thus,
Symbolize Eternity.

A prairie diamond,
By contrast,
Shaped from a nail,
Complete circle is not,
Having a gap
Yet to be filled.

The complete portion
Is God's promise
Already fulfilled—
His Atonement,
Grace,
Mercy,
The fullness
Of the Gospel Plan.

The gap,
However small it appears,
A significant chasm,
Deep and wide,
Fraught
With all the opposition—
Good and evil—
That life can,
Even must,
Hurl at them,
Which the couple must bridge
In partnership with God—
Doing their part
So God can do His—
To complete the circle;

Agency and Consequences

To cross the threshold
Of Eternity together.[2]

  Sensing the tender and priceless gift just given, Sarah quietly said with tears in her eyes: "Paul ... I don't know what to say except thank you. It's beautiful. We'll treasure it forever."
  Paul quietly turned and headed towards the same door he went through in a rage only ten weeks before. When he arrived at the door, he turned back, looked at his friends and smiled a huge smile. Then he said: "Thank you for taking a couple of your Sunday afternoons to visit me. You can't begin to know what they meant to me and how those visits helped me. I'll be out of rehab in a month. I'll stop by and we can make an appointment to visit. I have a lot to share with you and I'll be asking for your help."
  Then there was a slight pause. A tear rolled down Paul's cheek and then he recited:

"So at night
I set fruit and grains
And little pots of wine and milk
Beside your soft earthen mounds,

And I often sing."[3]

  "Thank you, Sarah, for not giving up on me. You didn't fail. Your faithful obedience unlocked the heavens and angels have been sent to help me.
  "George, of all the men I know, you're the only one worthy enough to be by Sarah's side. I sense you know what God will expect of you," Paul solemnly concluded. He was then out the door and gone.
  George and Sarah stood for a moment in silence. Sarah could not help replaying the scene of ten weeks earlier in that same place, looking at that same door and comparing it with what just happened. She turned to George, looked at him and simply said: "I love you. Thank you."

G. Kenneth Cardwell

22. Honeymoon

George and Sarah then thanked all of Sarah's staff who told them: "Get out of here."
Sarah changed out of her wedding gown into the same dress she wore when George proposed to her and they left. They made a quick stop at George's place where he changed his tux for knee-length cargo shorts, a short-sleeved shirt and moccasins. He then moved Sarah's luggage from the car into his truck and they were off again.

"Where's your luggage?" Sarah asked inquisitively.

"It's already there," George quipped.

"So, it's back to the big, beastie truck is it?" Sarah jabbed.

"Yup; and in about two hours, you'll know why," George said kindly. And besides, this old boy's got a bench seat, so slide on over here Mrs. Kindman," George invited and to which Sarah happily complied immediately.

"Lay your head on my shoulder and go to sleep if you want," George suggested.

"Don't think I can. I'm too wound up; too excited. I want to be awake for this entire experience," Sarah said as she laid her head on George's shoulder and, for the first time in their association, she laid her hands on his thigh.

George put his right arm around Sarah's shoulders and asked: "Do you remember what Paul said about angels being sent to help him?"

"I do. And I had the strangest and yet wonderful feeling come over me when he said it. Why do you ask? Did you feel something too?" Sarah responded solemnly.

"I did feel something and here's why. The day after we got Paul out of that hole, Sam and I took soil samples all around its wall. You see, every place else we dug trenches and manholes, that storm caused them to cave in and slough off. He should have been able, no matter how drunk he was, to climb out of that hole; but he couldn't. The wall of that hole and all the connecting trenches, which did cave in, look like someone put in a big, invisible, circular form so the wall remained shear all the way around. Well, I got the results of

Agency and Consequences

our soil samples back from the lab three or four weeks ago and they were just what I expected. That hole should have caved in just like all the others. I think a miracle has occurred and Paul has been spared and given some sort of direction—kind of like Saul, who became Paul, in the New Testament," George postulated. "I just can't come to any other conclusion," George said with a tone of resignation.

"I always knew Paul was a special person," Sarah affirmed. "I hope you're right. If you are, Paul will be a great man yet and do a lot for our town," Sarah said with confidence.

* * * * *

It was about two-thirty Saturday morning when George and Sarah arrived at a large, beautiful and very secluded hunting lodge high in the mountains. George had been there earlier in the week to make sure the place was clean, food stocked and fire logs lain in the huge, stone fireplace.

"Well, here we are," George announced as he unlocked and pushed the door open and flipped the light switch. In the next instant, he picked Sarah up and carried her in.

When George put Sarah down, she was absolutely delighted, even a little giddy. "WOW! How did you find this place?" she exclaimed.

"It's ours," George replied as Sarah put her hands up to her face not believing what she just heard.

"You're kidding. George, you're teasing me again, aren't you?" Sarah said trying to laugh as she whirled around tying to take it all in.

"No, I'm not teasing. My dad and mom built it as their secret, little get-away place years ago. I oughta know because I ran the backhoe that dug the trench all the way up the dirt road we just drove to lay the power, water and sewer lines in. Outside, up the hillside a ways, there's a five-hundred gallon water tank, buried so the water won't freeze in winter, which supplies water to the lodge. Way down, at the bottom of the dirt road, there's a pump house that sends the water up to the tank when the level in the tank drops to about one-hundred gallons," George explained as he realized he was getting a little carried away.

"Huh, so, anyway, now that dad and mom don't use the lodge hardly at all anymore and I only have one sister who lives half way across the world, well, it's essentially ours to use whenever we want to," George said.

Sarah threw her arms around George's neck, gave him an approving, passionate kiss and said: "It's perfect."

"Why don't you take a look around while I bring in your stuff and get a fire going in the fireplace," George suggested.

"I think I'll just do that," Sarah said with a mischievous look as she sashayed towards the kitchen.

* * * * *

For about the next half-hour, George hauled Sarah's luggage in, put a few of their favorite CDs on the player and checked the fireplace flu while Sarah quickly got her bearings.

The lodge's main room was the great room with a large stone fireplace at the peak of a large triangle that formed the north end of the room. On either side of the fireplace were large windows that formed the two sides of the triangle. The windows extended from the hard wood floor to the pitched ceiling giving a view of the mountains that was breathtaking. The windows had no curtains or blinds; but were coated to let light in from the outside but not allow anything on the inside to be seen from the outside. From the windows on one side, the morning sunrise could be seen and from the other, the evening sunset. In front of the fireplace were a large, plush sofa and a mound of pillows and blankets all on top of a large area rug. Hanging from the vaulted ceiling by an old logging chain was an old, weathered wagon wheel converted into a chandelier with large, candle-shaped bulbs. The downstairs also included a fully modern kitchen, a dining set, a fully stocked walk-in pantry with a chest freezer, laundry room, half bath, large water heater, furnace and a combination closet/equipment room with a bar-b-cue, camp stoves, lanterns, snow shoes, sleds, camping and hiking gear, snow mobile suits, all sorts of tools, etc. The

Agency and Consequences

upstairs was a loft bedroom with a king size bed, a large walk-in closet and a bathroom with an over-sized walk-in shower, whirlpool bathtub and double sinks.

* * * * *

As soon as George got Sarah's luggage up to the loft, she slipped into the bathroom to freshen up. She immerged and walked to the top of the stair and looked with awe, as her heart began to pound and a tear tried to swell in her eye, upon the man she loved skillfully lighting the fire. She thought back to her high school years and how so many of her friends could think of little else but having sex. Now, these many years later, she was grateful she waited. But, it had been hard for her too, especially these past eight weeks, not to be preoccupied with it.

There is a strange, compelling and relentless urge that seems to find its way into every cell of your soul—your whole heart, mind and body. Marjorie Holmes said it so well as she described Mary, the mother of Jesus, coming into womanhood. "Modesty quarreled constantly with this brash discussion of the state they seemed to value above all else. The coming to bed with a man, the loving and begetting. But how could she blame them [her old high school friends] when her own thoughts could dwell on little else."[1] She had dreamed for years of this night. She wanted it; she wanted him. And yet ….

* * * * *

As George finished starting the fire, Sarah began to descend the stair from the loft dressed in her white bathrobe. At that moment, George turned from the fireplace; and was struck dumb. Mesmerized, George gazed at her coming down barefoot, hair down her back. Though lighted only by the flickering flames from the fire, she was a regal shaft of light. He remembered how she recently told him she admired Tolkien's character Ĕowyn, "White Lady of Rohan," "Maiden of the Rohirrim," "…child of kings, slender but as a steel-blade, fair yet terrible."[2] A perfect description he thought. He couldn't help wondering: "Who is this woman really? Who am I that I have the honor and sacred responsibility to be her husband?" He thought of the words of a former Church leader who said: "A beautiful, modest, gracious woman is creation's masterpiece."[3] For the first time in his life, he began to understand what that meant for here was its embodiment—the proof of its truth.

* * * * *

Sarah reached the bottom of the stair and just seemed to glide to him. She slipped into his arms, looked trustingly into his eyes and prayerfully asked: "Would you dance with me for a while?"

They started to dance. There was no hurry as they held each other firmly and as Sarah laid her head on George's shoulder. In a little while she began to feel as though she were becoming part of him and he part of her; she was melting into him and he into her. They were in a cocoon and metamorphosis was taking place. They were becoming one. She knew he was ready and didn't want him to have to wait any longer.

"George?" Sarah whispered in his ear.

"Yes, Sarah?" George whispered back.

"I think I'm ready. Would you help me take off this robe?" Sarah softly invited with a slight bit of apprehension.

No more was said. George leaned back and tenderly looked Sarah in her eyes. The unspoken question: "Are you sure?"

George's look of complete, unselfish concern for Sarah sealed it; her mind and heart were now sure. She looked back at him, her lips in a closed, Mona Lisa smile, her eyes and mouth singing a silent, soaring duet and the lyric was: "Thank you for being so sensitive and 'Yes'," both at the same time.

George untied the belt of Sarah's robe as she began unbuttoning his shirt. Soon they lay together in the pile of blankets and pillows, their bodies warmed by the fire in the fireplace. And here they journeyed together into that hallowed, sacred place of Souls, Symbols and Sacraments,[4] into the fire of Eternal Burnings and Whiteness, where those less prepared can never go, apprehend nor comprehend, but seek only in vain.

* * * * *

For the next eight days, George and Sarah had a wonderful time together. They Bar-b-cued, back packed for two days and got thoroughly soaked in a high mountain thunderstorm just as they were putting up their tent for the night. They cleaned the fireplace (played in the soot), cooked hot dogs, roasted marshmallows and made smores. They enjoyed watching a couple of George's action movies on the big screen with the surround sound system as high as they wanted and a couple of Sarah's more romantic, chick flicks. But, all too soon it was time to go home and start living life together.

G. Kenneth Cardwell

23. Paul's Confession

IT was about three weeks later, as George and Sarah got settled in their pew for church services, they noticed (along with everyone else) Paul walk in. Paul scanned the chapel. When he found them, he walked over and asked if he could sit with them. "Of course," they both said in unison as they slid more toward the center of the pew to make room for Paul.

Although Paul did not partake of the Sacramental bread and water, he quite obviously enjoyed the meetings. Following the meetings, Paul could not help asking George and Sarah as they talked in the building foyer: "So, how's the old married couple doing?"

"Well, Sarah hasn't kicked me out yet," George said with a wry smile on his face.

"I don't intend to either. I think I'll keep him ... at least for another day or two. We'll just have to see how it goes," Sarah quipped as she jabbed her fingers into George's ribs.

"Why do you have to keep doing that?" George complained.

"To let you know who's the boss," Sarah chortled.

"All right you two," Paul interrupted. "You've been married barely a month and you're fighting already. Is the honeymoon over already?" Paul chimed in picking up on the teasing.

"I think it must be," George admitted getting very serious. "Those French style fingernails (or whatever they're called) are weapons I can't compete with. You should see my ribs. I'm clawed up, Paul. Man, if I'd known this woman was a tigress eight weeks ago, I'd have backed out," George said as he maneuvered in anticipation of another jab from Sarah.

"Alright, George, I'll back off for now," Sarah said offering a truce. "But, later on, buddy, when were alone ..." Sarah, whispered in his ear as she kissed him on the cheek.

"That's enough about us. How are you doing, Paul," George sincerely asked.

"Well," Paul paused for a moment, "I'm doing very

well. I've been dry since you lifted me out of that 'dastardly' hole of yours," Paul confidently replied. "But, I would like to set a time and visit with the both of you together. I have quite a bit I need to tell you and I want to ask for your counsel on some rather sticky issues," Paul asked with some urgency in his voice.

"Sweetheart, do you have any meetings this afternoon?" Sarah asked George.

"Actually, I'm free this afternoon," replied George picking up on where Sarah was headed.

"Well, if you're not busy now, why don't you come over and have lunch with us and then we can talk for as long as you need," Sarah invited. "We've got a ton of leftovers from the reception we catered at the restaurant last night. You may as well help us eat some of it before we give the rest to the homeless shelter tomorrow morning," Sarah said with that tone which mortal men can hardly resist.

"Done; can I bum a ride with you and I'll send my chauffer home with his family," Paul inquired.

"Sure, if you don't mind walking. It was such a nice day we walked this morning," George said.

By then the threesome where out the building as Paul sent his chauffer and his family home, Sarah quickly changed her pumps for loafers and they started the half-mile walk to Sarah's Place.

"So, that's what ladies keep in those big bags they carry around—a change in wardrobe," Paul teasingly observed. "What else have you got in there?" Paul pressed.

"None of your business, mister," Sarah said sharply with a huge grin.

"Paul, that's sacred ground you're on there my man. Suggest you cut bait and run or you'll be in a hole far worse than the one I dug and you fell into," George counseled.

* * * * *

Soon, George, Sarah and Paul arrived at Sarah's Place and they all went upstairs to the apartment on the second floor. Sarah kicked off her shoes, slipped into a pair of slippers and asked George to set the table while she went back down stairs to get the meal ready.

G. Kenneth Cardwell

"So, are you living here in the apartment?" Paul asked.

"Yes. We talked it over and it just seemed the best way for now until children start to come. This way, when the restaurant closes, Sarah doesn't have to drive to my place at whatever hour in the morning she can get away," George explained.

Paul didn't seem like he wanted to give any preliminaries to what was on his mind, so he helped George with the table and then they just sat in a couch and browsed a couple magazines.

"I'm not allowed in Sarah's kitchen down stairs," George quipped. "That's her man cave or woman cave or something. If I'm asked to help her on a Friday or Saturday night rush, I'm bussing dishes or running the dishwasher or something; but I better not set foot in that kitchen. Everything down there is just so, so. She won't even let me help clean it," George reported anticipating a question from Paul about why he didn't go help Sarah with the meal.

"So, what if she wants to ride on one of your big Caterpillars or a backhoe with you; would you let her?" Paul inquired.

"That's different. You don't have FDA inspectors looking around the cab of a bulldozer or backhoe," George said a bit snidely. "Ah, it will just take a little time. The only reason I really want to go into her kitchen is to sneak up behind her, put my arms around her waist and kiss her hello when I get home. So now, I'm not so secretive and when she hears the door close as I come in, she meets me at the kitchen door, apron and hair net on, a knife or stirring spoon or meat fork or whatever she's using at the time in hand and she lays a big one on me. Marriage does have its advantages," George confessed.

About then, Sarah sent the meal up on the dumb waiter and she was close behind up the stairs. "So, what have you guys been talking about," Sarah inquired as she pulled the trays of food from off the dumb waiter.

"Not, much. Just guy talk," George offered.

"Yeah, right. You're still complaining I won't let you in my kitchen with your muddy boots on weren't you George

Agency and Consequences

Kindman," Sarah accused with fake smugness.

"Sarah, are you saying George can go into your kitchen if he's cleaned up and not tracking half the sand and gravel of the county into your kitchen?" Paul asked sensing he'd not been told the exact truth.

"Of course he can …. If he doesn't touch anything including me while I'm working," Sarah replied with a wide grin.

"She says I'm too much of a distraction; well, you know …" George said with a bit of studly pride.

"All right; I think we'll stop there. We ought to keep some things private," Sarah said in a commanding tone.

* * * * *

Following their meal, George and Sarah sat comfortably on the couch and Paul settled into the love seat. He then began with what happened when he went off to college; how he tried just about everything—drugs, wild women and gambling. He explained how he got in over his head in debt with the loan sharks and the mob. They demanded payment, but not even the generous allowance he got from his parents could cover what he owed. So, they threatened to kill his parents. He never dreamed they would do it. But, when they were killed in that automobile accident, he knew the mob had made good on their threat. They waited for him to get his inheritance; then they came calling again with a huge interest amount attached to the premium.

Then they made their second threat. They had heard about this "dame" in his hometown he had a big soft spot for and so, if he ever said anything to anyone, they would send some people to Sarah's Place posing as customers and Sarah would be dead before they left. Since they carried out their first threat, there was no reason to believe they wouldn't carry out their second one.

As she listened, Sarah began to understand so much. Paul's plea as he stood by the door after that last meal and why he folded up like a deck of cards all made sense now. She snuggled closer to George and began to tremble. She couldn't help wondering, could these threats still be carried

G. Kenneth Cardwell

out? What is Paul planning?

George sat holding Sarah, making mental notes and organizing questions he would most certainly ask when Paul finished. The light-hearted fun of only an hour ago had now turned to deadly serious matters.

Paul explained how he wanted to come clean, but he couldn't put Sarah's life in jeopardy. He felt trapped and powerless. So, to hide how he felt for Sarah and make sure no one in the town got close enough to him where he would feel safe enough to confide, he became an obnoxious, drunk. Only Ruffles ever heard the truth until now.

Then, the night of the storm came. He started to walk home after all the bars had closed, but never made it; he got only as far as that dastardly hole of George's.

"I was unconscious in that hole until morning. When I awoke, I thought it would be a piece of cake to climb out. I had a drink and then I clawed and kicked at the wall and made no progress in getting out," Paul recounted.

"Paul, may I ask you something?" George interrupted.

"Sure," Paul answered.

"Did you notice, at anytime while you were in the hole, there was a ladder half-buried only a few feet down one of the connecting trenches?" George asked.

"No. I never did. Why?" Paul responded.

"Sam and I noticed a ladder there the morning after we found you when we examined the hole and took soil samples," George reported.

Sarah squirmed just a little under George's arm. She had borrowed the ladder secretly when she buried her box in the trench, but when she tried to pull it out, she lost her grip and it fell over in the trench. She was glad they found it; she didn't have to feel guilty of being a thief anymore. She would've said something; but then she would have had to explain why she was there at the manhole. That was her secret. Now, she wondered if her box was still there, had she buried it deeply enough or did George and Sam find that too? If George doesn't say anything about it, she reasoned, it was surely still buried.

"I must have been pretty drunk or hung over," Paul confessed.

Agency and Consequences

Paul continued his story telling how after his first attempt to get out of the hole he must have gotten angry and smashed his whiskey bottle. After that, he must have fallen asleep, went into a coma or something. He told how his whole life seemed to pass before him and, as it did, how utterly terrible he felt. He felt sorry for the pain he had caused so many because of his bad behavior and his insensitivity to those who cared about him.

At this point, something happened that he was still trying to understand fully. What he did realize was what a pathetic, dark, vile creature he had allowed himself to become.

He then saw an image of himself stand before him. The image was not the man he was, but the man he could be. This man spoke to him and showed him there may still be some possibilities for the kind of life that would truly be happy and fulfilling.

Remembering their conversation on the way to the lodge, George and Sarah looked at each other, and quietly said together: "It was a miracle."

Paul then said he woke up and the rain was starting to fall hard again; but he knew he had to make an effort to get out of the hole. It was kind of like a baby bird breaking out of its shell—he had to make the best effort he could. He said he almost made it and then a bolt of lightning hit the big oak tree just a few yards from the hole. He remembered dangling by some tree roots but didn't remember if he had gone much farther. He just remembered being totally exhausted and letting gravity have him as he fell back into the hole. "And that's where I was when you and Sam found me," Paul said looking at George.

"That image of who I can be is burned into my consciousness," Paul said solemnly. "It won't let me rest until I do what I have to do—what I have to do to make things right. But, that's the part where I need your help, because making things right may put Sarah and now, you, George, in danger," Paul said in a very agitated, concerned voice.

"During those years I was a drunk, when I was sober during the day, I wrote down everything I could remember about my associations with the loan sharks and the mob. I have names, addresses, phone numbers, conversations and dates from my day planners. I put it all together. Now, I need to find a way to give all of it to the right person so the two of you won't get hurt. The problem is I just don't know anyone I can really trust. It also means I will be going to prison for a while too. I was part of too much; I held the coats of too many while they stoned innocent people.[1] Sarah, you were right; there is a whole lot more than just my alcoholism," Paul said feeling relieved he had now gotten it all off his chest.

"Paul, I just don't know how to help you; I don't know ...," Sarah said as George broke in.

"I do. I have a friend from college. He's with the FBI investigating racketeering stuff, I think. Let me give him a call. I'll be very discrete, only hypothetical, if you know what I mean. And I'll get back to you in a few days," George offered.

They stood up, Sarah went to Paul and they gave each other a hug as Sarah, with great emotion, said: "Thank you for loving me enough to protect me. That means more than I can express. I love you, Paul. I'm glad you're back. I'm glad to be your friend."

"C'mon, Paul, I'll take you home," George suggested. "I'll be back in about thirty-minutes, sweetheart," George said tenderly to Sarah as he gave her a kiss. He and Paul then went down the stairs and Sarah found the couch, went to her knees and tearfully thanked God for both the men in her life, for their selfless love. She pleaded that somehow all of them would be protected from the evil men in Paul's past; and Paul would find complete peace and become whole through his repentance.

Agency and Consequences

24. Ruse and Arrest

A few days later, George came home for lunch and announced to Sarah his friend, Robert (Bob) Black, of the FBI was coming for lunch. He'd be driving a dirty pick-up and would be dressed in work clothes so it would appear George was just doing business with a subcontractor, which was not uncommon. And more often than not, Sarah joined them, so her staff would think nothing of the threesome having lunch when they arrived for work and started preparing for the evening ahead.

* * * * *

"Well, first of all, the best thing to do is to get your friend, Paul's, record and see if there really is anything that will lead to any arrests. We have several investigations going on right now and maybe this record will give us what we need to button some things up," Bob suggested to George and Sarah in a subdued tone of voice as they ate lunch.

"But, how do we protect Sarah?" George insisted.

"And George, too," Sarah said with great concern.

"If memory serves, we already have some things linking your friend, Paul, to some drug and money laundering schemes a few years back. Let me see if there's enough to merit a search warrant of his place. That way it will look like we tracked it down our selves and he never said anything to anybody. How does that sound?" Bob offered. "That way, you guys are, from this moment on, completely out of it. It's either that or we put you both in the witness protection program," Bob concluded.

George and Sarah looked at each other with astonishment and George said to Bob: "Let me call you in a day or two."

"That will be fine. But since you've given me some pretty good information, I will have to move on it one way or the other sooner rather than later," Bob said with some firmness.

"Bob, George will call you first thing tomorrow morning. We'll decide tonight what we feel is best," Sarah confirmed.

"Sarah, thank you. And thank you for the wonderful lunch. Now I know why this place has such a wonderful reputation. I think I need to bring my wife, Janet, here for a date night some Friday, evening," Bob said cordially as they got up and started towards the door.

"That would be wonderful, Bob; we'd love to meet her. But, if you do come on Friday or Saturday, you ought to call a couple days in advance for a reservation. We are, as the kids say who work at the fast food places, 'slammed' on those nights," Sarah said with a little pride in her voice as she handed him her business card.

* * * * *

It didn't take George and Sarah long to decide setting up the search warrant was the best option. The only thing they wanted to do was give Paul a head's up and make sure a copy of his record would be put into a safe place—just in case.

George picked up the phone and dialed. A few seconds later he said: "Paul, George here. Hey, I know this is short notice, but I have an answer to that Gospel question you asked last Sunday and I was wondering if you had a few minutes and I could come by and discuss it with you, in say 30 or 40 minutes?"

"Sure George. I really appreciate you doing the research. I don't have much of a Gospel library here. Should I get anything ready for your visit?" Paul responded.

"There's only one thing. Your question was really a good one; so, if you could make a copy of your complete question so I can put it in my files, it may become useful in the future," George suggested.

"I anticipated that already and I have a copy made. See you in just a few minutes," Paul acknowledged.

"I'm on my way," George said as he hung up the phone, grabbed his scriptures, jumped in his car and sped off to Paul's estate.

* * * * *

When George arrived, shadowed by Ruffles wagging

Agency and Consequences

his tail excitedly, Paul met him at the front door and escorted him to the back of the mansion and out to the greenhouse. "This is one of my favorite places. Lately I've taken to come here to read and pray. Imagine that; Paul Tenter becoming a prayerful man. In any case, we'll have our privacy here. So, what have you got?" Paul inquired.

George then explained the options Bob, his FBI friend, had outlined. He explained he and Sarah felt the search warrant option appeared to be the best for them given their businesses and all. Paul agreed and said he'd make it work.

Paul then reached into his pocket and produced a thumb drive. "Here's a copy of the record. When the FBI comes, they will find the original copy on my computer and a printed copy in my wall safe. This is a scanned copy of the original printed copy so they won't be able to examine my computer and determine that another copy was made. If they ask if there are any other copies, I will tell them the only two that exist are the ones they've seized," Paul explained.

"Sarah and I will put this copy in a non-descript envelope and put it in our safety deposit box. We'll expose ourselves and this copy only when and if you get word to us to do so because someone has tampered in some way with your originals. Agreed?" George asked.

Paul responded with great emotion as he realized his friends were willing, if necessary, to protect him: "George, you and Sarah are ... well, I'm overwhelmed."

"You know George, if this issue were only about me, I can't think of a single reason for doing what we're about to do," Paul confided as the full weight of what was now in motion settled into his consciousness.

"Well, the show now begins. Thanks for coming, George and please give Sarah my best," Paul said as he shook George's hand.

George pulled Paul to himself and gave him a hug and said: "Paul, your willingness to protect Sarah all these years is an act of love that Father in Heaven will take into account if you continue to work at becoming all He knows you can be. It was and is an act of charity that is as Christ-like as any I know. Your method may have been miss-guided; but there

83

were no tinkling cymbals or sounding brass;[1] your intentions were nothing but full of love and concern for a daughter of God and her protection. There is, will and should be, a place in her heart for you for all Eternity. You are a great man and I'm honored to be your friend."

* * * * *

When George got home, Sarah was only about half way through the dinner evening. He went up stairs and was tempted to put the thumb drive into the computer and see what was on it. But, he thought better of it.

After the dinner evening ended, George went down stairs to help Sarah with the final closing procedures. When they got up stairs, George reported everything was set. He showed her the thumb drive, they put it into an envelope and Sarah put it into their safety deposit box the next morning.

* * * * *

The FBI moved quickly. Within hours after George called Bob with Sarah's and his decision, a team of agents went into Paul's estate bearing a search warrant to look for anything that might be related to certain drug organizations, money laundering, etc.

Paul was the flawless thespian. After all, he had years of practice; but now his performance had to be perfect. There were none and never would be any hints the raid was arranged following his conversation with George and Sarah. He would protect them at the cost of his own life. As planned, agents found two copies of the record Paul had made. The first was on his computer and a printed copy was in his wall safe. The FBI then arrested Paul and placed him in protective custody.

The news of his arrest was broadcast across the country with the headline: "After years of painstaking investigation, agents of the FBI finally zeroed in on Paul Tenter, heir of the Tenter Fortune. Armed with a search warrant, agents entered the Tenter Estate this afternoon and seized a record, made by Mr. Tenter himself. This record allegedly names several, nationally known crime bosses linking them to many unsolved crimes that occurred during

Agency and Consequences

the time Mr. Tenter was allegedly involved with these individuals while attending State College."

Shortly after Paul's arrest, Sarah went to his estate, retrieved little Ruffles and took him back over to Alice's. When hearing this news, Paul realized he would most likely never see his dog again. He, then, broke down and sobbed uncontrollably.

25. Restitution

OVER the next several months, the FBI made numerous arrests based on the information in Paul's record.

One important part of the investigation revealed the truth about the death of Paul's parents. The fact Paul's parents were older and it had been raining on that particular night, no body suspected foul play. Therefore, the police never conducted a thorough examination of the car. Because several of Paul's old associates confessed to staging and carrying out the "accident" that killed Paul's parents, the record was set straight.

Because he turned state's evidence, after the trials, Paul was sentenced 20 to 25 years in the State Penitentiary. The other suspects were sent to Federal Facilities with some awaiting execution dates.

To make sure his affairs would be managed, Paul did all he could while in protective custody, prior to going to prison. He hired a respected law and accounting firm (the same one George and Sarah used for their businesses) to arrange for:

Alice and her husband, Ben, to keep Ruffles, all expenses paid.

His estate personnel were to be kept on the payroll and all maintenance and upkeep to the property would be done.

Philanthropic funds were set up that would be dispersed anonymously. These funds were predominately for programs to help kids go to college and well respected organizations focused on humanitarian aid to the poor, needy, un-wed mothers and alcohol and drug abuse.

Finally, he asked George to make sure any disciplinary procedure with the Church was carried out, as those in authority felt inspired was best.

Paul Tenter was now prepared to pay his debts to society and to God.

Agency and Consequences

26. Doubles

DURING the midst of these events, on an Indian Summer evening about four months after George and Sarah were married, Sarah came up to the apartment a little earlier than usual having asked Alice if she would finish up for her. A twinkle was in Sarah's eyes and Alice recognized it immediately. She responded to Sarah's request saying, with a knowing smile: "Absolutely ...."

When Sarah entered the apartment, she kicked off her shoes and sat on the bed next to George. She bent over and whispered in his ear: "Sweetheart, would you dance with me for a while? Tomorrow is Saturday so I'll let you sleep in," she said with soft and convincing persuasion.

George rolled over just has Sarah was taking the combs out of her hair and it fell softly over her shoulders and down her back. "I would be honored to dance with the most beautiful woman on the planet," George whispered back as he got up and flipped the radio onto the local oldies station.

George and Sarah took each other in each other's arms and danced for fifteen or twenty minutes and then Sarah whispered: "George, I'm ready; would you please help me get out of this dress."

The light of a full moon streamed into the apartment window as George and Sarah slipped off their clothes and between the sheets of their bed and entered into again that hallowed, sacred place of Souls, Symbols and Sacraments,[1] into the polished whiteness of Eternal Burnings.

Later, as they lay snuggled together, Sarah spoke quietly as she ran her fingers around George's mouth: "Do you remember that weekend a few weeks ago when I asked you to take me up to the lodge?"

"Sure I do; why do you ask?" George quietly responded.

"Well, it worked. I just hope when they come, I don't lose interest in being with you like some wives do after they ..." Sarah tenderly responded as George excitedly interrupted.

"Sarah Marie Kindman, are you; I mean are we going

87

to have a baby?" George said as he pulled Sarah closer to him.

"No, we are not going to have a baby," Sarah replied seriously, but with a little tease her voice.

"But, didn't you just say ..." George started to protest as Sarah broke in.

"I said '... when THEY come.' It appears Father in Heaven is helping us make up for lost time. You shot a double barrel full up there at the lodge and we're having twins you study man," Sarah said in her best gravelly voice as she gave George a big kiss.

"Twins ... did you say twins?" George said squeezing Sarah again as the excitement danced in his eyes and voice.

"Yes, I said twins. As near as we can tell at this point, we have a little boy and little girl growing inside me," Sarah explained.

"If that's true, I wasn't the only one shooting a double barreled shotgun at the lodge. You had to have two eggs ready at the same time. Talk about me being a stud .... What do they call a woman who's, well, you know, a female stud?" George said grinning ear to ear.

"A mother," Sarah said with some firmness. "Don't you go calling me a mare or a cow or anything else," she commanded as she poked George in the ribs with her fingernails. "I guess I'm just a 'fertile Myrtle,'" Sarah concluded with a giggle, still tickling George's ribs with her long fingernails.

"Why do you have to be so rough on me?" George questioned as he counter attacked, tickling Sarah's stomach where he'd learned she was very ticklish.

Then it was attack and counter-attack as they rolled around the bed, trying to escape the other's tickle fingers while at the same time trying to get a tickle on the other; both laughing until their sides ached. And then George and Sarah just settled into a comfortable, side-by-side, facing each other posture that included lightly running their fingers across each other's skin.

"So, what would you like to name them?" George asked.

"I hadn't even thought about that yet. What would

Agency and Consequences

you like to name them?" Sarah responded.

George thought for few seconds and said: "Let's call the girl Sarah Elizabeth after you and my mother."

"I never thought about naming a daughter after me, but somehow that seems right. OK ... so why don't we name the boy after you and call him George Kenneth Kindman Jr.?" Sarah suggested as she pulled herself even closer to George.

"You're teasing me now aren't you, Sarah?" George asked as Sarah was obviously in a very frisky and playful mood.

"Do you mean about naming the boy after you or me wanting to enjoy being with you some more?" Sarah replied in between kisses.

"I like the idea of naming our oldest children, especially since they're twins, after us," George said as Sarah continued to kiss him.

"Good; then it's settled. And yes, I am teasing you. Every minute I get to spend with you; feeling you close to me, is a treasure. Do you know what I really like? I like it in the middle of the night when, once in a while, you roll over, gently take my pajamas off and take me," Sarah admitted, punctuated with more kisses. "Because you're so gentle with me, that means it's more than just sex. But, at the same time, I like feeling you want me. And right now, I want you. I want you for as long as you can last," Sarah whispered, giggling seductively as she felt George responding.

"I've been seduced," George quietly acknowledged as he surrendered to the Venus in bed with him.

A short while later, they got up, showered and put their pajamas on and went to sleep.

* * * * *

A little after dawn, George woke up and just lay there looking at Sarah. In his mind, the melody and lyric of the song *"My Cup Runneth Over"* played softly:

"Sometimes in the mornin' when shadows are deep
I lie here beside you just watching you sleep
And sometimes I whisper what I'm thinking of
My cup runneth over with love

G. Kenneth Cardwell

Sometimes in the evening when you do not see
I study the small things you do constantly
I memorize moments that I'm fondest of
My cup runneth over with love

In only a moment we both will be old
We wont even notice the world turning cold
And so, in these moments with sunlight above
My cup runneth over with love
My cup runneth over with love
With love[2]

    In a few minutes, George quietly slid over to Sarah; gently he rolled her onto her back, straddled her and started to unbutton her pajama top. She opened her eyes and looked at him full of desire and whispered: "I was hoping you'd do that. Please, go slow and take me where no woman has ever gone before." Sarah closed her eyes as her heart began to pound and her breasts began to heave and she gave her supple soul totally to the captain of her voyage.

Agency and Consequences

27. *Wonderful and Spontaneous*

AT breakfast that morning, George asked: "Sweetheart, who besides the doctor and us knows we're pregnant."

"Nobody for sure; I think Alice suspected something when I asked if I could come up to the apartment a little early last night," Sarah replied. "Do want to keep it a secret?" Sarah queried.

"Not at all; I want the whole world to know George and Sarah Kindman are going to be parents. I've been dreaming, hoping, praying and I love them all ready ... Little George and Little Sarah .... Wow, it's hard to believe; it's a miracle," George said with amazement.

"Why is it hard to believe? We've been trying to make it happen almost every minute we weren't doing anything else for nearly four months," Sarah said with a mischievous smile.

"George, it's been the most wonderful time; I never in my wildest imagination ever ... well, I mean ...," Sarah was stumbling as George was looking at her with a little amazement even though he wasn't really amazed.

"Sweetheart, are you saying you thought about, imagined ...," George said with a huge grin. "Why what would the neighbors say if they knew?" George teased.

"Of course I thought about it, especially after we were engaged and don't act so surprised, so did you. We even talked about it together once or twice," Sarah said a little defensively.

"Sweetheart, ... oh ... how do I say this? I don't want to sound overly mushy or like a sex maniac, but George, I've loved it. Just being with you, the snuggling, the dancing, talking with you on the couch. Sharing breakfast like we just did; singing in Church together; praying with you; bar-b-cuing and hiking at the lodge; our picnics together; watching a movie together. Hearing the sound of your voice when you come home; even going over budgets; cooking for you; laughing with you; not to mention all of our teasing each other and just being best friends .... I could go on and on.

91

Sweetheart, that's all the meat and potatoes in our relationship.

"But ... sharing my body, my spirit—my soul—with you and you sharing yours with me, has been the sweetest desert that never gets too rich because its been more than just being physical—it's been the most incredible spiritual experience of my life.

"Last night and this morning—oh, sweetheart, how could any woman not want what I have, experience and enjoy with you. I'll remember these past several hours with you for the rest of my life and I'll laugh and cry with joy just thinking about them," Sarah emotionally said as she started to weep. She picked up her napkin and dabbed her eyes.

"Thank you for honoring and respecting me the way you do. You treat me with such tenderness and courtesy not only in public, but in private. I can't help but feel the most blest of women," Sarah continued with the deepest of appreciation.

"And now, knowing inside me, there are two little bodies our love and God's miracle are creating, just fills me with inexpressible joy. Thank you for being the father of my children; I hope I can be the mother of yours you and they deserve," Sarah said with such tender emotion, that welled up in her bosom, she could hardly express it without her voice breaking.

"There's no doubt in my mind and heart you are and will be forever the kind of wife and mother Mother in Heaven will be pleased to acknowledge as one of Her worthy daughters," George softly replied.

"You know we're going to have to start thinking of a bigger place right away now. So, why don't we keep our eyes open and if either of us sees something that looks promising, let's take a look," George said with obvious excitement and pride.

As George and Sarah got up from the breakfast table and George headed towards the door saying he had some paperwork at the office to get done, he turned and took Sarah in his arms and said: "Sarah Marie Kindman, my wife, lover, confidant, best friend and mother of our children, I love you with all my heart."

Agency and Consequences

George and Sarah kissed and Sarah, her eyes still full of tears, and still seeing in George's face and eyes, the strength and tenderness of real manhood, said: "Oh, George Kenneth Kindman, I've tried to say what I feel, but I fear there are not words to say what's really in my heart this morning. Just know I love you too with all of my heart."

George and Sarah kissed again. "And by the way, I think it's time to get the tuxedo out again, don't you?" Sarah quipped as her lips were still against his and a grin quickly formed as she pressed the fingers of her right hand into George's ribs and gave him a big tickle.

"That does it, Mrs. Kindman," George said commandingly as he picked Sarah up and bounded up the stairs with her. When he arrived at the apartment, he kicked the door behind closed and tossed Sarah a good five feet to the bed. By now she was giggling and wiggling with delight as George was now tickling her stomach, arm pits, her neck, anything that would elicit a response.

Soon, it was a tickling free for all. Both were giggling uncontrollably as each attacked and counter-attacked trying to get the advantage.

* * * * *

"What was that?" Sarah asked several minutes later. "Holy cow, how did that happen?" Sarah queried again.

"I don't know, but I'd sure like to do it again, some time," George responded as he and Sarah were snuggling again on top of the bed.

"Yeah, I thought we were on Mt. Everest last night and this morning; but we hit the moon with that one," Sarah said. "I'd like to know how to do it again too. I just hope nobody heard us up here. This was a lodge kind of experience where no one should hear us getting really into each other," Sarah observed as she couldn't help looking at George with all the tender affection in her soul.

"I think instead of being in a plush Cadillac on a smooth road or even in a fast, sports-car convertible with the top down and the wind blowing through our hair, we were just in a four-wheel drive, off-roading and mudding," George said grinning from ear to ear.

"What? Why are you looking at me that way?" George asked.

"That's the first time you ever handled me with the slightest bit of roughness and it was fun; it was wonderful and spontaneous. I think it awakened something in me. Don't get me wrong; I like being treated like a queen, but I have to say the last few minutes were an absolute delight. I think it opened a new door for us to explore together," Sarah said thoughtfully as she smooched George with a giggle.

"So much for my being tender and courteous …. I wasn't too rough was I? I would never want to hurt you, especially since you're now in the motherly way," George said with concern in voice.

Sarah snuggled even closer and began to run her fingernails ever so slightly down George's back as she whispered: "I never felt in the least unsafe or you were really angry with me for tickling you. You just gave me a wonderful surprise when you picked me up, carried me up the stairs to our apartment and tossed me onto our bed. George, it just had that feel of being a little raw, edgy and earthy which made it the most sensual and sexy thing you've ever done with me. It was a wonderful and unexpected present; and I loved it," Sarah reassured as she kissed him in a way she intended as an invitation to surprise her again sometime with something similar.

"Thank you, sweetheart. I hate to break this party up, but, we'd better get going if you're going to be ready for tonight's opening. I still have several hours of work at the office to get done," George reminded.

"I guess you're right. Kicked out of the Garden of Eden again,"[1] Sarah said as they both got up and headed for the shower.

Out of the shower and dressed again, George kissed Sarah goodbye as she sat in her bathrobe in front of the vanity combing out her hair. "Don't forget, you need to be home in time to wear the tux again tonight," Sarah reminded.

"That sounds terrific. I'll be home sometime in mid-afternoon," George replied as he opened the apartment door and headed down the stairs.

Agency and Consequences

28. Revelation

GEORGE arrived at his office and started working through the paperwork on his desk. There were bills to be approved and a proposal to finish. As he was filing some paper in one of his file cabinets, he just happen to open the drawer with the Strange Treasure he'd placed there the morning after he and Sarah had become engaged. He'd literally forgotten about it. But, now, as he stood there and looked at it, a strong impression came into his mind and heart. He knew what the impression was and where it came from; he also knew he should and would obey.

George found a solid, old, plastic gun case with a good seal, locks and key. He also took a brand new plastic tarp from his inventory. He removed some of the foam cutouts from the box, placed the Strange Treasure within it and then replaced as much of the foam as needed to make sure all the china and crystal were well protected.

George next took a piece of his company letterhead and wrote a note. He folded the note and put it in a company envelope, placed it in the box, closed the lid and locked it. Then he rolled the gun case in the new tarp. After folding the tarp over the gun case and tucking all the excess tarp under the case, he used a roll of Duct Tape and carefully secured all the edges so they would not come loose and so as little moisture as possible would seep in.

Then George took another piece of company letterhead and wrote another note. He placed this note and the key within another envelope. Finally, he wrote one more note on company letterhead. He placed this note and the envelope with the key into a manila folder. He then picked up the phone and made a phone call.

*****

About a half-hour later, George was at the picnic spot where he and Sarah liked to come and where they became engaged. He took out a used tarp, pick and shovel from his truck. He laid the tarp on the ground and then carefully removed a section of sod slightly bigger than the length and

G. Kenneth Cardwell

width of the wrapped gun case and laid it on the tarp. The soil was quite easy to dig except for the tree roots, but the pick made quick work of them. Soon, he had dug a hole about three feet deep.

George placed the wrapped gun case in the bottom of the hole and backfilled all the soil into place, carefully tamping and compressing, as he went. Finally, he replaced the sod and emptied a five-gallon can of water on it making sure all the grass roots were saturated.

In a few days, no one would be able to tell the picnic spot had ever been dug up. The Secret Treasure was now securely buried.

Part Three

Better That One Should Perish

G. Kenneth Cardwell

Agency and Consequences

29. Right For Each Other

FOLLOWING the long day ending with the evening at Sarah's Place announcing they were having twins, George and Sarah Kindman flopped into bed without a whimper. When they woke up, George announced he had some things to say: "Good morning Mrs. K. Before we get up and get ready for Church, I need to say a few things."

"Alright, I'm listening," Sarah said as she moved over and snuggled up close to George.

George, then, proceeded to say what was on his mind and in his heart: "First, Sarah, you said some really wonderful things yesterday at breakfast. I'm not as eloquent as you, but there was someone who said what I'm feeling. Parley P. Pratt, while in Philadelphia with the Prophet Joseph Smith, says this meeting with the Prophet: 'had merely lifted a corner of the veil and given me a single glance into eternity.' Sarah, that's how I feel with you. It's as though 'a corner of the veil is being lifted.'"[1]

Taking a book from the night stand and opening it to a marked page, George sat up in the bed and continued as Sarah laid her head in his lap: "Brother Pratt also said:

> 'It was during this time that ... the first idea of eternal family organization, and the eternal union of the sexes in those inexpressibly endearing relationships which none but the highly intellectual, the refined and pure in heart, know how to prize, and which are at the very foundation of everything worthy to be called happiness.
>
> '... I learned that the wife of my bosom might be secured to me for time and all eternity; and that the refined sympathies and affections which endeared us to each other emanated from the fountain of divine eternal love. ... I learned that we might cultivate these affections, and grow and increase in the same to all eternity.
>
> '... I learned the true dignity and destiny of a son of God, clothed with an

eternal priesthood, as the patriarch and sovereign of his countless offspring. ... I learned that the highest dignity of womanhood was, to stand as a queen and priestess to her husband, and to reign forever and ever as the queen mother of her numerous and still increasing offspring.

'I had loved before, but I knew not why. But now I loved—with a pureness—an intensity of elevated, exalted feeling, which would lift my soul from the transitory things of the groveling sphere and expand it as the ocean. I felt that God was my heavenly Father indeed; that Jesus was my brother, and that the wife of my bosom was an immortal, eternal companion; a kind of ministering angel, given to me as a comfort, and a crown of glory forever and ever. In short, I could now love with the spirit and with the understanding also.'[2]

"I apologize if I'm not very original, but Brother Parley says it better than I could in a hundred years," George said softly.

Sarah looked up at George and reached up with an arm and placing her hand behind his neck pulled him down to her, gave him a kiss, and whispered: "Thank you, Mr. K."

"Second," George continued; "I think we need to put what happened yesterday, with respect to the bedroom gymnastics, into perspective. Don't get me wrong; it was hot and steamy and I think we both felt like we were in another dimension. But for me, the most important thing is just being with you; having the private time together where our whole attention is on each other. I suspect, when Little George and Little Sarah come, that will be more difficult to come by. So, I'm just hoping instead of treasuring the explosion that takes us to the moon, we treasure being together and on those occasions when we go to the moon again, we count them simply as an added bonus. What do think and feel about that?"

"We must be really right for each other because I was

thinking the same thing. I think that's what I was trying to say yesterday at breakfast. Our base is the meat and potatoes and the desert, whatever gets served up, will be just fine with me," Sarah responded with great affection. "So, do you think we have time for just one scoop of ice cream before getting ready for Church?" Sarah invited with anticipation.

G. Kenneth Cardwell

30. Parenting

IT was about seven months later George and Sarah saw Little George and Little Sarah come into the world. In the mean time, they were able to secure two adjacent lots next to Sarah's Place. On one lot was a large, old brick and frame home they had completely remodeled and brought up to code. On the adjacent lot, they removed an old, dilapidated house that was close to being condemned. They installed beautiful privacy fencing around the entire property and had the place beautifully landscaped with plenty of room for what they hoped would be a growing family to play and work.

Within the next sixteen years, George and Sarah saw another six children fill their family making a total of five beautiful girls and three handsome sons. Each of these children as he or she grew was given plenty to keep him or her happy and occupied. They built a tree house in one of the large trees in their back yard and installed a zip line from the tree house to the swimming pool. And they enjoyed summer and winter campouts at the lodge.

George and Sarah had adopted a philosophy that none of their children would ever get an allowance. They would have plenty of opportunity to earn their own money. Each was set up with a savings account from an early age and was given assigned chores and opportunity to earn the money he or she needed. At Sarah's Place, each spent time learning to buss and wash dishes, wait tables, scrub floors, stoves and ovens. Each knew what it was to ride in the cab of a Caterpillar bulldozer and backhoe.

Part of George and Sarah's philosophy was a child's self-esteem had more to do with developing their self-confidence through learning and doing than it did from receiving "warm fuzzies." They liked a paragraph from Randy Pausch describing his little league football coach:

> There's a lot of talk these days about giving children self-esteem. It's not something you can *give*; it's something they have to build. Coach Graham worked in a no-coddling zone. Self-esteem? He knew there was really

Agency and Consequences

only one way to teach kids how to develop it: You give them something they can't do, they work hard until they find they can do it, and you just keep repeating the process.[1]

So, when each child wanted to try something, there were only three rules:

First, it must not interfere with anything else they or the family was already committed to (which included school and church activity).

Second, they had to give it their best effort for at least one year. At the end of the year, if it wasn't something the child was passionate about, they could quit—no harm, no foul.

Third, each child was required to have some free time to run, play and even get into a little mischief. Their children were expected to enjoy being children and grow up without being overly structured. There was enough of that anyway.

Connected with this idea was a principle they had garnered from the experience of Nephi in the Book of Mormon. They called it the "Shame on them; shame on me" principle. Nephi had been commanded to build a ship by the Lord and needed his brothers' help to do it. They, however, were reluctant and refused their help saying: "We knew that ye could not construct a ship, for we knew that ye were lacking in judgment; wherefore, thou canst not accomplish so great a task."[2]

Nephi knew he could build a ship; he knew he could do whatever the Lord asked him to do.[3] But his brothers had no such faith and confidence and to justify their lack of faith and confidence, they sought to level the field by pulling Nephi down to their level.

The principle George and Sarah taught often was this: "Shame on the person who tries to tear or knock you down and steal your dreams and hopes; but shame on you if you believe them."

The other thing George and Sarah insisted on was the evening meal and Sunday dinner together as a family and family night each Monday evening. As some of their children became teenagers and more busy, they modified this rule to say each member of the family must be at the evening meal or Sunday

G. Kenneth Cardwell

dinner at least five times each week. These meal times were the anchor of their family life as family prayer was offered, scriptures were read and lively discussions on events of the day were had. Often, when a question was asked, instead of just answering it, an assignment was given to do some research and then present a report to the rest of the family. Consequently, the family encyclopedia set, internet services and library cards were well used.

In addition, George and Sarah found time to give service to their community and Church filling teaching or committee assignments and leadership roles whenever called. And, at least once each month, one or both of them visited Paul Tenter at the State Penitentiary.

* * * * * *

As Little George and Little Sarah entered their high school years, things got really interesting. As it turns out, each was a near mirror image of the older version—Little George looked like Big George and Little Sarah like Big Sarah. Often Little Sarah would stand in the receiving line with her mother at the restaurant, and guests could hardly tell them apart. It was likewise with Little George. When he climbed into the cab of a big machine, you couldn't tell him from his dad. Little George's expertise became the backhoe. Taught by his dad, he could cut a trench with laser-like precision.

What you could tell, however, was when Little Sarah climbed into the cab of a big dozer. While she was as solid and sure around these machines as either her dad or brother, even in her steel-toed cowboy boots, jeans and safety helmet, her womanly figure was a dead giveaway. But make no mistake, with Little Sarah at the controls, the biggest dozer in her dad's fleet was a precision instrument, a surgeon's scalpel and she loved it.

Working together was one of Little George and Little Sarah's favorite things to do. They seemed to have a rhythm working together. Sarah would prepare a stretch down to grade and Little George would follow cutting the trench to the precise depth.

* * * * *

Little Sarah loved bulldozers so much at the beginning of

summer, between her sophomore and junior years in high school, her dad gave her an older Cat D9. She decided to rebuild it. So, with the help of a Certified Cat Mechanic, she spent her summer tearing down and completely rebuilding her own dozer. She devoured and practically memorized every technical document she could find. When she didn't understand the math, she engaged the help of her high school math teacher. By the end of summer, she had the calculus mastered sufficiently to understand all the power curves, fly-wheel horse power, turbo chargers and hydraulics to name just a few. She could turn a hand wrench, use an air wrench; with a welder, she could lay down a bead or resurface the cutting edge of a plow.

During the next year, Little Sarah's skills even became better, not only as an operator, but as a mechanic and engineer. She came up with an improvement that, when she built and tested it, her older D9 could out run and outperform her dad's newer models.

Soon, Cat engineers and executives were visiting Little Sarah and her dad to see her work for themselves. With Big George's negotiating skill, she sold the patent rights to her invention and made a very handsome profit.

The contract specified the following in exchange for Little Sarah's patent rights:

- a brand new D9T bulldozer, which she named Hidalgo, after the great mustang and long-distance race champion,
- a Kenworth truck tractor, which she named Traveler, in honor of General Robert E. Lee's famous horse,
- a flatbed trailer for hauling Hidalgo,
- a full-ride university scholarship,
- a large sum of cash,
- royalty payments for the next 10 years from each Caterpillar machine sold with her invention installed or sold later as an add-on to either Caterpillar equipment or other manufacturer's equipment.

G. Kenneth Cardwell

31. Questionable Date

IT was during her senior year in high school Little Sarah came to grips with the fact she was not a typical high school young woman. She liked to leave from school, take Hidalgo and help any one of the farmers or ranchers in the vicinity clean the manure from his corals or help the Forest Service build a firebreak. For many of these jobs, she was paid very handsomely. So, the kids in school, not so kindly, nicknamed her *"The Dozer Drivin' Momma."*

Little George, on the other hand, was popular, played on the football, basketball and baseball teams.

The bottom line was, Little Sarah, though she was stunningly beautiful and she knew how to dress and wear makeup as well or better than any of the girls in the school, didn't fit in with most of the girls and she intimidated the boys. After all, she knew more about engines, transmissions, fuel ratios, fuel injectors and turbo chargers than anyone else in the school and didn't feel the need to play dumb just to protect some guy's ego.

And so it was Little Sarah carefully flirted with and then decided to accept an invitation from a young man, Josh Bangeter, to go to Senior Prom. When Little George found out, he took her aside privately and asked: "Sarah, do you know who this guy is? The only reason he asked you to the prom is because you're a challenge; you're prey to him. This guy's reputation is really in the toilet. Do you know how many girls he's knocked up and how many more he's made out with and then bragged about it? All he wants is to put another notch in his gun handle, if you know what I mean."

"George, he can't be all that bad. If he were, somebody surely would have said something. If what you say were true, at least one investigation would have taken place. And besides, nobody else will ask me; they're all scared of me (why, I really don't know) and I'm tired of staying home and greeting all the prom goers at the restaurant when they come in later for something to eat," Little Sarah argued in defense.

"Look, Sarah, all I'm saying is 'be careful.' Make sure you keep some Mace and your cell phone in your purse when you're

Agency and Consequences

with this guy," Little George advised.

"Yeah, right. Now I think you're being a little extreme, don't you think? And besides, I've been thinking, maybe if I let down a little on this chastity stuff, I'll get more dates and have a little more social life," Little Sarah responded.

"Now you're scaring me, Sarah. That would be the worst thing you could do for yourself and you would break mom and dad's hearts not to mention it would be a very serious offense to God. All you'd be doing is adding the word 'Easy' to your nickname and making it even worse. I can hear it now: 'Hey, look, there comes The *Easy* Dozer Drivin' Momma now,'" Little George warned as he emphasized the word "*Easy*."

"How dare you say that, George? I'm going to the prom tonight with Josh and that's it. Not you, mom or dad is going to stop me. Got it!" Little Sarah shouted as she stormed to her bedroom, slamming the door behind her, to get ready for the prom.

* * * * *

A little while later, Little George caught his mom and dad at the kitchen table and said: "Mom and dad, if you have an extra prayer lying around, pray for Sarah. I'm more than a little concerned with her choice of dates for the prom this evening. I've tried to talk to her, but I think I just made it worse. I'll try and keep my eye on her, OK? Well, I'm going to be late picking up Mary. See ya later. I love you," Little George said before either Big George or Big Sarah could say anything.

It was just then the doorbell rang and Josh Bangeter was at the door to pick up Little Sarah. When George opened the door and saw Josh, his heart dropped. He too, as the current Stake President of the Church, knew something of Josh's reputation and fully understood Little George's concern. But, he greeted Josh cordially. However, before he could say what he felt appropriate to say, Little Sarah came down the stairs and was out the door with Josh saying, "See ya later daddy. I love you."

"Sweetheart, I wasn't aware of who Sarah's date was tonight; were you?" George asked his wife with grave concern.

"No, to be honest, I don't think I even knew she had a date," Sarah responded.

107

G. Kenneth Cardwell

"Well, I know you have to get back over to the restaurant; but before you go, I think we should follow George's advice and say a prayer for Sarah," George suggested.

George and Sarah went into their living room and prayed for both of their children out that night and their dates; but were more earnest in their pleadings on behalf of their daughter, Sarah.

Agency and Consequences

32. Narrow Escape

THE Senior Prom was held at a local hotel. They had converted three of their meeting rooms into a large room with a hardwood dance floor and festive decorations. A live band from Capital City was well adept at playing all the popular genres of music.

When Little Sarah and Josh came in, it seemed all eyes were on them and they were, at least for a while. Little George and Mary, however, were never far away. Little George was worried about his sister. Any wrong move by Josh and he was determined to get in the middle of it.

At first, Little Sarah was excited to be there, to be with Josh. But after a short while, it was clear Josh was warming up and trying to get Little Sarah that way too. About half way through the evening, Josh maneuvered them close to the door and said as he took Little Sarah's hand: "Let's get out of here."

* * * * *

Soon, they were in Josh's BMW and headed out into the country. Josh turned onto a little off road, where there were no streetlights. He locked the doors, pulled to a stop and turned off the engine. He climbed into the back seat and began to be physical as he reached down and lowered Little Sara's seat and pulled her into the back with him. "What are you doing?" Little Sarah asked a bit surprised (but thinking about her conversation with Little George, she wasn't really).

"Just thought we'd have a little fun, Sarah; wouldn't you like to have a little fun?" Josh said trying to be seductive as he kissed Sarah and reached for the zipper on the back of her dress.

In a flash, Little Sarah knew she was in trouble. If she somehow managed to get out of the car and start running, she'd never out run him and she would likely be raped. Yes, she had thought about losing her virginity, but not like this, in the back seat of a car and with a kid who thought nothing of her except as a piece of meat. This wasn't the way her mom and dad had their first experience together. She remembered what she had recently read in the book, *Freedom Writers Diary*, about a girl who had lost her virginity in only slightly better circumstances (at least this girl was with someone she liked):

> 'My boyfriend and I had been together for two years before we decided to have sex. Then when it came time for what was supposed to be my special moment, I thought there would be caressing and passionate kisses. Instead, it was a five-minute bang, bang, bang. I looked at him after we were finished and asked him, "Is that it?" I thought losing my virginity was something that would be worthwhile. Instead, it's something I now regret.
>
> 'Now I'm not a virgin and everyone looks at me as though I am a tramp or a ho.'[1]

Little Sarah was not going to make the same mistake this girl made. She thought fast. This would take some guile. "Josh?" Little Sarah said as she kissed him back and ran her hands through his hair. "Surely you won't deny a girl's request to lose her virginity in a clean bed rather than the back seat of a car out in some cow field would you? Please, take me to a motel. I hear you have a deal going at Charley's. And then you can teach me how to make a man really happy."

"All right!" Josh said with exuberance as he crawled out from under Little Sarah and back into the front seat. Little Sarah barely had her dress zippered back up when the car was roaring back out to the main road. She finally made her way back into the passenger seat and to keep the illusion going, she stroked the back of Josh's neck.

* * * * *

When they got to Charley's Motel, Josh was out of the car and into the Motel Office almost before the car stopped. As soon as he entered the office door, Little Sarah was out her side of the car. She left the door open so Josh wouldn't hear it close and was immediately running as fast as she could go around the back of the motel and into the park. Sarah's Place and her home were just on the other side of the park if she could make it.

Josh was only in the motel office for thirty-seconds (he

Agency and Consequences

did have a deal—a friend worked as the desk clerk and when Josh came in, he would just hand him a key). When he came out of the motel office and saw the passenger door of the car open and Sarah gone, he knew where she was headed. She had a lead, but running in a formal gown and heels made Sarah no match for him.

Josh caught Sarah half way across the park. He grabbed her from behind with his right arm around her arms and chest and clamped his left hand across her mouth. "Listen you little bitch; you led me on. So, here's the deal. We're going to do it right here in the park under this tree. You can enjoy it or not; that's your choice. Just remember, I have a motel registration slip (he was lying) that says you came willingly and everyone will know you gave yourself to me on prom night," Josh said angrily.

At that moment, before Josh could get Sarah on the ground, she imagined the spiked heel of her shoe as the ripper on the back of Hidalgo and stomped that spiked heel of her right shoe into the top of his right foot with all the concentrated force she could muster.

Josh let out a scream and reactively let go of Sarah as the spiked heel of her shoe felt like a rail spike going through his foot. She turned quickly and, as hard as she could, kneed him in his groin. Josh doubled over and was on the ground. Sarah flipped off her shoes, grabbed her dress, pulled it up as high as she could and made for home as fast as she could run.

* * * * *

Little Sarah burst into her house and yelled: "Dad, dad, where are you?"

"I'm here in the living room. Why, what's going on, honey," Sarah's dad responded.

Little Sarah ran straight to her dad, crawled onto his lap and sobbed," Daddy, please hold me and tell me I'm safe."

George put his arms around his trembling and frightened daughter, pulled her close and tenderly comforted her: "Sarah, you're safe. Daddy's got you and nobody is going to hurt you." In about five minutes, Little Sarah asked: "Would you take me to the hospital emergency room? Please, daddy, this is important. I'll tell you the rest on the way."

"OK; let's go," George responded.

G. Kenneth Cardwell

When George and Little Sarah got in the car, she told her dad about how she felt so different from all the other girls at school. She explained how she thought, if she accepted a date with Josh Bangeter and lost her virtue, she would become more acceptable with the kids at school. "I forgot the shame on them, shame on me principle," Little Sarah admitted.

"That's hard not to do sometimes, sweetheart," George said understandingly to his daughter.

"Daddy, this afternoon, George tried to warn me, but I wasn't listening and I almost made the biggest mistake of my life. When we got to the dance, Josh started to come on pretty strong. At first, I was excited, but somehow I began to sense that all he wanted was the sex. He didn't care about me any more than a stud, about to mount an in-heat filly, cares about her. So, then, it didn't take long to figure out having my first sexual experience that way wouldn't have been nearly as wonderful as it was for you and mom. And more importantly, I finally figured out for myself sex, outside of marriage, is wrong—wrong for me, disrespectful of you and mom and a serious offense to God—a much too big a price for superficial popularity."

"Sarah, I'm proud of you. You're quite a young woman. So, if you didn't have sex and you're still virtuous, why are we going to the emergency room?" Dad asked.

"Because Josh will tell everyone we did it anyway. The only way I could get away from him was to trick him into taking me to Charley's Motel where I had a chance to get out of the car and run home. He still caught me half way across the park, was going to rape me and then claim we were both at the motel as willing partners. But I think I broke his foot when I drove one of my high heels into his foot and then I kneed him in the groin as hard as I could. So, we're going to the emergency room so I can be examined and the doctors can certify I didn't have sex tonight and I'm still a virgin," Sarah responded.

"Sarah, you really want to do that?" her dad asked seriously.

"Yes, I do. I want my honor and the honor of this family to be protected. And if it takes a vaginal examination to do that, then so be it. Besides, it's my fault anyway; if I had listened in the first place …," Little Sarah said as she started to sob again feeling the weight of her unwise choice and it's near tragic

Agency and Consequences

consequences.

* * * * *

George and Little Sarah arrived at the emergency room and registered. Fortunately, the triage line was short and Sarah went in for her examination within just a few minutes. Then one of the doctors recognized George and asked: "Hey, aren't you the guy that found Paul Tenter in that hole several years ago?"

"That was nineteen years ago now; and yes, one of my employees and I found him," George replied.

"So, do you know how Paul is doing; he's up in the State Pen now isn't he?" the doctor queried.

"Well, Paul's doing as well as can be expected. I visited him last month and he is at the State Pen," George answered as he took a seat in the waiting room.

* * * * *

About thirty minutes later, Little Sarah came out with the female doctor who did the examination. "You must be Mr. Kindman; I'm Dr. Anders," the doctor said smiling as she held out her hand to shake George's.

"Yes, I am. So, how's Sarah?" George responded.

"Well, she's emotionally still a little shaken, but otherwise, she's in great shape and still a virgin. Here's the original document she asked for on hospital letterhead and signed by three members of the hospital staff who all participated in the examination. She didn't want just one doctor or nurse; she wanted three to sign this document. She even had the legal knowledge to dictate what it should say and made sure we put a copy in her file," Dr. Anders said with admiration.

"I wish more young women would take back their honor in this way. Most women just hold it inside thinking the trauma and hurt will just go away; and the lies, rumors and gossip won't make it worse. But they do; I know from personal experience. I refused the first time too. I just bottled it all up inside; but the lies, rumors and gossip got so bad, I figured the easiest thing to do was just go out and make them all true," Dr. Anders reported.

Then a big tear rolled down Dr. Anders' cheek as she said: "That was my biggest mistake. I got pregnant. Then I had

113

an abortion. I think about it every day. I'm married now to the love of my life and my husband knows the whole story; but I think something is missing in our relationship; there's a cloud; I feel like I've cheated us both, but mostly him."

"Don't let that reprobate, who thinks he's a man and God's gift to women, get away with what he did tonight. And if you need me to do anything else, even testify, if it should come to that, I'll be there in a heartbeat," Dr. Anders concluded with conviction.

George and Little Sarah thanked Dr. Anders for her service and for sharing her story and they left for home.

* * * * *

As George and Little Sarah drove home, Sarah's mind raced. Her thoughts quickly returned to Dr. Anders' advice: "Don't let that reprobate, ... get away with what he did tonight." A second later, her focus landed on a couple of movies she had seen recently. These were *True Women*[2] and *The Blind Side*[3]. Both of these movies portrayed women of magnificent strength, who, though they wished and hoped for lives that were more in line with their dreams of cultural refinement, were nevertheless willing to take the lead, step into the breach of danger and protect their families, their honor and virtue. In that moment, the vision of a plan settled into her mind. She knew what she would do next.

"Daddy, there's one thing more. I know what you're thinking. I want you to leave Josh to me. This is between him and me. Please trust me on this. I haven't got it all figured out yet; but I'm going to do what Dr. Anders suggested—I'm not going to let Josh get away with what he did and tried to do to me tonight," Little Sarah said with a determination George knew well. It was the same determination he knew so well in Sarah's mother.

"All right, honey. But, just remember, I got your back and you can't take that from me. Do you understand?" George said firmly.

"Yes, daddy, I understand. I love you, daddy," Little Sarah said with that sense of peace and security that always came when she knew her dad was in her corner.

Agency and Consequences

33. All Safe and Sound

JUST moments after returning home, Little George and his date, Mary Greenfield, came running into the house. "Dad, Dad," Little George shouted; "have you seen Sarah? We lost her at the dance and have been looking all over town and then we saw Josh's car parked at Charley's Motel," Little George said with grave concern in his voice.

"Sarah is fine; she didn't do what Josh wanted her to do. She's upstairs changing and will be back down in a minute or two," Big George said with a smile. "She's very thankful for …. Well, I'll let her tell you herself when she comes down," Big George acknowledged as he gave his son a hug and then whispered: "I'm personally thankful for your concern and your counsel to your mother and me earlier this evening. I'm certain our combined faith and prayers helped your sister to avoid a serious tragedy in her life this evening."

Sarah then came down the stairs and seeing her brother, ran to him and gave him a huge hug and then sobbing said: "Thank you, George, for trying to warn me this afternoon. I'm sorry I was too stubborn to listen." Turning to Mary, she then said: "Mary, may I borrow my brother for about fifteen minutes. I need him to escort me back into the park to retrieve my heels."

"Sure; but don't be too long. He needs to get me home by curfew or he'll be in big trouble with my dad," Mary said smiling.

* * * * *

Little Sarah and Little George were gone just over ten minutes as they walked to the park, found the heels Sarah had kicked off so she could run home and then walked back. During their walk, Sarah briefly explained what had happened and about the trip to the emergency room and she asked him: "George, I'm going to ask you the same thing I asked dad, would you please stay out of this? I know you've been taught to protect women and I appreciate you being in my corner and I promise to let you know if I need help. But, within the next week or two, Josh is going to know not to mess with Sarah Elizabeth Kindman and I hope any other young woman again the way he tried with me. His studly pride was hurt tonight; I out smarted him. He's going to say some things normally you would be obliged to knock his lights out for. Just know he's literally going to be digging a hole for himself. Will you promise?"

"Yes, Sarah; but if Josh even looks like he's going to hurt you in any way ..." Little George affirmed as Little Sarah broke in.

"You'll have to get in line behind dad," Little Sarah informed with a smile feeling very safe knowing both her dad and brother would be keeping their eyes on whatever came next.

* * * * *

As Little Sarah and Little George returned to the house, Big Sarah also came in from the restaurant and asked, as she saw her twins and Mary in the living room: "So, how was the dance tonight?"

Little Sarah gave her the Readers' Digest version of what happened that evening and then asked: "Mom, this may be inappropriate with Mary here; but if you and dad don't mind, would you be willing to share with us how you felt when you and dad had your first sexual experience together? I'm asking because I nearly blew it tonight. But, to be real honest, how will I ... I mean, how will we really know its right? I'm not talking about being married first; I think I understand that part. But, even some marriages don't seem to have what you and dad and Mary's mom and dad have. That's what I want to know ...."

"You want to know how you recognize the right companion to marry and then how do you keep the spark alive afterwards; is that what I hear you asking?" Big Sarah reflected.

"Yes, that's part of it, but I also want to know what to expect ... the first time," Little Sarah, a little embarrassed, admitted.

Big Sarah looked at her husband who gave her an affirmative nod and asked Little George and Mary if they wanted to be included in the discussion. To which they both indicated "yes"; but Mary was due home as her curfew was expiring shortly.

Big Sarah went to the phone and dialed: "Alice, hi, it's

Agency and Consequences

me, Sarah. I have a request and if you're not comfortable just let me know. A situation occurred with Sarah tonight and it has raised some questions George and I are going to explain as best we can. Little George and Mary are also here and they have expressed an interest in being part of the discussion. The subjects are virtue, chastity and what it's like for married couples to be together. If you have an objection to Mary being here, we'll send George home with her right now; otherwise, the discussion will go on past her curfew and if you don't mind, we'll put her up in our spare bedroom tonight and we'll meet you at Church in the morning."

"Thank you, Alice. Give Ben our love and we'll take good care of Mary tonight," and Big Sarah hung up the phone.

"Well, we may as well get comfortable. Sarah, please see if you have some clothes Mary could put on. Son, why don't you and I change and sweetheart, would you mind getting some milk and cookies or some kind of snack," Big Sarah directed.

G. Kenneth Cardwell

34. A Most Important and Sacred Subject

SHORTLY, everyone was gathered back into the living room, and then Big George said: "This is a sacred subject and shouldn't be discussed flippantly so George, would you please offer us a prayer and then I'll begin."

Little George offered a prayer giving thanks for Sarah's safety that evening. He also asked they would all learn and be strengthened by what was discussed. Finally, he offered a blessing on the snacks.

Following the prayer, Big George said: "The Lord said in *The Family, a Proclamation to the World*: 'We declare the means by which mortal life is created to be divinely appointed.'[1] That means in the right place, after the right ceremony and with the right person, wholesome sexual relationships are approved by God.

"The whole issue of sexual intimacy between a married man and woman is centered in the temple. As I have attended the temple over the years, I've pondered this subject many times. I've listened to the ceremonies very carefully and prayed about this subject often. Sarah and I have discussed it and prayed together about it."

"Dad, that seems a bit strange—even corny to pray about sex," Little Sarah injected.

"Yes, it may seem corny to pray about sex, but I can think of no subject more important to pray about. Let me see if I can explain it. Sarah, go ahead and jump in if you feel the need," Big George assured.

"I count six times in the temple ceremonies where sexual relations are either specifically mentioned or implied. No subject is referenced more often. When I say it's referenced, that relates to having children and posterity. Now, the way God ordained for children to be born is a consequence of sexual relations between a man and a woman who are legally and lawfully married," Big George explained.

"President Kindman, can you tell us what those references say in the temple ceremony," Mary asked.

"I can't tell you the words, but I can tell you where.

Agency and Consequences

First, is the washing ceremony and second is the anointing ceremony. Both of these ceremonies are part of what is called the initiatory ordinances.

"Third, and this one is important. During the portrayal of Adam and Eve in the Garden of Eden and as found in the scriptures, Adam and Eve are commanded to multiply and replenish the Earth.[2] This commandment is so important Adam and Eve chose to eat the fruit of the tree of knowledge so they would become mortal. Thereby, they would be able to keep this commandment. Here's what Eve said regarding this choice: 'Were it not for our transgression we never should have had seed ...'[3] [meaning children].

"Fourth, in the temple, we make a specific covenant to keep the law of chastity. This covenant is as binding on men as it is on women—there is no double standard.

"Fifth, there is reference to a righteous, eternal posterity at what is called the veil ceremony.

"And sixth, when a couple is married in the temple, like Adam and Eve, they are commanded to multiply and replenish the earth.

"All this, in my mind, suggests this subject is very high on our Father in Heaven's list of priorities.

"Now, I want to read you part of a letter written by a friend of mine to his son in the mission field. This missionary son was concerned for someone close to him who had made and was still making choices that would disqualify him to marry in the temple. My friend responds to his son's concerns in a way I think is unique and goes right to the heart of our subject this evening. He writes:

> 'I'm with you on the civil vs. Temple Marriage. I don't know if you have had the opportunity to witness an actual sealing in the Temple. There is no pomp and ceremony. And for most people in the world, that's what it's all about—a big show, a lot of expense—all in an effort to give the appearance of something important. But in the Temple, it's the most joyful, solemn, happy and serious of occasions. The rooms are small with only the closest,

worthy friends and family in attendance. Some believe that to be rather exclusive (meaning it keeps people out as well as admitting only the most select). And they're right.

'Sealing rooms in our modern temples are the counter part of the Holy of Holies in the Old Testament Temples. They are an extension of the Celestial Room (in early Temples, there was an altar in the Celestial Room where marriages could be performed). Today, because of the many different ordinances being performed in parallel; that is, simultaneously, sealing rooms are now placed outside the Celestial Room architecturally. But, they are quite literally, an extension of the Celestial Room within which the capstone ordinances of the priesthood are performed—the creating of and welding of families together for Time and Eternity.

'There is only one ordinance that remains for which all the other ordinances are but preparatory. It is the most abused and maligned of all the ordinances. It is the ordinance most openly attacked by Satan. This ordinance completes the circle and begins anew the cycle for another of God's Children. This is the ordinance we refer to (Elder Jeffery R. Holland calls it a Sacrament) as sexual intimacy between a worthy man and woman who have been washed, anointed, clothed in the garment of the Holy Priesthood and are then endowed with knowledge, revelation (if one is in tune), covenants, signs, tokens and dressed in Holy Robes. In fact, much of the instruction given in the endowment directly relates to the proper relationship between a husband and wife.

'From the beginning of time with Adam and Eve, it has been God's intention that this

Agency and Consequences

last, which is also the first, ordinance—sexual intimacy—was only to be performed after the sealing of a man and woman by the Holy Priesthood in a marriage for Time and Eternity. Every other kind of arrangement, even at its very best, this settling for something less, is what Marian D. Hanks, a former General Authority, had in mind when he described such caving as settling for the "plausible second choice."

'For, when it's all said and done, this is the one ordinance that most clearly defines the difference between Gods and Goddesses and all other beings in the universe. It's not intelligence. It's not the ability to create worlds, suns, galaxies or any other physical structure in the universe. It's not administrative ability. It's not social grace. It's not physical attractiveness. it's the ability of procreation. It's having the ability, worthiness and maturity to bring into existence a unique, spirit personality from the co-eternal intelligence that exists throughout space.

'If this is true, does it not stand to reason that how we think about, prepare for and remain faithful to the specifications for that ordinance in mortality will define the difference between us and all others in the world. Every other commandment and righteous principle we are given is calculated to enhance and foster the relationship between a married man and woman that culminates in this ordinance.

'This is why marriage and family are at the center of the Gospel. This is what this mortal existence is really all about. It is preparation for becoming like our Heavenly Parents. This is also why Satan is so desperate and ruthless in his attack of marriage, family and the intimacy that should only exist within the sacred bonds of legal and lawful marriage.

'Satan would lead us to believe that sexual intimacy is nothing more than a natural and wonderful function of our physical bodies. While that is true as far as it goes, it is more, much, much more. Because it is a Sacrament, an Ordinance, it is Spiritual. It is the culminating expression of love, trust, commitment and loyalty between a man and woman. As already mentioned, it is, when enjoyed within the bounds of Temple Marriage, the Ordinance that most closely emulates the full relationship that exists between a Celestialized Man and Woman.'[4]"

"So, Dad, what this friend of yours is saying, and I assume you agree, is sexual relations are only intended by God to be participated in after a man and woman are married by priesthood power and sealed for time and eternity. Basically, anything less than that is a cheap substitute. Have I got that right?" Little George asked.

"Yes, that is God's intention. However, I should clarify sexual relations, participated in by couples legally and lawfully married by government or other ecclesiastical authority, are not condemned by God. But the fullness of unity that can come with having the sealing power of the priesthood associated with those relationships, in my friend's view as well as my own, makes these other marriages 'the plausible second choice.'

"Sexual relations of any kind where there is no marriage between a man and a woman are an abomination and second only to premeditated murder in seriousness. Why? Because a mockery is being made of that, which in time and eternity, brings about life—spirit life in the heavens and mortal life here on earth," Big George explained with great seriousness.

"So, when I left here with Josh for the Prom last night and it was in my mind (and I suppose to some extent in my heart) to lose my chastity without the sanction of a marriage, the only thing I could do that's worse would be to kill somebody in cold blood?" Little Sarah asked in great seriousness as tears began to flow.

Agency and Consequences

"Yes, honey. Only in your case, because you have been taught plainly for many years, you wouldn't have *lost* your chastity, you would have *given* it away," Big Sara said solemnly as she moved over and took her daughter in her arms.

"If I had gone through with it with Josh, could I ever have gotten my virtue back again? Would I ever have been clean and eligible to enter the temple and do it the right way? Or would I have been, pardon my word here, screwed forever?" Little Sarah asked bluntly.

"Yes, Sweetheart, you would have been able to have your virtue restored. But, it would have taken a lot of effort in repentance. The sorrow you're feeling right now because you only thought about it with some seriousness would have to have been much, much deeper and more intense. You would have to confess to the Bishop. Then, after a strictly supervised period of time, when you and the Bishop both felt you had been forgiven and you had forgiven yourself, the Bishop, as the common judge in Israel, would declare you clean. All through this process, if you were sincere, you would feel the Lord's Atonement working in your life healing and repairing your damaged soul—that is, your body, mind, spirit and emotions," Big Sarah continued to explain.

"But, it wouldn't have been easy," Big George emphasized. "Because of the seriousness of the sin, this would have been a long, difficult process over several months at least. Before the Lord reveals to the Bishop your repentance is complete, He would need you to have shown your repentance was thorough and the likelihood of the sin being committed again very, very remote," Big George carefully explained.

"But why would I have had to confess to my bishop? Wouldn't just going to the Lord in prayer be enough? Is it really the bishop's business to know stuff like that about people?" Little Sarah asked feeling like her privacy could be infringed in such situations.

"It's because the Lord loves you and all of his children, Sarah," her dad responded with a depth of experience that surprised and softened her. "You see, sweetheart, when people commit serious sin, they lose the spirit; they are no longer entitled to have His guidance in their lives. And so the Lord has provided that His judges in Israel can serve as intermediaries—

literally in a Savior role—to help those who have lost the spirit choose a new direction in life. If the counsel of such men, who strive day in and day out to be worthy, is followed, those who have lost it can, and will, regain it. Confession to a bishop or stake president is, therefore, an act of faith—a reaching out to God's love, mercy and grace," President Kindman testified solemnly while Little Sarah sobbed quietly as she wiped a few tears from her eyes.

"Is this why your friend Paul lost his membership in the Church and most likely won't get to be rebaptized until he gets out of prison?" Mary asked.

"Yes, Mary, that's exactly right," Big George answered. "The sins Paul committed in his life were very serious. But, Paul has been very diligent in his repentance. His sorrow has been God-like in every respect. And I do believe, with all my heart, when he is released from prison, he will be ready for rebaptism into the Church. Because of his past, there will most likely be some restrictions in some of the callings the Church will be allowed to extend. But in God's eyes and in our eyes, as his brothers and sisters, he will be clean," Big George explained with great love and sincerity.

"I have one more question, dad, regarding what your friend wrote his son. I think I understand, but he suggested sexual intimacy is the highest ordinance or maybe I said that wrong; all the other ordinances lead up to it. What does that mean?" Little George asked.

"Well, it means this. While all the ordinances are necessary and must be performed with proper authority and in the correct order, there is a hierarchy in the ordinances. Some ordinances are preparatory to other ordinances. For example, I believe when we bless babies and give them names, besides giving a name there are two purposes. First, through the power of the priesthood, that little spirit is welcomed into the mortal world and hopefully feels a sense of comfort in coming from his or her Heavenly Parents to his or her earthly parents. It must be an awful shock to that spirit being combined with a physical body it has absolutely no control of and which it must begin learning to control. Second, a blessing is often pronounced which is intended to guide or prepare that new soul throughout its life.

"Next comes the first ordinance of salvation, the

Agency and Consequences

ordinance of baptism. This ordinance is preparatory to receiving the Gift of the Holy Ghost, the second ordinance of salvation. As a preparatory ordinance, baptism is performed by the Aaronic Priesthood, which is the preparatory priesthood.

"The Sacramental bread and water are administered also by the preparatory Aaronic Priesthood to prepare us for a new week and to help us keep improving our lives through repentance.

"The preparatory Aaronic Priesthood then leads, if a young man is faithful, to the Melchizedek or Higher Priesthood. This allows a young man to enter the temple and receive the ordinances there. In the temple, we begin with the initiatory ordinances, which are preparatory to the endowment, a presentation of knowledge, instructions and covenants.

"And then finally, we come to the ordinances of sealing where families are welded for time and eternity together.

"Each of these ordinances and the priesthood are designed to prepare and lead both men and women to what the Lord designed as the most exclusive, godlike experience of all—sexual intimacy between a sealed man and woman.

"But, President Kindman, why don't women have to have the priesthood to enter the temple," Mary asked.

"I don't think I know all the answers, but let me share what I've come to believe is true. First, women are generally more sensitive to spiritual things than men are. I'm a spiritual pygmy compared to my wife and most of the great women I know including your mother, Alice. I often am in awe and tears when I sense the power and influence of righteous womanhood in my life and in our stake and wards.

"Second, I believe the priesthood was given to men to help men become equal to women. When a woman, who's really in tune with the spirit, becomes pregnant and later as she nurses a baby (if these experiences are her opportunity), there is a connection, a bonding that occurs between her and her baby no man on this planet can come close to understanding or experiencing. It is only through a man's righteous exercise of the priesthood, when giving a blessing or in being of service to his wife and family and others, that he has an opportunity to approach this kind of experience and bonding.

"Third, as one of our past general authorities said: 'The

priesthood is held in trust to be used to bless all of God's children. Priesthood is *not gender*, it is blessings from God for all the hands of his servants He has designated.'[5]

"In our temples, women perform some of the priesthood ordinances just as the men do. And all women have the potential of becoming queens and priestesses—surely positions of power, authority and service.

"That said, righteous womanhood combined with righteous priesthood is the most awesome power for good in the universe. And that welding of a righteous woman and a righteous man that occurs in the temple is strengthened and revitalized by wholesome sexual relationships," George concluded.

Agency and Consequences |

35. *Council and Counsel at Midnight*

"**W**ITH that introduction, now, let's talk about Sarah's questions," Big Sarah suggested. "How do you know when you've found the right one? How do you keep the spark alive after the first time you're together and finally what can you expect the first time?" Big Sarah reminded.

"First, let's clear the air. I won't go into detail on this, we can have another discussion on it later, but except in very rare circumstances, like Adam and Eve or Joseph and Mary, there is not a 'one and only' partner. We each have to choose. Dad and I chose each other; Mary's mom and dad, Alice and Ben, chose each other. This takes work. Often it means kissing a lot of toads before you find the prince if I can say it that way. You need to be smart, prayerful, living the commandments and being patient.

"I don't think, and this is my opinion, a big, long laundry list or specification of what you're looking for in a partner such as a certain color of hair, or certain body type, or can they play the piano, or is he this or is she that, or anything else is very helpful, if you get my drift. I think those things tend to cloud your spiritual receptors to the most important things. Instead, ask: 'Is he or she committed to the gospel? Is he or she worthy to enter the temple? Does he or she have balance in their lives? Are you both able to resolve problems in a mature way? Do you have some sense of the value of money and are you good stewards of all the resources the Lord has given you? And finally, do you both have the same attitude about having and rearing children? In other words—if you are a righteous woman, the most important thing you need in your life is a righteous man and vice versa. Then, if you have the ability to communicate openly, with honesty and loving kindness[1] on a consistent basis with each other about these issues, you have a good chance to experience the happiness and joy God wants for married couples.

"So, when you meet that righteous someone, you ask yourselves individually and maybe together: 'Can we and will we work together towards the Celestial Kingdom, no matter what comes and no matter how long the road ahead may or may not turn out to be?' If you're both comfortable and are positive in your feelings about moving ahead, then you go to the Lord and ask for confirmation. After you've both prayed and listened, in both your mind and heart for the Spirit,[2] if either of you doesn't or both of you don't feel the peace that means 'Yes,'[3] you part as friends and continue your search. Otherwise, if that peace comes to both of you, you get engaged and move on with your lives," Big Sarah explained.

"But, mom, why did it take you and dad so long to decide?" Little Sarah asked with serious intensity.

"Honey, it wasn't a question of deciding. Your father and I loved each other for years before we became engaged. Your father bought the wedding and engagement rings I wear years before he gave them to me. We didn't become engaged sooner than we did because I was on a mission. It wasn't a formal mission like going out to proselyte or serving a work mission; it was a very specific and private mission where the Lord put it into my heart to try and reclaim one of His precious sons, Paul Tenter. Then, came the time when I was released from that mission. Your father and I became engaged a week later and married eight weeks after that. The Lord had a timetable and your father and I were both patient enough, although it was really hard and frustrating at times, to wait until the Lord said it was time for us. When he let us know, we acted and we've not ever looked back.

* * * * *

"Now I want to talk about your third question next because it follows the natural order of things. Your father and I (Mary, I'm not leaving you out, it's just easier to say it this way), had a wonderful first time together. We spent our honeymoon week up at the family lodge. I didn't even know we had a lodge until your dad opened the door and carried me across the threshold. Anyway, while I looked around, your dad brought in my luggage, put some very romantic CDs on the player and lit a fire in the big fireplace.

"As soon as my luggage was brought in, I went up stairs to freshen up. When I came out of the bathroom, I just looked at your dad from the top of the stairs for a few moments. As I stood there, I couldn't have been more grateful I was clean; I was

Agency and Consequences

grateful I knew your dad was clean. Like all of you, both of us had thought about what that first time would be like. As I looked at your dad from the top of the stair, I wanted that night together to be special and I wanted your dad with all that means; but I was a little scared too.

"One of the other things we learn in the Proclamation on the Family is a man has a very sacred and special responsibility to treat the women in his life, especially his wife, with respect, honor and protection.[4] As a woman, in that sacred ceremony in the temple, I gave myself to him; I entrusted myself to him with a covenant that he would honor, respect and protect me. So, as I descended the stair with the intention of giving my whole soul to him, it was in faith.

"Your father has told me, as I came down the stairs, he felt very keenly that responsibility to honor, respect and protect me. Now, make no mistake, Sarah and Mary, you have as much responsibility to honor and respect the men in your lives as they do you. Consequently, you need to live in such a way that both expects and invites a man to treat you the way God expects him to treat you. But, there's something different for a man, I don't know that I fully understand it. In the Book of Mormon there is a scripture that teaches us something about that special responsibility a man has. Here's what the scripture says as it relates an old father giving his last instructions to his sons before he dies:

> 'O that ye would awake; awake from a deep sleep, yea, even from the sleep of hell, and shake off the awful chains by which ye are bound, which are the chains which bind the children of men, that they are carried away captive down to the eternal gulf of misery and woe.
>
> 'Awake! And arise from the dust, and hear the words of a trembling parent, whose limbs ye must soon lay down in the cold and silent grave, from whence no traveler can return; a few more days and I go the way of all the earth.
>
> '... Arise from the dust, my sons, and be

men, and be determined in one mind and in one heart, united in all things, that ye may not come down into captivity; that ye may not be cursed with a sore cursing; and also, that ye may not incur the displeasure of a just God upon you unto the destruction, yea, the eternal destruction of both soul and body.

'Awake, my sons; put on the armor of righteousness. Shake off the chains with which ye are bound, and come forth out of obscurity, and arise from the dust,'[5]"

Sarah concluded as she read the last two paragraphs tearfully.

"And just as this righteous father commanded his sons to 'Arise from the dust ... and be men,' men are commanded to do the same thing in the temple. Every time I witness that scene, especially when I see your dad rise to his feet, it sends a tremor through my soul. Then, I wonder: 'Who am I that God Himself would command His sons to live a life of righteousness that includes and places such a high priority on honoring, respecting and protecting me (and all women) in such a powerful way?' I've come to two conclusions to that question:

"First, as a daughter of Heavenly Parents, I'm very special to them and I deserve to be thus treated by the men in my life.

"Second, when you expect, invite and then allow a man to treat you as God expects him to treat you, it literally fills you with joy and fulfills you as a woman in a way that is incomprehensible and not possible in any other way."

"Sister Kindman," Mary broke in. "I have some questions: First, what do you mean by 'allow a man to treat you the way God expects;' and second, if what you say is true, why are so many women abused? Why are so many women confused about their relationships with men? I mean, even in school, it isn't just the boys who are out to exploit the girls; I know lots of girls who are just as predatory as Josh Bangeter. How have we gotten so mixed up?" Mary asked in a confused but wanting to know tone.

"Mary, those are good questions. I don't think I know the exact answers; but with regard to the first question, allowing a

Agency and Consequences

man to treat us women as God expects him to treat us is a multi-faceted thing and has nothing to do with women being, what some have wrongly referred to, as the weaker sex.

"Think of the great women in history who have stood with great strength and faith and have often done what no man could do. I think of Esther, Joan of Arc, Mary Fielding Smith, Marie Curie and Florence Nightingale. I look at my own daughter, Sarah, and her love of big earth moving machines and the skill with which she operates them. As with Sarah, many of these women have done what they've done despite the false traditions that what they were doing was not womanly in nature.

"Where a man places women on his personal list of priorities, has a lot to do with the way he treats us. But, our gentle, constant and loving expecting, inviting and allowing a man to treat us as God expects him to, reinforces and encourages him.

"A man's elevated feelings towards a woman on his 'list of priorities' involve the simple courtesies of helping her with her coat (even though she's capable of doing it herself), opening doors, walking on the street side of a side walk. It has to do with sharing loads within the home and counseling with her and sincerely asking for and considering her opinions and making sure she is comfortable with a decision when it's made. It means making sure she has the opportunity to grow continually and pursue her own interests. It has to do with making sure she knows he loves her by both what he says and what he does.

"Now, as I said, a woman has those same responsibilities where the men in her life are concerned, but men, as a general rule, typically struggle with these things. There's peer pressure that suggests being a man means you're dominant and if you do all these things, you're a wuss. So, it usually doesn't come very naturally to a man.

"But, for me at least and for your mother, Alice, being treated this way is magical. Sure, I can get my own doors, put on my own coat, make decisions all by myself and I often have to do those things for myself when George isn't around or with me. Unfortunately, many women insist this kind of treatment is belittling to them, that it suggests they are somehow less capable. My experience is just the opposite. Being treated this way reminds me I'm not a man; I'm not in competition with my husband nor men in general. It reminds me I am special to my husband and to my God. And the best part, something happens to a relationship, to a marriage, where this kind of respect and honor are expected, invited, allowed and then appreciated.

"Now, to your second question, I know Satan wants to destroy souls; he wants to destroy yours, mine, my husband's, your parents', everybody's. So, he tells lies; and too many of us believe him. Here are some of the thoughts I've had on those questions.

"First, this goes to the subject regarding what real manhood and womanhood are. Women who don't really understand their true role in God's plan—even if they've heard the plan—are often susceptible to being deceived by Satan or by those already deceived by him and who are preaching his lies. So, the first lie Satan usually gets women to believe is they are not daughters of Heavenly Parents; they have no royal heritage; they are only on earth to be used by men, or to be their toys, or, as you said, to in some way take advantage of men themselves. Here are a few of his specific lies.

"He tells women, in order for men to like them or worse love them, they have to give themselves to them before there's any commitment.

"He tells them they can get pregnant, have children, they don't need a husband and children don't need a father.

"He tells young men and older men they can get a woman pregnant and they have no responsibility to the woman or the baby; that it's the woman's fault she got pregnant.

"A lie related to these last two, because it usually follows one or both of them, but with a pernicious twist, and more often sold to and believed by women but in some cases men, is children are more important than a spouse. This appears to happen particularly when premarital sex occurred and there was no real bonding between the partners. In other words, as Sarah felt last evening, the couple was no more than a pair of animals in a breeding shed; the woman was no more than a brood mare and the man no more than a stud, when pregnancy occurred. Consequently, the sexual act itself did nothing to foster unity, love, adoration, respect or commitment between them. Then, when the child comes, especially for the woman, it becomes her priority, the primary focus of her love and attention, 'the center

Agency and Consequences

of her world.' The man, who may have tried to do the honorable thing and get married, support the woman and the child, may now feel betrayed, left out, second in the life of his wife.

"What they both fail to realize, because the stack of lies they've embraced has numbed them to each other, is the best thing they can give the child and each other is to place each other first. To the Ephesians, Paul said: 'For this cause shall a man leave his father and mother, and shall be joined unto his wife, and they two shall be one flesh.'[6] The Lord said in the Doctrine and Covenants: 'Thou shalt love thy wife with all thy heart, and shalt cleave unto her and none else.'[7]

"Taking our barnyard analogy a little further, I believe what's good for the gander is also good for the goose. Thus, '… none else,' for both wives and husbands, means children come second in the relationship.

"But, instead of cleaving to each other and none else, a flimsy relationship, based on these lies, often becomes a vicious circle, when the wife, now a mother, makes her husband second in her life. The husband responds by showing little or no attention and love to either his wife or the baby. She then complains he's uncaring and worthless. From there, it often ends up in the divorce courts and then they do it all over again with someone new," Big Sarah taught with conviction.

"Mom," Little George quietly broke in, "I've never felt like I was second and I've never heard or felt any of the other kids in our family who thought he or she was second either. If kids are second, how come we've never felt that way?"

Big Sarah wiped a tear from her eye as she lovingly responded: "Because your dad and I are first in each others' lives and we truly do love each other, you, your brothers and sisters feel safe and secure. In addition, Father in Heaven has blessed us with the ability to love each of you in a way each one of you feels the unique love, we truly have for each of you. But more than that, as a consequence, you also feel a measure of the Eternal Love your Heavenly Parents have for each of you.

"But," Big Sarah injected parenthetically, "even in the best of marriages, putting your spouse first after children come can be—very difficult. The bond between a mother and her children can be so consuming, she can literally forget the first choice of her loyalty," she said as she tenderly looked at Big

George with tears in her eyes. Looking back at little Sarah and Alice, she firmly counseled: "Ladies, you must never forget and fight the inner battle to keep your priorities and loyalties in order."

Big Sarah then continued: "Another lie Satan tells is the only difference between men and women is their up-bringing and there are no core intellectual, emotional, spiritual as well as physical differences. This lie becomes even more malicious when some, who have a body of one gender, believe they should really be the other; or it's OK to be attracted to someone of the same sex. After all, they are convinced, who and what we are is just a freak accident of nature anyway.

"To still others he says being a mother and home maker is servitude without respectability and or honor.

* * * * *

"One of his lies is there is nothing wrong with exposing your body to anyone who wants to look; after all, it is beautiful so why not show it off."

"Sister Kindman," Mary injected; "I have a question. I've been taught at home and in Church to be modest. Why is that really such a big deal?"

"Mary, Paul said our bodies are temples.[8] Now, think of a temple. They're beautiful on the outside. They are constructed of the best and most beautiful materials we, as a Church, can afford. The grounds are kept immaculate—the trees are trimmed, the lawns cut and manicured; the flowerbeds are always updated for the season.

"The interior of the temple is likewise kept in excellent repair and clean. After dedication, only those with a properly endorsed recommend are allowed to see or participate in what goes on within.

"That's also the way our bodies should be kept. Our bodies are no different from a dedicated temple—only those with a properly endorsed recommendation should be allowed to see beneath the exterior covering of our bodies. These persons are only our spouses and under appropriate conditions, qualified medical personnel. Does that explain it a little better?" Big Sarah asked warmly.

"Yes, Sister Kindman; that cleared up a lot for me," Mary

Agency and Consequences

responded gratefully. But there was still a sense of not really understanding in her voice.

"Mary," President Kindman queried kindly, "you're still unsure about why modesty is so important aren't you?"

"It all makes sense; but I just don't understand why our bodies are considered to be temples," Mary said seriously.

"Well, that's because they are made from temple materials—the atoms, elements—the minerals and chemicals—of the earth itself," President Kindman replied in a direct, but humble manner. "Consider the following scriptures," President Kindman followed."

"'And the Gods watched those things which they had ordered until they obeyed.'[9]

"'All truth is independent in that sphere in which God has placed it, to act for itself, as all intelligence also; otherwise there is no existence.'[10]

"'And again, verily I say unto you, the earth abideth the law of a celestial kingdom, for it filleth the measure of its creation, and transgresseth not the law'"[11], President Kindman quoted.

"So, what does all that mean?" President Kindman asked rhetorically.

"It means, as far as I can tell, the earth was built and then tested and proved in its obedience before it was allowed to become the testing ground for all of us in our mortal state. It was for that very purpose the earth was dedicated, consecrated and set apart. The earth has a degree of agency. With that agency, it is abiding the measure of its creation and will be exalted. Our bodies were made from the earth—atoms, elements—the minerals and chemicals that have been tried, tested and proved to be obedient. Thus, each of our bodies, made from these consecrated, dedicated and set apart materials, is a temple—a temple that has already learned to be obedient. Designed after the pattern of our Heavenly Parents' bodies, our bodies were given to us for the purpose of helping our spirits become as obedient as they, that is our bodies, already are. In other words, if we allow them, our bodies will help us return back to our Heavenly Home with honor," President Kindman explained thoughtfully.

"Mary, now do you understand?" President Kindman asked

kindly.

"For once, I think I do. It's all pretty magnificent isn't it?" Many responded with quiet enthusiasm.

"Daddy," Sarah asked in a confused tone, "If that's true, why is it still so hard to be good? Why do so many people become addicted to drugs, pornography, sex, gambling and even food and run the risk of losing their right to return Home with honor?"

"Sweetheart, those are questions with very complicated answers I don't think I can answer completely. But here's what makes sense to me," President Kindman responded a little tentatively.

"While our bodies are an indispensable and priceless help to us, they are not perfect. While they are made of obedient materials, because of the fall of Adam and Eve, those materials are *fallen*. In addition, they are still subject to the direction of our spirits. So, when the spirit makes unwise choices based upon the '*natural*' or '*fallen*' desires, passions, emotions and thoughts of the body, or the direct temptation of the adversary, a person gets into trouble. The consequence of such unwise choices, if not repented of quickly, is, not only does the body become addicted, so does the spirit. However, because the body, despite its fallen nature, is constantly trying to be obedient, when given the opportunity, it will overcome an addiction long before the spirit does. Then, it will help the spirit repent and overcome the addiction. If death occurs before the addiction is completely overcome, the spirit must overcome it on its own—often a near impossible task. And why is it harder after death to repent?" President Kindman asked as Little George, Little Sarah and Mary looked quizzically at each other.

"Here's what Samuel the Lamanite said:

> 'He hath given unto you that ye might know good from evil, and he hath given unto you that ye might choose life or death; and ye can do good and be restored unto that which is good, or have that which is good, or have that which is good restored unto you; or ye can do evil, and have that which is evil restored unto you.'[12]

Agency and Consequences

"Alma may have said it even better:

> 'And now behold is the meaning of the word restoration to take a thing of a natural state and place it in an unnatural state, or to place it in a state opposite to its nature? O, my son, this is not the case; but the meaning of the word restoration is to bring back again evil for evil, or carnal for carnal, or devilish for devilish—good for that which is good; righteous for that that which is righteous; just for that which is just; merciful for that which is merciful.'[13]

"What that all means," President Kindman commented "is don't expect to have all the bad habits and issues of your life magically disappear when you die. They will be restored to you; that is, you will retain them when you leave this life. Just as they are now, they will be ingrained into the cells of your spirit. You will then have to deal with and overcome them without the aid of your obedient body," President Kindman concluded as he nodded to his wife indicating she should take over.

* * * * *

"Now, getting back to the lies," Sister Kindman continued, "another says as long as a couple is in 'love,' or if the two partners are consenting, then sex is OK. This lie gets us to confuse lust for love to the point many in the world can't tell the difference anymore.

"One variation of this lie suggests there is something wrong in a couple's relationship if they haven't had sex by the third date. And another suggests there's something wrong with you if you're not having sex, married or not, at least three times a week.

"Satan glorifies sex saying 'since it's natural and feels so good, then it must be right.' He then reinforces this attitude by saying the traditions and commandments of morality and chastity are out of date and don't apply in this modern age. And of course that's all made to appear to be the truth given the technologies of condoms, erectile dysfunction drugs, the pill and other forms of pregnancy prevention. But he carefully and cleverly leaves out or down-plays any notion of consequences, like pregnancy, disease, responsibility and the worst of all, the burden and unhappiness that come with sin. They, who have bought into this falsehood, don't understand or ignore the fact only God can revoke a previously given commandment.

"Sister Kindman," Mary broke in again. "This is something I really don't understand. We all know the scripture that says 'wickedness was never happiness;'[14] but I know lots of kids and adults who don't keep the commandments and they're smiling, laughing and appear to be very happy. Sometimes I ask myself: 'why should I keep the commandments; those who don't are just as happy, maybe happier, than I am?'"

Big Sarah looked at Mary and her children, George and Sarah. They all nodded in agreement. Then, with great tenderness, she answered saying: "The Savior himself gave the answer to that question when he visited the Nephites. Here's what He said: 'But if it be not built upon my gospel, and is built upon the works of men, or upon the works of the devil, verily I say unto you they have joy in their works for a season, and by and by the end cometh, and they are hewn down and cast into the fire, from whence there is no return.'[15]

"So, they are happy, at least for a time. But it can't last because happiness is based upon righteousness and righteousness is based on keeping the commandments of God.[16]

"Another of Satan's tricks is to get us to believe: 'You only go around once.' 'You never know what's going to happen tomorrow so you gotta do all the living you can today— experience it all right now.' And then, if you get aids or some other social disease in the process, he tricks you into being philosophical rather than repentant about it and say to yourself: 'Well, we all gotta die some time and their ain't no way better than another and their ain't no time better than another either.' That, of course, is a lie because how we're living, the direction we're going and the intent of our heart when our time comes are crucial to our eternal salvation and destination.[17]

"How did I do; did I answer your questions, Mary?" Big Sara queried.

"Yes, Sister Kindman. I think you did," Mary responded a bit hesitantly.

Agency and Consequences

Sensing Mary's tentative response, Big George added asking: "Mary, do you understand the fundamental principle behind your questions and Sarah's answers?"

"President Kindman, I'm not sure I know what you're asking. I guess that means I don't know," Mary replied honestly.

"Mary, I wish all the young men and women in our Stake were as honest as you. Sarah alluded to the fundamental principle in the very beginning of her answer to your questions. It is this: 'Do you really believe, down to the nucleus of every cell in your soul you are a daughter of Heavenly Parents who truly love you, who have a plan for you, who placed you here on this earth for a wonderful purpose?'

"Peter spoke of '... holy women ... who trusted in God ....'[18] These were women who were in every way the equal of the righteous men in their lives," President Kindman emphasized warmly.

"Now, for men and young men, we have long had the following ideal when the Savior challenged: 'Therefore, what manner of men ought ye to be? Verily I say unto you, even as I am.'[19] While we all have the Savior as our ideal of how to live a perfect life, I believe women and young woman would do well to try and imagine the kind of woman our Heavenly Mother is and what she might say if she were to visit you personally. Might she ask: 'Therefore, what manner of woman ought ye to be? Verily I say unto you, even as I am,'" Big George challenged.

"You see, Mary, if you don't believe you are in fact a daughter of Heavenly Parents who love you, have a plan for you and who placed you on this earth with a divine purpose; if you have no idea of what true womanhood really is then little, if any, of what Sarah said to you will make any sense. It will be nothing more than foolish gibberish.

"Why? Because if there is no God, then any life style we choose is acceptable. If we have no purpose on this planet except to eke out an existence as best we can in competition with every other being and life form on the planet, then getting all we can in the here and now, taking advantage of one another sexually, cheating in our business dealings, even murdering, plundering and raping our neighbors have no eternal consequences. Therefore, by definition, these behaviors are no more right or wrong than any other behaviors engaged in by anybody else. It then becomes truly survival of the fittest, with every man, woman and child concerned only for him or herself. Korihor, an Anti-Christ in the Book of Mormon, described this condition terribly well when he argued: "… Every man fared in this life according to the management of the creature; therefore, every man prospered according to his genius, and that every man conquered according to his strength; and whatsoever a man did was no crime."[20] The definition of what is right or wrong is then based largely on what you can get away with and to a lesser extent on what society, at any moment in time, will tolerate; absolutes become none existent," Big George explained.

"Mary, does that help in clearing up the confusion you've been feeling?" Big George asked kindly.

"Yes, President Kindman, it does. I guess I've been a little lazy in really coming to a firm belief and knowledge of who I am," Mary confessed.

"I think you're not the only one, Mary. Thanks for asking what I was afraid to ask. Dad is right, too many of us are afraid to ask those hard questions and face them straight on. If I hadn't been afraid to really ask those questions and honestly seek answers, I wouldn't have been so foolish last night. I think we both have some work to do," Little Sarah admitted.

"The important thing is all of us have a better understanding of the questions. Now, let each of us take those questions to the Lord in prayer with real intent and see if He doesn't help each of us to know more firmly who we really are, why we're here and what our unique missions are," Big George challenged.

* * * * *

"Dad, there have been several mentions tonight of Heavenly Parents. I know the *Proclamation on the Family*[21] speaks of Heavenly Parents and Eliza R. Snow's words in our hymn, *O My Father*,[22] speaks of a Mother in Heaven. Why don't we hear as much about our Mother in Heaven as we do our Father in Heaven or Jesus Christ," Little George asked with a puzzled inflection in his voice.

"Son, that's a question I've pondered over long and

Agency and Consequences

often. I believe it has to do with the concept of men protecting women your mother spoke of earlier. Think of it this way. Ask yourself: 'what do we do in our society with things we deem to be a masterpiece, rare or very valuable?' Answer, we guard them, we protect them with special security systems, we even create the ideal environment to preserve them and keep them from decay. President David O McKay said: 'A beautiful, modest gracious woman is Creation's masterpiece.'[23] If that is so, and I believe it is, then our Father in Heaven is setting an example for all His sons. He is doing all He can to protect His precious bride from the abuse of the thoughtless and irreverent; He's protecting that which is most holy from dogs and His most valuable pearl from the swine."[24]

* * * * *

"Well, getting back to my story," Big Sarah said with a chuckle; "when I reached the bottom of the stair, I went to your dad and asked him to dance with me. As I said, I was a little apprehensive. So, for several minutes we just held each other and danced next to the fire. I loved your dad very much and I realized he was ready to go to the next level, if you know what I mean? And so it was important to me that I not deny him that. That's when I told him I thought I was ready and asked your dad to help me take off my bathrobe.

"Now ... ladies this is important. This is what makes the difference between the tawdry, animalistic desire thrust upon Sarah by an unbridled, out of control, pogo stick and the way your father treated me during our first experience together and every time since then. Your dad looked at me and silently asked—he didn't need to say the words out loud: 'Are you sure?' At that moment, I knew if I needed another hour, or another day or even another week, even though we were married, your dad would force nothing on me. My heart melted. I was ready to give myself completely to this man who loved me enough to deny himself until I was ready. I was speechless too at that point, but with my eyes, I said 'thank you for being so sensitive' and 'yes' at the same time. And it was a wonderful experience; it was joyful, exquisite, full of desire and passion. We had earned the right to be together without any shame. We felt God's approval and were enveloped with the Spirit," Big Sarah explained with great tenderness and respect.

"So, what you're saying is it was nothing like the scene in the movie *Coal Miner's Daughter* when Doolittle forced himself on Loretta on their wedding night and showed no feeling or sensitivity for her at all?[25]

"While you and dad have always said your first experience was wonderful, I've always wondered if what I saw in that movie is *really* the way it is. Then, last night ... well, that just reinforced in my head sex is just a necessary evil to bring children into the world and the less of it the better. I began to wonder if sex was something I ever wanted to experience at all," Little Sarah quietly said trembling again.

"That's a perfect example of a man and woman who just didn't know any better. And no, honey, it doesn't have to be that way. The experience your dad and I shared was wonderful. It can be as wonderful for you, for George, for Mary as it was for your dad and me," Big Sarah reassured.

"Sweetheart, I feel like sharing a couple things at this point," Big George injected kindly. "First, one of Satan's ploys to get us to live lives out of harmony with the Gospel is, if he can't get us to give away our virtue through premarital or extramarital sexual behavior, he may try to get us to despise it, feel guilty about it, think it's something dirty and unworthy, just a necessary evil as Sarah suggested, even when it is appropriate.

"I've spent a lot of time counseling with parents who think the only way to keep their kids from inappropriate sexual behavior is to scare them to death about it. Admittedly, there are times when the consequences of the misuse of sex must be explained clearly and without pulling punches. But, I'm afraid most parents, who use this tactic as a matter of course, simply cripple their kids.

"Then, when marriage does come, the honeymoon often becomes a nightmare. One (and sometimes both) of the partners, if they've been educated this way, is completely unprepared to enjoy the experience. They are often so racked with guilt and shame and their defense arsenal of horror stories so impenetrable, any chance of really enjoying what they were designed to enjoy is damned up, locked in a steel vault, inside them. They simply aren't prepared to give themselves permission emotionally, spiritually, intellectually or physically to

Agency and Consequences

grow into this next stage of their journey towards being like their Heavenly Parents.

"Tragically, I'm finding more and more young adults are delaying marriage, at least in part, because they're scared, sometimes terrified, of the intimate sexual relationship that should come with marriage; and Satan is laughing with each deception. Here's what Parly P. Pratt said about this:

> 'It was during this time that ... the first idea of eternal family organization, and the eternal union of the sexes in those inexpressibly endearing relationships which none but the highly intellectual, the refined and pure in heart, know how to prize, and which are at the very foundation of everything worthy to be called happiness.'[26]

"In other words, if I understand what Brother Pratt is saying, '... those inexpressibly endearing relationships ...' require our being well educated, we need to be refined and pure in heart to enjoy them properly. That those relationships, when properly expressed between legally and lawfully married couples, are at the very foundation of true happiness.

"A modern Apostle gives this powerful perspective: 'Romantic love is not only a part of life, but literally a dominating influence of it. It is deeply and significantly religious. There is no abundant life without it. Indeed, the highest degree of the celestial kingdom is unattainable in the absence of it.'[27]

"Secondly, we all feel desire and wonder what that first experience will be like. What Sarah has shared is our experience. Hopefully, as Sarah said, yours, when the time is right, will be just as wonderful. That feeling of anticipation is in all of us. And even for Sarah and me it continues to be there although it's not the same as it was those many years ago at the lodge. There's a poem by the modern church poet, G. Kenneth Cardwell, which he wrote after twenty-one years of marriage to his sweetheart, that says what your mother and I feel at this stage in our lives.

G. Kenneth Cardwell

Anticipation

From the day
Of our engagement,
It was in our eyes,
Our bodies teamed
With growing excitement—
Anticipation—
Consummated the evening
Of our marriage.

Now,
More than
Twenty-one years
Have past.
Our family is
All but raised;
We've worked
Our way through
Near-death illness,
Near-intractable
    Misunderstandings,
Near-bankruptcy,
Near-crushing heartache,
Near-consuming joy,
Near-no-days of not saying:
    "I love you."

So, as I take you
Into my arms,
And pull you close,
The depth
Of your gaze
Sends tremors
Through my soul;
And I can
Hardly restrain all
That your fully
Mature womanhood
Ignites in me—

Agency and Consequences

Anticipation.

Then,
With signal unspoken,
We wrap ourselves
In each other
And nothing
Of that first night
Can compare with
The electricity,
The oneness,
The wholeness,
The glory,
The fulfillment,
The anticipation
Of Eternity.[28]

"So, if you guard it, nurture it and treasure it, it will grow and the love you feel in the beginning with your first experience together will be as but a seed in comparison with the mighty tree of your relationship in the years to follow," Big George counseled as he looked at his wife with unspeakable love.

And then Big Sarah continued: "And so ... how do you keep it alive afterwards. In a phrase: 'never become complacent with each other.' You keep it alive by making sure your spouse is always and foremost your number one priority. Here are some ways to do that together and individually.

"You keep it alive by solving the issues that come up between you as quickly as you can. Sometimes as quickly as you can is seconds, sometimes minutes, sometimes it's a whole lot longer. Marriage is the crucible in which the hottest of refining fires burn. Learning to quench those fires peaceably and amicably before they incinerate a marriage is maybe the greatest challenge of marriage. The bottom line here is use the principle of repentance whenever needed, swallow your pride and apologize. In that process, seek to understand the other before defending yourself.[29] After all, you're both on the same team; so focus on what's best for your marriage and family. If you're both doing that, a miracle happens—each one's personal needs will have a way of getting met as well.

"The next thing I feel is important is to linger a while when one of you is leaving or coming, such as leaving for or coming home from work, and wants to say goodbye or greet you with a kiss. I hear about too many couples who spoil one of the greatest opportunities to keep their relationship nurtured and fresh by being too busy or preoccupied with other things than to spend even thirty to sixty seconds at least twice a day in this ritual.

"In the beginning of our marriage, George would come home and I'd be in the restaurant kitchen baking pies or doing some other thing. He'd be covered with whatever sand, gravel or mud he'd been 'playing' in that day and he'd walk right in, put his arms around me, tell me he'd missed me and loved me. He would then want me to turn around and share a kiss with him. Now, that's something I really wanted to do too. Our problem was the FDA … huh, that's the Food and Drug Administration. All that mud or whatever else was on his feet, in his clothes and everything else, just wasn't acceptable in the restaurant kitchen. So, we compromised. I would listen for him to come in, put on what I call our 'hugs and kisses apron' and go to him. And that's what we still do. But, here's why it's important. You need to communicate verbally you love each other every day. But just as important, you need to hold each other and look into each other's eyes and see each other with spiritual eyes.

"The Lord counseled Emma Smith: 'Let they soul delight in they husband, and the glory which shall come upon him. And verily, verily, I say unto you, that this is my voice unto all. Amen.'[30] In other words, spouses, men and women, are to delight in each other and the glory that shall come upon each of them. We are to clean the darkened glass and see each other and know each other as God sees and knows us.[31]

"I feel when we take a few moments when we are covered in mud or flour, with a hair net or a hard hat on, with dirt and grime under our nails and look into each other's eyes and see the real soul that's in there, it makes a huge difference in a marriage.

"Add to that, attending the temple regularly together and seeing each other dressed in white, holding hands and praying together in the Celestial Room, recharges and strengthens those visions of glory we can come to see in each other. Indeed, if we are in tune, we may be privileged to see each other in revelation. Again, as Parley P. Pratt described it, as God "... [lifts] a corner of the veil and [gives you a] single glance into eternity.'[32] Then you'll see and know each other as God sees and knows each of you. And if we see glory in each other, then we should also see it in our selves.

"Next, make your bedroom the most romantic room within your home. This room, as much as possible, should be a husband and wife's private room where the two of them can feel totally alone and comfortable together. As much as possible, husbands and wives should solve their problems somewhere else and not bring them to the bedroom with them.

"The master bedroom should, in my opinion, be as close to temple-like in decor, in orderliness, in light and in spirit as possible. Central to this concept is your bed. The bed is like the alter in the temple sealing room. Why? Because a couple should kneel often together, holding hands and pray together at this alter. And, the most sacred of all relationships occurs most often upon that alter.

"Upon this alter, a couple make their most sincere, real intent, attempts to sacrifice everything that is personally selfish and strive, by renewing their personal covenants with each other and God, to become one as God intends for a married couple to become. It is upon this alter a couple make themselves unselfishly available, as partners with God, in bringing His Sons and Daughters into mortality so they can progress in their journeys of becoming like their Heavenly Parents.

"On my list next, never, ever, ever use sex as a weapon against the other. Sex, in my opinion, should never be used as a tool of manipulation. As soon as it is, that is unrighteous dominion,[33] regardless of which partner is using it. If a couple truly believes the temple sealing has the power to make them truly one, then each partner belongs to the other (that doesn't mean servitude nor the loss of individuality) and neither has any right to use this most sacred, uniting experience as a means to take advantage of the other. For both men and women, I believe the root of these issues, where sex is used to gain some kind of advantage or to punish, is usually incorrect or corrupted attitudes regarding what real manhood and womanhood are.

"In the man's case, it's often a distorted feeling of needing to be in control, of seeing his wife as an object to be dominated, controlled and sometimes as his 'servant.' In the animal world, when the male of a species takes the female in sex, he often becomes dominate over the female. This is not the Lord's way for His Sons and Daughters.

"For a woman, feeling comfortable in a sexual relationship is so bound up with her sense of trust, it's easy, when her feelings have been rubbed a little or even a lot the wrong way, for her to let that work on her feelings of trust. If that happens, it very often gets in the way of a truly enriching and satisfying relationship with her husband.

"In either case, sex becomes mostly one-sided; and too often becomes a source of power to the one using it, either by forcing it on the other or withholding it, to gain some supposed advantage over the other or as some kind of punishment. What sex should be, what it was intended to be, is empowering to the relationship—helping men to feel and become manly after the manner of Heavenly Father and for women to feel and become womanly after the manner of Heavenly Mother.

"Another item of importance is both partners need to be aware of the need to take good care of themselves. The years will take their toll, but each partner in a marriage should do his or her best to be as attractive as they can for each other.

"Finally, married couples shouldn't think they have to hit the moon, as we like to call it, every time they get together. Rather, they should focus on becoming each other's best friend so the most important thing is just being together.

"Because our bodies are mortal, they change. Those changes, caused by any number of things—hormone levels may fluctuate, there may be sickness along the way. And so a couple's sexual experience together over time will also change. That's all part of the mortal experience.

"Consequently, each sexual experience a couple has together will be different. We like to compare it to driving a car. Sometimes, we are in a big, plush Cadillac driving on a nice smooth road; other times we've been in a speeding sports car with the top down and the wind blowing in our hair; and other times, we've been in a four-wheeler off-roading and mudding in

Agency and Consequences

the mountains. We take each experience as it comes and no matter what kind it is, we just enjoy the ride and being together.

"And one of the really great results of these experiences together is through our love and God's miracle, eight wonderful children have come into our family. Every one of them was conceived with joy; and, with great anticipation, we've waited for each one to arrive," Big Sarah Concluded with a warm smile as she looked with great fondness at her son and daughter.

"And on this final point," Big George injected; "compare this scenario of becoming pregnant with that of the unwed couple or more often the unwed mother. In those situations, there is usually just the opposite of what Sarah described. Instead of joy and anticipation, it's usually a feeling of desperation; there are thoughts of and often acts of abortion; there are blaming and accusations such as 'why weren't you using protection?' There's worry about 'how am I going to finish school' and or 'how are we or how am I going support this baby.' If the father is known and has any honor, what kind of support is he going to give? Should the couple get married? Should the baby be given up for adoption (a practice encouraged by the Church when the child has little prospect of being raised by both a loving father and mother who are legally and lawfully married). And the list of tragic, unneeded, unwanted problems is almost numberless," Big George cited with experienced passion.

* * * * *

"Sarah, have we answered your questions?" Big Sarah asked her daughter.

"Yes, mom ... I'm so glad you and daddy are my parents. Most parents wouldn't have handled this situation over the last few hours the way you did nor would they have been willing, with daddy having some pretty early meetings in just a few hours, to stay up until two in the morning and be so open with us. I think and feel I understand a whole lot better now. I want a marriage like you guys have. I hope I can be as patient as you were. It was obviously worth waiting for," Little Sarah said sobbing thankfully.

"Yes, honey it was worth waiting for. You, your brothers and sisters were all, each one, worth waiting and preparing for the Lord's way," Big Sarah said as she gave her daughter a hug and a kiss.

"Well, let's have a closing prayer and hit the hay; Sarah would you offer the prayer, please," Big George asked looking at his daughter with a smile of being very pleased with her.

Following the prayer, as Big Sarah was putting away what remained of the cookies and milk, George came into the kitchen, put is arms around his wife and whispered: "Thank you, dear. I feel that was a very productive discussion."

Big Sarah turned in George's arms and as she put her arms around him, quietly said: "We are a great team when the Spirit is with us aren't we? Now, I have a favor to ask," she said with a look George knew exactly where she was headed. "I've been on my feet most of the day and I'm not sure they will get me up those stairs tonight; would you mind ...?"

George picked up his wife and as they headed for the stairs, she whispered in his ear: "I think these clothes are going to be a bit of trouble all by myself too."

George and Big Sarah were giggling half way up the stair as Little Sarah heard them and opened her bedroom door just a little and peeked out. When she saw her mother and dad reach the top of the stair and head toward the master bed room, she thought: "They've been married almost twenty years and they're still on their honeymoon. How neat is that?" She realized then, it was possible to fall in love and then grow in love throughout a marriage. She vowed to herself to find the person with whom such a marriage would be possible.

Agency and Consequences

36. Braiding the Whip

DESPITE the long night, Little Sarah was up and off to Church early in the morning. Her first stop was to see if she could meet with Bishop Stanford before church. As it turns out, Bishop Stanford was also her high school principal. So, when Sarah poked her head into the Bishop's office and asked if he had a few minutes, he feared the worst. She and Josh was the subject of all the gossip and of course, he couldn't help but notice them himself as he chaperoned the dance the previous night. Bishop Stanford invited Sarah into his office, closed the door and asked: "Sarah, how may I help you."

"Bishop," Sarah began, "I almost made the most terrible mistake in my life last night ...." Sarah, then, told the complete story, showed Bishop Stanford the certificate she had received at the hospital and said something of the long discussion she, her brother and Mary had with her parents until 2:00 that morning. She concluded by expressing her deepest regret for having thought the things she thought and asked if it would still be OK to take the Sacrament that day in church.

"Sarah," Bishop Stanford said with great sympathy, "you're a remarkable young woman. I'm so pleased with you and so is your Heavenly Father. My sense is you didn't sleep much last night did you?"

"No, I didn't. I spent most of the night on my knees asking Heavenly Father to forgive me for almost bringing such dishonor to Him, to my parents and to myself. And while I didn't lose my virtue literally, I realized that in my heart, for a while now, I didn't consider it very valuable. I felt impressed to come and talk to you and see about making it right. Bishop Stanford, I've been pretty foolish. I'm not like most of the other young women my age. I like bulldozers, mechanics, engineering and all the math that explains horse power, turbo charger pressures and things like that. I intimidate all the boys I know and the girls think I'm a freak. You must have heard what they've nick-named me: 'The Dozer Drivin' Momma.' So, anyway, I stupidly thought if I went out and gave myself away I would be more acceptable to the rest of the kids my age. I'm so sorry," Sarah confessed tearfully.

"Sarah, it took a lot of courage to come and see me this morning. There are only two things I want you to do. First, I want you to take the sacrament with a special prayer in your heart today. Really focus on the Savior's Atonement. I think the Lord will let you know how He feels about how you feel.

"Second, you keep right on loving bulldozers, mechanics and all the stuff that makes you the unique young woman you are. The time will come when it will all pay even greater dividends than it already has.

"Most of the kids at the high school who make fun of you are jealous. They haven't paid the price you have; consequently, they haven't accomplished what you have. Not one student in that high school, except you, has a full ride scholarship to Purdue University locked up. Not one, except you, has the ear of the CEO and the VPs of Engineering and Research and Development at the Caterpillar Tractor Corporation. And, as far as the young men are concerned, there isn't a young man in that high school, except maybe your brother, George, who has the maturity and good sense to know the caliber of a young woman you are. That one, I'm afraid, may take some patience on your part. Don't you dare settle for any man not your equal and who doesn't or can't accept you as his equal. Am I clear on that?" Bishop Stanford firmly counseled.

Sarah looked at Bishop Stanford and realized how much he knew about her and how much he really cared for her as her Bishop and as her friend. Then a warm glow came over her as she realized the counsel given to her was not just from a man, but it came from her Father in Heaven through His appointed servant.

"Yes, Bishop Stanford, I'm clear. For the first time in my life, I'm really clear. Thank you," Sarah said as the clarity of Bishop Stanford's counsel rang like a bell through her soul. She would never again doubt who she was nor the direction she was going.

"I have just one request of you now, not as my Bishop, but as my high school principal," Sarah asked politely.

"And what is that?" Bishop Stanford asked.

"Well, I want to give a demonstration of bulldozer operation. It won't be on school time or on school property. I

Agency and Consequences

don't have all the details yet, but I was just wondering if I could put up some posters and pass out some flyers at the school when I've got all the arrangements made?" Sarah explained.

"I don't see why not. Just keep me in the loop and when you've got it all set up, let me know and I'll make the arrangements at the school," Bishop Stanford responded.

"Bishop, thank you again. I'll be in touch," Sarah said as she stood up and shook Bishop Stanford's hand as she exited his office.

* * * * *

A few minutes after leaving Bishop Stanford's office, Little Sarah noticed Brother and Sister Franklin enter the church foyer. She quickly went over to them and greeted them. This was a special couple to Sarah and for many years she had helped them clean the manure from the corals of their dairy farm. Except for the few gallons of fresh, whole milk they sent home with her each time she finished, she always refused to accept payment. After the pleasantries and checking on their son, Andrew, serving a mission in South America, Sarah inquired: "Brother and Sister Franklin, may I ask a favor of you?"

"Of course, Sarah; how can we help you," Brother Franklin responded.

"Well, you know your field that's lying fallow across from the high school. I was wondering if I could use it to give the town a demonstration on bulldozer operations. We'd rope off a large section where Hidalgo would be parked and I'll have a couple friends help anyone who wanted to climb up on him and go through the cab and look at the controls. I'm going to see if the police and fire departments will help with parking cars around the outside of the demonstration area. Then during the demonstration, I'd explain a little about how much dirt Hidalgo can move at a time ... you know ... all the stuff people say 'wow' about. And then I plan to show how fast I can dig a pretty good sized hole, use the ripper on the back end and finally fill the hole back up. What do you think?" Sarah asked hopefully.

"Sarah, I don't have a problem with anything except digging the hole. There's about twelve to eighteen inches of really good topsoil on that piece of land and I sure as heck don't want it at the bottom of the hole when you're done," Brother

153

Franklin confided.

"How about if I strip the topsoil from the hole demonstration area ahead of time and put it into a separate pile. Then when I'm done, I'll put it back in place. Would that be acceptable?" Sarah offered. "In fact, what might even be better, before the demonstration, we can do a quick survey of the hole area where we take measurements of the topsoil depth every so many feet and then we can drive survey sticks into the ground. Removing the topsoil would then be part of the demonstration. It will take a little longer, but it will show how I can control Hidalgo's blade to the exact depth we want to take off," Sarah proposed with confidence and excitement.

"Are you sure you can do that?" Sister Franklin questioned with some doubt.

"Yes, I can. And if you'd like me to give you a private demonstration in the next day or so, I would be more than happy to do so. Besides, I'll bet it's about time to clean out your corals anyway," Sarah countered with restrained confidence.

"Can you come over tomorrow afternoon?" Brother Franklin asked.

"I'm out of school just after noon and I'll be at your place by 2:00 o'clock," Sarah replied.

"We'll see you at 2:00," Brother Franklin agreed.

*****

Well, Bishop Stanford was right. Little Sarah sat quietly and prayerfully during the Sacrament service that morning. The words of the Hymn, *I Stand All Amazed*,[1] pierced through her heart. She listened, as she never had before, to the prayers, especially the one offered by her brother, George. As she did, she felt the warm enveloping comfort of the Holy Ghost healing the wounds on her soul and testifying all was forgiven. It was a singular experience as she sat next to her mother and gentle tears of joy trickled down her cheeks. She now realized, on a completely personal level, Christ suffered and died for her and she could not get through this life and back home to God's presence without Christ's love, mercy and grace. And just as important, she felt the ability to forgive herself. It was time to move on. She remembered the words of a poem she read recently and began to understand.

Agency and Consequences

Weekly Healing

Sacrament meeting—
My son
Just blessed the emblems;
I'm melancholy,
Mind and heart
Resting upon events
Not too distant.

Dear Father,
Lift me,
Turn me out
A cheerful man;
Help me wait
Upon Thee;
In thy wisdom
I trust.

Peace—
O' the healing
Of this day,
Of this ordinance.
Life—
With all it brings,
Awaits;
But now, I'm ready.[2]

* * * * *

At 2:00 o'clock the next day, Little Sarah drove Traveler pulling a lowboy flatbed with Hidalgo securely chained down[3] onto the Franklin Dairy Farm. With practiced ease, she maneuvered the huge rig into position for getting Hidalgo off the flatbed. Brother Franklin was waiting and greeted her: "You're right on time. Can I help you with anything?"

"Sure," Sarah replied with big smile. You can tip those ramps to the ground at the back of the trailer and I'll get started releasing the tie-downs," Sarah instructed.

G. Kenneth Cardwell

* * * * *

Soon, Sarah was in Hidalgo's cab doing her equipment and safety checks. Then she turned the key and pressed the start button and Hidalgo roared to life. There was something in the vibration of that beast of a machine that bound and merged Sarah to it. It was a rhythm; a melody; a voice from a world only few understood; and she understood it better than most.

Each time she pressed the start button, Sarah could envision the electrons marshalling as an army within the battery and marching at lightning speed along wire nerves bringing the great beast to life. She could envision the huge starter cranking as the solenoid gear engaged the flywheel and in that same instant the fuel pump pressing fuel through the injectors into the huge cylinders.

She saw the giant pistons begin their dance, going from a dead stop, then accelerating to an impossible speed and then decelerating to a dead stop again, only to accelerate once again to that same impossible speed and decelerate to the dead stop. Every two complete cycles per piston, it was the same excruciating dance of power, exhaust, intake and then compression.

She could see the turbines of the turbo charger spinning, spinning, whining their high-pitched siren. Energized by the hot exhaust of combusted diesel fuel, they sucked in enormous volumes of air and forced them into the cylinders, to be compressed and heated, waiting for the mating, the impregnation of the fuel, that would then explode in that confined, superheated, compressed space forcing the dizzying dance of pistons.

She visualized the water pump moving gallon after gallon of coolant through the great voids in the engine block and back to the giant radiator where the excess heat is transferred to the outside air. A process that saved the beast from its self, from the product of that excruciating dance of pistons, that would otherwise build up and warp the monster engine and cause the pistons to seize in mid-cycle, never to dance again.

Finally, she saw in her mind's eye the hydraulic system, the muscles of the beast, come to pressure and become hard as

Agency and Consequences

granite, prepared to flex, to do her bidding, at her command.

To Sarah, Hidalgo, this big, beautiful, machine was a marvel, even a miracle, of balance—of heat and cold, weight and power, friction and slip, steel and plastic, electronics and hydraulics. And each time she sat in his seat, her hands and feet at his controls, she was part of him; they were one.

* * * * *

All her gauges showing normal, Little Sarah checked to make sure no one would get hurt should she roll Hidalgo crookedly and off the trailer sideways. She now backed Hidalgo ever so slowly, over rear trailer tires, down the ramps, off the trailer and onto the ground. Once solidly and safely on the ground, she opened the cab door and asked loudly: "Brother Franklin, what do you want me to do first, the corals or the topsoil demonstration?"

"Let's do the topsoil demonstration first. It's not that I doubt you and your ability; it's just I'm so dog on curious how you do it; I can't wait to see it done," Brother Franklin admitted.

"Not a problem. I'm more than happy to explain it and show it to you," Sarah explained as she climbed out of Hidalgo, went to her truck and from a large tool box behind the cab, she took out a large bundle of stakes, a large marker, a small sledge hammer, a large steel tape measure and a core tool.

"Can you put this stuff in the back of your pick up and I'll follow you out to any spot you want to do the test," Sarah requested.

With Sarah's equipment loaded in Brother Franklin's pick up, they headed out behind the farmhouse where Sister Franklin came running out and climbed into the pickup truck next to her husband.

When they reached the site, Sarah shut Hidalgo down and met Brother and Sister Franklin. "Here's the way this works," she began. "There are some pretty sophisticated methods for making sure, when we grade an area for a building or a road, we take exactly the right amount of dirt away or we fill a low spot with just the right amount. These methods take advantage of both laser and global positioning systems,"[4] Sarah explained.

"For this demonstration, and for the town, we'll do

something much simpler, but accurate enough you'll lose very little if any top soil. So, if you'll take out eight of those stakes, we'll drive the first one into the ground right here and leave it the exact same height above ground as Hidalgo's blade which is six feet, four inches. We'll need to stand on the tail gate of your pick up to drive it in the ground," Sarah instructed. "Next, we'll drive the next one in the ground exactly thirty-feet from this one and then place the next two in a straight line between the first two at 10 foot intervals. Once those stakes are in, we'll go back to our first stake and measure sixteen feet, perpendicular to the line of stakes we've driven and parallel to Hidalgo's blade. Then we'll do exactly the same thing we did before except we need to make sure each stake on that side is exactly sixteen feet from the one on this side," Sarah explained further.

Soon all the stakes were in the ground with exactly six feet, four inches from the ground to the top of the stake. "Now that all the stakes are in the ground, we need to determine the depth of the top soil at each stake. Normally, we just figure six inches; but since you said the depth was between twelve and eighteen inches, I thought we ought to measure it. That's why I brought this simple coring tool. We'll drive it into the ground, pull it back out and then measure the depth of the top soil. We then measure from the top of each stake the number of inches of top soil and draw a straight line and mark the number of inches with this marker on the stake. Usually, we also write some additional information on the stake, but for this little demonstration, that won't be necessary," Sarah continued to explain.

When all the cores were taken and the depths marked on the each stake, Sarah took out her calculator and calculated the average depth of top soil in that location to be approximately 15.8748 inches or 1.3229 feet. Since the length of the demonstration area was 30 feet, the total number of cubic feet of top soil to be removed was 563.563 or 20.8727 cubic yards. Hidalgo's blade being 14.2 feet across has a rated capacity of 17.7 cubic yards.[5] So, Sarah determined it would take two passes with Hidalgo to clear all the top soil from the demonstration area. She next measured down from the top of each stake and drew another line exactly eight inches from the top. Then she asked: "Do you see those wires that look like antennae sticking out from the top of the blade?"

"Yes, I was wondering what those were," Brother Franklin responded.

"Well, those wires are on spring-loaded hinges and when I drive Hidalgo between each pair of stakes, I want those wires to touch those stakes right at those marks we made; first, the one I just made and then, on the second pass, on the bottom one. If I hit those marks, we'll take mostly the top soil from the demonstration area. I said mostly the top soil because the depth of the top soil changes slightly as I progress forward and from left to right. So, on the second pass, I'll be making slight changes in the depth and angle of Hidalgo's blade. That means I'll most likely get just a little of what's under the top soil in a few spots," Sarah continued to explain. "Does it make since to you?" Sarah queried.

"You know, I think it does. It's really pretty ingenious," Brother Franklin remarked.

"I'll bet you still have to be pretty on the ball and careful to make sure you hit each of those lines just right," Sister Franklin observed.

"Yes, you do have to keep your eyes on the markers ahead and on the position of the wires on the blade. Are we ready?" Sarah asked with a smile.

"Yup, I think we are," Brother Franklin responded.

* * * * *

With that, Sarah was up in Hidalgo's cab and, within seconds, he again roared to life. It was almost as if he sensed it was time to go to work. Sarah often thought of the words from the book, *Seabiscuit*, by Laura Hillenbrand as she described Seabiscuit entering the racetrack for the famous match race against War Admiral: "… This day Woolf felt something new, a gathering beneath him, something spring-like. The horse was coiling up."[6] Hidalgo, the name of another famous horse, it seemed, was coiling up, anxious to get to work, to do what he was designed to do.

Sarah brought Hidalgo up to the demonstration stretch, made the necessary adjustments to the blade and moved between the first pair of stakes, the wires on the blade swiping the pair of stakes exactly at the same time and dead on the marks. Moving at an easy walking pace, Sarah guided Hidalgo with practiced precision making the adjustments in the angle and depth of the blade in quick, tiny bursts as she flicked Hidalgo's controls with rapid exactness. By the time they reached the thirty-foot stake, Hidalgo's blade was over half-capacity full of top soil as Sarah pushed the pile of soil from the demonstration area and stopped, backed slightly and then pirouetted around and began her second pass going in the opposite direction. Again, she quickly aligned Hidalgo exactly center between the stakes, the blade penetrating the soil with the wires again swiping the stakes at precisely on the depth marks for the second run. Sarah, again, made the blade adjustments as required and in just under seven seconds, for the second pass, the demonstration strip was cleared. Sarah pushed this second pile past the end and stopped. Meanwhile, Brother and Sister Franklin were looking in almost disbelief at how clean the strip was. Here and there, due to the minute anomalies in the top soil depth there were little patches of top soil left behind. Presently, Sarah joined them and flatly asked: "So ... what do you think?"

"I think you know what you're doing," Brother Franklin admitted.

"That's what I get paid the big bucks for," Sarah quipped. "So, can I do the demonstration for the town here? I promise, I'll leave your field just like I found it when I'm done," Sarah gently pleaded.

Brother and Sister Franklin looked at each other and quickly nodded affirmatively to each other and then Brother Franklin gave permission saying with a bit of tease in his voice: "Of course you can ... so long as you clean those corals out before you leave tonight."

"No problem. Thank you so very much. Would a week from this Saturday be OK; say about three in the afternoon?" Sarah inquired.

"That would be fine," Brother Franklin confirmed.

"Great ... If you'd pull those stakes from the ground and haul them back to my truck, I'll put all this soil back and then head over to your corals," Sarah requested.

The piles of top soil Sarah had stripped from the demonstration area were quickly put back into place and compacted as she drove Hidalgo over the site a few times letting Hidalgo's tracks compress the soil back into place.

* * * * *

Shortly, Sarah was working on the corals carefully dragging the manure away from the fence lines into windrows. She then pushed it all out and into large piles. Brother Franklin would then use these piles of manure as fertilizer by loading them into a spreader that would disburse the manure on his hay and grain fields.

When Sarah was finished, she drove Hidalgo back to her tractor-trailer and loaded him onto the lowboy. Sarah quickly chained Hidalgo down and was ready to leave when Sister Franklin came from the house carrying two gallons of whole milk for Sarah and her family. There were exchanges of 'thank you' and Sarah left.

* * * * *

In the days that followed, Sarah prepared posters and flyers. She visited with the police captain and fire chief and made arrangements for their support. She stopped by Charley's Motel to verify some information. Her most important visit, however, was with a local insurance agent and a specially invited guest. This specially invited guest would insure her plan could be carried out without any legal repercussions.

During these preparations, Sarah's mother and father couldn't help wondering what she was up to. When asked, she would only smile and say: "Come to the demonstration and find out."

One evening as Big George and Big Sarah were preparing for bed, Sarah asked George: "What do you think our daughter is up to?"

"She's carefully braiding her whip,"[7] Big George replied with quiet assurance.

And so she was. She even solicited her brother into the plot asking him to bring the company's maintenance vehicle for a special task.

A growing excitement was saturating the town. Somehow, everyone sensed this was to be a demonstration worth attending. The stage was now set.

G. Kenneth Cardwell

37. The Demonstration

THE Saturday of the demonstration was a bright, late spring day. Little Sarah was up very early. Her first task—power-wash Hidalgo, Traveler and the trailer. All her equipment must be spotless, shinning like jewels. Then she drove Traveler and the trailer with Hidalgo over to the demonstration site where everything appeared to be in readiness. The portable bleachers and portable restrooms were in place; the demonstration area was roped off and the necessary stakes were laid out. A large, 10-ton boulder had been moved onto the grounds. The generator and sound system were set up and ready. Even the trash barrels were in place. Her inspection completed, she lowered the landing gear on her trailer and disconnected Traveler from the trailer and drove home.

* * * * *

At home, Little Sarah went to her room and took a nap. About noon, she rose, showered, ate lunch and then dressed. It was then she notice her mom home and not at the restaurant getting ready for the evening dinner. "Hey, mom what are you doing home?" Sarah asked.

"We got everything ready this morning so everyone could come to your demonstration," Big Sara replied to her daughter.

"So, where's dad?" Little Sarah queried.

"Your dad has gone to the airport to pick up Mr. Sheffield who's coming in from Peoria on his corporate jet for the demonstration," Big Sarah said with a big smile.

"You mean Mr. Sheffield, the President and CEO of Caterpillar Tractor, is coming?" Little Sarah said with surprise in her voice.

"Yes, the very same Mr. Sheffield and he's staying overnight with us and going to church with us tomorrow. And there's another surprise too," Big Sarah said with some excitement.

"Oh, please, I'm going to be a nervous wreck already; so … OK, what is it?" Little Sarah asked hesitantly.

"Your Aunt Gerti is coming down; and she's staying the

Agency and Consequences

night too," Big Sarah announced.

"You're kidding ... Aunt Gerti is coming! That's wonderful. Oh, I can't wait to see her. Mom, thanks. But, now I gotta go and get Hidalgo off his trailer and ready. See ya. I love you," Little Sarah said as she moved towards the door and then stopped, turned around and walked back to her mother and threw her arms around her and said tenderly: "Mom, thank you; thank you; thank you. I know I haven't said much about what's going to happen this afternoon. I appreciate the trust you and daddy have in me. It means everything to me."

* * * * *

At one-thirty, Little Sarah got back into Traveler and returned to the demonstration site where she unloaded Hidalgo from the trailer and drove him to the demonstration area. She parked and placed placards about and on him that gave some of his specifications. She also took a manila folder from Traveler's cab and placed it in Hidalgo's cab behind the seat where no one looking into the cab would take undo notice.

By two o'clock, the police and fire personnel were in place to park cars and ready for any emergency. At two-thirty, the crowd began to arrive. They brought their coolers loaded with soft drinks, chips, sandwiches and whatever else they desired. Soon Sarah and her brother, George, were helping children, parents and all others who wanted to, climb up and on Hidalgo, look into his cab and answer questions about his abilities and specifications.

What Sarah did not expect at this point was the arrival of newspaper and television reporters with their trucks. For whatever reason, the interest in this demonstration was wider than she could have imagined. She wondered: "Did the real reason for this event get leaked?"

By pre-arrangement, when Josh Bangeter arrived in his BMW, George directed him to park his car in a pre-designated spot. And, of course, he thought it some special honor to which he was entitled. When he walked out to the demonstration area, he was still limping from the stab in the foot by Sarah using her high heel two weeks earlier. But, he smiled, thinking he had bested her. At every opportunity during the past two weeks, his story of how good it had been with Sarah Kindman got bigger and better than the time he told it before. And since neither she nor her brother, George, was saying anything to deny it, he believed he was getting away with it.

Of course, when Little Sarah's family with Mr. Sheffield and Aunt Gerti all arrived, Sarah was ecstatic. She hugged her dad, mom, Aunt Gerti and shook Mr. Sheffield's hand. She thanked him for coming (she still didn't know how he knew she was doing the demonstration—it just never occurred to her to ask). As they shook hands, Mr. Sheffield asked: "Sarah, we don't want to rain on your parade here, but your father and I would like to be first on your program today. Would that be all right?" Mr. Sheffield asked very sincerely.

"Sure, huh ... I don't know what's going on; but, I guess that would be all right," Little Sarah responded tentatively.

"Sarah, finally, that puts the shoe on the other foot and you in the same boat as the rest of us. We, none of us, know for sure what's going on here today, is that right?" Big George said with a warm teasing smile.

"All right, dad, you got me. But, there are a couple of others who know what's going on besides George and me," Sarah countered. "Here's the microphone. I only arranged for one wireless mike," Sarah explained as she removed the battery operated transmitter from the belt of her skirt.

* * * * *

With that, Sarah's family went to their seats, Little George headed off to the parking lot while Big George, Mr. Sheffield and Little Sarah stood out in front of Hidalgo. Big George holding the transmitter in his left hand and the microphone in his right welcomed the audience: "Ladies and gentlemen, boys and girls, on behalf of my daughter, Sarah, I want to thank all of you for coming this afternoon. Now, I don't really know what we're going to see today, Sarah's been pretty mum about that. But, I know her skills and abilities and so I'm certain it will be a great show. Standing next to me is the President and CEO of Caterpillar Tractor Corporation, Mr. Robert Sheffield. He has some words he would like to say at this time."

George handed Mr. Sheffield the microphone and kept the transmitter in his other hand, since Mr. Sheffield held a large framed object in his free hand. "Ladies and gentlemen, as

Agency and Consequences

President and CEO of Caterpillar Tractor Corporation, I'm honored to be here today with my good friends, the Kindmans. A week ago, I called George and told him the patent application we had sent to the U.S. Patent Office on Sarah's invention had been finally completed and approved. I also told George, even though Sarah had sold her patent rights to Caterpillar Tractor, I wanted to come and present her with a framed copy of the patent certificate. At that point, George told me about the demonstration Sarah was doing so we decided I could come and surprise Sarah here today. She has had no prior notice this was going to take place today.

"I don't know how many of you are aware, but this young lady, Miss Sarah Kindman, is not only one of the very best bulldozer operators in the country (her dad is maybe a little better), she is one sharp engineer and mechanic. Her invention, which you will see today as Sarah has installed one of her prototypes on Hidalgo (I like that name), makes the fuel injection system more efficient by getting even greater atomization of the fuel as it is injected into the cylinders. What this means very simply is a more complete burn of the fuel, which means we can get more power from less fuel and cleaner exhaust. All of which means we can build a bulldozer that is less expensive to operate and cleaner for the environment. That's huge for our company. So, without any further adieu, on behalf of Caterpillar Tractor Corporation, I would like to present this framed copy of the Patent Certificate to Sarah E. Kindman for her invention, Super Atomized Fuel Injection System or SAFIS," Mr. Sheffield concluded as he handed the framed patent certificate to Sarah as the audience applauded.

Little Sarah received the framed certificate and held it over her head for everyone to see and then gave it to her dad as he gave back to her the microphone and transmitter. Big George and Mr. Sheffield then took their seats in the bleachers with Sarah's family.

* * * * *

Little Sarah replaced the transmitter on her belt, the microphone on her head and said: "Wow ... what a surprise. Mr. Sheffield, thank you for coming today. I appreciate all you and Caterpillar Tractor Corporation have done for me.

G. Kenneth Cardwell

"As we begin today, I want to thank all of you for coming. I feel honored so many of you would take a couple hours out of your Saturday afternoon, come out here and sit in the sun and watch a teenage young woman drive a bulldozer around a field. I would also like to thank some others, without whom, this demonstration would not be possible.

"First, Mr. and Mrs. Franklin whose land we are all sitting on. On most years, this piece of ground would be growing alfalfa or oats, both feed for their dairy herd. It just happens this year this ground is lying fallow. That said, since we are on the Franklin's property, I would ask you to be especially careful with your trash. Please use the trash barrels provided or take your trash home with you.

"Second, I would like to thank Principal Stanford of the high school and all the businesses in town for allowing me to plaster the walls of the high school and the windows of your businesses with posters and flyers.

"Third, a big thank you to our fire and police departments who are here to park cars, provide traffic control and to be of assistance should anyone need any emergency help."

Sarah continued her 'thank you' for the all the equipment provided and finally the biggest thank you of all was given to her family and particularly her brother, George, for his backstage assistance.

Then Little Sarah began: "Did everyone who wanted to, get the opportunity to get a good look at the bulldozer, named Hidalgo? If you didn't, as soon as I can get Hidalgo loaded and moved after the demonstration, I'll have him on display at my mom's restaurant until about 10:00 P.M. this evening. So, kids, if you didn't get to see this beast of a machine, ask your mom and dad to have dinner at Sarah's Place and come and see Hidalgo."

Mr. Sheffield in the stands whispered to Big George: I wish my sales personnel were so creative.

"She does love showing off that machine," George replied with a big grin.

At that point, Little George came out, picked up all the placards around and on Hidalgo and gave Little Sarah a very discrete thumbs up that all was going well in the parking lot. "A hand for my brother, George," Sarah cheered as he walked

Agency and Consequences

briskly off the demonstration site.

"Hidalgo is a top of the line, large bulldozer built by Caterpillar Tractor Corporation of Peoria, Illinois. As he stands right now, he weighs in at just over 107,500 pounds. His power plant is a CAT C18 ACERT diesel powered engine fitted, as Mr. Sheffield said, with a prototype Super Atomized Fuel Injection System or SAFIS. This engine generates a gross 464-horse power and 410-horse power at the flywheel.

"Hidalgo is approximately 26 and one-half feet long and over thirteen feet tall. The blade in front is 14 feet, 2 inches wide and 6 feet, 4 inches in height and weighs over 14,400 pounds. Under good conditions, this blade can dig almost 2 feet deep into the ground at a time. The rated capacity of this blade is about 17.7 cubic yards of material. That equates, given this particular soil, to just about 36,000 pounds of material. In other words, if you own a standard, half-ton pickup truck, Hidalgo can push as much dirt as nearly 36 pickup trucks can haul, at one time.

"The big device on the back of Hidalgo is called a ripper and is used for tearing loose rocks, breaking up compacted soil and sometimes asphalt roads. This ripper can penetrate into the ground about four feet with a force of 34,580 pounds of pressure and weighs 10,700 pounds.

"The maximum speed Hidalgo can move in top gear going forward is about 7.3 miles per hour. In reverse, he's a little faster at 8.9 miles per hour.[1]

"The demonstration this afternoon will be in five parts. First, you will notice a series of stakes in the center of the area. These stakes are 16 feet across from each other and 10 feet apart. The entire length, from the first pair to the last pair, is 100 feet. These stakes have been previously marked with several lines and a number. Before the demonstration, my brother, George, and I set these stakes and at each one, measured the depth of the top soil. Normally, when we clear top soil, we just figure a nominal depth of six inches. The top soil depth on this dairy farm, however, is over twice that depth averaging in this demonstration area just over 15 inches. We don't want to mix the top soil with the sub soil underneath and when we're all done, we want to put it all back like it was. So, on each stake, there is a number indicating the depth of the top soil and a solid black line at the number of inches from the top of the stake to that depth. Each stake, you will notice, is the same height above the ground as the top of Hidalgo's blade or 6 feet, 4 inches.

"There is on the top and outside edge of Hidalgo's blade a long, straight wire attached to the blade by a spring-loaded hinge. My objective is to take Hidalgo between those stakes with my guide wires precisely brushing the marks on the stakes so Hidalgo's blade can skim the top soil off the sub soil as cleanly as possible. By my calculations, we have to remove about 1,879 cubic feet or close to 69.5 cubic yards of top soil. That should take almost exactly four passes removing close to four inches of top soil per pass.

"Second, we will dig a hole in the area were we've cleared the top soil. This hole, at its deepest point, will be about ten feet deep (including the 15 inches of top soil) and ten feet long. A ramp on either end of the hole will be 25 feet long and when we're completed, will be at an angle of just over 18 degrees or a slop of 3 to 1. This hole will require the removal of 4,225 cubic feet or just over 156 cubic yards of material and will be piled in the first forty feet of the of the cleared area to your left. This will take between 11 and 15 passes to dig.[2]

"Following these two parts, I'll make a couple of comments about what was accomplished and some facts I hope will be interesting to you.

"The third part of the demonstration will be to roll that big 10-ton rock around. If all goes well, we'll roll it down and out of the hole and over the mound of dirt we take from the hole.

"The fourth part of our demonstration is a surprise which will be explained when we get to that point.

"Then lastly, we will put all the sub soil and top soil, we've taken from the hole, back into the hole.

"So, here we go. I'll talk to you and tell you what's going on as I put Hidalgo through his paces. Please notice, how maneuverable he is. Hopefully, it will be kind of like a ballet or a dressage event.

Little Sarah then climbed into Hidalgo's cab and within moments the great beast of a machine came alive. Instead of like his name's sake, a horse, "the bull wheel sprocket above and slightly ahead of the rear track idler wheel ...,"[3] gave him

Agency and Consequences

the appearance of a huge cat, crouched in his ambuscade, ready to pounce on its unsuspecting prey.

Sarah knew it was all about to happen—for better or for worse. She wondered at this moment: "Have I taken on too much—am I being judge, jury and executioner all in one." She thought of the words from her favorite play, *Camelot*, when Arthur felt betrayed and he demanded a man's vengeance. But instead, he decided to rise above the hurt, feeling like a victim and took the higher road ... to reach for the stars, to live and cultivate new attitudes where violence was not strength and compassion was not weakness.[4] For two weeks, this moment has been all she had thought about. Was she justified in what she was doing? Or was she only seeking revenge, which according to Arthur is, "That most worthless of causes?"[5]

Then Sarah thought about all the other young women who had been taken advantage of and would be in the future if they weren't warned, if Josh Bangerter was not exposed as the foul, poor excuse of a person he really was. After all, didn't she have his dad's support? Right there in the cab with her, didn't she have authorization to .... She took a deep breath, closed her eyes and prayed: "Dear Father in Heaven, I've felt I needed to do this for the past two weeks; I've made all these preparations; but now I'm wondering if my motives are right. Am I justified in doing what I've planned to do?" She waited and at that moment she felt enveloped in a warm, comfortable and peaceful spirit. And then a scripture came to her mind from the Book of Mormon and she understood just a little bit of the feelings Nephi must have felt when the Lord said to him: "It is better that one man should perish than that a nation should dwindle and perish in unbelief."[6] Sarah had her answer and finished her prayer.

She took Hidalgo down in front of the bleachers and ran him their length. She then turned and lined Hidalgo straight between the first pair of stakes. She dropped Hidalgo's blade precisely four inches and hit the first marks on the stakes with the guide wires right on the first set of marks on the stakes. Those, in the audience, who brought binoculars, were amazed how, at each pair of stakes, she lined up Hidalgo within what appeared to be a zero tolerance. She pushed the first load from the demonstration area, backed Hidalgo from the pile of top soil, pirouetted around and headed back for the second run in the reverse direction. Again, hitting her marks on the stakes and narrating the entire operation as she went. On the last run, she hit the final markers and all in the crowd were amazed when they saw the difference in color of soil that lay beneath the top soil and how little of this different color dirt she was scraping up.

The top soil removed, Sarah pulled Hidalgo up front and center to the crowd and explained: "That's one pretty effective method for removing just the right amount of material from an area you want. This method, however, is rather primitive and becomes cumbersome when clearing a large area. On larger projects, where we often have to be even more precise, Hidalgo has the ability to receive laser or GPS signals that can control his blade to within $1/100^{th}$ of an inch. You'll notice because of the slight anomalies in the depth of the top soil, we scraped some of the sub soil and left some of the top soil in small patches behind. Now, let's dig the hole.

This time Sarah aligned Hidalgo just as she had before, lowered his blade precisely at the first set of markers and then she took just enough to start. Then she dug deeper as she went and then shallower again. As she started to lift the blade on the other side, she came out right at the forty-foot mark. She pushed the dirt up to the edge of what would be her exit ramp and began a pile of soil at the same slope as her ramp would be. She, then, backed Hidalgo all the way back to the start position. This time she lowered the blade at just past the first pair of stakes at about 1 foot, lowered the blade and again adjusted so it was full when she came out precisely at the forty-foot mark. She then pushed the dirt up the pile until it fell off the blade on the back of the pile. She repeated the process again and again and again. In all, she made the trip 13 times.

When she backed out the last time, Sarah again moved Hidalgo front and center to the audience. She turned him off, came out of the cab, climbed some steps and stood on a platform she had installed over the top of Hidalgo's engine cowl. She then addressed the audience: "How many of you young people (or even older folks) don't like arithmetic?" A large number of hands went up. "You know, when I was a little girl in elementary and junior high school I didn't like arithmetic much either. But, when my dad started teaching me how to operate

Agency and Consequences

bulldozers, he made me learn how to figure how much dirt I was moving or had to move to do a certain job. He also said I had to know how much each kind of material weighed per cubic yard and all sorts of different stuff like that. Why do you suppose we have to be able to calculate all that?" Sarah asked.

    A few hands went up and Sarah pointed to one young man who responded: "Is it so you can calculate how much it will cost to do a certain job?

Sarah repeated to the whole audience what the young man said in his answer and then said: "That's exactly right. It's so we can calculate what it will cost to do a job. Here's a quick example. Let's suppose we needed to move all that dirt we just dug out of that hole somewhere else using dump trucks. I calculated earlier we had to remove almost 70 cubic yards of top soil and just over 156 cubic yards of sub soil from the hole. Now, since there are 27 cubic feet in a cubic yard, dealing with the volumes we do, cubic yards is just easier. But guess what? Those piles of top soil and sub soil don't equate to my original numbers any more. Anybody want to guess what's happened to the volumes of material as a consequence of our digging out that hole?"

Not so many hands went up this time, but Sarah picked a young teenage girl this time who responded: "I think once the dirt is all loosened up, it's kinda gotten fluffier."

Sarah again repeated the answer to the audience and then said: "That's the perfect answer. That's exactly what happens. The dirt is not compacted like it was before and it's fluffier. We call that 'swell.' In this case, the top soil is now about 15 percent fluffier than it was before making a total volume of 80 cubic yards instead of close to 70; and the sub soil, because it's a sandy clay loam mixture, will swell about 25 percent from its original 156 cubic yards to almost 196 cubic yards.[7]

"In addition, remember when I told you my dad had me learn how much all that dirt weighs? Well, this kind of material, in its non-compacted state, weighs about 2,025 pounds per cubic yard. We have a total of 276 cubic yards of dirt at 2,025 pounds per cubic yard for a total of about 558,900 pounds or over 279 tons.[8]

"And all that will have direct impact on the time it will

take for a particular size of loading equipment to load the trucks and the number of trips a truck or fleet of trucks will have to make to move that dirt. All that equates to time—time in operator labor and machine time that equates to fuel and maintenance. It all adds up to cost—dollars all of us of pay for utilities, highways, airport runways, landscaping, basements and foundations for buildings. So, all you young people, it doesn't matter what field of work you will decide to go into, arithmetic and mathematics are most likely essential tools to do the work and I encourage you to become good at arithmetic and mathematics.

Next up is to roll this big rock that's over there. Often, especially when building roads where they have to blast cliffs and things like that, there are always big rocks and boulders that have to be moved. Sometimes we roll them into low spots and use them as fill; other times we roll them onto banks or a berm to keep down erosion. Whatever the situation, there is usually a need to move rocks and boulders. So, here we go.

Just as Sarah was about to return to Hidalgo's cab, a man in the crowd spoke loudly and said: "Miss Kindman, I have a question."

"Yes, sir; please ask," Sarah responded politely.

"You mentioned at the beginning your bulldozer had the ability, through laser and GPS technology, to be precise down to 1/100th of an inch. When you're grading a highway or some other large area, isn't that getting a little over precise; I mean, it's only dirt; it can't be that important," the man in the crowd asked just a little bemused.

"Sir, I understand how you could think that way. In the short run, will it have any effect on how a car handles if a new highway is 1/100th of an inch lower or higher? Probably not. But for us, in the business, when we have hundreds of lane miles of highway to grade, it does make a difference. Here's the quick and dirty arithmetic. For every 1/100th of an inch this bulldozer grades too deep, it means digging up an additional 14.2 cubic feet of dirt every 1,200 feet of grading. For every mile graded, that's 62.48 cubic feet or an additional 2.3 cubic yards. A four-lane highway with 12-foot wide lanes and an emergency lane on each side would equate to about 316.8 cubic feet, or 11.7 cubic yards, of extra dirt per mile of highway. That all translates to

Agency and Consequences

fuel, wear and tear on machines, labor, more time, more material to haul or dispose of someway, somehow—in other words, more dollars to do the job. Sir, thank you for the question," Sarah said with a smile.

"Sarah really has her numbers down, doesn't she?" Mr. Sheffield smiling asked George, as he was watching from the bleachers.

"She's dead on. Every time she's helped me prepare a proposal, we've won it and made good money. Yeah, she's pretty amazing," George replied with bit of pride in his voice.

Back in Hidalgo's cab, Sarah pressed the switch and Hidalgo was his big, beastie self again, anxious for the next task. When Sarah reached the boulder, she positioned Hidalgo to catch the boulder on left side of his blade. She narrated indicating: "Often, because of the clearance on one side or the other, it may not be possible to push from the middle."

As she got the boulder moving, she showed how she could roll the boulder by lowering the blade, tilting it so the edge would catch under the bottom of the boulder and then raising the blade. "In real soft soil, this is often the only way a boulder, that has a tendency to dig into the soil, can be moved," she explained.

She next demonstrated how she could move the boulder from side to side across the front of her blade by angling the blade in one direction and then the other. "Sometimes, because boulders have weird shapes they will do this on their own and you need to move your blade back forth to keep the boulder in the middle—sort of like moving the front wheel on your bike to keep from falling over," she narrated.

Finally, she pushed the boulder down into the hole and then carefully she maneuvered it up the exit ramp and set it like a cherry on the top of the pile of sub soil removed from the hole. And there she left it and then she backed down into and out the hole. It was now time to execute the main purpose of this whole demonstration.

As she came of out the hole, Sarah explained over the sound system it was time for Part 4 of the demonstration and this was going to be a big surprise to someone in the audience. She announced part of the demonstration would feature the awesome power of the ripper mounted at the back of Hidalgo.

G. Kenneth Cardwell

She explained her brother, George, had been preparing the essential participant in this demonstration and she was taking Hidalgo out into the parking lot to retrieve it.

As Sarah drove Hidalgo into the parking lot, as many in the audience who could, mostly those on the top row of bleachers, stood, turned and watched. In a moment, they all gasped and many were saying in unison: "Did you see that?"

Sarah had maneuvered Hidalgo and backed him right up next to Josh Bangeter's BMW, she raised the ripper, backed up until Hidalgo was touching the BMW's front bumper and then sent the ripper right through the BMW's engine compartment.

Hidalgo was now dragging Josh Bangeter's brand new BMW 335i coupe into the demonstration area. When they reached front and center of the audience, Josh realized what was happening and started to run onto the field, but was immediately seized by the police. Josh was immediately told everything that had been done and was about to be done was authorized by the legal title holder of the car, his father, and he was to sit down, watch and listen.

At this moment there was a terrible crunching sound as Sarah backed Hidalgo over the front of the car just enough to release the ripper's grip so she could lift it out of the car. Once the ripper was extracted, Sarah moved Hidalgo off the car and then parked him along the car's side so the audience, and particularly Josh, could see both the car and her. She shut Hidalgo down, took the manila folder from behind her seat and again took position on the platform atop Hidalgo's engine cowl.

"Ladies and gentleman," Sarah said with firm authority; "we now have come to real reason for this whole demonstration today. I apologize for the ruse; only four individuals in this whole town knew its real purpose, these are my brother, George, Mr. Melvin Gardner of the Farmer's Insurance Agency, Mr. Brad Bangeter, the owner of the car I just drug in and myself.

"I want to tell you a story that happened only two weeks ago this evening. And I want every young woman and every young man to listen and listen very carefully. For you parents with younger children, I apologize in advance. The story I feel needs to be told is most likely in the PG-13 category and I am deeply sorry so many young ears will hear things this afternoon much earlier than they should have to.

Agency and Consequences

"You see, I'm not what you'd describe as a normal young woman. As you've seen today, I like bulldozers; I like everything about bulldozers; I have a passion for operating them, working on them and designing them. It's a wonderful thing for me. Already, I've made a lot of money. The patent you heard about today will, most likely, make me more money in the next ten years than most of you would make in several life-times. I don't say that to brag, I have been given a gift which I've tried to share wherever I can. In addition, I already have a full ride scholarship secured to Purdue University starting this summer that includes an on-going internship at Caterpillar Tractor's Research and Development Laboratory where improvements to my invention will be pursued. Consequently, I've had very few friends in high school because I was perceived as being weird and as for guys inviting me on dates, well, that didn't happen often for obvious reasons.

"So, I decided to change all that by doing something incredibly stupid. I played up to the biggest playboy in the school, Josh Bangeter. I thought if I went out with Josh, and he did what he was notoriously infamous for—getting girls in bed with him—that would make me more popular and I would get more dates. Well, when we left the prom together, two weeks ago and Josh drove me out in this BMW to a cow pasture, dragged me into the back seat and tried to seduce me, I realized, just in the nick of time, this wasn't the time, place or person with whom I wanted to have a first sexual experience. I felt like trash. I was nothing but a piece of meat. Josh Bangeter cared no more about me than a stud mounting an in-heat filly.

"Well, I thought fast, and admittedly with a lot of guile, I tricked Josh into taking me to Charley's Motel. And while he was in the office getting a key, I got out of this car and ran for home. Josh caught me half way across the park and told me we were going to do it anyway and the motel register would prove we were both there as willing partners.

"That isn't true," Sarah said as she held up a document from the folder. "Here's a notarized copy of the motel register for that evening. Neither Josh's name nor my name is on that register. Every name on this register is accounted for. There was no one registered in that motel that night under an alias. Josh Bangeter was not, I was not in that motel two weeks ago. So, every story Josh has been telling about me and him getting it on that night is nothing but a bald faced lie designed to protect and enhance his already sordid, sleazy and debauched reputation.

"Here's what is true. Josh has been limping for two weeks. You want to know why? Because just like the ripper on Hidalgo punched a hole through the engine compartment of this BMW, I punched a hole through his right foot with one of the four-inch spiked heels of the pumps I was wearing that night. After that, he got my knee in his groin, I kicked off my shoes and ran home. And to prove I didn't have sex that night, I had my dad take me to the emergency room at the hospital for a vaginal examination. And here is the certificate signed by three hospital personnel stating in no uncertain terms I did not have sex and I was still a virgin," Sarah testified with restrained anger and confidence.

Oh, how she wished at that moment there had been no need to say what she had just said. The thought of the tender souls of the innocent in the audience, who would now be full of questions before their time, that parents would now have to answer, filled her mind and heart. She felt love and forgiveness for Josh and for herself sweep through her and they seemed to penetrate right down to the nucleus of every cell in her soul.

Like her mother standing before Paul Tenter that night at her restaurant and like Ëowyn on Pelennor Fields, Sarah stood majestic and silent on the platform over Hidalgo's engine cowl. Luminous, a shaft of light, in a white ruffled blouse, white knee-length skirt, white belt and hose and white heeled boots, face grave, fair yet terrible, with both longing and tears in her eyes, heart aching, full of yearning and compassion, made it impossible to blench.[9]

"Josh," Sarah said looking at him with the greatest of compassion and tenderness all there had ever seen, "I forgive you. There is no animosity or anger in my heart. What I've done today, what I will yet do, is all done with the hope it will cause you and everyone in this audience to think about how precious is the virtue of chastity.

"To all you young men and young women who wonder about the real value of chastity, despite all you see and hear on television, in the movies, on the inter-net, in gym locker rooms, it is more precious than rubies or diamonds or even life itself.

Agency and Consequences

Chastity is not yours to take whenever passion and lust raise their ugly heads. It's not to be given away by anyone to anyone except within the sacred bonds of legal and lawful marriage. And then, it's not given away at all, it's shared and treasured and protected all the more."

Sarah paused for a few moments as her still stunned and admiring audience silently digested what had happened and what they had heard in the past few minutes. Then she said: "Well, to move on to part five of this demonstration, let me make sure all here, especially Josh, know Mr. Brad Bangeter, the legal and lawful title holder to this vehicle has given me, Sarah E. Kindman, full authorization to do whatever I choose to do with this car," as she showed the notarized affidavit.

"Therefore, so this vehicle will never, ever again, be the place of seduction, the place where innocence is sacrificed, it has been carefully prepared for burial. Prior to being drug out here from the parking lot, my brother, George, drained all the fluids from this vehicle and removed the battery. This will minimize, to an absolute minimum, any leaching of gasoline, oil, battery acid, radiator, brake and power steering fluids into the ground and eventually into the water table," Sarah assured.

With that, Sarah was back in Hidalgo's cab and in mere seconds he was purring again with deep, diesel engine resonance. To avoid getting broken glass on Mr. Franklin's field, Sarah again backed Hidalgo to the front of the BMW and drove the ripper through the engine compartment. With that, the car was drug down into the hole where Sarah drove Hidalgo over the top of the car several times. The sound of breaking glass, shattering plastic, exploding tires and cracking metal, was almost ghastly.

Soon, Sarah backed Hidalgo out of the hole and drove him to the far side of the demonstration area. It was then everyone guessed why she deposited that huge, 10-ton boulder on top of the pile of sub soil. Sarah lifted Hidalgo's blade a couple feet off the ground and charged up the pile crashing into the boulder with terrific force, sending it almost air-borne into the hole and crashing with explosive authority right on top of the already smashed BMW.

Next, Sarah began the task of pushing all the sub soil back into the hole. It would be a bit of a task to get all the soil back into a hole that was now partially filled with a smashed car and 10-ton boulder. But she pushed it into place one blade full at a time and then carefully drove Hidalgo over and over the material allowing his more than 107,000 pounds to compress the soil as she went. When she was finished the ground was only slightly mounded. Then she replaced the top soil and then finished by dragging her blade in reverse, smoothing everything until the car's burial site was barely noticeable.

Josh Bangeter sat there enraged. He was obviously humiliated. Flanked by police, he was powerless—he couldn't even leave. Sarah had seduced him into showing up and had given him the best seat in the house. The sights and sounds of his car being mutilated and buried alive indelibly etched into his psyche a pattern for revenge. He vowed no woman would EVER get away with and do to him ever again what Sarah Kindman just did.

Sarah then took Hidalgo to front and center one more time. She shut him down and again took a position on the platform above the engine cowl. The audience, except for Josh Bangeter, all came to their feet cheering and applauding. She stood silent, looking at the audience, listening to their applause, feeling a reassurance she had done the right thing and yet there was a pang in her heart. She now understood what another Book of Mormon prophet named Jacob must of felt, when confronted with having to address the same subject, said to his audience:

> And also it grieveth me that I must use so much boldness of speech concerning you, before your wives and your children, many of whose feelings are exceedingly tender and chaste and delicate before God, which thing is pleasing unto God; but, notwithstanding the greatness of the task, I must ... tell you concerning your wickedness and abominations, in the presence of the pure in heart, and under the glance of the piercing eye of the Almighty God.[10]

Finally, Sarah said: "Ladies and gentlemen, boys and

Agency and Consequences

girls, honored guests and family, this concludes the demonstration today. I'm honored and grateful for your warm and enthusiastic applause. Thank you for coming. May I ask you again to please check around you and make sure all your trash is appropriately deposited or secured to go home with you. Thank you all again and have a pleasant rest of the week end."

* * * * *

At that moment, several newspaper, radio and television reporters rushed onto the demonstration area and formed a semi circle around Hidalgo's side as Sarah climbed down to the ground. "Miss. Kindman, may I ask you a few questions?" they all seemed to say at once.

Sarah, having learned to be the gracious hostess, said smiling: "Sure ... I have just a few minutes; but, I reserve the right to not answer any particular question."

First reporter: "Miss Kindman, why did you decide to do this demonstration today with such a public humiliation of Mr. Bangeter?

"I did what I did today for several reasons," Sarah responded. "First, when I was at the hospital having the tests done two weeks ago, I met a woman who had a similar thing happen to her and she did nothing. Eventually the rumors and lies were so pervasive, she decided the answer was to just go out and make them the truth. She encouraged me not to let the person who attempted to take advantage of me get away with it. Second, it was important for me to reclaim my honor and that of my family. Third, it was done publicly because Josh Bangeter chose to go public with his lies."

Second reporter: "Do you think this demonstration will encourage other young people to be more open about exposing those individuals who try and all too often succeed in seducing other young people?

"I hope so. But what I hope even more is young people and older people will value the virtue chastity and decide it's worth protecting and keeping it intact. And as I said earlier, only sharing it within the bonds of legal and lawful marriage," Sarah answered.

Third reporter: "Do you think others will go to the same extremes as you did in making their point? Digging a ten-foot deep hole with a D9 Caterpillar, then smashing a very expensive automobile and burying it in the hole you dug is pretty extreme don't you think?

"Stealing someone's chastity, parenting children who will most likely never have a normal childhood and will grow up repeating the same sinful practices, generation after generation, is even more extreme. Had I not had permission from Josh's father, who was the legal title holder of that car, to do what I did, I would have found some other way. In any case, I would have exposed Josh Bangeter one way or another," Sarah said with deep conviction.

"One more question only," Sarah said firmly.

Fourth reporter: "You mentioned your invention would make you a great deal of money within the next ten years; how much do you estimate that will be?"

Sarah smiled and thought "why does it always end up being about money" and replied: "To be real honest, I don't know what the final numbers will be. Caterpillar Tractor Corporation has a contract with my father and me. It's a private matter where my dad and I are concerned. We are under obligation to say nothing of the details where Caterpillar is concerned. The invention is now their property. Hidalgo and a couple other machines in my dad's fleet have prototypes installed and we are doing field testing and keeping very careful records on things like performance and fuel consumed. That's all I can say about it."

"Thank you ladies and gentlemen; but now it's time to load this guy up and put him on display at my mom's restaurant. You should all come over, use your expense accounts and have the best meal in the region," Sarah invited as she climbed back up into Hidalgo's cab.

Agency and Consequences |

38. Celebrity Status

WHEN Little Sarah got home, the parking lot to Sarah's Place was jammed. The restaurant had a line out into the lot waiting to get in. Her dad had reserved the necessary space to put Hidalgo on display. And the police department rerouted traffic while Little Sarah maneuvered Traveler and the trailer into position to unload him.

News reporters were having a field day talking to people who had attended the demonstration as they waited in line to get into the restaurant. For all in the line, what they had seen at Sarah's demonstration, was the subject of the cacophony of chatter between them. The majority of the opinions were in favor of what she did and said. But the dinner-goers were mostly impressed with her courage to take a stand, to take back her honor.

With Hidalgo unloaded and the placards placed around and upon him, it wasn't long before a line of kids and teenagers were lined up for a look and to ask questions. Many in the line were classmates of Sarah, who, for the first time, seemed to take an interest and who seemed genuinely impressed by her accomplishments and skill. A few of the girls, particularly, were very openly impressed by her willingness to put Josh Bangeter in his place. Sarah couldn't help but wonder if they missed the real point of the whole thing.

As the evening wore on, the line to see Hidalgo wound down. Little Sarah went in to the restaurant and got something to eat in the kitchen. Her mother came in and all they could do was hug each other and cry. Finally, Big Sarah said: "You should do a demonstration every Saturday. For the first time in the history of Sarah's Place, we had to send some people away because we ran out of food. I think your dad, Aunt Gerti and Mr. Sheffield are waiting for you at home. Your dad said: 'Don't worry about Hidalgo, Sam Noble has volunteered to load him up and take him back to the yard.'"

* * * * *

Little Sarah walked from the restaurant to her house and was greeted by her dad. And just as with her mother, all they could do was hug and cry. Sarah then hugged Aunt Gerti (who wasn't really her aunt, she was just called "aunt" as she was a dear and close friend of her parents since their college days and who was widowed not long after her marriage). Then she greeted Mr. Sheffield with a warm handshake as he said looking intently at his young friend: "Young lady, I've never in my life witnessed anything like what I saw this afternoon. I know you haven't been able to see any of the news casts this evening, but you are a celebrity—unwittingly for sure, but a celebrity nonetheless. I think your life, as of this moment, will be nothing you could ever have imagined before this afternoon."

Little Sarah excused herself, went to her room, changed and offered a prayer of thanks for all the good that happened that day. She then went back down stairs and spent a wonderful late evening with family and friends.

* * * * *

The following day at Church was, despite all the attention Little Sarah received, a tender and sensitive day. Just as she had two weeks before, she again felt the warm assurance of the Spirit as she partook of the emblems of the Sacrament.

That afternoon, at home, the telephone didn't stop ringing. Calls came from everywhere—the Tonight Show, Late Night, Good Morning America, The Today Show, 60 Minutes and a dozen other lesser-knowns.

During the next few days, decisions were made. Right after school let out (Little Sarah and Little George's graduation), they'd go as a family to California for the Tonight Show, Disneyland and the rest of the sights in Southern California. Little Sarah and Big George would then go to New York and do the circuit. A flat car was leased to move Hidalgo on the Rails and a truck tractor and lowboy trailer would be leased locally to move Hidalgo to the show sites.

For the Tonight Show, they pre-filmed part of the show at a local construction site where Little Sarah gave Jay Leno personal instructions on operating a bulldozer. Sarah was Jay's second guest on the Tonight Show, following a scantily clad bombshell of an up and coming actress. Sarah came on the stage in a beautiful, completely modest, white, knee length dress and matching four-inch heels. As she came out on the stage, there

Agency and Consequences

was an audible gasp from the audience—she was a commanding presence in body and spirit. The next several minutes were filled with questions, answers and the film clip of Jay operating Hidalgo. In addition, Jay couldn't help but quip: "I pity any man who tries to take advantage of you. Never mind your dad on the doorstep with a shotgun. You'll come after him yourself with a 54-ton bulldozer." During the next commercial break, Sarah changed into a jump suit. Following the break, she gave a short demonstration in the NBC parking lot. It was then time to put Hidalgo back on a train and go to New York.

New York was a whirlwind. The David Letterman show, Late Night, and the two big morning shows were each unique and challenging experiences. On each occasion, Little Sarah began to understand a little more clearly she could make these experiences opportunities to promote modesty, the virtue of chastity and wholesomeness. While she was admired for doing what she did, she also became aware, for the most part, it was all sort of an oddity to people. Even to the smart, cordial and aware television hosts with whom she interviewed, in the final analysis, like the foolish, immature girls in her high school, she concluded, most people just didn't get it.

Following the New York trip, they shipped Hidalgo to Caterpillar Tractor Corporation in Peoria, Illinois where Traveler and his lowboy were waiting. Little Sarah was dropped off by her dad at Purdue University in West Lafayette, Indiana.

As Mr. Sheffield predicted, Sarah could not have dreamed all that had happened in the past few weeks. Little did she know, for her and the Kindman family, it was only a taste of what lie ahead.

G. Kenneth Cardwell

Part Four

And The First Shall Be Last

G. Kenneth Cardwell

39. Transition

THE next several years for the Kindman family were, in a word, transitional. Little Sarah and Little George went off to university; little George, a year later, off on a mission for the LDS Church; another son and daughter graduated from high school; and then within a year, the same son was also off on a mission.

Upon returning from the mission field, Little George married his high school sweetheart, Mary Greenfield, Alice and Ben Greenfield's daughter. It was about this time Little Sarah graduated, with honors, from Purdue. But she wasn't finished. She decided to continue and get her masters and Ph.D. through an accelerated program (three more years of full-time hard work). The saving grace for Sarah was the opportunity, several times a month, to go to Peoria and work with the Caterpillar engineers on the refinements to her invention and other projects. And, as always, she carved out a little time to be at Hidalgo's controls.

* * * * *

Maybe the most significant event during this time span was the release of Paul Tenter from the penitentiary. George and Sarah threw a big welcome home party at Sarah's Place for him. Paul was a different man when he came out of prison. He hadn't had a drink for over twenty years; he had worked hard to repay his debts to both God and society; and shortly after returning to church, he accepted an assignment to be the organist in his local church ward. Paul had loved the organ since his youth and playing it was a skill he had renewed and refined while in prison.

One of the tender moments for Paul, upon his return, was to visit the grave of his beloved cocker spaniel, Ruffles, who had died three years prior to his release. The Greenfields had buried him at the edge of their apple orchard under one of their trees. Their children had made a marker and put a little picket fence around the spot.

G. Kenneth Cardwell

The capstone of this period was, within two years, upon President George Kindman's recommendation, Paul was rebaptized into the Church.

40. The Phone Call

SHORTLY after receiving her Ph.D., Little Sarah took a full time post at Caterpillar Tractor as a senior research engineer. Over the next couple of years, Sarah's work at Caterpillar was impressive. What she still enjoyed the most, however, was getting out into the field, firing up Hidalgo and pushing dirt around. As she did at home, she found ways to donate her skills and Hidalgo's strength.

But, now Sarah developed a new passion. Asked to serve as young women's president in her Peoria Church Ward, she fell in love with the teenage girls for whom she now had responsibility. Her desire to help them come to know their own potential as daughters of God and to value all righteous virtues (particularly chastity) became almost an obsession. It was, in fact, during the young women's summer camp, the phone call came.

* * * * *

Little Sarah was sitting with her girls at the evening campfire when a member of the Stake Young Women's Presidency came and told her she needed to call her father on his cell phone as soon as possible. She went to the camp office and called saying: "Hey daddy, what's up?"

"Sarah," her dad said, with a very tired and anxious voice; "I just got off the phone with your mom and she told me how to reach you. I need your help."

"Sure, dad; anything, how can I help?" Sarah said to her dad knowing if her dad needed her help, especially while she was at camp with her young women, there was a very good reason.

"There's a big forest fire up near Boise, Idaho. There are a lot of homes in its path and we're losing. I need you and Hidalgo here by tomorrow night," Sarah's dad explained.

"Dad, that's not possible. I can't drive him there that fast and I can't get him on a train and be there by tomorrow either. How do you think I can be there by tomorrow night?" Sarah asked sincerely.

"This fire has been declared a national disaster and there

will be an Air Force C-5 Transport waiting for you at Scott Air Force Base near St. Louis at noon, central time tomorrow. Can you be there?" George asked his daughter.

"I'll be there," Sarah said in a way reassuring to her dad.

"That's my girl. I know you've got to get things arranged there at the camp and get Hidalgo ready for the trip. I suspect this will be a long night for you. Thank you, honey. I love you," George said with relief in his voice.

"I love you too dad. See you tomorrow night," Sarah said as she hung up the phone.

* * * * *

Sarah returned to the campfire and explained to her girls it was her dad who called and he needed her right away to go to Boise, Idaho to help fight the big forest fire up there and she had to leave immediately. She then asked two of her girls to go find a member of the Stake Young Women's Presidency and she began immediately to strike her camp and load her truck.

Within just a few minutes, Sarah's girls returned with Sister Fletcher, first counselor in the Presidency, to whom she explained the situation. Sarah realized her vehicle would be needed to get the girls and their gear home at the end of the week, so she suggested Sister Fletcher ride home with her and then drive her truck back to camp in the morning. After conferring with the other leaders, the suggestion was agreed to and Sarah and Sister Fletcher were on their way to Sarah's home in Peoria.

* * * * *

On the ride home, Sarah and Sister Fletcher talked about each other's background. Sister Fletcher recalled hearing about Sarah when she hit all the TV shows following her demonstration. She was frankly amazed with Sarah's passion for bulldozers. Sarah explained she wasn't the only one amazed by it.

About half way home, Sarah learned Sister Fletcher's husband was out of work. She also learned how tough it had been for them the past several months. There was no complaining in Sister Fletcher's voice. It came out in just a matter of fact way impressing Sarah deeply. It reminded her of the stories of the pioneers facing their problems—Sister Fletcher

Agency and Consequences

and her husband just kept moving forward with faith.

* * * * *

They arrived at Sarah's home at almost mid-night and quickly unloaded Sarah's truck. Sarah invited Sister Fletcher in and, like everyone visiting Sarah's home for the first time, Sister Fletcher was struck with amazement. Sarah quickly showered and gathered up the things she would need for the trip to Boise. Sister Fletcher was surprised when Sarah brought out her Winchester Model 94 lever action rifle and a box of ammunition.

"One of the hardest things about this kind of work—building fire breaks in big fires—is you sometimes find animals badly injured by the fire or falling trees, stuff like that," Sarah said explaining with a bit of a lump in her throat.

Within just a few minutes, Sarah had her gear in the truck and said: "Let's go."

"Aren't you staying here tonight?" Sister Fletcher asked in a surprised voice.

"Nope; I've got a sleeper in Traveler, my tractor. All I need for you to do is take me to my rig and drop me off," Sarah explained matter-of-factly.

* * * * *

When Sarah and Sister Fletcher arrived at the Caterpillar yard where Hidalgo, Traveler and the trailer were stored, the guard at the gate was already expecting her. "Heard you was coming Miss Kindman. Got a big fire up in Boise I hear," the guard said.

"That's right. Charlie, I'm going to sleep in Traveler tonight and will be out the gate by about six," Sarah told the guard.

Sarah and Sister Fletcher drove up to where Traveler and Hidalgo were parked and Sister Fletcher was even more amazed. "Gosh, that's a big thing. You drive that machine?" Sister Fletcher asked with incredulity.

"One that big since I was seventeen; smaller ones since I was a little girl. My dad says I was pushing and pulling levers on bulldozers before I could walk," Sarah said with a hint of pride.

Sarah and Sister Fletcher unloaded Sarah's gear into Traveler's cab with the fully loaded sleeper berth. "I've always wanted to look inside one of these," Sister Fletcher said. "It's really quite amazing isn't it?" Sister Fletcher said with awe.

"Meet Traveler. When I get back, I'll take you for a ride. I think you'd like it, "Sarah said.

Sarah, then took the key to her pickup, a full size crew cab Ford F150, and gave it to Sister Fletcher. She then gave her five, crisp twenty-dollar bills saying: "The truck will need some gas."

"Now, before you go back to camp in the morning, I want you and your husband to take this envelope to the Peoria State Bank and ask for Mr. Gardner," Sarah said in a firm, concerned voice.

"What's this about?" Sister Fletcher asked.

"Mr. Gardner will explain it to you and your husband in the morning. Just don't open the envelope. Mr. Gardner will do that," Sarah said in a way Sister Fletcher realized there was no use arguing or questioning.

"Thanks for riding home with me. Please tell my girls I love them and I'll be home just as soon as this job is finished," Sarah requested kindly as she climbed into her tractor cab to get some sleep before the long day ahead.

* * * * *

Just before six in the morning, Sarah was up and in Traveler's driver seat. She started him up and carefully pulled Hidalgo loaded on the lowboy up to the gate of the Caterpillar yard. She stopped, got out and went into the guard building carrying her travel bag and a clothes bag.

"Good morning Miss Kindman," Charlie said with a big smile. "S'pose you're off to the big fire out west are you?"

"Yeah, I guess I am, Charlie," Sarah replied returning a smile. "May I use your restroom to freshen up a bit?

"Sure, sure, Miss. Kindman; go right ahead," Charlie responded.

About ten minutes later, Sarah came out of the restroom donning a jump suit, steel-toed cowboy boots and Caterpillar baseball cap. "How's your wife getting along since her surgery?" Sarah asked Charlie sincerely.

"Oh she's doin' alright. Still hard for her to get around much though. She get's awfully tired fast," Charlie reported

Agency and Consequences

with a tone of concern in his voice.

"Well, please give her my best and tell her she's in my prayers," Sarah said kindly looking Charlie in the eyes as she took his hand to shake it and slipped him a roll of twenty-dollar bills.

Then, as Sarah put her hand on the door to leave, in through the other door on the other side of the gate, came two Illinois State Patrolmen. "Sarah Kindman? I'm Sergeant Hollingsworth and this is Corporal Chadwick, we've been assigned to escort you and your bulldozer down to Scott Air Force Base," Sergeant Hollingsworth asked, introducing himself and his partner at the same time.

"Good morning, officers. Yes, I'm Sarah Kindman. Glad to have you with me on the way down. Are you hungry? I hope you are; because I'm famished and I'd planned to eat breakfast on the way. I'm buying," Sarah said in a way the two officers just looked at each other and both realized even if they weren't hungry they were stopping anyway.

A few minutes later with Sergeant Hollingsworth leading the way and Corporal Chadwick following, Sarah's Kenworth and lowboy loaded with Hidalgo were out the gate of the Caterpillar yard and headed toward Scott Air Force Base.

Their route took them first along Interstate 74 heading towards Bloomington, Illinois. After just a few miles, Sergeant Hollingsworth led the caravan into a truck stop. Sarah paid for an ample breakfast and she and the two officers enjoyed good conversation. Following breakfast, they continued east to the I-55 junction. They then headed south towards Scott AFB.

* * * * *

Meanwhile, Sister Fletcher and her husband had a sleepless night wondering what could possibly be in the envelope Sarah gave them. At eight-thirty, they left their home and were at the Peoria State Bank waiting for the doors to open at nine. When they entered the bank, before they could inquire for Mr. Gardner, a very pleasant gentleman approached with a warm smile greeting them: "You must be Mr. and Mrs. Fletcher. I'm John Gardner," as he extended his hand to shake their hands.

"Yes, we are," Brother Fletcher said as Mr. Gardner directed them into his office.

G. Kenneth Cardwell

"Please be seated," Mr. Gardner invited as he closed the door and moved to his seat behind his desk. "May I please have your envelope," Mr. Gardner requested.

Brother Fletcher handed Mr. Gardner the envelope as he took an opener out of his desk and opened it. "Sarah Kindman is a remarkable young woman," Mr. Gardner noted. "She left a message on my cell phone early this morning telling me you would be in this morning. I bet you've been wondering all night what this is all about?" Mr. Gardner posited with a large smile as Brother and Sister Gardner looked at each other and then at Mr. Gardner.

"Huh ... well, yes we have, Mr. Gardner," Brother Fletcher acknowledged.

"Here's what I'm authorized to tell you," Mr. Gardner said kindly. "Sarah Kindman is a very gifted, hard working, young woman who has made a considerable amount of money in her young life—principally through an invention she sold to Caterpillar when she was only seventeen. A large portion of that money was put into a philanthropic account which she decides to whom it will be given. This letter authorizes me to issue you a certified check in the amount of fifty-thousand dollars to be used in any way you see fit. The only condition on this gift is you tell absolutely no one about the source of this money. The only ones to know anything about this gift are you two, Sarah Kindman and me. Should you break this condition, the money becomes a loan and not a gift. Here is a very simple two-page agreement stating what I just explained that you will be asked to sign. Take a few minutes to look it over and if you can agree to be silent about where the gift came from, I'll prepare the check.

Brother and Sister Fletcher were both in tears at this point as they read together the agreement. And it was just as Mr. Gardner explained. The money was free and clear—a gift. The only condition was silence about where it came from. They both signed the document and were soon out the door with a certified check for fifty-thousand dollars that would keep them from losing their home and get them out of the deep hole they were in due to being without work.

Agency and Consequences

41. Flight to Mountain Home

AT about 11:00 A.M., Sarah, with her highway patrol escort, drove Traveler onto Scott Air Force Base through the south freight entrance. Because all the necessary clearances were in place, she was waived through to the tarmac after a short wait at the gate.

In order to get Hidalgo on the transport, he had to be unloaded from the trailer, so when Sarah was directed to the staging area, she parked Traveler and unloaded Hidalgo from the lowboy.

At noon, a big C-5 transport was on the tarmac ready for Sarah to drive Hidalgo and then Traveler and the trailer up into its belly. Once Hidalgo and Traveler were on the cargo deck, cargo masters anchored everything down. Sarah then took her place up near the pilots in the cockpit of the big plane. This was a first for Sarah and she was actually looking forward to the flight with such a different perspective.

* * * * *

In very short order, at about one P.M., the big C-5 Galaxy was in the air headed for Mountain Home Air Force Base near Boise, Idaho. For the next three and a half hours, Sarah and the flight crew munched on sandwiches; drank fruit juice and soda pop. They chatted about driving bulldozers, flying cargo planes, putting out forest fires, wacky college professors, why she wasn't married, why the pilot, Major Jim Worthington, wasn't married and why the two of them should get together.

As it turns out, the pilot, Major Jim Worthington was a member of the Church and a returned missionary and something in his eyes caught Sarah's attention. It was for everyone an enjoyable time with the kind of joking and teasing Sarah had grown up with.

Flying west, they gained an hour, so at around three P.M. mountain time, the big plane touched down at Mountain Home Air Force Base. The Galaxy was hardly parked when ground crews swarmed around and the big cargo doors were opened.

G. Kenneth Cardwell

* * * * *

As Sarah climbed down from the cockpit into the cargo bay, her dad was there smiling, exhausted, overjoyed to see his daughter. "Daddy, it's so good to see you. You look exhausted," Sarah said in a joyful but concerned voice.

"I'm dead dog beat; I don't mind telling you. That's why I called you. I need to work with someone who knows what they're doing. It's bad, very bad and a lot of homes will go up in smoke within just a couple of days if we don't get you up there and go to work," George said with resolution.

"Daddy, it looks to me like you need some sleep. Are we going to start as soon as we get there or ..." Sarah said getting even more worried. The last thing to do was to put her exhausted dad back into the cab of 54-ton bulldozer and expect him to be safe or effective.

"I'm sorry honey; I didn't mean to miss-lead you. We've got to get you and Hidalgo up there ready to hit the fire at first light. The rest of the crew will manage; they have to manage, until we're ready in the morning," George clarified. "It looks like they're about ready for you to get your babies off this plane. I'll call your mom and let her know you're here safely. She's been a bit anxious," George said.

* * * * *

As Sarah was about to climb up into Hidalgo and drive him off the plane, Jim came over and shook her hand and thanked her for the pleasant time on the flight. Sarah reached into her pocket, pulled out a business card, and said: "I don't want to be too forward, but if you're ever back at Scott with some time on your hands, I'm not too far away," she said with a warm inviting smile.

"That sounds real tempting," Jim said smiling as he backed away from Hidalgo and headed out down the cargo ramp ahead of Sarah and her big beastie machine.

When Jim reached the bottom of the ramp he overheard some of the Forest Service officials comment to news reporters: "The only person better than Sarah Kindman in a D9 bulldozer is her dad, George Kindman. And now because both of them were there, they would see a dramatic change in being able to control the fire."

Agency and Consequences

Jim was now really intrigued. So, he lingered behind to just watch as Sarah expertly moved Hidalgo down the cargo ramp and parked him. When Sarah got out she noticed him standing there watching and so she hollered at him and said: "Come on Major, you can help me drive Traveler and his trailer off the plane." Jim didn't need to be asked twice. He caught up with Sarah about half way up the ramp and as Sarah unlocked Traveler's door, he opened it for her. Sarah looked at him, remembered the lessons of her mother, and very genuinely said: "Thank you." She climbed in, touched the power lock to unlock the other door and waited for him to get in.

"It's not as big a cockpit as you're used to, but it's pretty roomy," Sarah said as she hit Traveler's starter. She checked his gauges, released the brakes and moved him and his trailer off the plane. "I guess we both like big machines," Sarah said to Jim.

"I think you're right. I've wanted to fly all my life and flying transports for the Air Force is great training for the airline industry.

"Say, I heard some guy down there saying the only person better than you at operating a bulldozer is your dad. That must be pretty special. You and your dad the best in the business," Jim complimented.

"Yeah, well, if I had as much cab time as my dad, I'd be better than he is. But, right now, I spend most of my time in an R and D lab at Caterpillar, so I don't get the time actually operating I'd like," Sarah quipped with a little laugh.

Sarah reached the position where she would load Hidalgo back onto Traveler's trailer. "Come on Major, you can help," Sarah invited, obviously enjoying Jim's company for the moment.

Sarah and Jim walked to the rear of the trailer and Sarah instructed him on how to lower the ramps just as her dad came upon them. "Oh, daddy, I'd like you to meet Major Jim Worthington. Jim, my dad, George Kindman, the best bulldozer operator in the country," Sarah said with noticeable pride.

"So, Major, are you the one I should thank for getting my daughter here safely?" George asked with a big smile as he took Jim's hand and gave him a firm shake.

"Well, I'm one of them. I'm the pilot; it was my pleasure

to fly her here. We had a good time," Jim said warmly as he cast his eyes in Sarah's direction.

"I trust you guys in the cockpit didn't get out of line with her. You've heard what happens to you if you get out of line with Sarah haven't you?" George said loud enough for Sarah to hear with a huge tease in his voice.

"Daddy," Sarah said with much protest. "Now, that isn't fair. Jim barely knows me and I don't want you ..." Sarah caught herself.

"You don't want me to what?" George said knowingly.

"You know what. Just leave it alone," Sarah insisted.

Jim couldn't help but laugh as he observed Sarah and George having their little battle and he knew right away Sarah liked him and knew George wasn't fooled by either of them. "OK you two. I've only met you and you're fighting about me already. Trust me, I read the newspapers and saw the TV news casts. I wouldn't dare do anything to have this woman take after me with that bulldozer," Jim said as though he were right at home.

George and Sarah looked at each other and laughed. The tension was released and now it was time to get to work. Sarah fired up Hidalgo and moved him up onto the lowboy. George then showed Jim the art of using tie-down chains. When Hidalgo was secure, Jim and Sarah said good-bye, this time with a hug and not just a handshake. Jim opened Traveler's door, she climbed up behind the wheel, and George got in the passenger side.

Jim stood on the tarmac, gave Sarah a wave good bye, and wondered. Sarah looked at Jim through her rearview mirror and wondered.

As Sarah drove, George navigated and they talked. "So, the Major looks like a pretty good young man," George observed.

"I think so, daddy. He is a member of the Church and a returned missionary from Bolivia. He wants eventually to fly for the airlines. I just barely know him; but I think there's an interest for both of us. I just don't know how we'll get the opportunity to date and really get to know one another and ..." Sarah said with a little disappointment.

"Sarah, if you've started a little fire and it feels right, you'll find a way to give it the fuel and oxygen it needs," George said reassuringly.

Agency and Consequences

* * * * *

After about four hours driving, they reached the base camp. Sarah and George unloaded Hidalgo and parked him next to George's dozer. It was then time for some chow, showers and bed.

When Sarah crawled into Traveler's bunk that night, two men were on her mind. She couldn't help but be worried about her dad and how so completely tired he looked. And while the warmth of their hug goodbye still lingered, she drifted peacefully asleep with the face of Jim Worthington on her mind.

42. Tragedy

THE next morning, things started early with breakfast and briefings. By five-thirty, George and Sarah, with their dozers, headed for an area only one-half mile from the big new sub-division in the mountain's foothills. Using their on-board GPS systems and private radio system, they coordinated an attack on the brush and trees that left everyone amazed. Watching George and Sarah work together was like watching a pair of champion ballroom dancers. Both dozers were fitted with 2nd generation prototypes of Sarah's invention and this was a real test of whether or not it made a dozer more fuel efficient and powerful, everything else being the same.

Working side-by-side, George and Sarah were clearing a break almost one-mile wide. They began by clearing the back end of the break by pushing the brush and trees about 50 yards toward the front of the break. With this initial strip cleared on the back, they then began pushing all the combustible material away from the leading edge of the fire another 150 yards. This would, hopefully, because of prevailing winds, keep burning material from landing in a fuel rich area close to the homes.[1] It was a race against time and they were accomplishing it faster than anyone could imagine. Some cuts required more than one pass as they pushed huge trees over other trees and then returned to get those left behind. For the next five days, for sixteen to eighteen hours a day, it was the same tough grind. And it was hard on both machines and operators.

*****

About mid-way through the sixth day, George and Sarah were working near a sharp bend above a dried riverbed where the spring runoff and flash floods had severely undercut the riverbank. They had walked the area the evening before and put in warning stakes with bright red streamers to warn them of the unsafe ground. As Sarah was watching her dad, she noticed him move his machine into that dangerous area just above the bend; but their warning stakes were not there. Just as she called over

Agency and Consequences

her radio to warn him of the danger, the unthinkable happened. The undercut ground beneath George's dozer gave way and his machine crashed to the dried riverbed beneath and flipped over on its cab. Immediately, Sarah got on her walkie-talkie and called for help. After giving the specific details of the accident and their location, she shut down Hidalgo, grabbed her first aid kit, clamored over the riverbank and made her way down to the riverbed.

George's machine was now lying on its side mortally wounded. Having fallen through the undercut riverbank, its back end first, it hit the bottom, went over on its cab and then rolled to its left side where it stopped. The engine had stopped and like a dying pachyderm, the great beast just lie there, steam coming from the broken radiator. Sarah climbed up on the right side of the cab hollering: "Daddy, are you alright? Daddy, are you OK?"

The dozer's cab was crunched almost flat as it had taken the entire weight of the dozer when it fell backward onto it. From inside, Sarah heard a faint voice: "Sarah, I'm here. I can't move. I'm pinned in here like a sardine in a can."

Sarah immediately realized she could not get him out and again used her walkie-talkie: "Base this is Sarah. My dad is trapped inside the cab of his dozer. Need jaws of life and cutting torches. He is alive; but I cannot assess medical condition. Certain he is severely hurt."

"Sarah, this is base. Ground and helicopter rescue teams on their way. ETA less than two minutes," the base dispatcher responded.

"Daddy, hold on. Help is less than two minutes away. Daddy, just hold on; everything will be alright," Sarah tried to reassure as calmly as she could.

It seemed for Sarah and George an eternity as the two minutes they waited passed until the helicopter with the rescue crew arrived. Only a minute or two later, fire equipment with the special tools to extricate George from the cab of his dozer was also on the scene.

The rescue team worked quickly and efficiently as they cut the crushed cab away from George's body and then carefully removed him from the wreckage. It wasn't hard to tell George was in bad shape and Sarah could hardly contain herself as she looked at him being worked on by the paramedics. Very quickly they had George ready for the helicopter ride to the trauma center in Boise. Sarah was also given special treatment with a ride in a police car, sirens blaring, to get her to her dad's side as quickly as possible.

*****

When Sarah arrived at the hospital, the emergency room doctor's prognosis was very bleak as he said to her: "I think you should say your good byes to him quickly. I'm sorry, there's no more we can do for him; he hasn't long."

As she went into the treatment room, George opened his eyes, smiled and said: "Somebody removed our stakes and I didn't hear your warning in time. That fall, as the undercut in the riverbed gave way, was a real doozy. How's my dozer look?"

"It's busted up pretty bad, dad," Sarah said trying to be comically poetic.

George chuckled and then coughed. He gathered himself and then seriously said, as he took Sarah's hand: "Sarah, I haven't had a better week of work in my life than this last week with you. Thank you for being here. I love you more than I have the capacity to express. I am so pleased with the woman you've become.

"Many years ago, the day after your mother told me we were pregnant with you and your brother, the Lord gave me to understand I wouldn't have the privilege of growing old with your mother. My time is here. I've had the most wonderful life a man could have in this life.

"Please tell your mother the last thing on my mind and in my heart was a vision of her and of the love I have for her.

"Tell your brothers and sisters I love them and they are the jewels in my crown.

"Tell your brother, Tommy, the greatest honor he could bring me is to stay in the mission field, keep working hard and come home with nothing left in the tank.

"Finally, my dear Sarah, my first born, the Lord has prepared a wonderful companion for you. Open your heart and your eyes a little more and you'll recognize him," George concluded as he closed his eyes and slipped away from mortality.

Sarah crawled onto the gurney beside her father's body,

Agency and Consequences

kissed him and let herself weep. A few minutes later, she gathered herself together, completed the necessary paperwork the hospital needed and then took out her cell phone, found a private place and called home.

* * * * *

Big Sarah was just getting ready for the evening dinner at the restaurant when the phone rang in her office. There was something foreboding in the ring and she felt a presence in the room she knew instinctively belonged to George. As she picked up the phone, she already knew George, her beloved husband, was dead. So, without even waiting for the news, already sobbing, asked: "Sarah, how did it happen?"

Sarah explained to her mother how they had surveyed the area they were working that day the evening before and had carefully marked the danger areas. She continued by telling how, when they got to that area of the work site, their warning stakes had been removed and by the time Sarah recognized the danger, as she watched her dad working ahead of her, she called out the warning on their radio, but it was too late. She described what she saw next, her dad and his dozer falling, as the undercut in the bend of the dried riverbed gave way under the weight of the huge bulldozer.

Sarah next explained the suggested arrangements to send George's body home and she asked if Sam Noble, her dad's crew chief, could fly up to Boise and take charge of getting Hidalgo and George's dozer recovered and shipped home before the proprietary, 2nd generation prototypes of the invention were stolen.

Big Sarah agreed with the arrangements for getting George's body sent home and indicated she would arrange for their local mortician to meet the plane and receive the body. She also said she would call Sam and ask him to go to Boise immediately and supervise getting the dozers recovered.

* * * * *

The following morning, Sarah and her dad's body, arrived home at the local airport aboard a private jet sent by Robert Sheffield of Caterpillar Tractor. All the family, the press and, it seemed, half the town were there to greet them. Principal among them was Paul Tenter. No one seemed more grief-stricken than he. George had been his priesthood example and line leader for many years. His counsel, encouragement, friendship and listening ear had been pinnacle in Paul's repentance, recovery, reactivation and re-baptism. He stood there, forefront in the crowd; and yet, he was an alone and desolate creature. His soul shuddered and shrank as he anxiously wondered how he would stay on firm ground without his beloved friend.

Because George had been warned so many years previously he would not live to grow old with Sarah, he had convinced her, without telling her anything of his inspiration, of the wisdom of selecting and paying for burial plots and funeral services. He had also completely planned his funeral service and left the instructions in a sealed envelope with their attorney. And so, later that afternoon, their attorney, their bishop, Ben Greenfield (Alice's husband), the funeral director and Big Sarah and her family met to make the final arrangements.

* * * * *

The funeral was conducted a week later to accommodate family and close friends to arrive from out of town. It was held at the local tabernacle of the Church, which was filled to capacity, and was conducted by Bishop Greenfield. George had asked his daughter, Sarah, to give the family prayer and his crew chief, Sam Noble, give his life history, which he did with some carefully selected anecdotes. He requested Paul Tenter play his favorite piece on the organ, *Carillon de Westminster*, by the French composer, Louis Vierne. His three sons (Tommy, in abstention), with close business and church associates, including Robert Sheffield, served as pallbearers.

During Bishop Greenfield's closing remarks, he made particular mention of Little Sarah's report of George's final words. He noted how George had known he would not grow old with Sarah and how he had quietly prepared, not knowing the exact day or the manner in which he would be taken. For Bishop Greenfield, this was a testimony of God's love for this faithful son and His trust in him—a love and trust that allowed God to share such knowledge with him. Bishop Greenfield remarked no one, not even his beloved, Sarah, knew anything of this personal

Agency and Consequences

revelation until he shared it with his daughter in the last seconds of his life. And yet, he lived his life with passion, without any fretting or worrying about whether or not: "is this the day?" And then Bishop Greenfield asked: "Is it really any different with each of us?"

* * * * *

At the gravesite, as a lone bag piper played the hymn, *Amazing Grace*, George asked his wife, Sarah, to read the poem, also titled *Amazing Grace*, by the poet, G. Kenneth Cardwell.

Amazing Grace

A solitary figure
At attention stands
In manly skirt.
With lop-sided antlers
And his bellows full,
The drone summons Earth;
Focusing heart and mind on all that's dear.

He moves now
With stately stride
As King to throne.
Bedrock drone supports, inspires,
As pipes sing a hymn,
An echo of Heaven's grace;
And one sees beneath and beyond the tears.

Arriving at distant spot
Where drone, Earth,
Song and Heav'n are one,
He invites me to be
A soul more complete;
Bellows full, pipes singing,
Dressed—unashamedly—in manly skirt.[2]

Following the hymn and reading of the poem, George's oldest son, George, then dedicated his grave.

G. Kenneth Cardwell

* * * * *

For Big Sarah Kindman and her family, these were tender days. But they rejoiced in the knowledge their husband and father was not gone forever. He had only gone ahead to prepare for them. His role as a humble, meek and faithful Patriarch, presiding gently over their family was not ended; but continued. And they were sure, because they had already felt it, his influence and guidance would ever be with them—and in some ways, would be more strongly felt than before.

Agency and Consequences

43. New Beginnings

A week following George's funeral, Mr. Robert Sheffield, Caterpillar Tractor's CEO, sent one of the company planes for Little Sara and she flew back to Peoria, Illinois. When she arrived at her office, there were several bouquets of flowers and many cards of condolence. But, there was one bouquet and card that especially caught her eye. The card read: "Dear Sarah, I read and saw the news reports of your dad's accident and death. I felt it a sincere pleasure and honor to have met him. I recognized immediately a man that was truly great. I mourn your loss with you and your family. Warm Regards, Jim Worthington. P.S. I have three days leave a week from this Friday. I can catch a hop to Scott if you'd like to meet. I'll call you on your cell tonight at eight central."

Sarah read the card over and over. As she did, she felt a warm comfortable spirit; but her trained mind worried: "Jim could just be or become a substitute for her dad, the only man she had ever loved at any level." Then, she seemed to hear her dad's voice repeating: "... my dear Sarah, my first born, the Lord has prepared a wonderful companion for you. Open your heart and your eyes a little more and you'll recognize him," the last words her dad said to her.

* * * * *

Sarah spent the rest of her day reading and responding to emails, mostly from those expressing condolence. She then took Jim's bouquet and card and went home.

She fixed a simple meal and waited. She felt like an anxious schoolgirl. Eight o'clock came and almost immediately, her cell phone rang. She picked it up and said: "Good evening, Sarah Kindman."

"Good evening, Sarah Kindman," a resonant baritone voice said warmly. "This is Jim Worthington. Do you have a few minutes to talk?" Jim asked politely.

"Yes, Jim, I have a minute or two," Sarah said feeling immediately comfortable and astonishingly in a teasing mood.

"Then, I'll be brief and just ask you if you would 'meet me in St. Louis' as the musical goes—well actually, would you

207

meet me at Scott Air Force Base a week from Friday at about six in the evening," Jim asked.

"Well, maybe. But, I would like to know what you'd plan to do next?" Sarah responded.

"Well, if you accept, that's a surprise. I would however make sure we get separate rooms on separate floors at a hotel and I'd pay all your mileage and for the whole weekend. It's all on me; no going dutch," Jim outlined in a persuasive and kindly tone.

"Wow, that sounds like an offer awfully hard for a girl to resist," Sarah replied trying to be cool.

"Then don't. I promise to take good care of you and we'll have a great time. We'll go to Church on Sunday and we'll be back at Scott in time for you to be home to get a good night's sleep before going to work on Monday. What do you say?" Jim, patiently asked again.

"Do you promise to hold my hand?" Sarah teased letting the cat out of the bag.

"Of course I promise to hold your hand. Is it a date?" Jim asked the third time.

"It's a date. Just tell me how to get to the gate at Scott and I'll pick you up at six p.m. or as you would say eighteen hundred hours a week from Friday. Jim, I'm already looking forward to it," Sarah assured.

"I'm looking forward to it too," Jim acknowledged and then asked: "Do you have a pencil and paper handy?"

"I'm ready to write," Sarah acknowledged. Jim then gave her detailed instructions to the visitors building at the Shiloh gate to the base.

"Jim, do you have more time to talk?" Sarah asked warmly.

"Sure, take all the time you want," Jim responded sensing Sarah's need to talk and felt honored she would feel comfortable, at this time of her life, to possibly confide in him.

"Jim, I want to thank you for the flowers. I received a lot of nice bouquets, but yours was exquisite. I really appreciate your thoughtfulness," Sarah said trying hard to not be too emotional.

"It was my pleasure. How are you and your family doing," Jim asked with genuine concern.

Agency and Consequences

Jim and Sarah talked until about mid-night as Sarah shared the details of the accident, funeral and all the feelings of the last couple of weeks. After a little while, as the events surrounding Sarah's dad's passing were thoroughly exchanged, they moved onto more personal, getting to know each other, conversation, such as Jim telling Sarah he tinkered a little on the piano. It seemed to Sarah, Jim was someone familiar. That didn't mean a match made in heaven. To her, it meant she and Jim had backgrounds, experiences and personalities that combined to feel like putting on a pair of very comfortable shoes.

After they hung up for the night, Sarah found herself having a difficult time going to sleep. It was just as her dad said when he and she were driving from Mountain Home to the fire just about three weeks ago. She and Jim were finding a way to give their feelings some fuel and oxygen. But would they be able to build the fire carefully enough so it would be warm, comfortable and steady rather than blaze and burn out because of a lack of fuel and oxygen for the long term. She didn't know and she was sure Jim didn't know. She only knew it was worth the risk.

* * * * *

Thousands of miles away, at an air force base in Europe, Jim had gotten little sleep himself and was now scurrying to get to work. A C-5 Galaxy was waiting with another important load of cargo for the U.S. Military.

* * * * *

The next twelve days seemed to go at a snail's pace for Sarah and Jim. Neither, despite their disciplined characters, could stay completely focused on their everyday tasks. Even though they were now exchanging emails and slipped in a phone call every few days, the anxiety and anticipation were building.

Finally, the Friday for their date arrived. Sarah loaded her suitcase in her truck and went to work. At three in the afternoon, she changed from her business suit to an evening dress and was out the door of her office. Colleagues at work had been and were supportive, full of good wishes and lots of kind-hearted teasing. But, it was Mr. Sheffield, himself, in the parking lot, who stopped her, gave her hug and said: "This is from your dad. You don't know this, but I talked with him the day before the accident. As you know, he was a very spiritual man and he had a premonition. So, he called me and asked me to keep an eye on you.

"I sincerely hope this weekend is a wonderful experience for you and your Air Force Major. Friends in the Air Force tell me he's top-notched. It appears he's worthy of you. But, be careful. Call me if you need me for anything and when you get home, you have an appointment at nine, Monday morning, in my office. You can't come home and talk to me and my wife at the end of your date in our bed room the way I know you would with your dad and mom if you were still home and it were possible. So, this is the best I can do," Mr. Sheffield said affectionately.

Sarah, now in tears, hugged Mr. Sheffield in return and said: "Thank you. Thank you so very much."

Agency and Consequences

44. Date in Missouri

SARAH arrived at Scott just before six. Jim was already at the visitors building near the Shiloh gate waiting. When she saw him, she quickly found a place to park, opened the door of her truck and stepped out. For a moment, they just looked at each other, she in a beautiful evening dress and he in his dress blues. Then the electrical charge was applied to the two separate electro magnets in their hearts. They ran to each other and took each other in their arms. There were no words; the kiss came naturally and spontaneously. It said everything—everything that needed to be said.

As they walked to Sarah's truck, she guided Jim to the passenger side and when he tried to open it, it was still locked. "I guess I was in a hurry," Sarah said with a warm smile. "The key is still in the ignition," she said as Jim made his way to the driver's side saying with soft authority: "Don't you dare open that door when I've unlocked it."

From the open driver's door, Jim reached in and pressed the door unlock button. He, then, walked briskly back to Sarah, opened the door and took her hand as she climbed in the truck. When she got in, she raised the center console on the seat, slid over to the middle and slipped the seat belt about her waist. Meanwhile, Jim grabbed his suitcase and put it on the floor next to the back seat with Sarah's. As Jim got in the driver's seat, adjusted it for his longer legs and fastened his seat belt, they looked at each other again and shared another tender kiss.

"You're really trusting, to let me drive your truck, aren't you?" Jim said with a grin.

"I was a lot more trusting when I said 'yes' to being with you this weekend," Sarah responded smiling but with a tone of sincerity that conveyed to Jim she was a woman not to be trifled with.[1] She was here at this moment because she trusted him and because she wanted to be here. There was no desperation. She simply liked him; maybe she was beginning to love him. This weekend was a test; his measure would be taken. And yet, he felt absolutely at home and comfortable with Sarah and so he didn't mind that his soul was about to be examined; he rather

211

looked forward to it.

"So, where are we going," Sarah asked inquisitively.

"I told you, that's a surprise. I just hope I can remember how to get there and that we'll have time for a quick bite first," Jim responded.

"Jim quickly put Sarah's truck on I-64 towards St. Louis. About twenty minutes later, they crossed the Poplar Street Bridge over the Mississippi River, passed the Gateway Arch and continued on passing Bush Stadium and Union Station. Soon they exited I-64 and turned north onto Grand Avenue. As soon as Sarah saw the Fox Theater she knew: "We're going to see Camelot. Oh, Jim how did you know that was my favorite play?" Sarah beamed excitedly.

"Well, the week before the accident, after we met, I Googled 'Sarah's Place.' I then sent your mom an email. She confirmed with your dad we actually met and I appeared to be someone they could trust with a little information about you. And, as they say, the rest is history," Jim confided with a little pride.

"You're a sneaky devil aren't you? I've talked to my mom almost every day since the accident, while at home and since I got back to Peoria, and she hasn't said a word about you. And so, what else did my mom tell you about me," Sarah asked a little sternly as she jabbed Jim in the ribs with her fingers (having seen her mother do the same thing when she wanted to know something).

"Hey," Jim objected; "I am driving right now. Your mom said you like bulldozers," Jim responded, stating the obvious to avoid really answering.

"You already knew that. I guess there's no point in pursuing this at the moment. I don't want you wrecking my truck. But just you wait Major …," Sarah meekly threatened, actually quite pleased she had impressed Jim enough he tracked her down. "Hmm," she thought; "obviously, he's not intimidated by me. This guy might be worth keeping after all."

Luckily, Jim found a place to park along one of the side streets near St. Louis University, just a few blocks from the theater. As they walked, Sarah took up her cross-examination again: "So, Jim, what else did my mother tell you about me?"

"Well, let's see," Jim responded thinking this a good time

Agency and Consequences

to let Sarah know he'll answer when he's really ready, wanting to keep a few things close to the vest: "Your mom said you're about 5 feet, seven inches, tall in your bare feet ... and, oh, yeah, she wants grand children ... soon.

"And another thing your mother told me about you is you're strong willed; you don't take no for an answer easily; but she also said you're humble and your intentions are as pure as gold," Jim said softly as he gently, but firmly guided her into an alley out of public sight and hearing. He then turned her so he could look her in the eyes.

"Sarah Kindman, I noticed something very special in you from the time you climbed into my cockpit as we prepared to fly to Boise to that fire. You are as strong, beautiful and independent a woman as I've ever met. I will never try to control or dominate you, but I expect the same in return. Please, don't badger me that way about what your mom said to me. Your mom and dad were pretty careful, doing their best to make sure I could be trusted not only in being with you but in sharing some things that would help me to first, be your friend and if we were both agreeable, possibly something more. That suggests a couple of things to me. First, what your mom and dad (through your mom) shared with me is sacred; and two, by definition, as it logically follows, you're sacred too. That said, like all sacred things, I will not trifle[2] with you by answering flippant questions.

"I know this may seem too bold at the moment; but Sarah I feel something very strong and tender inside for you. I haven't been able to stop thinking about you and my soul just seems to vibrate since we met. But you need to understand, I am very comfortable in my own skin; I'm pretty sure about who I am and what God expects of me. I really strive to live the commandments and to feel good about carrying a temple recommend in my wallet. I've believed for a long time the most important quality I can give a woman in marriage is to be a righteous man and the most important quality a woman can be for me is to be righteous as well. I realize we haven't got to that point yet, but I have to tell you, I'm hoping it does.

"I guess what I'm saying is I don't want anything to wreck our progress towards that possibility. But, I am prepared to go another direction if it doesn't. I apologize if your question, asked quite possibly in fun, set me off. It's just I feel ...," Sarah interrupted at this point by putting her arms around Jim and giving him a very caring and passionate kiss.

As she hugged him, Sarah whispered in Jim's ear: "Thank you for taking hold of me in such a firm and loving way. I've needed that for a long time. Only daddy has ever been able to do that for me."

Sarah now realized this man was his own man. He had obtained information about her in good faith; he liked what he was told and badgering him about sharing it, would be a waste of time at best and at worst, it could drive him away. Besides, he found out Camelot was her favorite play and he was using that information to make a special night for her. So why spoil it.

Sarah stepped back from Jim a couple of inches: "Jim, I apologize. I'm being a nag and have no right to be. Instead, I should have thanked you for caring enough to find out about me and for bringing me to this wonderful theater to see and enjoy my favorite play. I hope you'll forgive me for acting so badly and being so ungrateful?

"This may seem too bold at the moment, but I'm falling, maybe growing is a better word, in love with you Jim Worthington. No one has ever treated me in a way that makes me feel so special. You've cared about me enough to reprove me sharply and then express love for me.[3] That means more than you know. I've only had that experience before with my parents and with God, himself, as I've partaken of the Sacrament. You now belong to a select group. You are a righteous man and I hope I'm a righteous enough woman that will help us comfortably get to the next level together, side by side, hand in hand. I've felt the same things you've felt. Now, I don't want to be accused of badgering you, but do you forgive me for being an old, sway-back nag?" Sarah gently asked as she lightly kissed Jim again.

"You're anything but an old, sway-back nag and yes, I forgive you for asking me what your mother told me. Do you forgive me for lecturing?" Jim asked giving Sarah a kiss of his own.

"You didn't lecture. If you had, I would have gone to sleep. I needed to hear what you said; but if it makes you feel better, I forgive you anyway. Don't you think we should go to the

Agency and Consequences

play? Don't they have food at the Fox?" Sarah queried, again expressing excitement to see Camelot and indicating she was hungry.

* * * * *

    The performance of Camelot was impeccable, according to Sarah and she and Jim thoroughly enjoyed it. They were too late for food, so by the time the play was over, they were famished. So, it was over the bridge, across the railroad yard to the Italian district of St. Louis called the Hill and Tony's for supper. Afterwards, it was out to St. Charles County and the Embassy Suites where Jim had made reservations for two nights and, as promised, in separate rooms on separate floors.

* * * * *

    The following morning, after a late breakfast, Jim now in a pair of cargo shorts and a golf shirt with running shoes and Sarah in a denim skirt, white blouse and penny loafers, went to St. Charles, Missouri's old main street. They delighted in funnel cakes, exploring the wonderful array of shops and the Foundry Art Center built in an old converted American Car and Foundry factory building. Sarah was particularly intrigued by a shop called WSI, where they sold all kinds of knobs, hinges and other hardware to restore or repair antiques. They had lunch at the incomparable Mother in Law House, which Sarah judged to be on a par with her mother's restaurant. But, mostly they enjoyed a long, leisurely stroll in Frontier Park along the Missouri River, stopping often to sit on a bench and just talk.

    One of their stops, in the park, was in front of the large statue of Meriwether Lewis and William Clark, co-captains of the famous Lewis and Clark Expedition, more accurately called, the Corps of Discovery that departed from St. Charles, when Lewis rejoined the expedition, May 21, 1804. As they sat there talking, Sarah asked Jim: "What's the significance of the dog sitting with Lewis and Clark?"

    "You don't know about Seaman, I take it," Jim answered. "Well, Seaman was a big Newfoundland Meriwether Lewis got somewhere, nobody knows for sure, as he started down the Ohio River. One story suggests Lewis paid twenty dollars, a month's salary in those days, for him in Pittsburg, Pennsylvania. Pittsburg is where the boats were built they used to travel up the Missouri River, to explore the territory gained in the Louisiana Purchase. The purpose of the expedition was to find, hopefully, a nearly all water route, 'the Northwest Passage,' from the Pacific Ocean to the interior of the American Continent.

"Seaman played an indispensable role in the expedition that would, most likely, have failed without him. Several stories tell how Seaman fearlessly protected the expedition's campsites; he helped hunt and even brought down a young bull elk in a river by breaking its neck and dragging him to shore for food. Another story tells how, before joining Captain Clark, on the way down the Ohio River, Seaman jumped into the river amidst a large group of squirrel attempting to swim across the river. Seaman grabbed a large number of the squirrel one at a time, killing them and bringing them back to the boat. Apparently, all on the boat that night, including Seaman, had a very hardy supper of squirrel meat. On another occasion, Seaman went into a beaver pond after a wounded beaver that had been shot and was severely bitten by the critter and nearly bled to death and would have if Lewis hadn't stitched him up.

"The only time Lewis threatened to kill anyone on the expedition was when a small band of Indians, whose diet included dog meat, captured Seaman. Lewis told John Colter, who later became a famous mountain man, whom he sent with two other men to recover the dog: 'If they don't surrender Seaman at once, fire on them,'"[4] Jim reported with great fondness for the subject.

Sarah was genuinely impressed. There was a glistening in Jim's eyes and tenderness in his voice as he told Seaman's story. She asked: "Why do you like that story so much?"

Jim thought for a moment and then he sincerely said: "First, the story of the Lewis and Clark Expedition is one of the great stories of faith, preparation, courage and endurance in our history. It's on a par with that of our pioneer forebears, whom I believe could not have succeeded if Lewis and Clark had failed. That said, secondly, Lewis and Clark were obviously inspired and lead by God. Third, Seaman was no doubt one of God's noble beasts. Many animals have played major roles in helping God's

Agency and Consequences

purposes come to pass and Seaman was one of them."
 Jim and Sarah strolled along the riverfront, hand in hand, talking, teasing and laughing until dusk. Then they enjoyed supper at the out-door restaurant, The Winery, which was also superb, even without any wine.

| G. Kenneth Cardwell

45. Prepared for the Extemporaneous

THE next morning, Jim and Sarah attended church in the LDS building located on Old Highway 94, just a little south of downtown St. Charles. As soon as Sarah was recognized, she was asked if she could address a joint Relief Society and Young Women's meeting. A request she was happy to accept as long as Jim could be with her. Just prior to the joint meeting, she asked Jim to accompany her out to her truck. From inside the truck box on the back, she asked Jim to retrieve a large duffle-type bag and a portable screen. Upon seeing this stuff, Jim remarked: "I gather you do this often?"

"Almost everywhere I go," Sarah said with a smile. "I always take everything with me, except for the screen when I fly commercial. Don't the Boy Scouts teach you to be prepared?" she said as she gave Jim a quick 'thank you' kiss.

* * * * *

Because multiple congregations were using the building and due to the size of the meeting, it was held in the cultural hall. While Jim and Sarah set up Sarah's equipment, chairs where quickly set and everyone quickly assembled—even all the men and young men. Everyone was interested to hear Sarah's presentation.

Bishop Cutler conducted the meeting. As soon as he concluded the regular business, he turned the meeting to the Relief Society President, Sister Tanner, to introduce Sarah.

"Brothers and Sisters, we're honored today as Sister Sarah Kindman and her friend, Air Force Major, Brother Jim Worthington, just happen to be visiting with us. As you may know, Sister Kindman made the news several years ago as she defended the virtue of chastity in a very unusual manner, which she will explain. Sister Kindman holds a Ph.D. in mechanical engineering from Purdue University and is a Senior Research Scientist at Caterpillar Tractor Corporation in Peoria, Illinois. Presently, Sister Kindman serves as the Young Women's President in her Peoria Ward. And as you may have seen on the news only a few weeks ago, her father was killed in an accident as he and Sister Kindman were fighting the big forest fire up

Agency and Consequences

near Boise, Idaho. We'll now turn the balance of the time to Sister Kindman," Sister Tanner said introducing Sarah.

* * * * *

"Wow, what a nice group. Thank you for that very kind introduction. Before I begin, I'd like to say a few words about my special friend. Brother Worthington and I have known each other now just over a month. We met when the Air Force assigned him to fly Hidalgo, my bulldozer, and me from Scott Air Force Base to Mountain Home Air Force Base so I could join my father to fight the fire out there. Jim is a very accomplished pilot and handles a C-5 Galaxy, one of the largest aircraft in the world, just as well as my father handled the largest of bulldozers. I'm honored to have Jim as my companion today," Sarah said as she warmly smiled at Jim.

"Because it seems, wherever I go, people want to know my story, I've put together a Power Point® presentation that takes about 15 minutes. After the presentation is concluded, I'll say a few words about the virtue of chastity and will then be pleased to answer questions and bear you my testimony," Sarah explained in her always warm, cordial, but very professional manner.

Sarah's Power Point presentation began with her mother and dad's wedding, then the birth of her brother George and her. She showed pictures of her family, her mom's restaurant, the family lodge, Aunt Gerti, Paul Tenter's home coming, George and Alice's wedding, high school and university graduations, girls camp with her girls and of course the bulldozer demonstration, followed by clips from the Tonight Show and her New York Tour. It included photos of her trip to Boise, with even Jim in one of the shots at Mountain Home and the last photo taken of her and her dad the morning of the accident as they stood, arms around each other, in front of Hidalgo. The last few frames were of her dad's funeral, ending with the bag piper standing alone in the distance, playing the last strains of Amazing Grace. Sarah narrated the presentation herself, with well-chosen music playing in the background.

"Brothers and Sisters, that's a fifteen-minute synopsis of my life. Before taking questions, I should say a few words about the incident that inadvertently made me a well-known person.

G. Kenneth Cardwell

"As you saw in the presentation, I did a bulldozer demonstration in my hometown during the spring of my senior year in high school. At this demonstration, with written permission from the legal title holder, I completely demolished and buried ten feet in the ground a brand new BMW 335i coupe. I did this in response to a young man who tried to seduce and take advantage of me. When I tried to run away from him, he caught me, threatened to rape me and then said he'd claim I was a willing participant. I again got away from him by stomping his right foot with one of my high heels and kneeing him in the groin. Long story short, he then claimed publicly we had been together that evening, dishonoring my family, our beliefs and me.

"My major error that night was thinking, because I was perceived as weird by most of the kids in my high school, I could change that by accepting a date from someone I knew had a well-known reputation for exploiting young women.

"My dear brothers and sisters of all ages, I testify the virtue of chastity (yours and mine) is worth more than any other gift our Father in Heaven has given to us except for the gifts of His Son, Jesus Christ, and our individual agency. I submit it's worth any cost to keep and preserve. I wish I had time to share with each of you all my dad and mom said to my brother and his friend (now his wife), Mary, and me, late into the wee hours after my scary date.

"A few months ago, on a business trip to Europe, I had the opportunity to see some of the most magnificent art pieces ever created. At that time, I picked up a book about Leonardo da Vinci. This book records that, on the back of one of his portraits, da Vinci painted a scroll. On that scroll, he wrote the following motto: 'Virtutem Forma Decorat.' In Latin, this literally means: 'beauty adorns virtue, indicating that outer beauty is only the ornament of inner virtue.'[1] Brothers and Sisters, this is a motto we should all embrace.

"President James E. Faust said: 'Virtue encompasses all traits of righteousness that help us form our character.'[2] He then added this quote he attributed to '... an old sampler found in a museum in Newfoundland, stitched in 1813: "Virtue is the chiefest beauty of the mind, the noblest ornament of humankind. Virtue is our safeguard and our guiding star that stirs

Agency and Consequences

up reason when our senses err.'"[3]

"Suffice it to say, not one of us has the right to give our own or take from another, the virtue of chastity. Doing so is an abomination and a mockery of that precious and unique ability God has given His Children to be most like our Heavenly Parents. Chastity is to be shared only between a man and woman who are legally and lawfully married."

Sarah paused a few moments to let what she said sink in and said: "That's all I think I need to say about that."

"I'll now be glad to take questions up until about 10 minutes to the hour at which time I'll bear my testimony and turn the meeting back to Bishop Cutler. So, what are your questions?" Sarah queried.

A young woman asked: "Sister Kindman, your dress is very beautiful. Did it cost a lot?"

"Thank you for the compliment. Jim thought it was beautiful as well. As to what it cost, I suppose I could have paid a lot for it. But, I learned from my mother long ago, never pay full price for anything unless you absolutely have to. This dress, in an upscale designer store, would probably sell for well over $100.00. I was on a business trip to New York a couple of months ago and found it in a close out place and paid $20.00 for it," Sarah said trying to teach a lesson.

From a young man in the group: "I hear you're a pretty good mechanic. Could you help me soup up my car?"

"I would be pleased to, but you'll have to get in line behind all the young men in my stake and bring it to Peoria," Sarah responded with a bit of a laugh.

An adult leader asked: "How would you rate getting an education in your life?"

"First, I believe the most important education has a lot more to do with learning by faith than it does with earning degrees. I was very fortunate to have experiences in my life, that luckily or maybe better said, providentially, taught me the most important things about living commandments and being faithful and true to tried and tested principles.

"Secondly, getting prepared to work and make a contribution to our society and earn a living for our families is also critical. I never received any allowance from my parents. Each of us eight kids learned very early to work. We bussed dishes, mopped floors, cleaned ovens, stoves and restrooms. We waited tables and eventually learned to cook in my mom's restaurant. We also learned to work at my dad's excavating and trenching business. That's where I learned to operate bulldozers. While that's one of my great passions, there's more to it than just getting in the cab, starting the engine, pulling levers or pushing foot pedals. Part of that education was learning how to do proposals and calculating every aspect of a job. Then the summer between my sophomore and junior years in high school, I learned to be a mechanic. I tore down and completely rebuilt my first bulldozer. My high school math teacher taught me how to do trigonometry and the calculus. I worked sixteen to eighteen hours every day, six days a week to learn everything I could about bulldozers. Yes, I believe educating one's self is important," Sarah said emphatically.

"Another adult leader asks: "Besides your work with Caterpillar Tractor and operating bulldozers, what do you like to do?"

"Well, right now, I enjoy being with Jim," Sarah said with a smile and a little blush. "I also enjoy working with my girls in my ward. I love musicals—Jim took me to the Fox on Friday to see my favorite, Camelot. I love camping and hiking, being out of doors in general. I'm a woman and I guess that means I love to shop and look for a good bargain. I enjoy going to the temple and being taught by the Spirit, feeling Father's love and receiving revelation."

A young woman asks: "What was the hardest thing for you growing up?"

Sarah sighed, while looking at the young woman with great empathy. Then she said very earnestly, as a tear ran down her cheek: "The hardest thing for me growing up was learning, accepting and then enjoying, down to the nucleus of every cell in my being that I am a woman and the daughter of loving, Heavenly Parents who sent me to this Earth for a purpose. Every individual in this room must come to know who he or she is. I could talk on this subject for hours—I have with my girls in Peoria. But, coming to learn, accept and enjoy being who YOU are and not worry about trying to be like, emulate or overly impress anybody else, to the degree you lose your own sense of self, is one of the most important quests of your life. Now, that

Agency and Consequences

doesn't mean becoming self-centered. In fact, it's just the opposite. Learning who you are will come most readily as you look for your own unique way of giving service to others.

"What is it you are passionate about? Is it music, science, math, sewing, plumbing, carpentry, cooking, flying, theater, literature, writing, gardening, teaching, animals—the possibilities are endless? For you young men in Scouting, earning merit badges is a wonderful way to explore your possible passions.

"I found mine, that is, my first passion, using my bulldozer to clean manure out of corals at local dairy farms and cattle ranches near my home, by grading roads, with my brother digging a trench behind me with a backhoe for utility pipes and by fighting forest fires with my dad. My second passion has become my girls in Peoria. I'm grateful for that calling. It's added a lot of balance and variety to my life.

"So, find out what your gifts are. Become passionate about sharing and giving them away to others and if you're keeping the commandments, seeking earnestly to know who you are and to know the Lord, you'll find the Lord and yourself.

"I need to add something to what I just said. When you've discovered a passion, or even something that might be a passion, then you need to adopt the 'Shame on them; shame on me' principle. My parents taught this principle in our home constantly and they reminded us of it every time one of us wanted to cave in to the opinions or teasing of others. This is what shame on them; shame on me means.

"Do you remember the story in the Book of Mormon when Nephi was commanded to build a ship? What did his brothers say? It's in 1 Nephi 17:17-19. They called him a fool; they said he couldn't do it; they said he lacked judgment; they said building a ship was too much for him to accomplish.[4]

"Brothers and sisters, when we know we're doing the right thing; when we know we're on the right course in our lives and others start putting us down; when others try to bring us down to their level; shame on them for being so faithless. Shame on them for not rejoicing in our goals and ambitions. Shame on them for not rejoicing in our talents. But, do you know what's even worse? What's worse is if we believe them. If you or I abandon our righteous objectives, whatever they are, for the scorn of the world,[5] shame on you; shame on me; shame on us.

"Consider what would have happened if Nephi had listened to and followed the deriding, self-serving, uninspired remarks of his brothers and caved in. What if he had said: 'Ya know, maybe you're right; I am being a bit foolish; this is too big for me; I just wasn't thinking straight?'"

Just then, without raising his hand, a young man blurted out, "What if there's something you really want to do and your parents or somebody else really important in your life, says you can't or you shouldn't do it?"

"That's a tough one," Sarah said kindly. "Here's what I've learned. Just ask yourself a couple questions. Now this requires some real soul searching at times. You've got to be honest with yourself. Ask yourself first: 'Is what I want to do REALY something I want to do or is it just a way to rebel and do *my thing*?'" Sarah said as she gestured quotation marks with her fingers.

"Second: 'Will what I want to do help me keep the commandments and strengthen my testimony? In other words, will it help or hinder my relationship with Christ?' Mormon really said it best:

>'Wherefore, all things which are good cometh of God; and that which is evil cometh of the devil; for the devil is an enemy unto God, and fighteth against him continually, and inviteth and enticeth to sin, and to do that which is evil continually.
>
>'But behold, that which is of God inviteth and enticeth to do good continually; wherefore, everything which inviteth and enticeth to do good, and to love God, and to serve him is inspired of God.'[6]

Sarah paused for a moment. Feeling the spiritual power and tender emotion present in the meeting, she took a deep breath, and said: "Well, brothers and sisters, thank you for allowing Jim and me to barge in on you and for sharing your services with us. We've enjoyed being here and with you, renewing our covenants just as you have.

Agency and Consequences

"The past few weeks have been very tender for me. I was holding my dad's hand when he passed away. It was I who had to call my mother and tell her what happened. Through all of that and the days that have followed, despite the loss of losing my dearest friend for the first twenty-seven years of my life, there has been a peace in my mind and heart[7] I cannot describe nor adequately share. It's like a warm hug being constantly shared with beings you know are there but can't see with your natural eyes.

"Brothers and sisters, I know our Father in Heaven lives.

"I know we have a Mother in Heaven whom our Father loves, protects and honors as every righteous husband loves, protects and honors his wife; and I know she loves our Father and each of us, just as Father loves us—more than we can comprehend.

"I know my Savior, Jesus Christ, loves me too. I know He died for me, suffered for me, felt every sickness, tiredness, ache, pain and heartache possible for me.[8]

"I know the Gospel was restored through the Prophet Joseph Smith. I've stood in the Sacred Grove and know what Joseph said he saw and heard he, in fact, saw and heard.

"I'm grateful to know the powers of righteous priesthood and righteous womanhood sealed together in holy temples can be, if honored and worked for, the most powerful influence for good in the entire universe.

"I know our canon of scripture is true and if read, studied, meditated and pondered over on a daily basis will be the iron rod[9] that will lead us home to the tree of life—Eternal Life with our Heavenly Parents and the Lord, Jesus Christ.

"Of these things I testify, in the name of Jesus Christ, amen," Sarah tenderly and tearfully concluded her testimony.

* * * * *

After the meetings, Jim and Sarah were invited to have dinner at Bishop Cutler's home with him and his family. Following the meal, they headed back over the Missouri and Mississippi Rivers to Scott Air Force Base.

As they arrived at the Shiloh gate, Sarah remembered another lesson taught by her mother. When saying goodbye to the one you love, linger a while and look deeply into their eyes and look for the glory. As Jim and Sarah kissed each other goodbye, Sarah said: "Jim, my mother taught me when saying goodbye or hello to the one you love, you should linger a while and look for the glory in each other's eyes and countenance. I think I see it in you. Jim Worthington, I love you. Thank you for being so supportive today at church and for the best weekend a girl could ask for."

Jim smiled, remembering his thoughts at this very spot on Friday evening—he must have passed the examination. But, instead of feeling a sense of pride, he felt overwhelmed with humility. It had been a wonderful weekend.

They had cried together, laughed together, spoken frankly and tenderly to each other. And then Jim said: "I feel like the most honored man on the planet Sarah Kindman. That you would even give me the time of day is beyond my wildest dreams. Thank you for feeling about me as I feel about you. I do love you, too. And yes, I see the glory in your face and eyes. Would you allow me to offer a prayer and then ask you for permission to see you again?"

"Yes and you have my permission with one condition," Sarah replied warmly.

"OK ... huh ... what's the condition," Jim wondered out loud.

"Our next date must be in Peoria. You must come to my home and I promise to have made arrangements for you to stay with someone who will keep an eye on you and make sure you don't get into trouble," Sarah teased.

"Condition accepted," Jim agreed. He then paused and with his right arm around Sarah's shoulders and his left hand holding both of hers, he offered a prayer of thanks and a request for guidance in their relationship and safety for their journeys.

Jim then got out of Sarah's truck, grabbed his suitcase and walked to the gate. Sarah blew him a kiss, slid over behind the wheel, adjusted the seat, put on the seat belt and headed for home.

Agency and Consequences

46. Obstacles

AT nine o'clock the next morning, Sarah was in Mr. Sheffield's office to report on her date. "So, how did your date go. Tell me about it," Mr. Sheffield asked in a fatherly tone.

"I've never had such a great time. Jim took me to see Camelot at the Fox Theater. We went to Old Main Street in St. Charles on Saturday and spent the day talking; we ate lots and we went to church Sunday. Jim is the most kind, strong, gentle man I've ever known, except maybe for my dad," Sarah responded with a bit of a lump in her throat.

"That's wonderful. But, I should remind you, your dad had a lot of years and lots of training from your mother to make him the kind, strong and gentle man he was. Don't make the mistake of comparing Jim to your dad too closely. What you want is potential and it sounds like Jim has that," Mr. Sheffield counseled.

"I'm sorry; I don't mean to compare. You're right; it never occurred to me the dad I knew and remember had a lot of time to become the man he was. You're right, though, Jim has all the potential. I just hope I have an equivalent amount," Sarah said hopefully. "One thing I learned is Jim is not intimidated by much if anything. He certainly wasn't intimidated by me," Sarah said smiling in a grateful tone.

"Sarah, does Jim know anything about your financial position?" Mr. Sheffield asked earnestly.

"No. Not yet. That's why I've asked him to come here for our next date as soon as we can get our schedules to mesh," Sarah replied with a bit of worry. "Frankly, I'm concerned when he sees me in that big, all-paid-for, house, it may be more than his very male ego can handle. I think he's hoping we would build our nest egg together and ...," Sarah said as she reached in her purse for a tissue.

"Sarah, my sense is he will handle it, provided you two figure out a way for him take some ownership in what happens in the future. You two will have a unique challenge. The burden of being breadwinner will not be typical for Jim. You will have to make sure you love and appreciate that his manhood has more to do with the other qualities he brings to your relationship. Now that has to do with more than just the physical side of things. You must, when the time is right, involve him. He must be an equal partner. My guess is he will bring some gifts, abilities and insights to your life and projects that will more than compensate for the fact he doesn't need to bring home the bacon. Even still, he should probably work at what he's passionate about; isn't that flying? ... at least for a while," Mr. Sheffield advised.

"I guess we have some things to work at right away, don't we? Mr. Sheffield, thank you for being my surrogate father. Dad would be very pleased. And I appreciate it more than I can express," Sarah said softly, realizing the road ahead was already fraught with challenge as she left Mr. Sheffield's office.

*****

Over the next several days, Jim and Sarah made arrangements for their next date in Peoria. It would be in two weeks when Jim would be close enough to get a hop into Scott, rent a car and drive up to Sarah's.

During the interim, however, Jim arranged to visit with Sarah's mother for a day. The obvious matter of business—ask permission to invite Sarah to be his wife. So, as Jim and Big Sarah sat at a table during the afternoon of his visit at Sarah's Place sharing some pie and ice cream, Big Sarah asked: "Jim, my daughter has told me a lot about you and she's quite taken. Tell me, what does your heart tell you about her?"

"I love her deeply. From the moment I met her in the cockpit of the C-5 I was flying to take her and Hidalgo out to Mountain Home to meet your husband to fight that fire, I knew there was something special about her. And, I've continued to have that same feeling. As you told me, she is independent, but I like that in a woman; there's a lot of security in that just in case something should happen later."

"You mean like the accident that took my husband?" Big Sarah followed up.

"Yes. I suppose that's what I mean. I'm sorry if I touched a tender nerve," Jim apologized.

"No apology needed. George and I talked about that a lot. It's something a couple must prepare for as much as possible. Let me ask you another question. Given Sarah's

Agency and Consequences

independence and strong tendency to get overbearing and want to do things her way more than her share of the time, how would you handle her without exercising unrighteous dominion?"[1] Big Sarah inquired with a little concern.

"That has already come up. When I told her I had talked to you right after I met her, while she and your husband were fighting the forest fire, she became real insistent I tell her everything you told me about her. When it became badgering, I took her aside where we couldn't be seen or heard; I looked her straight in the eyes and told her I would never seek to control her and I expected to be treated the same way," Jim replied.

"And how did she respond?" Big Sarah asked, following up.

"She apologized for being a sway-back nag. And she thanked me for taking hold of her and claimed I was now in a very select group that included only you, your husband and the Lord Himself," Jim reported with a little bit more confidence.

Big Sarah smiled broadly; then, as she reached across the table and laid her hand on Jim's, said affectionately: "Jim, my husband, George, was a very good judge of character. When he met you, after your flight to Mountain Home, he called me and said: 'I just met Sarah's future husband.' So, if you're seeking permission to ask for Sarah's hand in marriage, with all the love and support I can give, on behalf of my deceased husband and our family, you have my blessing.

"But, there's one more thing. Sarah hasn't told you everything yet. I'm not in a position to tell you what she must tell you and talk to you in all seriousness about. When she does, it could change everything. It will certainly test the feeling you have for her at this moment. I don't mean to be mysterious. To put your mind at ease, Sarah is as pure and clean as the new fallen snow; she has committed no major sin. But, with all my heart, I hope the two of you can work your way through this obstacle," Big Sarah said with great sincerity.

* * * * *

When the weekend arrived, Jim found himself northeast of Peoria just outside Chillicothe, Illinois, not far from North Peoria Lake, at the gate to Sarah's property. As he looked passed the gate and down the drive, he saw it wound through a wooded area that blocked the view of any house that might be there. He turned his car through the gate onto the drive and followed its path. As he rounded the last bend, he skidded his car to a stop and got out. He took a second look and couldn't believe what he saw as he said aloud: "What in the world ...? Is this some kind of joke?" He took off his sunglasses and just gawked at the huge house in front of him, as its white brick exterior glittered like a million diamonds in the sun. He double-checked the address and the GPS on the dashboard. Both indicated he was at the right place. He felt overwhelmed.

"Well, here goes," Jim said aloud as he got back into the car.

As Sarah had suggested, Jim drove past the circular drive that passed by the front door and around to the left side of the two-story house (it looked like a mansion to him) to the garage.

What he found was an eight-door garage with the last two doors, at the extreme left, open. He pulled up and found Sarah in the eighth bay servicing a car that was up on a hydraulic lift with a young man helping her. In the next bay, there was a service pit with a car over it and another young man down in the pit changing the oil in the car. In the sixth bay was an assortment of machines and tools for overhauling engines, transmissions and other vehicle parts. Across the ceiling, spanning the three end bays and able to travel both front to back and from side to side, was an overhead crane with an electric winch and travel motors, no doubt for lifting out engines and anything else needing a lift. In the next bay, there was an assortment of lawn and garden machines including a riding mower with a trailer and an all terrain vehicle. Next was a trailer loaded with a small Cat® 247B Series 2 Multi Terrain Loader and a backhoe attachment sitting on the floor. At the far end of the garage, closest to the house, Sarah's truck was parked. The second and third bays were empty.

As Jim got out of his car, Sarah noticed him and came running. Holding her greasy hands behind her, she leaned forward and gave him a kiss hello. Sorry I can't hug you just yet, but I'm so glad you're here. I'll open the second bay door and you can pull in. If you'd like, I have a pair of coveralls hanging over the wall and you can join us.

As the second bay door went up, Jim pulled the car in. He

Agency and Consequences

turned off the engine and found the pair of coveralls lying over the cement wall that divided the garage from a spacious walkway or hall leading to the main house. He pulled on the coveralls and walked to where Sarah was changing an oil filter, or rather she was showing the young man standing next to her, how to change an oil filter.

"Jim, I'd like you to meet Peter Dunsforth. He's a Priest in my ward and the son of my Bishop. We're doing a few bits of maintenance on Bishop Dunsforth's family car. First, we're changing the oil. Then, we're going to look at the brakes, give the exhaust system a once over, change and gap the sparkplugs, replace the shocks, top off all the fluids and finally, inspect and clean the injectors. We should be finished in about an hour and a half. And down there, in the pit, is Peter's best friend, John. He's changing the oil in his car and then he'll join us up here. Peter and John, this is my very close friend, Jim Worthington," Sarah said making introductions.

"Jim, if you plan to get greasy, I suggest you coat your hands with some of the dishwashing liquid on my tool bench. If you do, it will help your hands clean up more easily when we're done," Sarah kindly advised. "But, it's up to you," she added, not wanting to be bossy.

Jim quickly joined in and showed he wasn't completely unfamiliar with the basic tasks, like changing sparkplugs and oil and checking fluids. He was even quite adept at changing pads on disk brakes. But, when it came to inspecting and cleaning injectors, Sarah was the pro. In all these tasks, however, she would first demonstrate and then let the two young men have a go at doing it themselves. But, when the bolts, securing the shock absorbers wouldn't break free, Sarah got out her oxy-acetylene torch and expertly cut the bolt heads right off. She then demonstrated how to use a large punch and hammer to knock the bolts out.

At about seven-thirty, they were finished and the two young men thanked Sarah for her time and help, pulled their cars from Sarah's garage and went home.

* * * * *

When Sarah had lowered the two garage doors, she and Jim washed up together at the garage sink and then she looked at Jim, as a tear rolled down her cheek. They embraced and kissed each other as Sarah whispered: "Gosh, I've missed you. I love you ya know. I'll bet you're starved."

"I've missed you too. I love you and yes, I am hungry," Jim responded warmly.

"Come on then, dinner should just about be ready," Sarah directed as she took Jim's hand and they walked down the hallway at the back of the garage to the house.

They entered the house via a spacious laundry and mudroom where they took off their coveralls and shoes. "Why don't you take a few minutes and take a self-guided tour while I finish getting our dinner ready. Meet me back here in fifteen to twenty minutes; but don't get lost, I might not be able to find you," Sarah chuckled as she gave Jim a light kiss and went into her kitchen.

* * * * *

From the laundry, across an eight-foot wide hall, was the kitchen, patterned on a smaller scale, to the kitchen at Sarah's Place, but which also included a roomy table and chairs for casual eating. Adjacent to the laundry was an elevator to the second floor and basement with a stair going to the second floor on the left of the elevator door. The stair made one third of the ascent on the side, then a third on the back and the final third on the other side of the elevator. The stair to the basement began on the right of the elevator door and descended in like manner as the one going up.

Down the hall on the right, past the elevator was a large dining room, capable of seating about two dozen comfortably around a large oval table. Across from the dining room, were a large half bath and a music niche. The half bath had a door at the other end that lead to a large enclosed pool, whirlpool and sauna.

Presiding over the music niche, was a full-sized, Steinway grand piano. Jim looked at the shimmering ebony instrument and could not resist. He raised the lid to its full open position, sat down on and adjusted the bench; then he ripped off an enthusiastic "The Entertainer" by Scott Joplin. For the next several minutes, the music reverberated from the music niche into the large great room.

The great room was sunken a couple of feet lower than the rest of the floor. It featured a large stone fireplace directly opposite the entrance foyer, a vaulted ceiling with skylights and massive exposed beams. Plush, leather couches were arranged in a semi-circle around the fireplace and dozens of pillows were placed on the semi-circular steps leading to the floor. Both the steps and floor were made of natural stone. The great room was obviously an amphitheater designed for large groups of people to converse and/or to listen to presentations of one kind or another.

On the far end of the great room, was the grand staircase leading to the second floor. Across the hall-space, in front of the great room, was the front entrance foyer. The entrance itself was a double entrance with an inner and outer set of doors. As one entered the foyer, there were an elevator and stairs on the right (similar to those found across from the kitchen) and a half bath and coat closet on the left.

Feeling he needed the exercise, Jim climbed the grand staircase, which appeared to be a rise of about twelve feet, to the second floor, also with a ceiling height (not counting the vaulted ceiling of the great room and the space above him) of about twelve feet.

Outside the elevator, was a hall space leading to the grand staircase and the hall to the private area of the house. At the end of the hall space was a large floor to ceiling window appropriately draped, but which still allowed the outside light to enter the home.

Across the hall-space from the elevator and stair was a large, open library. The stacks of books were along the back separated by four aisles and a center aisle dividing the stacks. Each aisle had lighting activated by a motion detector. To the front of the library, facing the great room, was a large desk, a worktable, several chairs and reading couches with individual reading lamps and side tables. A door on the sidewall of the library led to the master suite.

The hall running past the library looked out over the great room and featured a beautiful, cherry railing that continued down the grand staircase. A large, double door, at the moment open, separated the upstairs living space from the open space. Once inside the private area, on the left, another set of double doors, also open at the moment, led to the master suite. As Jim entered the suite, he was astounded at the elegance he saw. At his left, a king-size bed with rich, cherry wood side tables, a beautiful chandelier and matching lamps gave the room a celestial feeling. At the far end, were ceiling to floor windows with elegant drapes and shears. On the right of the master suite, was a spacious walk in closet and a large bath that could be entered from either the bedroom or closet. The bath featured a whirlpool tub, oversized (no shower curtain needed) walk-in shower, commodious linen storage and a spacious double sink vanity with huge, well-lighted mirrors.

Across the hall from the master suite was a home theater with doors to the hall on both the right and left. Just like a regular theater, each door opened to a walkway and at the end, turned up to the seating as the ceiling followed the slope of the roof.

At the end of the hall on the right, was the elevator and stair. Just past the elevator, the hall turned right and there were six large guest rooms each with a queen-size bed, television, phone, writing table and chairs. Between each pair of rooms was the bath for each room with the closet for each room on the opposite wall. Thus, each room was well insulated from every other room. At the end of the wing of guest rooms was a stair well that led down to the garage bays and out to the pool area.

Jim finished his tour, having not seen the basement, by descending the stair at the end of the second-floor guest room hall. He exited the stair well at the end of the garage. As he walked the hall along the rear of the garage back to the kitchen, his mind was reeling. "This place is not at all like most of the posh places I've seen across the world—audacious, gaudy opulence. Instead, this place is like Sarah herself—inspiring, uplifting, enlightening, simply elegant. But ...."

* * * * *

"So, what do you think?" Sarah asked, as Jim came into the kitchen and the aroma of ham, spiced with pineapple and clove tantalized his olfactory nerves.

"I'm overwhelmed," Jim responded flatly.

"That's why I wanted you come here this weekend.

Agency and Consequences

There's purpose in my madness," Sarah said as she invited him to sit at the table. "Jim, I'd appreciate it if you would offer us a blessing on the food. It's been a while since I cooked for anyone but myself," she said with a hint of doubt as she took Jim's hand in hers.

As they ate, Sarah said: "Jim, you told me you 'tinkered' on the piano? You are full of surprises."

"Well, I did minor in piano performance in college. I joined the Air Force to make a living. And I'm not the only one with surprises," Jim said with an edge of concern in his voice.

"Sweetheart," Sarah responded firmly looking Jim squarely in his eyes, "I needed you to see this. And there's more. This house sits on a hundred acres of mostly wooded ground. There's an enclosed pool, with a retractable roof, between the garage and great room. There's a large storage room, a game room, full bath and space to add additional rooms when needed in the basement. You see, I love to entertain; I just don't get to as often ...."

"Sarah," Jim interrupted, obviously somewhat disturbed; "I don't know how much you make at Caterpillar; but you gotta be up to your eyeballs in debt and that bothers me," he said in a very concerned tone.

"Jim," Sarah said warmly, looking at him very steadily; "that's why I wanted you to come and see for yourself. The fact of the matter is it's all paid for; I don't owe a single dime on anything you've seen. Jim, I'm a very wealthy woman. I'm not in a position at this moment to tell you exactly how much is in the bank nor the size of my stock portfolio or what I have in other investments. I work because I love to work.

"When I bought this property and built this house, I had no idea within a few months of finishing it, I would meet and fall in love with you. I didn't ask you to come here to show off my wealth. Everything I have can go on sale tomorrow or be given away if you can't be comfortable loving me as I am. But my hope was and is you can. Most of the money I make, I give away and donate to worthy causes I've chosen to contribute to," Sarah confided.

"I apologize for assuming and obviously jumping to a very bad conclusion," Jim stated sincerely. "But ... but ... huh, where did it all come from? Did you inherit it from someone or ...?" Jim, asked kindly but still in a state of shock.

"As you know, my dad gave me an old bulldozer when I was a sophomore in high school. The summer between my sophomore and junior years, I completely tore down and rebuilt that dozer. In doing so, I read every technical document I could lay my hands on; and I had my high school math teacher tutor me in trigonometry and calculus. By the end of my junior year, I had built a prototype device that increases the atomization of the injected fuel into the engine cylinders. That device, when my dad and I sold the patent rights to Caterpillar, made us both very wealthy. That's how I got Hidalgo and his tractor-trailer rig. It paid for my degrees at Purdue and I'm still receiving royalties from every engine Caterpillar sells with that device installed or from devices sold as aftermarket add-ons. In addition, my most recent contract with Caterpillar stipulates that I (or my assigns) get a percentage from every sale of every new patent or configuration up-grade connected with that device for the next fifty years (I'll be seventy-five years old when the money stops). And all that, of course, is in addition to my six figure salary, as a Senior Engineer at Cat's Development/Research Center, located down the road a short distance in Mossville. So, now, as Paul Harvey was wont to say, you know the rest of the story," Sarah reported.

"Wow ... and double wow." Jim said as he stood up, tipping his chair to the floor. He righted the chair and began pacing around the table. "I had no idea about all this. Now that you mention it, I do remember reading about your invention, but the financial details ...," Jim sighed and took a deep breath. He now knew what Sarah's mother had spoken about at their meeting a few days ago. This, however, was not the time to mention that.

"We've always kept the money part very close to our vests. My dad and I never talked about it except in very vague terms. Cat is, likewise, extremely closed-lipped. And, I want it to stay that way. Obviously, when I pay my tithing, I have to count on the confidentiality of the Bishopric and Ward Clerks. As I said, I try to give most of my money away to worthy causes—individuals, families and organizations. I don't mind paying a fair income tax, but I would just as soon make sure most of it goes where I know it's making a difference in the trenches, with real

Agency and Consequences

people needing a lift," Sarah explained.

"Jim, look at me," Sarah asked firmly, but kindly.

Jim sat back down and looked at Sarah as she said: "Sweetheart, do you understand why I had to share all this with you before our relationship went any further?"

"Yeah, I do. That sounds funny," Jim acknowledged with a smile.

Sarah took Jim's hands in hers and said simply: "Sarah Elizabeth Kindman is just an ordinary woman who's been blessed with some gifts that have made her a lot of money at a very young age. She had absolutely no idea or feeling, when she started tinkering in her dad's maintenance shop on that device, it would lead to all this. She's paid a heavy price over the years as the kids in her high school thought she was weird and most of the men she dated in college ... well, when they found out, would basically run away or act more like a groupie.

"She feels very much as Erin Gruwell must have felt in the film, *Freedom Writers*, when her dad said "... you have been blessed with a burden ...."[2] So, she's trying very hard to have faith in her temple covenants, and not let this burden spoil her or ruin her ability to feel the Spirit and live the way she knows Father wants her to live.

"Jim, since the spring of my senior year in high school, only two weeks before I did that bulldozer demonstration in my home town, where I took back my honor and that of my family, after a young playboy tried to steal it from us, my greatest desire has been to be a righteous wife and mother. Since then, on the advice of my Bishop at that time, I've been looking for a man who would lead me Home as his equal. I've been looking for someone who wouldn't be intimidated either by me or by my money or worse, someone who isn't looking for a free ride. I think I've found him.

"Jim Worthington, I love you with all my heart. I'm hoping we will dare to risk finding a way to share this burden equally together and be partners for eternity. But, out of necessity, at this moment, I'm hitting the ball into your court," Sarah warmly challenged.

"Sarah, with all my heart, I love you, more than words can express. I guess I think and feel like one of my investigators, while serving my mission. When he realized, for the first time, that just maybe the church he had believed in all his life wasn't the real deal after all, it was hard for him to accept the fact he would have to change; and that his whole life would be turned upside down and inside out all at the same time. That's not to say, there's anything wrong with you; it's just this is something I never, in my wildest imagination, dreamed of. Sarah, I just don't have either my heart or brain wrapped around what you've shown and told me tonight," Jim confessed.

"I guess there's going to be a long talk with Heavenly Father tonight. Were you able to make arrangements for me as you promised?" Jim asked sincerely.

"I did. Bishop Dunsforth said you could stay at his home. But it is rather late and getting there is a bit tricky; so, if you're not too uncomfortable, you can have the room at the end of the hall up stairs, the farthest away from my room. All the doors do have locks. That's not too unlike different rooms on different floors at the Embassy Suites. It's up to you," Sarah invited. "And, if that makes you too nervous, I have a roll away we can set up in the basement. There is another full bath down there," Sarah offered.

"It has been a long day and I'm exhausted. I think I'll take you up on your suggestion and use the bedroom upstairs, as long as you're comfortable. I wouldn't want anyone to think ...," Jim said with concern.

"I'll just call Bishop Dunsforth and tell him the truth. Nobody else needs to know," Sarah reassured.

"Well, I'll go get my suitcase. Can I use the elevator to go to the second floor?" Jim asked with a smile.

"Sure, I guess it will hold you," Sarah teased.

"Before we say good night, could we kneel together in prayer," Jim asked sincerely.

"Sure; I'd be honored to pray with you. Let's go to the great room," Sarah suggested.

They went to the great room and Sarah took a couple pillows from the steps and placed them on the floor in front of one of the couches. They kneeled down, each put one arm around the other and placed their free hand in each other's. Sarah asked: "May I be voice?"

"Of course," Jim responded.

Sarah prayed thanking Father in Heaven for the wonderful

time she and Jim had had together since they met. She acknowledged they needed His help in resolving the issues discussed that evening. She acknowledged both she and Jim loved each other but whether or not their relationship should go to the next level was something they both needed to be comfortable with. She prayed for help they would both make the right decision, whatever that decision happened to be. She prayed for wisdom in the night and despite the personal prayers that would most likely go into the wee hours, they would get the sleep and rest they needed.

Following the prayer, they stayed kneeling for a couple of minutes, spiritually listening and feeling. They then slipped easily into each other's arms and kissed each other good night. Jim then said, as they looked at each other: "I like what you taught me last time we said goodbye about lingering and just looking into each other's eyes and face. You are the most Christ-like person I've ever met. I am hoping Father will help me be comfortable. I think I want the challenge you offered. I hope you're not embarrassed or offended when I tell you I want you, all of you, every particle of you and that means more than just ...."

Sarah's eyes flooded as she responded: "Jim, if the Lord helps you to be comfortable, and you're willing to take me on and share the great burden I bring, then if you were to ask me ... at the right time, in the right place, after the right ceremony, I would be the most honored of women to give you all of me, down to the nucleus of every cell in my soul. And I would be just as honored to receive all of you in the same way."

Jim and Sarah arose from their knees and walked back towards the kitchen. Jim then went to his car, retrieved his luggage and took the elevator by the kitchen to the second floor. It seemed a long walk for Jim as he set down his luggage outside the elevator and walked away from his room towards the master suite. He paused briefly, looked into the open room as a full moon bathed and gave it surreal warmth and, just for a moment, wondered what it would be like to .... He quickly checked that thought, turned back and went to his room.

Sarah, meanwhile, called Bishop Dunsforth, cleaned up supper and then she retired, offering a long, heart-felt prayer and then remained on her knees listening and feeling for guidance for both Jim and her.

* * * * *

      At about two in the morning, Sarah awoke and felt a spiritual nudge to go down stairs. She got up, put on a robe and walked out to the balcony above the great room, down the grand staircase and across the great room to one of the floor-to-ceiling windows. She parted a drape slightly with the back of one of her hands. As she did, she saw Jim exit the house from the stair well at the end of guest room wing. She watched as he walked around the pool deck; he paused, splashed a little water, continued walking, then exited the pool enclosure and walked into the woods. A tear trickled down Sarah's cheek as she returned to her bed; but she found herself on her knees again pleading for the man she now loved more than life itself and all the wealth she had. She offered thanks for the wonderful influence for good Jim had been in her life during past several weeks and prayed Father would help him make the decision that was right for him.

Agency and Consequences |

47. Sharing the Load

SARAH allowed herself to sleep in until seven-thirty at which time she arose, showered and put on a light, cotton, flower print dress. She didn't know if Jim were still in the woods or if he had returned to the house and his room. So, she went to the library and answered emails and prepared an agenda for her property staff meeting at noon.

At about ten, Jim walked down the hall and found Sarah at her desk. "Good morning to the woman I love," Jim said beaming as a bright countenance shown in his face.

Sarah arose from her desk and responded warmly: "Good morning to the man I love." Jim and Sarah embraced and kissed and Sarah sensed a confident passion in Jim that made her tingle.

"Can we talk?" Jim asked politely.

"Of course," Sarah responded as she gestured to a love seat nearby.

"It was a long, wonderful night last night. I ended up in the woods, found where you're building a large fire pit, spied a wonderful tree house and made friends with a couple of raccoons," Jim reported chuckling. "I think I'd like to see it all in the day time," Jim concluded.

"I think I could arrange that, later today if you'd like. The tree house, by the way, would make a spiffy man cave," Sarah hinted looking intently into Jim's eyes.

"Or a dog house when you kick me out," Jim quipped in response.

"And, what does that mean?" Sarah asked hopefully.

"It means last night I had an experience not unlike what Oliver Cowdry experienced as recorded in Section 6 of the Doctrine and Covenants," Jim said as he stepped to Sarah's desk and retrieved her triple combination and then read:

> 'Verily, verily, I say unto thee, blessed art thou for what thou hast done; for thou hast inquired of me, and behold, as often as thou hast inquired thou hast received instruction of my Spirit. If it had not been so, thou wouldst

241

not have come to the place where thou art at this time.

'Behold, thou knowest that thou hast inquired of me and I did enlighten they mind; and now I tell thee these things that thou mayest know that thou has been enlightened by the Spirit of truth; yea, I tell thee, that thou mayest know that there is none else save God that knowest thy thoughts and the intents of thy heart.

'Verily, verily, I say unto you, if you desire a further witness, cast your mind upon the night that you cried unto me in your heart, that you might know concerning the truth of these things. Did I not speak peace to your mind concerning the matter? What greater witness can you have than from God? And now, behold, you have received a witness; for if I have told you things which no man knoweth have you not received a witness.'[1]

Jim slipped from the love seat to his knees on the floor and holding Sarah's hands asked: "Sarah Elizabeth Kindman, will you marry me; will you be my wife for time and all eternity. I promise to do everything in my power to be your husband and the father to your children I know you deserve and Father in Heaven expects me to be?"

"Don't you think you should ask my mother first?" Sarah couldn't help teasing with a smile hoping to get a "You gotta be kiddin'" reaction.

"I already have ... and she said 'go for it,'" Jim said with a big grin as Sarah looked back incredulously thinking just for a second, "You gotta be kiddin'." Just as quickly, she smiled back as she realized there was no point in asking the obvious question: "When?"

Sarah, trembling, in tears, slipped from the love seat to her knees, looking at Jim intently and with all the love in her being said: "Jim Worthington, I accept your proposal of marriage. I promise to do everything in my power to be your wife and the mother to your children I know you deserve and Father

Agency and Consequences

in Heaven expects me to be."

They took each other in their arms, sealed their engagement with a kiss and then just held each other. Jim then whispered: "Sarah, there are three things I'd like you to help me with."

They got back into the love seat and Jim requested: "First, I'm a pilot, not a Wall Street financial wizard. I don't know how long, if ever, it will take me to be as conversant or knowledgeable about the world of money and finance as you or your advisors. All I ask is to be included and when I ask a question, even if it's the same one I've asked a dozen times before, will you be patient with me and help me to learn? Until I can relate this stuff to what I already know and understand and it becomes a second language to me, I'll need you to keep it simple.

"Second, I need to have something to do around here. So, will you teach me to run the mower and maybe even that neat little bulldozer with the ... I think it's called a backhoe attachment ... out in the garage?

"And third, the dress you're wearing is beautiful. I've noticed you wear a lot of dresses, more than most women I know. And when we saw Camelot, I noticed you quietly mouthing a lot of the words. And when Arthur did the soliloquy between the verses of 'How to Handle a Woman' where he said: 'Never be to disturbed if you don't understand what a woman is thinking. They don't do it often,'[2] instead of appearing offended, like many women I know would be in today's world, you seemed to be delighted. Somehow, the dresses, the delight in those words seem to be all connected and I want to understand. Would you try and teach me?"

"Well, Jim, dear—gosh that sounds wonderful—let me start with your first question. I'm not a Wall Street financial wizard either. My dad and I were very careful at choosing advisors we could trust. I meet with them at least monthly on a conference call and at least twice a year, I fly to New York and visit with them personally. Locally, I do my banking at the Peoria State Bank where Mr. John Gardner handles my accounts and my local philanthropic efforts. And yes, anything you don't understand, please ask as many times as you need to and I'll graciously answer. If I don't, just give me one of those looks I've come to understand and I'll get the message," Sarah answered jabbing Jim softly in his ribs.

"What look is that?" Jim queried as he jumped with the jab in the ribs.

"You know very well what that look is. It's the same look I used to get from my dad when I was getting too close to the boundary line and going out of bounds," Sarah said. "It's a look I need from time to time and I'm counting on getting it from you."

"Now, to question two. You can have your first lessons on driving the mower and the 247B this afternoon if you like. The mower will come most easily. But, with your pilot abilities, you'll be flying the mini-dozer in a couple of days," Sarah said confidently.

"Question three is a little more involved and yet it is really simple. I wear dresses and enjoy them because first, I'm not a man; and second, I enjoy being a woman and they remind me of those facts. As to the words in Camelot, there are some better ones, also written by Alan J. Lerner, expressed by Henry Higgins in 'My Fair Lady' when he sings:

> 'Women are irrational,
> that's all there is to that!
> Their heads are full of
> cotton, hay, and rags!
> They're nothing but
> exasperating, irritating,
> Vacillating, calculating,
> agitating,
> Maddening, and
> infuriating hags!
> ... why can't a woman be
> more like a man?
> Yes. Why can't a woman
> be more like a man?'[3]

"The simple answer to why women don't think or behave like men is we're not supposed to. We simply are not, physically (that's obvious), emotionally, spiritually or even intellectually designed like a man. And quite frankly, I'm grateful for that. I

Agency and Consequences

don't think women and men should be or were ever intended to be competitors in any way when it comes to those special relationships in marriage and family. And even in society and business, I don't understand the unisex mentality that tries officially and outwardly to ignore our fundamental differences and ends up, in the everyday reality, in the movies, in print (especially the magazines at the checkout stand at the grocery store or gas station) being hypocritical, simply because there's no escaping the truth.

"In my case, I can run out the equations on turbo charger pressures or horse power as quickly and accurately as any man on the planet. And I'm not the kind of woman who goes berserk at the sight of a spider or mouse or some other seemingly unpleasant critter. But, I do fuss over what I wear every day, my hair, my nails, color coordinating my outfit every day and all that sort of stuff. And for reasons I can't even begin to understand, let alone explain, I would be totally embarrassed if I were to wear something someone remembered me wearing within at least the last couple of weeks. And I suppose, as we get more intimately acquainted, you will discover a whole lot more about me that will, as it did Henry Higgins and King Arthur, cause you to take long walks and talk to yourself.

"Jim, as you said two weeks ago about yourself, I'm comfortable in my own skin; I simply love and enjoy being a woman. My hope is I enjoy being a woman as much as you enjoy being a man. And I can't wait to learn how to be and work together as men and women were intended by God to be and do," Sarah confessed as she snuggled as close to Jim as she could get.

"Are you hungry? I sure am. I've waited all morning to fix breakfast so we could eat together," Sarah reminded as her stomach rumbled.

"Yeah, I am; but I forgot something," as he reached into his pocket and pulled out a small jewelry box and opened it. "Happy anniversary," Jim said as he presented Sarah with her engagement ring.

"Oh, Jim, it's beautiful," Sarah exclaimed as Jim placed the ring on her left hand ring finger.

"Oh, one other thing. Our honeymoon trip is on me and is a surprise. It's probably the last thing in my life I'll get to pay for totally on my own. And so, I reserve the right to keep it a secret until we get there. Agreed?" Jim said with tender firmness.

"Agreed. I've learned my lesson about being a sway-back nag," Sarah said as they walked hand in hand down the hall towards the stair to the kitchen.

* * * * *

Sarah quickly fixed fried eggs (over easy for Jim), hash browns and bacon for their brunch. As they ate, Sarah asked: "Sweetheart, I have one request as we start our marriage. I want to start our family right away. I hope that's OK with you."

"That's what I hoped you'd want. It's fine with me. So, when do you want to start?" Jim said with a twinkle in his eyes.

"You're getting anxious aren't you? I guess that means we ought to set a date, huh?" Sarah said smiling with the same look of anticipation Jim had.

"Yes, I guess we should. Where do you want to do the ceremony?" Jim asked realizing this should be Sarah's choice.

"If you will agree and it's convenient enough for your family, I'd like to have the ceremony at the St. Louis Temple. I've gone to St. Louis many times to shop and go to the Cardinals baseball games and I just feel the St. Louis Temple is a special place for me. I've had so many revelatory experiences there. It just feels like home to me," Sarah reverently answered.

"Is there a particular sealer there you know whom you would like to perform the ceremony?" Jim asked following up.

"Well, I've done sealings there several times and Brother Richard Oscarson and I have become good friends. He's a former Patriarch, Mission President and Stake President. He, with his wife Linda, who is such a sweet lady, were the Temple President and Matron in St. Louis not long ago. I hope someday to be the kind of woman I see when I look at sister Oscarson," Sarah responded tearfully.

"Then it's settled. Why don't you call the St. Louis Temple and see if you can get hold of Brother Oscarson and ask what his schedule is and when he's available and set the date. I'll be sure and be there. Just give me enough time to confirm honeymoon arrangements, OK," Jim suggested.

"You know, if we can arrange it just right, we could have

Agency and Consequences

the ceremony in the morning and then go to the Embassy Suites in St. Charles where we had our first date for a couple hours afterward and then come here for the reception," Sarah suggested smiling just a little seductively.

"Now, you're a little tigress. That's awfully tempting. Too tempting to resist," Jim acknowledged," smiling with approval.

* * * * *

About then, Sarah's property and housekeeping managers, Brother and Sister Wagoner, arrived for staff meeting. Jim was invited, introduced and within an hour, everything was discussed relative to property maintenance and the Stake Youth Conference at the estate the following Friday and Saturday. Jim realized so much had happened since he got to Sarah's home, she simply hadn't had time to inform him of this event and so took it in stride.

When the question arose about getting a high ropes course completed and staffed with competent, certified instructors, Jim's response was: "I have some time off due and I could stay the week and help. I am a certified ropes course instructor." Sarah was delighted.

What else made this conference special for Sarah was her whole family, less brother, Tommy, still in the mission field, would be there to help with the food. She had already arranged for a private jet to pick them up and they would be there Wednesday evening.

* * * * *

After the staff meeting, Sarah and Jim changed clothes. Jim then asked: "Can I make a phone call and can we postpone the mower and mini-dozer instructions? I want to call a friend, Walt Dickerson, and his wife, Vicki. Both are certified ropes course instructors. I want to ask if they can come and help. Then I want to survey the ropes course. Do you have a long tape measure, a writing pad, pencil and something I can mark trees with—long pieces of ribbon would do nicely."

Sarah hardly knew what to think. Jim was taking ownership of this event for the conference. She looked at him as he waited for a response. "Of course. How can I help? Sarah responded.

"Hold the tape for me while I take measurements and then use all your wonderful negotiating skills and get us the equipment we'll need to build the course," Jim said matter-of-factly.

"Then let's go for it. I'll get the tape and other stuff while you make your calls," Sarah said enthusiastically. "By the way, isn't Walt Dickerson a member of the flight crew you were flying with when we first met?"

"Yup. He was the co-pilot. We often fly together," Jim said smiling.

Jim called his commander, arranged for the time off and then dialed his friend, Walt Dickerson and his wife, Vicki. Walt answered and said: "Hello, it's your nickel. How ya doin' Jim?"

"Walt, I'm doing great. I just got engaged." … "When? A couple of hours ago." … "Yeah, Sarah. She's the greatest. Say, how would you and Vicki like to meet her?" … "Yeah, I know you already met her, but Vicki hasn't and besides, I need your help." … "When? How about tomorrow night? Here's the deal. Sarah is running this big youth conference for our church next weekend and they want to have a ropes course. But, I need help building it and I need a couple of other certified instructors. There's plenty of room here at Sarah's and I'll pick up the tab on your airfare. Can you take a week off and come? I know it's short notice. But this is the chance to build the ultimate, mother of all high ropes courses," Jim said persuasively.

There was a pause as Jim overheard Walt and Vicki discussing their options.

"You can? Man … that is awesome. I'm going out now to draw up the first draft of the course. When you and Vicki get here tomorrow, we'll go over it together and you guys can rip it apart and we'll start over. But, I at least want to get something cooking in my head," Jim said exuberantly as Sarah came back into the kitchen and saw a little boy with a new bike at Christmas.

"Here's all the stuff you asked for. Wow, you look like a kid at Christmas," Sarah said smiling.

"What a day. First, I get engaged to the absolute greatest woman on the planet and then she lets me build the ultimate in high ropes courses with two of my best friends. It just doesn't get any better than that," Jim said with a grin from ear to ear.

* * * * *

Jim and Sarah got on the all terrain vehicle and headed into the woods. When they came to the tree house Jim saw the night before, he was dumb founded. It was a cottage built thirty feet off the ground in a huge oak tree. It had a lift, rope ladder and a balcony around the entire house. "That's perfect," Jim exclaimed. "We can use the tree house as both the start and finish for the course."

Jim then began surveying. He realized they only had four days of construction time and so he thought carefully about the challenge of each element and the difficulty of building it in the time available.

From the tree house to a large tree about thirty feet away, he sketched in a two line bridge. Next a telephone pole balance beam would span about twenty-five feet. After that, would be a multi-vine, also called the Tarzan swings, and then a zip line back to the ground and a rest area. A cargo net was next and a Raider Bridge back to the tree house. Participants would finish by repelling from the tree house to the ground.[4] This design, Jim thought, would allow participants to do either or both the first and second parts of the course. Realizing most people liked the zip line, he thought putting a rope ladder up to the top of this element would also be appropriate.

"So, what do you need me to get for you, sweetheart," Sarah asked as they rode back to the house to make some calls.

"Do you know anyone with some clout at the electric company?" Jim replied.

"It just so happens …," Sarah responded

The next couple of hours were a whirlwind as they ordered helmets, gloves, repelling rope, harnesses, cable and hardware over the internet and set up airfreight delivery for Monday morning. Sarah called her friend at the electric company, arranged for a used power pole and even persuaded him to have the power company deliver it. Finally, they arranged for a large, electric boom with a bucket.

"Jim, you look a bit concerned," Sarah noticed.

"I'm pretty sure, if the stuff we need gets here by noon on Monday we can get it all done. It will be some long days and I noticed you had a generator and portable lights so we can work into the night if we have to. I just haven't figured out how to get that blamed utility pole horizontally thirty feet in the air. We can build the cradles for it no problem; but getting it up there …," Jim said as his mind was working for a solution.

"Could we rig a block and tackle to my mini-dozer and lift it up? We could put a big eyebolt in each end and lift it. All I need is enough room to make the pull."

"Boy, I'm glad I'm marrying you. That's brilliant," Jim said excitedly. "We may not be able lift both ends at the same time, but I'll bet we can lift one end, tie it off and then lift the other."

* * * * *

In the early evening Jim and Sarah took a break and returned to the tree house. This was not a regular tree house. It had electricity, running water and a sewer line, a full bath, kitchenette, bedroom with a full size bed and a small study with big, soft, cushy pillows.

"When I was a little girl, we had a tree house. It became my escape place," Sarah confessed. "When I saw this big tree, after I bought the property, I knew right away I wanted a tree house built in it. I want you to have it as your private space, Jim. Fix it up anyway you like. Then, when you feel like my '… head is full of cotton, hay, and rags'[5] you'll have a place you can come, be alone and sort things out. Sometimes, you might even want to invite me for a candle light supper and dancing," Sarah said softly and lovingly.

"Why don't we both use it as an escape place? I'll put up a few mementos of my own and we'll make it our own little hideaway in the woods where we can listen to the frogs croaking and the crickets and cicadas singing. Maybe we'll get to watch a few birds nesting and raising their young. We can send secret messages to each other arranging for an occasional midnight rendezvous. Somehow, I have the feeling when we're struggling with something, this will be the perfect place to forgive each other," Jim said wisely.

"I like that idea," Sarah concurred kissing Jim. "I think it's about dinner time. Do you have a special request?" Sarah asked as they walked out to the balcony and got into the tree

Agency and Consequences

house lift.

    After their meal together, Jim invited Sarah to sit next to him at the piano bench. For the next hour, he played, to her delight, every song she could think of and a few she didn't know.

* * * * *

    The next day at Church, Sarah was all a glow showing off Jim and her diamond engagement ring. Her girls in Young Women were jumping up and down and just ecstatic for their Sister Kindman. "Have you set a date," they all seemed to ask together.

    "No," Sarah replied. "I still have to check with the sealer I'd like to perform the ceremony at the St. Louis Temple. But, we've decided the reception will be at my place (oops! I mean our place) and the honeymoon is Jim's surprise and he's not telling anyone, including me," Sarah explained anticipating the follow on questions.

* * * * *

    After church, Jim got in his rented car and rushed off to the airport to pick up Walt and Vicki as Sarah prepared a meal. Since Walt and Vicki would need a room, after seeing the tree house bedroom, they talked Sarah into letting them use it for their stay. "We'll let you know how comfy it is," Vicki said to Jim and Sarah as she gave a wink to her husband Walt.

    The next four days were grinding as Jim, Sarah, Walt and Vicki made final preparations for the conference.

    On the first day, Jim and Sarah returned Jim's rental car to the local agency; then they took Sarah's truck to the freight office at the airport and got the first load of equipment for the ropes course.

    Sarah spent the rest of the day finishing the excavation for the council ring and fire pit so workers could come in and install the benches and lay brick for the stage area around the pit. Jim, Walt and Vicki seemed to be always up in trees or the boom as they stretched wire, rope and built scaffolding for the various perches for each of the ropes course elements. When it came time to lift the utility pole into place, just as Sarah had suggested, a well-placed block and tackle and a long straight pull with the mini-dozer did the trick.

On Wednesday evening, Sarah rented a van and picked up her family at the airport. When everyone got settled, a meal in the dining room was the order of the evening. Of course, the excitement for Sarah's and Jim's engagement couldn't have been more exuberant.

Thursday, Big Sarah and her family were at work in the kitchen preparing the meals for the conference and storing them in Sarah's big refrigerator and freezer in her basement. Rented tables and chairs were delivered and set up in the first five bays of the garage for their make shift dining hall and the vehicles were parked outside. A dumpster for all the trash, including all the disposable eating utensils, plates, cups and napkins, was parked outside the garage. Finally, several porta-potties were set up out by the ropes course.

In the late afternoon, the Stake President and the Stake Young Men and Young Women Presidents came by for their final follow up. Everything was ready and on schedule. All that remained were a few odds and ends. These included making the hurricane lamps that would light the path from the fire pit back to the house where a dance would be held on the pool deck following the testimony meeting on Saturday evening. The Stake, Young Men and Young Women Presidents went to work following the instructions given by Jim and made two dozen hurricane lamps and then placed them on the path between the house and fire pit.

"Brother Worthington, I hear you and your friends have built a pretty spectacular high ropes course in just four days," the Stake President congratulated.

"Well, we think we have. Would you and your youth presidents like to try it out before it gets dark?" Jim offered with a smile.

"I think I would. How about the rest of you?" the Stake President inquired.

The Young Men and Young Women presidents looked at each other and the Young Women President asked: "Is it safe? What if I fall?"

"Not to worry," Vicki said. We harness you up, give you a helmet and a pair of gloves and you're tethered the whole time you're up there. If you happen to fall, each one of us is certified and has the ability to get you down safely."

Agency and Consequences

So, they walked to the tree house and took the lift up. "The kids will have to use the rope ladder," Jim quipped.

* * * * *

Following each evening of work, Jim performed a piano recital. It seemed he could play anything including show tunes, Gershwin, Barry Mannilow, the Carpenters, Bach, Tchaikovsky, Debussy and Prokofiev. When he played, he became a man possessed; he entered a dimension into which only he knew the password. Like Sarah at Hidalgo's controls, he was the master of his instrument.

As Sarah listened to the at once scintillating and emotional music that revealed the soul of the man she loved, she remembered the day she bought the piano. On that day, she almost decided on something a whole lot less than the Steinway grand; but the spirit whispered: "buy the grand." Now, these many months later, it all made sense to her.

48. Youth Conference

CONFERENCE check-in began Friday at 7:00 a.m. as the cars began entering Sarah's property and parked along the drive leading to the house. Most of the adults and youth attending the conference had never been to Sarah's house; and so there were many ogled eyes as they came toward the house and upon entering the main foyer. The check-in tables were located in the hall space in front of the great room. Everyone was given a packet that included a map giving the location of each activity. Sign up for activities, except for general events, was on a first come, first served basis. These included swimming, the ropes course and leadership and management training.

The opening, conducted by Sarah, was held in the great room. A hymn was sung, a prayer given and introductions of the leadership and instructors were made, which included Sarah's family, Jim, Walt and Vicki Dickerson and Mr. Sheffield, who had agreed to talk about Leadership and Management. A discussion of the activities, rules—which included an off limits to the second floor and other specifically marked areas of the house—and dress code was also had. The Stake President then gave the keynote address and then everyone was dismissed to the activities and learning sessions.

*****

At about five o'clock the following morning, Walt and Vicki Dickerson were snuggling in the tree house bed when Vicki said: "This has been an amazing week hasn't it? I mean, we couldn't have asked for a better belated honeymoon. After seeing and working with these great young people, I feel we ought to rethink our decision to not have kids. How would you feel if I told you I now want to have children?"

"I was thinking the same thing," Walt whispered. "But, there's a hitch."

"What's that?" Vicki asked quietly.

"Kids like that aren't an accident. There's something to what these kids are being taught. Look at Jim and Sarah and all those other adult leaders. Then, look at Sarah's mom and her brothers and sisters who came to help her. There's more there than what you see on the surface," Walt explained with a bit of awe and wonder.

"Yeah, I noticed that too. What do you think it is?" Vicki followed up.

"I think it's the church they belong to. Have you noticed it seems to be the focus and center of their lives?" Walt observed.

"Yeah, it seemed pretty obvious. So, what you're saying is, if we want children who have a good chance to become like the young people we saw yesterday, then we need to be members of the church that's providing whatever it is that makes it possible," Vicki said sincerely.

"Vick, I think that's exactly what I'm saying—you can't have the right side of the equation without the left side—the output is the equivalent of the input. But, I also get the sense it's more than that. Have you noticed how happy the leaders are? Have you listened to how they refer to their families and especially their spouses? I think whatever is in this church is as much for adults as it is for kids," Walt continued.

"If that's true, then we should look into it. I'm sure Jim and Sarah would tell us how to proceed without being pushy. I mean, I feel just like you do, but I don't want it crammed down my throat. I want to observe, study, compare and talk together about it. Walt, would that be OK with you?" Vicki asked in a way Walt knew it wasn't really a question.

"That's perfect," Walt confirmed.

"Now that's settled, aren't we still on our belated honeymoon?" Vicki whispered in Walt's ear.

* * * * *

The Saturday events of the youth conference were going well when Vicki got Sarah aside and asked: "I noticed the dress standards for the dance tonight in some of the pre-conference literature some of the kids had. I don't have anything that meets that standard. Is there a possibility I could borrow your car and go get something more appropriate?"

"How about I go with you?" Sarah responded with a smile. "Let me just let a couple people know we're slipping out for a couple of hours and let's go."

As Sarah and Vicki drove and shopped, Vicki recounted the observations Walt and she had and their conversation of that morning.

Sarah listened carefully and explained the Church is family focused and marriage was at the heart and center of it all. She explained marriage in the Church was for Time and Eternity and not just "... until death do us part." She explained how children born to such a marriage were born into an Eternal Family where, as each member of the family kept their covenants (promises with God), the family will remain intact and be linked generation to generation forever.

"But what if you're already married and you weren't married for Time and Eternity?" Vicki asked with concerned sincerity.

"That's easy. If you and Walt decide to join the Church, after a reasonable time-period—usually about a year—you and Walt can go to the temple and have your marriage sealed. If you have any children between now and then, they can be sealed to you. Both ceremonies are just as binding and sacred as if you were married for Time and Eternity in the first place," Sarah explained with warm conviction.

"Wow. Why do I feel warm inside listening to you answer my questions? Vicki inquired.

"Well, that warm feeling is the Holy Ghost letting you know I've told you the truth," Sarah replied simply.

"Sarah, I have another question. All my life I've been more or less a tom boy. Walt and I met on a high ropes course when Jim, Walt and I were doing our certifications. I love being out of doors, hiking, camping, white water rafting and that kind of stuff. I have this list of things I want to do like sky dive, scuba dive, climb Mount Everest, run the Colorado River. I know you understand because, as I hear it, you're one of the best there is at operating large bulldozers. But during this past week, I've felt something. I would never have bought the clothes I bought today before today. It's a stirring inside me. Walt and I talked this morning about starting a family; we were always afraid of bringing kids into the world until we saw and worked with all those youth yesterday and again today. What do you think it is I'm feeling? It's strange and yet I seem to recognize it; but I can't define it," Vicki asked as they were arriving back at

Agency and Consequences

Sarah's property.

Sarah drove in silence for a few moments thinking and praying at the same time. She then said, "Vicki, I feel impressed to tell you what you're feeling is womanhood. My experience is too many women who begin to feel what you're feeling try to ignore it. And if that doesn't work, they subjugate it. The consequence is they don't become the fully mature women they could be. Now, that doesn't mean you have to let go of the dreams you just spoke of. In my case, I'm still passionate about operating bulldozers. But, now I have new passions and dreams. I dream of being a fully mature woman so my soon to be husband can become a fully mature man (that works both ways by the way). I want to be a mother and have the privilege of partnering with my husband and with God in bringing a few of God's children into the world to participate in the test we call mortality. I want to be a fully mature woman so those special gifts women appear to have more fully than men do can be used to bless and heal the world in which we live.

"Vicki, when I see mature womanhood, I see it as the crown jewel in all creation. For example, my mother—she's absolutely the strongest woman I've ever known. I watched her, only months ago, loose to death the most precious person in her life, my dad. They were magnificent together. I don't think their honeymoon ever ended. When they looked at each other, even from across a large room, you could see the laser beams, packed with love, honor and respect, being exchanged. In my dad's eyes, she was a queen, they were best friends and lovers; they teased each other constantly in a fun way; they worked and served together; they loved each other first so we, as kids, could feel safe, secure and uniquely loved. That could not have happened if my mother hadn't made it a priority to develop and nurture her womanhood.

"I wish I could explain it better. Maybe we could spend some time with my mom after church tomorrow and ask her about it," Sarah shared as best as she could as she parked her truck.

"Thank you. What you said feels good. I still have that warm feeling. I would like to talk with your mom though. Womanhood feels neat. I think I like it," Vicki said smiling.

"Let's go to my room and get ready for the evening,"

G. Kenneth Cardwell

Sarah suggested.

* * * * *

That evening at the testimony meeting at the fire ring, just toward the end of the time allotted, Vicki arose and walked to the front. She stood in front of the fire, fidgeting, struggling to find a sense of composure. Finally, her quivering mouth released her opening words: "Ladies and gentlemen and all my new friends, my heart is racing 200 beats a minute and I felt a seemingly irresistible urge to stand and say a few words.

"A week ago, my husband, Walt, and I received a call from our dear friend, Jim Worthington. He asked if we could come and help him build a ropes course for this big event being led by his fiancée, Sarah. I have to admit, we had other plans for the week. You see, we really didn't have much of a honeymoon when we were married four months ago because only one day after our marriage, Jim and my husband, who are both pilots in the Air Force, got a phone call and had to leave right away. But, for some reason, we both felt we should come. And yes, the rumors are true; Walt and I have been staying in the tree house all week.

"When Walt and I were married, we discussed very carefully and in great detail, the world in which we live. We didn't like what we saw and decided we would not be guilty of bringing children into such a world. We had decided to surgically make it impossible for us to be parents. This morning, in the nick of time, we changed our minds. After being here this week and working with you young people and your leaders, we've decided to have a family. But, we realized in making this decision, there's a catch.

"You see, most of you in this council circle are the products of something wonderful. You may not see it; you may not feel it; but Walt and I do—very strongly. We can only guess as to what it may be; we have a good idea it has something to do with the church to which most of you, I suspect, are members. If this church is what it purports to be, we will find it out and we will join and live its teachings with all of our hearts. If it is a hoax, we will discover that instead and will do all in our power to expose it. But, I'm predisposed to believe it is true for the evidence is before me.

"Thank you all for being so kind to Walt and me. This has been the best week, the most wonderful of honeymoons, we could have imagined," Vicki concluded tearfully and then she returned to her seat.

G. Kenneth Cardwell

49. Agency and Consequences

THE following day was full as Sarah, her family, Jim, Walt and Vicki attended church together. Afterwards, they enjoyed a wonderful meal together and then all the women, with glasses of lemonade, convened on the pool deck for conversation.

Vicki had many questions and found not only could Big Sarah answer with knowledge, feeling and conviction, but all of her daughters and her daughter in law, Mary. The most intriguing answer to Vicki's questions came when she asked: "Don't you feel limited by all the rules of your church?"

Big Sarah looked at Vicki with great empathy and said: "That's an issue every one of us in the Church must, at some time, come to grips with. Do the rules or commandments limit us or do they in fact make us free?" Turning to her daughter, she asked: "Sarah, why don't you share your feelings on that question."

"Vicki," Sarah began, "the great gift of mortality is our agency or the right to choose what we will do with our life. The catch comes with the reality that we don't get to choose the consequences—good or bad—that are connected with those choices. As an engineer, I've learned there are laws that govern how things in the world operate. Those laws have been around since before the world was created and operate whether we are aware of them or not. For example, birds have been flying since creation. But it's only been for the past hundred years or so that mankind has understood the laws that make flight possible well enough to use them.

"Let's take the example of the law of gravity. Gravity is what keeps the planets in orbit around the sun; it keeps us from flying away from the earth. When Moses came down from Mount Sinai, let's suppose he came with an eleventh commandment that read 'Thou shalt not fall or jump off a thousand foot cliff for in the moment thou doest it, thou shalt surely die.' Until Isaac Newton came upon the scene, understanding why God would give such a commandment could not have been fully understood. Sure, we would know that falling a thousand feet would have fatal consequences; but the WHY we fall was not

Agency and Consequences

understood. The fact that two masses attract each other with a force equal to the gravity constant times the first mass, times the second mass divided by the square of the distance between them was unfathomable. Even today, most people don't understand this law even when it's explained to them.

"So it is with all the commandments or rules we receive from prophets. Commandments are the shortcuts to keeping the laws of the universe. We may not understand the laws regarding being chaste or keeping the Sabbath holy or paying tithing any more than people understood the law of gravity or the laws that make flight possible. But they are, nonetheless, operative. And our happiness depends on our keeping them, having faith that God knows the laws and all the consequences—good and bad—that are irrevocably connected to them."[1, 2]

"What I think you're saying," Vicki reflected, "is that commandments are given to us because we aren't able to understand the intricacies of the laws they represent. But if we keep the commandments, we avoid the bad consequences of a broken law and receive the benefits associated with keeping the law. Does that sound about right?" Vicki queried.

"I couldn't have said it better," Little Sarah said smiling as a tear trickled down her cheek.

"And so as we keep the commandments, we remain free to continue to grow, to make other choices and experience joy. Breaking commandments subjects us, and often others, to consequences that limit our future choices. These include things like addictions, prison, disease and illness and sometimes death. The tricky thing with this agency and consequences stuff is that they are not isolationist principles. One choice and its consequences add to the conditions and environment within which the next choice is made and its consequence experienced. In addition, we are all connected together. The exercise of agency by a single individual can impact thousands and even millions of people," Mary, Big Sarah's daughter in law, explained.

"You mean someone like Adolph Hitler?" Vicki responded in a questioning tone.

"Yes; but it also means someone like Buddha, Mohammad, Martin Luther and Jesus Christ. And maybe more close to home, a mother and father who set an example—good or bad—that will impact generations of their posterity," Mary expanded.

"Or how about one of your missionaries I've seen on his bicycle who left a college scholarship behind and is paying his own way to teach someone like me?" Vicki quietly and rhetorically questioned as a lump swelled up inside her breast while remembering visiting briefly with a pair of young elders in a Wal*Mart parking lot about week before Jim had called her and Walt.

Vicki felt both overwhelmed and saturated. She could not help thinking there was not a weak woman among them. They were women of great individuality, gifts, training and beauty. There was elegance in each of their beings. They were far from being prudish or puritanical and yet they spoke of intimacy with a man with respect, tenderness and a subtle, discrete anticipation.

That afternoon was a revelation for Vicki. These were women fully aware of the world around them; and yet they seemed to live above the sordidness that was so much of it. They saw through the fog and pollution of societal trends, political correctness and situational truth. It seemed to Vicki they saw things as they really were.[3]

While Vicki never, even for a moment, felt she was less of a woman than the women in Big Sarah's family, she felt she could be more than she was; she felt inspired, she seemed to have a vision of what she could become. And the feeling that she had felt while talking with Sarah as they shopped the day before was now even more intense. She and Walt would have a lot to talk about when they got home.

* * * * *

That evening, Sarah and Vicki took Jim and Walt back to Scott Air Force Base so they could go back to work. The following morning, Sarah took Vicki, her mother and family back to the airport for their flights back home and then it was off to her own office and a desperate attempt to get caught up after one of the most eventful weeks of her life.

Agency and Consequences

50. The Fulcrum

TWO months later, Jim, Sarah, their families and close friends convened at the St. Louis Temple where Brother Richard Oscarson performed, what was in Sarah's mind the most beautiful marriage ceremony she could have ever imagined.

Following the taking of the photos on the temple grounds, Jim took Sarah to the site of their first weekend together, the Embassy Suites in St. Charles, Missouri. Unlike her mother, this was not a time for serious reflection or feeling the least bit afraid. Since that night of near tragedy with Josh Bangeter and having all her doubts erased by her parents, this was the time for releasing all that had been bottled in and lying behind and beneath covenants. Behind the closed and locked doors of their wedding suite, Jim and Sarah Worthington exchanged their total souls with each other and experienced an ecstasy they could only cap with tears of joy. As it was with her parents, they journeyed together into that hallowed, sacred place of Souls, Symbols and Sacraments,[1] into the fire of Eternal Burnings and Whiteness, where those less prepared can never go, apprehend nor comprehend, but seek only in vain.

* * * * *

A short while later, Jim and Sarah returned to Peoria for their reception at their estate. It was a wonderful reception where, instead of gifts, their guests were invited to donate to a worthy charity. One of the best gifts, however, was Walt and Vicki Dickerson's announcement they were going to be baptized as soon as Jim and Sarah got back from their honeymoon and they were expecting their first child. Sarah's mom also had a surprise as she was there with Paul Tenter and they were quite obviously behaving like more than just friends.

The music for the reception was provided by Paul as he sat at the piano and played love song after love song. About midway through the evening, Jim sat down and played a medley for Sarah beginning with the theme from Love Story and moving into the "Laura's Theme" from Doctor Zhivago and ended with "If Ever I would Leave You" from Sarah's favorite play, Camelot.

Following Jim's medley, Paul walked to the piano and

said to all those at the reception: "It appears the groom has been holding out on us. Let's see if he can match this."

Paul then sat down and plunked out the old familiar "Chopsticks" melody that he quickly improvised into a flourish of variations that displayed a technical artistry few knew he had in him. The gauntlet was thrown down.

As Paul was taking his exaggerated bows, Jim walked to the piano. With a huge smile, he gently pushed Paul out of the way, sat on the bench, playfully interlocked his hands and stretched his fingers. He held his hands slightly above the keyboard and very carefully and deliberately played the children's primary tune, "Jesus Wants Me For a Sunbeam."[2] After the first verse, he played an interlude with a complex key change and launched into an extravaganza of piano virtuosity as he wove the simple tune into a series of ever increasing complex arrangements that never lost sight of the original melody.

When Jim finished, Paul walked over and raised Jim's arm into the air declaring him the winner of the dueling piano's contest. Then both men hugged each other and Paul returned to the keyboard to play for the reception.

* * * * *

Following the reception, Jim took his new bride and off they went to the airport where a private jet was waiting. Jim first did a walk-around, kicking the tires and looking at all the other things pilots do before flying a plane. Then, with their luggage, they got on board. Jim closed the door and asked Sarah to sit in the cockpit's right seat. He climbed into the left seat and began going through the pre-flight checklist. A few minutes later, the engines were running and they began their taxi towards the runway. In a few more minutes, they were racing down the runway; Jim rotated the plane and they climbed to their assigned altitude of 36,000 feet as they turned to a heading almost due west.

Jim then said: "Sarah, take the yoke firmly but lightly in your hands and put your feet on the rudder pedals. The master dozer operator you are, you should be able to fly this plane," Jim instructed and complemented.

For the next two hours or so, Jim and Sarah talked and shared visions of the future. Jim then took control of the plane

Agency and Consequences

and put it down with barely a bump in Sun Valley, Idaho. For the next 10 days, Jim and Sarah spent their days hiking, climbing and flying to the next spot on Jim's itinerary. They just completely enjoyed being together.

* * * * *

A few months later, Jim and Sarah would share an experience that would be one of the fulcrums of their married and individual lives. Jim had learned to operate the small 247B dozer and was busy cutting flowerbeds, putting in top soil and planting beautiful flowers while Sarah was on a business trip. Just as he was finishing up and before he could clean the machine and sweep the rest of the soil from the drive where it had been dumped, rain began to fall and his cell phone rang. He was quickly off to Scott for a last minute mission, having barely enough time for a shower and shave. He left, failing to leave a note for Sarah.

When Sarah arrived home, she immediately noticed the flowerbeds and was absolutely delighted. Then she noticed the remaining soil (now turned to mud) on the drive. Expecting to find Jim cleaning the machine, she instead found the garage doors all down. Upon entering the garage, she noticed the muddy 247B parked in its space. She was now worried—what had happened? She ran into the house and looked for a note. There was none either in the kitchen or in the bedroom. All she found were Jim's work clothes in the laundry hamper.

When Jim got home the following evening, he found Sarah just finishing power washing the 247B. When he went to kiss her hello, she nearly turned the power washer on him. "How dare you leave a machine like you did this one," she yelled. "It's no different than putting a horse away wet. Don't you ever, ever, ever, leave one of *my* machines in this kind of condition again. If you can't plan enough time to clean up after you use it, then don't use it. Do you understand me?" Sarah demanded.

Jim just looked at Sarah. "Sarah, I'm sorry. I got a call ...," he tried to explain as Sarah interrupted.

"I don't care. I don't want your excuses. I want *my* machines taken care of. This is not a debate," Sarah yelled over the power washer as her whole body shook with anger.

Jim turned without saying a word, walked out past the

pool and into the woods towards the tree house.

It was well after dark when Sarah, still trembling, took a flash light and headed out towards the tree house. Half way there, a bolt of lightning flashed above her and the thunderclap nearly knocked her to her knees. In mere seconds, she was soaked and the wind was blowing so hard she could barely stay on her feet. The tree house was only a hundred yards away, but it seemed like miles.

When she arrived, the power was out and so her only option was to climb the rope ladder. At times, she felt like a flag whipped on a pole. She called for Jim, but her voice was drowned in the wind.

At last, she reached the porch, crawled to the door and, on her hands and knees, entered. Jim was sitting on the bed with a lantern providing light while he read a book. Sarah pulled herself up using the doorframe and stood in the dim light of the lantern, soaked and exhausted. "I think you better get out of those wet clothes," Jim said softly as lightning flashed and thunder continued to roll outside.

"I'm too tired to even undo the buttons on my shirt," Sarah said as she leaned hard against the doorframe.

Jim got off the bed, helped Sarah to the bathroom and got the wet clothes off her. He took a towel and gently dried her body and got most of the water out of her long hair. He helped her put on dry under clothes, then picked her up and laid her in the bed. After taking off his uniform, he slipped into bed next to her. He turned her on her side and pulled her close. She was shivering from cold. But Jim could also tell she was still tense with her anger. Sarah wrapped her arms around Jim and began kissing him.

"Sarah, we have all night. I think we'd better talk through some things first. Will you try to listen and understand my point of view?" Jim asked as he gently stroked her cheek.

"I'll try," Sarah said quietly as another tremor rippled through her body.

"Sweetheart, I understand how you feel about your machines and how angry you must have felt when it appeared I put your dozer away with no thought of taking care of it. I'm also sorry I didn't leave you a note. I got a call just as it started to rain yesterday and I had just barely enough time to take a quick shower and go to work. That sometimes happens. Remember how Walt and Vicki didn't even get to go on their honeymoon? When I get the call, I have to go. That's my job. And sometimes, like this trip, I can't even call you and tell you where I am or when I'll be home. And I'm afraid until my tour of duty is up and I'm out of the Air Force, that's the way it's going to be. Now, I didn't mean to put the horse away wet. I just didn't have a choice. Do you understand? Can you live with that for a while and realize this incident just might happen again?" Jim asked intently but kindly.

"Jim, darling, intellectually I understand every word you've said. But there's a part of me that's still so angry with you right now. It scares me. I love you more than I can even begin to describe or express. But, I'm worried I can't control what I'm feeling because I don't even know what it is that's causing it. Does that make any sense or am I full of cotton, hay and rags?"[3] Sarah asked as she snuggled even closer to Jim. "Thank you, for being so kind a few minutes ago. I wouldn't have blamed you if you had said: 'Just go back to the house.'"

"First, you're welcome. Do you remember when I said this tree house would be a place where we'd forgive each other? Well, here we are working on our marriage, forgiving, talking, listening, feeling, holding on to each other.

"Now, to your concerns. I have some thoughts about them. I don't know if any of it will make any sense, but maybe it will be something you can consider and pray about. OK? Jim asked kindly.

"I'm listening. But I gotta tell you; I'm feeling very distracted at the moment," Sarah said with a seductive smile and a kiss.

"That's exactly one of the things I want to talk to you about," Jim said as Sarah injected.

"Do you think I'm too horny?" Sarah asked with surprise in her voice.

"No, I don't think you're too horny. I can't think of a man on the planet who would ever think, let alone complain, his wife was too horny. What I wanted to say was you are the most passionate woman I've ever met. Now, when I say passionate, I'm talking about how everything you do is 100 per cent.

"I believe one of the reasons the Lord has blessed you

with wealth is because He knows He can trust you with it. He knows you will be a good steward and you'll use so much of it to build His Kingdom, serve the needy and help worthy causes. In addition, it's the same with your work, your church calling and with all you own. You take care of things. It's like everything is sacred, and to the extent they are all obtained for the purpose of being consecrated to doing good, they are. So, when anything you've so consecrated is mistreated or abused—put away wet— that lights a fire in your belly. You're like a mother tiger protecting her young. Does that make sense?" Jim asked as he lightly massaged Sarah's shoulder.

"Yes, I guess it does but what does that have to do with me desiring to be with you?" Sarah asked as she felt the tension leaving her body.

"Because making me happy has become as much a passion for you as taking care of everything else that belongs to you," Jim said warmly. "And you know what, you're succeeding magnificently."

"Yes, my love, I do want to make you happy. But don't misunderstand. I'm a bit selfish here. I never imagined enjoying anything so much as making love with you. Do you remember when you taught me about Seaman and Lewis and Clark when we were in St. Charles on her first date?" Sarah inquired softly.

"How could I forget our first date," Jim responded.

"Well, you were so enthusiastic telling me that story, I decided to do some reading. One book I found, titled *Meriwether* by David Nevin, is an historical novel, so this particular incident from the book probably never took place. In the book, when Meriwether was a young man, a certain young lady named, Mary Beth, had a real crush on him. They were walking in the moon light one night when he was explaining to her how much he wanted to be invited by Thomas Jefferson to be part of an exploring expedition across the continent. He thought that would please her; but instead she was very upset. She wanted to marry him and have him stay home, make love and have children. She was even so bold as to confess she wanted him and dreamed of him ..."[4] Huh ... well, she may have been too graphic. But, Jim, that's how I feel about you.

"Something you don't know about my blowing up this afternoon is when I got home last night, I was so wanting you.

Being away on business for three days just about drove me nuts; I ached for you. And when you weren't here, not only did you leave before cleaning my—I should say our—machine, you left me alone, stranded on a desert island, with my whole soul brimming with desire. I tried to work; I took a cold shower; when I got into bed, it got worse. I got to the point the only thing that got me through the night and today was to let myself get angry, hateful and ugly. All the things I said to you this evening were well rehearsed," Sarah said tearfully as she confessed her deepest feelings.

    Sarah paused for a few seconds and looked into Jim's understanding eyes. "Sweetheart, I'm really sorry. I needed you last night and now I need you to help me get this, whatever it is, under control. There is one thing I know about it, it is partly your fault. Why? Because I just can't seem to get enough of you," Sarah said now smiling with a bit of tease in her voice.

    "Honey, thank you for being so open. Gosh, I love you. And, I forgive you. Please forgive me for not being here when you needed me," Jim asked sincerely.

    "You're forgiven. You're here now. We're all snuggled up together in our tree house and …," Sarah said almost purring.

    "I have just one more thing to say. Alma, in *The Book of Mormon*, as he was counseling his son, Shiblon, said: '… and see that ye bridle all your passions, that ye may be filled with love.'[5] The key words are 'all your passions.' I think, sometimes, we only think of the obvious passion. In your case over the past two days, two passions overwhelmed you. Like horses without a bridle, they went racing off, bucked a few times and left you in the briar patch," Jim firmly explained.

    "A little bit worse than putting the horse up wet, huh?" Sarah confessed.

    "Well, I don't know about that. What I do know, dear lady, the woman I love, you need to bridle those passions. That doesn't mean hobble them or break them until there is no spirit left like an abused horse. But, as an example, here in our tree house, in our bed room or in a private hotel room, we can romp and play together all we want. In a tennis match, there is no limit to how hard and fast you can hit the ball, all you must do is keep it in bounds. A spirited horse is a wonderful thing, but if he can't be ridden or trusted to follow the commands given through the bridle, he probably isn't worth a lot.[6]

"I want you to imagine six years from now and suppose we have a couple of little children by then. They've just had lunch, there's peanut butter and jam all over the floor and there's spilt milk that needs cleaning up, but little Jimmy or George or whatever name we give him wants to go play with his toy bulldozer in the sand pile. Will you leave the peanut butter, jam and milk on the floor for a while and go play? Will you teach him to clean up the mess when he's teachable (which might be after you've showed him for the 100th time how to properly grade a road with his toy dozer)?" Jim inquired incisively.

There were now tears in Sarah's eyes again as she whispered: "That's exactly what I've been imagining. That's exactly what scares me to death. I know, at least for the first few times when I blow up like I did today, you're thick-skinned enough to walk away; and like you are now, you'll try to help me get a handle on it. But, a precious little child? Jim, I'm terrified. I want to be a mother so bad, but I want to be a good one—like my mom was and is," Sarah said starting to tremble all over again.

"You aren't your mother. You're Sarah Elizabeth Worthington. The Lord loves you and I love you. You will be a fantastic mother. You're already a fantastic wife. But it's just like learning the calculus. It's not going to happen in a day or a week. I have some things to work on too. So let's just work together; OK?" Jim encouraged as he kissed Sarah letting her know he was ready.

"Can I give you a message," Sarah purred.

"Sure. It's a good thing tomorrow is Saturday," Jim replied as he rolled to his stomach.

"By the way, the flower beds are exquisite. They are what I noticed first when I came home yesterday," Sarah whispered in Jim's ear as she began to message his shoulders.

Presently, a soft lightning flash moved across the horizon; seconds later, thunder softly vibrated through the tree house. The rain was now a gentle love song playing on the roof and windows.

Agency and Consequences

51. Ordeal

IT was a beautiful fall evening as Big Sarah left the Stake Center after the Women's General Conference broadcast. There was a lot on her mind. The conference was inspiring and there was much to ponder. But, what was most on her mind these days was Paul Tenter.

She and Paul had being seeing a lot of each other. They had plowed all the old ground including that night almost 30 years ago at her restaurant. So much of what they both had wanted to say those many years ago, had now been said. She had loved Paul those many years ago, but had let him go when he made the choices he made. She had put him behind her and moved on wonderfully and full-heartedly with George. There had been no regrets and the marriage she and George built together was, in her mind, exquisitely wonderful. They had eight wonderful children together and now she was a grandmother. Life just couldn't have been or be any better.

She worried what she felt for Paul now was simply a rebound. She missed George terribly. But Paul wasn't George. She knew that intellectually, but the old flame that had cooled to a barely warm coal in her heart, was now flaming again.

She needed some time to think, to sort things out. She decided to take a drive out along the foothills, around the farms and ranches in the area. She opened her cell phone as she got into her car and called home. Her youngest daughter, Maggie, answered. Sarah explained to her she would be home in about an hour. She started the engine, turned on the headlights and turned off the radio. She backed the car from its parking spot, exited the parking lot and turned towards the country.

* * * * *

About thirty minutes later, Sarah slowed the car as she neared the little dirt road that lead to her and George's picnic spot—the tree still stood in majestic solitude up on the hillside where George had proposed to her. "If I was not in high heels and there was light," she thought, "I would go up and just sit on the soft fall layer of leaves and have a conversation with George

271

the way we used to do. But, ..." Sarah sighed.

Sarah pressed her foot down on the car's accelerator and proceeded to head home. She wasn't going but about forty miles per hour when she felt the thump, thump, thump. "Oh, darn," she said aloud. "It feels like a flat tire."

Sarah pulled the car to the side of the road to take a look. As she did, she noticed a pair of headlights in her rearview mirror. The vehicle pulled up behind her. A tall, lanky man wearing a hunting shirt, bloodstained boots, camouflage trousers and sporting a full beard stepped from a big, 4X4, off-road vehicle. The man strode with a slight limp up to the side of Sarah's car, tapped on her window and spoke loudly so she could hear: "Ma'am, can I help you?"

Sarah turned her head to look at the man through the window. The man was now crouched over looking straight at Sarah. The man looked old. His eyes were dark, cold and lifeless. It seemed, even through the laminated, safety glass of the car, his soul exuded a foul, rancid stench that was utterly malevolent.

At that moment, they both recognized each other and the man began pulling on the door handle of Sarah's car. "Get out of that car, Sarah Kindman," the man shouted. "I've got a score to settle with your family. Now get out of that car," the man continued to shout as he pounded on the window with his fist.

Sarah recognized Josh Bangeter and realized by his aggressive behavior, she needed to get away from him. She put the car in gear and stomped on the gas. The smell of the flat tire spinning and ripping off the rim was immediate. Josh jumped away from the car and ran back to his truck. In just seconds, he was chasing Sarah's fast moving car, which now had sparks flying from the now bare rim of the left front wheel running on the road.

Sarah struggled to keep control of her car and soon realized she would most certainly crash if she pushed it to the speed necessary to outrun Josh in his truck. Josh pulled up alongside and began pushing her onto the shoulder of the road. But that didn't satisfy him. He bumped her hard and sent her into an irrigation ditch alongside the road. Sarah's car went into the ditch so hard the airbags deployed keeping her head from smashing into the steering wheel.

Agency and Consequences

Josh jumped from his truck and quickly located a heavy crowbar in his truck box. In mere seconds, he was smashing the driver's side door window. He reached in, unlocked and then opened the door. "Don't fight me, woman," Josh yelled angrily, "or I'll kill you with this crowbar here and now. Get out of the car," he demanded loudly one more time.

Sarah weighed her options quickly and realized she had none except to comply with Josh's demands. She unbuckled her seatbelt and started to move out of the seat when Josh grabbed and then yanked her out of the car. He picked her up like a sack of potatoes walked to his truck and stood her up hard against its passenger door. He turned her around and pulled her hands behind her and tied them tightly with a short length of rope he fetched from his open truck box. As he did, Sarah did has her daughter had done those many years ago—she stomped on his foot with the high heel on her right foot. But, all that did is break the heel off her shoe against the steel toe of Josh's boot. Josh violently pulled her away from the door, spun her around and yelled in her face: "You Kindman bitches are all the same."

Josh opened the truck door, lifted her inside and then buckled the seatbelt around her. He slammed the truck door shut, slammed the truck box closed and ran to the driver's side, jumped into the truck, slammed his door closed, slammed the gear shift into second gear and took off like a drag racer back onto the road. Josh sped down the road, a demon possessed.

So far, no one had seen what happened and Josh needed to get off this road and head up into the mountains as quickly as he could, even if meant taking a rough, unimproved route. About five miles down the road, Josh made a quick right turn up a barely noticeable farm road and was soon invisible to any car passing along the road where he had kidnapped Sarah.

Josh began talking in a soft, pleasant, gentlemanly voice: "Well now, Mrs. Kindman, why don't we start over. You sure do look beautiful tonight. It was a real pleasant surprise to find you lonely, stranded and in need of a man back there on the road."

"Let me see ... if I remember correctly, your husband was killed about a year back and I'll bet you, being the faithful, church-going, virtuous woman you are, haven't been with a man in all that time. Well, tonight is your lucky night cause I'm going to fix that for you. It'll be just like we was married. Soft ...

gentle ... slow. We'll just take our time and get to know each other. Then, well ... well it will just feel so good. It'll be just like we was meant for each other ... the way it should have been with Little Sarah and me," Josh said in a mocking, sarcastic, vengeful tone. He then laughed a sick, boisterous, ugly laugh.

Sarah sat tied, erect, head up, eyes straight ahead and said nothing.

* * * * *

Meanwhile, Sarah's daughter, Maggie, was worried. Her mother always called when something delayed her from being home when she said she would be there. And when Sarah didn't answer her cell phone, Maggie decided to call her brother, George.

"George, this is Maggie," Maggie said as she heard her brother say "Hello."

"Hey, what's up sis; is everything alright?" George inquired.

"I don't know. Mom called and said she'd be home around ten, it's now eleven and she's not here, she hasn't called and doesn't answer her phone," Maggie answered in a concerned voice.

"Did she say where she was going?" George probed.

"She just said she needed to think and was going for a short drive," Maggie responded.

"Huh, that means she could be anywhere. Just a second, I've got a beep, maybe that's her," George said hopefully.

"George?" the voice said on the phone.

"Yes, this is George. How may I help you," George responded.

"George, this is Sheriff Tom Roberts and I'm out on County Road D, just past the old Hornsby Farm and we found your mom's car in the irrigation ditch. I think you better get here right away," Sheriff Roberts said with great concern.

"Is my mom OK; is she hurt?" George inquired with alarm.

"George, I don't know. She isn't here. It appears there's been some foul play," Sheriff Roberts reported.

"Alright, Tom, I'll be right there. And thanks for the call," George said with great anxiety.

"Maggie, I'm back. That was Tom Roberts. It appears

Agency and Consequences

there's been some kind of accident. Mom's car was just found up on County Road D. I'm not sure about mom's condition just yet. Tom wants me to go over there. Would you mind waiting up for a while just in case mom calls? I'll call you as soon as I know something," George instructed.

"Sure, but make sure you call me as soon as you know anything," Maggie firmly asked.

"No problem; and you do the same, OK? I'd better get going. Talk to you soon," George said and then hung up the phone.

As George laid down the phone, his wife, Mary, came into the kitchen where he had been doing some late night work when Maggie called, and asked: "Sweetie is anything wrong?"

"I just got off the phone with both Maggie and Tom Roberts. Mom isn't home and her car has been found in an irrigation ditch up by the Hornsby Farm and she's nowhere around. Tom thinks there is some foul play and asked me to go over there," George reported obviously a bit shaken.

"What can I do to help?" Mary asked with great concern.

"Do you think you could go over to Mom's and give Maggie some company?" George responded.

"Sure, I'll get the baby, pack up a few things and be over there in just a few minutes. Should I call anybody?" Mary inquired.

"I don't think so just yet. Let's wait and see what Tom has to say," George replied as he grabbed a jacket and his car keys.

George looked at Mary and said: "I need a hug." They hugged and kissed each other and George was out the door.

* * * * *

At about midnight, Josh pulled his truck up to a hunter's cabin far into the high forest. He got out of the truck, unlocked the cabin and came back for Sarah. He unbuckled the seatbelt and lifted her out of the truck. Sarah made no resistance as he mockingly carried her across the threshold of the cabin.

The cabin was surprisingly neat and there were the remnants of a fire still in the fireplace. Josh sat Sarah on the bed and then closed and locked the door. He asked Sarah if she needed to use the toilet. She nodded that she did. Josh untied her hands and walked her to the little shower room that had a toilet and sink. "Don't be long and don't have any clothes on when you come out or I'll ... rip!" Josh instructed firmly as he gestured he'd rip her clothes off if she came out with them on.

In the shower room, Sarah's first thought was to pray for help. She whispered with all the energy of her soul: "Dear Father, please help me. I've lived the best I could all of my life and I don't deserve what's about to happen to me. Please, Father, please intervene and protect me from being raped; in the name of Jesus Christ, amen."

Sarah waited and listened as a warm comforting spirit came over her and spoke into her mind. "Sarah, my dear daughter, I fully understand your condition. I lived a perfect life and didn't deserve the cross. As I said to my servant Joseph, I say to you:

> 'And if thou shouldst be cast into the pit, or into the hands of murderers, and the sentence of death passed on thee; if thou be cast into the deep; if the billowing surge conspire against thee; if fierce winds become thine enemy; if the heavens gather blackness, and all the elements combine to hedge up the way; and above all, if the very jaws of hell shall gape open the mouth wide after thee, know thou, my [daughter], that all these things shall give thee experience, and shall be for thy good.
>
> 'The Son of Man hath descended below them all. Art thou greater than he? Therefore, hold on thy way, and the priesthood shall remain with thee; for [his] bounds are set, [he] cannot pass. Thy days are known, and thy years shall not be numbered less; therefore, fear not what man can do, for God shall be with you forever and ever.'[1]

"And the paraphrased words I caused to be written by my servants Alma and Mormon:

Agency and Consequences

> 'And [I] doth suffer that [he] may do this thing, or that [he] may do this thing unto [you], according to the hardness of [his heart], that the judgments which [I] shall exercise upon [him] in [my] wrath may be just ….'[2]
>
> 'But, behold, the judgments of God will overtake the wicked; ….'[3]

"Know my daughter I am with thee. Fear not, amen," the voice in her mind concluded.

Sarah removed her clothes, let down her hair, wrapped a towel around her body and opened the shower room door. "I'm going as a lamb to the slaughter,"[4] Sarah thought to herself.

Josh was standing by the now blazing fireplace and even he was struck with amazement at Sarah's noble beauty. For a moment, he thought better of what he was about to do, but revenge was his master and it had completely taken over his soul. "I told you to come out with nothing on," he said as he walked up to Sarah and yanked the towel from her body.

Josh picked Sarah up, threw her onto the open bed and took his own clothes off as fast as he could. He crawled into the bed next to Sarah and pulled up the covers. He feigned gentle caresses. Then he raped her.

* * * * *

At the site where Sarah's car was found in the irrigation ditch, a full accident and crime investigation were taking place. As the incident was being reconstructed, it was determined Sarah's car had experienced a flat tire and Sarah had pulled to the side of the road. They could also tell a large four-wheel drive vehicle had pulled up behind her and the driver had gotten out and walked up to where Sarah had pulled off the road. They also could see where Sarah had attempted to drive the car with the flat tire and the four-wheel drive vehicle had spun its tires to give chase. There were also remnants of the destroyed tire from Sarah's car along the road. There were gouges in the pavement made by the car's tireless rim. Paint from the four-wheeler's body was found on Sarah's car as a consequence of the four-wheeler being used to push the car into the ditch. And Sarah's broken high heel was near the spot where the four-wheeler had stopped after Sarah's car had gone into the ditch. All this combined with the smashed driver's window of Sarah's car suggested strongly Sarah had been kidnapped.

Plaster molds of the four-wheeler's tire treads and the apparent assailant's boots were made. Other evidence, including the transferred paint, dozens of photographs and Sarah's broken high heel were gathered. The car was towed from the ditch. It was then taken to the police station where the forensic team would go over it with a fine-toothed comb.

About five miles from the incident site, the investigators noticed where it looked like the same four-wheeled vehicle had recently turned off the road and onto an unimproved farm access road. They took additional photographs and plaster molds of tread marks.

As Sheriff Roberts and George discussed the evidence and the fact Sarah was nowhere to be found and no one living in any of the scattered farm houses along the road saw or heard anything unusual, it was concluded Sarah was apparently kidnapped. They also concluded the kidnapper recognized who she was and very likely decided to kidnap her for ransom.

George decided rather than give that kind of news to Maggie and his wife, Mary, over the phone, he would drive home. They could then also call the rest of the family.

As soon as George walked into his mother Sarah's house, both Maggie and Mary started asking whether Sarah was all right. George explained what appeared to have happened with the flat tire and apparent kidnapping. They knelt in prayer and then George proceeded to call all his brothers and sisters and Mary called her mother, Sarah's best friend, and her dad, who was Sarah's Bishop.

As soon as George finished his call to his sister, Little Sarah, she called her CEO, Mr. Sheffield, and asked for a leave of absence until her mother could be located. He told her to get to the airport where one of the company jets would be fueled and ready and for Jim to fly her back home right then.

George also thought it appropriate to call Paul Tenter. Paul immediately got dressed and came to Sarah's house. The vigil was on.

By morning there were reporters, TV cameras and a gathering crowd wanting to help in anyway each could. Church

Agency and Consequences

services in Sarah's home ward were confined to just the Sacrament Service as search parties were organized and sent out to their respective search areas. Mary's mother, Sarah's best friend, Alice, opened Sarah's Place, called in her staff and provided meals and sack lunches to all the volunteers.

* * * * *

It was just after 10:00 in the morning. Josh had just raped Sarah again as he had every couple of hours since midnight. When he finished this time, instead of tying Sarah to the bed, and then sit by the fireplace and drink whiskey, he fell dead asleep, face down on the bed. Sarah just lay there not sure what to do when the Voice of the Spirit spoke in her mind saying: "Get thee up for Josh has murdered thee in his heart and will surely not leave thee alive until tomorrow. Leave him tied in his own bed and get thee out of this cabin. For the sword of my justice shall swiftly come upon him. Thy family and friends do search for thee and thou shalt be found soon."

Sarah wasted no time. She got out of the bed, put her under clothes on, found a convenient log and hit Josh at the base of his head knocking him out cold. She crossed his wrists behind his back, took one of the ropes Josh had used to tie her with, and lashed them together using a diagonal lashing she had tied so many times when her boys were earning their pioneering merit badges in Boy Scouts. She then did the same thing with Josh's ankles. She pulled the bed covers over him, found some clothes, boots, a jacket and the keys to Josh's truck. She put a couple more logs on the fire and then went out the front door of the cabin, climbed into the truck and soon was headed down the road away from the cabin.

As Sarah bumped along down the mountain road, she couldn't help but wonder about the message from the Spirit indicating "... the sword of my justice shall swiftly come upon him." She had been violently violated by a man whose sole intent was to show he was a man and he could prevail over a Kindman woman. Little Sarah had foiled his attempted rape of her back when she and Josh were seniors in high school. What distorted view of manhood and womanhood had so overtaken his soul that he had become no more than a wild beast intent on abusing a woman in the most cruel and violent manner? She wondered how many other woman had been hauled off or lured to that cabin, used for a time, discarded and maybe even killed? She felt an overwhelming sense of pity and remorse for the man. She knew God had spoken to her and Josh would soon, by some means, face his maker in no condition to do so with honor.

In that instant, Sarah looked to her left out the window. Along the ridge above her, she saw something she had never seen before in these mountains. A pack of wolves loped easily along, going in the opposite direction she was traveling, back toward the cabin. She stopped the truck, applied the parking brake and took it out of gear. She closed her eyes and prayerfully just wept for Josh. As she did, the Spirit whispered to her mind again saying: "My justice shall be just; for the blood of many cries from the ground for vengeance. He '... shall become meat for dogs ....'"[5] Her immediate response was to turn the truck around and try to save him; but she felt a powerful feeling of restraint. So, she just continued to pray.

About 15 minutes later, Sarah proceeded again down the mountain road. She wasn't sure where she was, but the road was heading down the mountain following a little stream of water off to her right.

She continued down for about an hour when the road came to an open clearing. Suddenly, a helicopter dropped down right in front of her. Men were aiming at her with rifles and a loud speaker blared: "You, in the truck, stop immediately. Get out and lay on the ground face down with your hands spread out in front of you."

Sarah got out of the truck and did as she was told. As Sheriff Roberts got close to her, she said: "Tommy, it's I, Sarah Kindman. I'm all right. I've been raped; but I need to talk to you."

"Sister Kindman, is it really you?" Sheriff Roberts asked with relieved surprise.

"Yes, Tommy, it's I," Sarah said as Sheriff Roberts laid his rifle down and helped Sarah get off the ground.

"We thought you were Josh Bangeter. We got his finger prints off your car and we knew it was a red truck that pushed your car off the road ..." Sheriff Roberts explained apologetically.

"Tommy, I'm so glad to see you," Sarah said, now crying

Agency and Consequences

as she gave the Sheriff a hug. "I left Josh tied up in his bed in a cabin about an hour or so up that road," Sarah reported.

"OK Sister Kindman. We'll go get him. But first, let's get you to the hospital," Sheriff Roberts said kindly as he lead Sarah to the helicopter.

"Tommy," Sarah said with great urgency. "You've got to get to that cabin quickly. I think Josh's life is in danger."

"Why's that?" Sheriff Roberts asked. "Didn't you say he was tied up?"

"Yes, he's tied up; but I saw a pack of wolves headed towards the cabin," Sarah replied with great concern. Then she said in a strong whisper so only Sheriff Roberts would hear: "Tommy, the Lord told me the blood of many was crying for vengeance. If I'm right, you'll find some bodies up there too."

"Sister Kindman, thank you. We'll go investigate right now," Sheriff Roberts said kindly as he helped her into the helicopter.

In a matter of just a minute or so, Sarah was on her way to the hospital. Sheriff Roberts was quickly on the radio letting the search team and Sarah's family know they had found her.

When Sarah arrived at the hospital emergency room, her whole family and it seemed half the town, along with the news media were surrounding the helicopter pad. Sarah was taken quickly inside with her family and Paul Tenter trailing right behind. News reporters were giving their reports that were as much speculation as fact.

* * * * *

About an hour later, Sheriff Roberts and a team of deputies surrounded Josh's cabin. Sarah had told him she had left him tied in his bed. However, they still approached the cabin with caution and called on a bullhorn for Josh to come out. But, nothing moved.

They approached the cabin carefully and soon noticed the back entrance was open. As they got closer, they observed the paw prints of a pack of wolves going into and out of the cabin. A trail of heavy bloodstains led from inside the cabin.

Upon entering the cabin, the ghastly reality of Josh Bangeter's end was fully evident. The pack of hungry wolves had entered through the back door and finding Josh tied helplessly in the bed, had quickly dispatched him.

*****

Back in the hospital emergency room, Sarah was examined thoroughly and the necessary evidence was gathered for a possible trial. Shortly after, Sarah was taken to a room where she would spend the night.

When word came Josh was dead—killed by a pack of wolves, Sarah broke into tears. Noticing her daughter, Sarah, had her laptop computer with her, she asked her to type the story as she then told it to her family and Paul. The details of her ordeal and the revelations she had received were almost unbelievable to them. As Sarah concluded, she bore her testimony saying: "Now I understand a little better my heritage and the Atonement. I know in our deepest, most terrible trials, God still loves us and sustains us. He doesn't always shield us from the evil use of others' agency; but he always will help us endure and make it an experience that will sanctify and purify us."

Sarah reached for and took Paul's hand, looked him in the eyes and said: "Paul, I went for that drive last night to think about us. I want you to know I love you. I'm going to need your help to heal. Is that OK?"

Paul bent over, gave Sarah a tender kiss and said: "I'll be right here beside you all the way."

A nurse came in and told everyone it was time for Sarah to get some sleep—she hadn't had any for nearly two days. The nurse pushed some medication into Sarah's IV and soon she was asleep.

George invited the family to say a prayer and then they organized a rotating, two-hour schedule of who would stay. Little Sarah took the first shift.

Just when everyone else left, Mr. Sheffield walked in the room. Little Sarah got out of her chair and she and Mr. Sheffield briefly hugged each other. "Mr. Sheffield, thank you for coming. But … why are you here?" Sarah asked with some surprise in her voice.

"Your dad was not only one of my best customers, he was one of my best friends. Whenever we were together, for business, on the golf course or having a meal, the one thing, the one person, who was always, always in his heart and on his mind

Agency and Consequences

was your mother. I've never met a man so devoted to his wife. So, I just had to come and see if there was anything I could do. My wife, Sally, also sends her prayers and hope that everything will be OK with your mom," Mr. Sheffield responded very tenderly.

* * * * *

Meanwhile, during the rest of the day at Josh Bangeter's cabin, the forensic team found precious little of Josh Bangeter's body. The bloody bed blankets and mattress would provide the DNA to prove it was his blood. In the days that would follow, assorted bones would be found scattered in the surrounding woods that also belonged to him.

In a chest, found at the foot of Josh's bed in the cabin, were found a bloodstained tarp, a hunting knife, a bone saw, a note book and charred human leg and arm bones that had obviously been cut with the bone saw from their bodies.

As Sarah had predicted, a search of the area soon revealed the location of a half dozen shallow graves. The remains of six women were found, all of whom, it would be learned, were on missing persons lists in nearby states. Not surprisingly, as each woman's remains was found, it was missing an arm or a leg. In each of the graves with the decomposed body was a tourniquet with a stick through it. The soil around each body indicated a lot of blood was lost while it lay in the ground.

The note book, or as Josh called it, *My Log of Sexual Revenge*, detailed each woman's name, where he found her and all the sordid and brutal details of her last hours alive.

It would start as a friendly, two consenting adults, hooking up and an apparent good time at the cabin, usually lasting a couple of days. Then Josh would force the woman to dig her own grave. He would put the tarp on the bed and tie his naked victim to the bedposts. He then did the amputation while the woman was alive using the hunting knife, the bone saw and a tourniquet to slow the bleeding. One can only imagine the agony of the woman as she lost an arm or leg in such a brutal manner. One can only imagine her horror, if she were conscious, of watching her own arm or leg put on a spit, roasted in the fireplace and then eaten by her tormentor. One can barely imagine the sickness in her stomach as he would offer her a piece asking: "Are you hungry?" But he doesn't just offer, he forces a piece in her mouth and makes her chew and swallow it. Most of the time, she would then throw up all over herself. By this time, the woman had lost enough blood she had no strength to resist as he would carry her to and put her in her grave. He then raped her, loosened the tourniquet and buried her alive as she bled to death. All this, in his mind, is like his car being mutilated and buried by Sarah Elizabeth Kindman.

As recorded in the Book of Mormon, like some of the Nephites in their last days, the evidence showed clearly what Josh Bangeter had become and the fate of the women whose remains were found:

> "... and after depriving them of that which was most dear and precious above all things, which is chastity and virtue—and after [he] had done this thing, [he] did murder them in a most cruel manner, torturing their bodies even unto death; and after [he had] done this, [he devoured] their flesh like unto [a] wild [beast], because of the hardness of [his heart]; and [he did] it for a token of bravery."[6]

Josh Bangeter had become a rapist, serial killer and a cannibal.

And as he had murdered and eaten the flesh of his victims, so it was done unto him. The pack of wolves ...? Well, they had never been seen before and were never seen or heard of again.

Agency and Consequences

52. Healing

SARAH left the hospital the next afternoon. She left dressed as if she were going to Church. She looked positively elegant. Outside the hospital, reporters were still on the prowl looking for a story. Sarah graciously took questions and said all she could say given there was still an on-going investigation.

* * * * *

In the days that followed, each family of the six women whose remains was found at Josh's cabin was brought to the city. The best accommodations were provided as arrangements were made to have their loved one's remains sent home—all paid for by Sarah and Paul.

Sarah also arranged to visit with Josh Bangeter's parents. This meeting was as tender and full of tears as there ever could be. Josh's parents were good, honest, virtuous people who had given much to the Church and the community. The rest of their children were strong, upright and faithful having served missions and had become fully contributing and exemplary adults, husbands, wives and parents. This stain upon them and their name put there by the life and death of their son and brother, Josh, was one they didn't deserve any more than Sarah and those other woman deserved to be victims; for indeed, they were all victims.

But the tragic results of this life gone so terribly astray were still being literally uncovered. Josh's notebook or log, found in his footlocker at the cabin, gave a history of Josh's travels. Police departments across the country were soon finding more and more remains like those found at the cabin. It was a burden Sarah was going to help the Bangeters shoulder and they would help her.

To help what was becoming a large number of victims, including illegitimate children, Sarah, Paul, Little Sarah and the Bangeters set up a relief fund. With the help of law enforcement, social workers and the courts, a procedure was established that made every reasonable attempt to confirm a woman's claim as a victim of Josh Bangeter. Some, because of embarrassment had left the area. Therefore, if they returned and their claim was validated, their travel expenses were reimbursed.

Despite all their attempts to provide these service to Josh's victims, Little Sarah found herself struggling as she realized Josh's motivation for doing what he did was apparently to satisfy his perceived need for retaliation and revenge. All due to the way she had exposed him and destroyed his car those many years ago. From evidence found in his *Log of Sexual Revenge*, he apparently had vowed no woman would EVER get away and do that to him ever again. And that pattern, those sights and sounds, witnessed at her demonstration, were relived each time he seduced a woman and then carried her off to his cabin.

Those many years ago, Little Sarah's hope in doing the demonstration was to warn young men and woman of the tragedies of illicit and predatory sex. She had also hoped Josh would realize he couldn't get away with that kind of behavior; that soon or late, someone would hold him accountable. Now, she felt all she did was incite him. As the number of victims grew and the thought that her mother could have lost her life haunted her, she often found herself in tears and feeling responsible.

Setting up the fund and working with the victims became very cathartic for Sarah, Little Sarah and the Bangeters. Little Sarah and Jim were often flying back for meetings and interviews with victims. But, for Little Sarah, it was the Bangeters themselves whose constant love and reassurance helped her to realize what she did at the demonstration was right. They reminded her it was they who had approved of and supported her fully on that day—it wasn't Josh's car she and Hidalgo crushed and buried—it was theirs.

Another benefit of setting up and administering the fund was Sarah and Paul spent a lot of time together. And as the work on the fund began to level off, they found other ventures to work on together.

* * * * *

It was now about a two years since George's death in the accident near Boise, Idaho. On a beautiful Saturday evening as

Agency and Consequences

Sarah and Paul were leaving the Stake Center after the Adult Session of Stake Conference, Paul suggested they take a little drive up the canyon. Sarah said, as Paul opened the passenger door of his Mercedes: "I think I'd like that."

They drove up along the switchbacks of the mountainside and came to a place where a scenic turnout had been created and they could look out over the valley below. Paul drove the car into the look out, got out, walked around to the other side and let Sarah out of the car.

There was a soft, warm breeze blowing and the scent of fresh-cut alfalfa from the valley below was strong. "Wow, just look at that down there. All those lights. I remember when there weren't half so many," Sarah said.

"Yeah, it's all George's fault. He excavated all the roads and put in all the sewer, water and power lines—at least he cut the trenches for it all," Paul quipped.

"It was a lot of work; some real long days. Sometimes he'd come home so tired and then he'd have a Church assignment to go to or I would need some help or one of the kids needed help with some home work. Then he'd get what he called his second wind and just keep going—happy, smiling, ready to tease or tell a joke," Sarah reminisced.

"Sarah," Paul said softly; "I'm sure I can't begin to comprehend how much you miss George. I know I can't ever take his place. I'm sure I'm not even half the man he was and still is; but I would be honored if you'd consider getting married," Paul asked a bit timidly.

Sarah turned and looked Paul straight in the eyes. "Paul Tenter, are you asking me to marry you?"

"I am," Paul replied with his more usual confidence.

"Then I accept. I accept with all my heart," Sarah answered warmly. "But, there's something you need to understand," Sarah said firmly.

"And what's that?" Paul asked a bit quizzically.

"You're right. You're not the man George was. I don't expect you to be. You're different. You've come a very different and difficult path to become the man you are. But, you're every bit of the worthy, spiritual and wonderful man George was. If you weren't, I would have been done with you long ago. From the time we dated in high school, I saw greatness in you. You've

287

become all I ever imagined you could be and more. You've helped thousands with your charity work; you've thrilled and inspired thousands more as you've sat at the consol of an organ. You've been a father to my children and grandfather to my grandchildren; you were there for me through the most difficult ordeal of my life. And what's most important, I think and feel George would approve. He loved you, Paul. It's when I saw his love for you the day he found you in that sewer hole my heart finally melted for him. And I've loved you since I was just a young woman. That takes a lot of man to hold a woman's heart that long," Sarah said feeling all warm inside.

"You did let me go; you didn't wait for me," Paul said intently.

"Yes, I let you go. The Lord released me from my responsibility to wait for you the night you left my restaurant in a rage and you yelled at me to leave you the hell alone. I did; you gave me no choice; and I had and will have for Eternity the most wonderful of marriages a woman could ever hope and dream for. Most days, I never even thought of you. I had a new life and new responsibilities as wife and mother. You had a new life to find and as you've said, some challenges to face and responsibilities to accept. Both of our lives have been and will always be in God's hands. Are you angry I didn't wait?" Sarah asked with some concern.

"No. I just hadn't heard the whole story told that way in all these years. Thank you for being straight with me. That's one thing I could always count on. I always felt darned uncomfortable; but now, I treasure it as a genuine blessing, an expression of your love," Paul said warmly.

"So, as Captain Von Trapp asked Maria: 'Is there anyone I should ask for permission to marry you?'"[1] Paul asked kindly as they were now kissing each other lightly.

"I guess the answer is the same for us as it was for the Captain and Maria—ask the children," Sarah whispered in between kisses.

* * * * *

The following day, after the regular session of Stake Conference, the entire Kindman family, excepting Little Sarah and Jim, were gathered for Sunday dinner. As the dinner concluded, Sarah brought the phone to the table and called her daughter. "Sarah, is Jim there with you?" Sarah asked as Little Sarah answered the phone.

"Yes, mom, he's right here. I'm glad you called; we have something to tell you. Who else is there?" Little Sarah asked with excitement in her voice.

"The whole family is here and Paul is here too. So what's your news?" Sarah asked with a tone and a smile that said she already knew what the news was.

"Well, after really trying hard for a long time, Jim and I are expecting a baby," Sarah said in that effervescent way that was all her own.

"As long as you enjoyed all the trying," George jabbed as his wife, Marry, jabbed him in the ribs.

"Well, as a matter of fact, it was just OK," Sarah responded.

"That's not what she told me," Jim chimed in.

By now everyone was laughing and jumping in with their congratulations.

"As you can tell, honey, we're all excited for you and Jim. And just so you know, I hope you had a good time getting this little one on the way. Dare I say it? Of course I dare. I did with every one of mine!" Sarah admitted. "It was wonderful."

"So, mom, was there any special reason for your call this afternoon or were you just inspired knowing Jim and I had some exciting news to share?" Sarah asked half suspecting what was coming.

"Well, I'm going to let Paul answer that one," Sarah said as everyone in the room and in Peoria looked at each other as they all said in unison: "It's about time."

"Well, since everyone already seems to know, I guess we don't have to go through the formality," Paul said matter-of-factly.

"Huh huh," the Kindman clan groaned all together.

"No way Jose," Maggie chimed in. "You gotta ask us. Right, family?"

"Right!!!" everyone shouted together.

"Alright; alright. Well, your mom and I ... well, we've known each other for a long time, since high school actually. And, well ... well we've been really good friends and ... well ... a

... since your dad was passed away, the flame between us has been rekindled and with your ... all of you ... I'd like to ask permission to take your mom's hand in marriage," Paul asked feeling very intimidated.

"How do you plan to support her, Paul?" George asked seriously.

"And do you promise to always be kind?" Maggie asked.

"Now remember, you must be frugal, don't expect to have everything your mom and dad had right away," Little Sarah chimed in.

"And have you asked mom yet?" Alice asked.

"Yeah, what if she doesn't want to marry you?" Tom chortled.

"You guys are brutal," Sarah interrupted. "If we thought you were going to give us the third degree, we'd have gone off and eloped," Sarah said smiling knowing her family was just enjoying the fun of the moment.

"OK," George said taking charge. "All in favor of giving mom permission to marry Paul, say aye."

"AYE," they all resounded.

"All opposed, say nay," George followed up in parliamentary fashion.

The room and phone were silent.

"The Ayes have it," George said officially. "Paul, welcome to the family."

"I'm not a member of the family yet," Paul retorted.

"If we know mom, and I think we all know mom, trust me, that won't take very long," George said as he extended his hand and the family laughed.

"Well, children," Sarah said as she stood up and tried to be just a little condescending; "I want to thank you for allowing your dear old mom permission to get married. You are now all excused from the table and don't you dare leave, any of you, until the dishes are done. And as for my oldest daughter, you take good care of yourself and let me know if I, in my old feeble way, can be of assistance."

Moments later they were all hugging and congratulating Sarah and Paul. It was a joyous afternoon and evening as the family rallied together again at this special time to give their support and love to their beloved matriarch and the man she had

Agency and Consequences

chosen as her companion.

* * * * *

Then, as George had predicted, Paul and Sarah were married just six weeks later in an early morning, for time only, ceremony at the temple. It was a wonderful experience for the entire family.

When they arrived home from the temple, Sarah's dear friend and Attorney for many years, John Shutzer, came only minutes later. When he entered the living room, there was a wry smile on his face and an old manila folder in his hand. He walked to where Sarah was sitting and said: "Sarah, I have a gift for you and Paul from George."

He handed Sarah the folder as she looked at her son.

"No, Sarah, not your son. This is from George. This folder has been in my safe at the office for almost 30 years," John explained. As you can see on the letterhead, my instructions were to give this to you on the day you and Paul were married. I have no idea what's in the envelope except for the key. I'll see you later at your reception." John excused himself and George accompanied him to the door.

Sarah examined the instructions to their attorney on the letterhead. The salutation on the envelope read: "To My Dearest Sarah and friend, Paul Tenter, on Your Wedding Day." The handwriting, on both the letterhead and one of George's old business envelopes, was, unmistakably, George's.

"Sarah, would you please get me the letter opener from the desk," Sarah asked her daughter as her hands nervously handled the folder and envelope.

Little Sarah retuned with the opener and handed it to her mother. Sarah nervously inserted the letter opener into the end of the envelope and carefully cut the end of the envelope open. Inside were a key and a single piece of letterhead with the following written in George's hand.

"To our favorite spot,
Go with shovel and pick.
To our favorite spot,
'Neath the oak's largest arm,
Where our blanket lay,

G. Kenneth Cardwell

> First remove the sod
> 3 by 2 feet and
> 'Bout three feet down,
> A Strange Treasure find.
> To our favorite spot,
> Where a diamond I placed
> Upon your hand,
> A Strange Treasure find."

"What does it mean, mom," George asked quietly.

"Where is this place, this 'favorite spot,'" Sarah asked.

"It's the picnic spot where your dad and I became engaged and where we went often alone to talk and pray. If I hadn't been in heels the night I was kidnapped, I would have gone there to think. I passed right by it; but …" Sarah answered as she wiped a tear from her cheek.

"What do you want to do," Paul asked gently.

"I think I want to get a shovel and pick and go see what's there.

George quickly grabbed a shovel and pick from the garage. They all piled into their cars and went in a caravan following Paul and Sarah. About thirty minutes later, they were all standing on the little hill where a single oak tree presided in magnificent glory. Sarah looked again at the paper and then pointed to the spot. "There, remove the sod in a 3 by 2 foot rectangle and dig down about 3 feet.

"Do I make the rectangle longer this way or that way," George asked.

"Your father didn't say. Just pick," Sarah responded.

"That was a play on words," Tom remarked ready with the pick.

There had been a gentle, soaking rain for two days prior and so removing the sod and digging were fairly easy except for the several substantial roots that were encountered.

At just over two feet down, the shovel struck something hard. "I think we're there," George remarked.

"Yeah, I think your right," Tom said as he shoveled more carefully.

Soon they had the top cleared and were working round the sides so they could lift the object, the "Strange Treasure," out of the hole.

"What do you think it is?" Little Sarah questioned.

"I haven't the foggiest idea. Your father was always one for surprises," Big Sarah answered.

"OK guys, all the men on your knees around the hole and let's see if we can lift it out," George instructed.

Quickly all the men responded as they got on their knees and all reached down and got their fingers around the edge of the object at the bottom of the hole. George quarterbacked: "On the count of three. 1 ... 2 ... 3." They all lifted together and out it came. They scooted it to the downhill side of the hole and then just stared.

"What in the world? Does anyone have a pocket knife?" Sarah queried.

Jim stepped forward, removed a knife from his pocket and presented it to Sarah. "No, Jim, I can't. Would you please remove the wrapping?" Sarah asked trustingly.

Jim carefully cut at the duct tape and unfolded the wrap from the box. "It's a gun case or at least it looks like a gun case," Paul observed.

Sarah handed Paul the key and asked: "Would you open it, please."

Paul took the key, bent over, unlocked and released one latch and then the other. He lifted the lid and as if he'd seen a ghost, he closed it again as he jumped back from the case and said: "I remember this. But, it can't be. Alice told me you took all this stuff and buried it or at least she thought you buried it."

Sarah's mind raced. It went back to that night when Paul was in her restaurant, when he left in a rage and told her to leave him alone. She had gathered up all the linens, china, crystal and silver from the table, boxed it all up and .... "No, it can't be," she said as she moved toward the case and lifted the lid herself.

But it was. Sarah put her hands to her face and said: "How on earth did this get here and how did George find it. I buried this stuff in the ...." And then it came to her.

"Oh, my gosh, that's it." She bent down and gently removed one of the crystal glasses from the case. She turned to Paul, looked at him and crying asked: "Do you know what this is?"

293

"Yes, Sarah, I do. This is the very table setting you had on the table we used that evening when I ... when I ran away from you, when I said all those awful things to you. But how did it get here? This isn't where you buried it, is it?"

"No, sweetheart, this isn't where I buried it. I buried it in the same hole you fell into the night of the storm all those years ago. I'd borrowed one of George's ladders and a shovel and took this set in the box I'd put it all in and dug a hole at the bottom of a trench that connected to the hole you fell in. I guess the storm must have uncovered it and George found it sometime when he was in the hole with you the morning he found you or the next day when he and Sam inspected the hole," Sarah surmised.

"There's another envelope here, mom. Maybe dad will tell you about how he found it," Maggie pointed out as she retrieved the envelope from the case and handed it to her mother.

"Jim, may I borrow your knife for a few moments, please," Sarah asked.

Using Jim's knife, Sarah carefully opened the envelope, removed another piece of letterhead and read:

"My Dearest Sarah and My Friend Paul,

"Today has been both glorious and sobering. You, Sarah, just this morning told me we were having twins—what a way to get started with a family. Then, a little later, as I was filing some paper at my office, I stumbled on this Strange Treasure.

"Yes, Sarah, I found it where you buried it. The morning after we retrieved Paul from the hole, I'd gone there early, before Sam arrived to do our inspection and found it. I decided not to leave it there. I'd rebury it somewhere else. A sewer trench just didn't seem fitting to me.

"Anyway, after I got everything all cleaned up, I stuck it all in my file cabinet and forgot about it until today when quite by coincidence I opened the drawer where I'd put it.

"Well, as I looked at it, the Voice of the Spirit whispered: 'George, my dear, faithful son, I have a work for thee; but part of that work shall be in Paradise. And so, I shall call for thee sooner than thou shalt like for thou shalt not grow old with thy beloved Sarah. But, I shall prepare another for her, even Paul Tenter. He shall protect her, watch over her, thy children and

Agency and Consequences

grandchildren until he and Sarah shall be old. And then, I will call them home.

'Take, therefore, this treasure and hide it up until Sarah and Paul shall be married. Leave instructions for them that they may discover it; that they may know I have commanded thee; and that I have watched over them and prepared them. And let this be a testimony to them and thy children and grandchildren that I am God and that I love all them that serve me and keep my commandments. "And this according to the mind and will of the Lord, who ruleth over all flesh."[2] Even so, amen.'

"And so, with full faith the Lord was in charge and all things would come to pass and work together for good,[3] I have been obedient.

"Please know I love you all. And Paul, as you once said: '...of all the men I know, you're the only one worthy enough to be by Sarah's side. I sense you know what God will expect of you.'

"My Deepest and Eternal Love,
George

"P.S.
'So at night
I set fruit and grains
And little pots of wine and milk
Beside your soft earthen mounds,

And I often sing.'"[4]

* * * * *

Sarah lifted her tear-filled eyes from George's letter and there, standing next to the oak tree only 10 feet away, was the most glorious being she had ever beheld.

"He had on a loose robe of most exquisite whiteness. It was a whiteness beyond anything earthly [she] had ever seen .... His hands were naked, and his arms also, a little above the wrist; so, also, were his feet naked, as were his legs, a little above the ankles. His head and neck were bare. [She] could discover

> that he had no other clothing on but this robe, as it was open, so that [she] could see into his bosom.
>
> "Not only was his robe exceedingly white, but his whole person was glorious beyond description, and his countenance truly like lightning."[5]

He looked at Sarah with Eternal Love, raised his hand to his mouth and blew her a kiss. Immediately, she was enveloped with that same Spirit of love and a joy that were indescribably exquisite. He and she stood transfixed as they looked at and communed with each other for a mere few earthly seconds. And then she saw:

> "... the light ... gather immediately around the person of him ... and it continued to do so until ... [it was] just around him; when, instantly [she] saw, as it were, a conduit open right up into heaven, and he ascended till he entirely disappeared ...."[6]

THE END

End Notes

Preface

1. 2 Nephi 2:27

2. Doctrine and Covenants 130:20-21

3. Doctrine and Covenants 133:61.

4. Mosiah 3:19

5. 2 Corinthians 5:17. (Note: all Biblical references are from the King James Version.)

6. Genesis 37:15-17.

7. Mosiah 27:14.

Part One: The Man and The Hole

Chapter 1. The Man and The Woman

1. J. R. R. Tolkien, *The Lord of the Rings* (New York: Houghton Mifflin Company, 1994), 504, 823.

2. Ibid., 823.

3. Ibid., 943-944.

Chapter 4. Subconscious Memories

1. Daniel Ladinsky, ed., "We should Talk about this problem," *I Heard God laughing: Poems of Hope and Joy*, Renderings of Hafiz (New York: Penguin Books, 2006), 4.

2. Exodus 20:14.

3. Genesis 39:9.

4. Proverbs 31:10.

Chapter 6. Last Dinner Together

1. Tolkien, 823.

2. Ladinsky, 4.

Chapter 7. Release and Good Bye

1. Tolkien, 822.

2. Genesis 24:39, 41.

3. Tolkien, 943.

Chapter 12. Judgment and Mercy

1. Ladinsky, 4.

Part Two: The Strange Treasure

Chapter 19. No Secrets and Engagement

1. Ladinsky, 4.

2. Genesis 24:39, 41.

3. 1 Corinthians 13:12.

Chapter 21. Starting Life Together

1. G. Kenneth Cardwell, Letter to Joseph F. Cardwell (St. Peters, MO: November 27, 2007).

2. G. Kenneth Cardwell, "Prairie Diamond" (St. Peters, MO: an Unpublished Poem, 2003).

3. Ladinsky, 4.

Chapter 22. Honeymoon

1. Marjorie Holmes, *Two From Galilee: A Love Story of Mary and Joseph* (New York: Bantam Books, 1974), 13.

2. Tolkien, 504, 823.

3. Clare Middlemiss, comp., *Man May know for Himself: Teachings of President David O. McKay* (Salt Lake City: Deseret Book Company, 1967), 261.

4. Jeffrey R. Holland, *Of Souls, Symbols, and Sacraments* (Salt Lake City: Deseret Book Company, 2001).

Chapter 23. Paul's Confession

1. Acts 8:58-60.

Chapter 24. Ruse and Arrest

1. I Corinthians 13:1.

Chapter 26. Doubles

1. Holland.

2. Ed Ames, *My Cup Runneth Over*, www.LyricsDrive.com, 2008.

Chapter 27. Wonderful and Spontaneous

1. Genesis 3:23-24.

Part Three: Better That One Should Perish

Chapter 29. Right For Each Other

1. Parley P. Pratt, *The Autobiography of Parley P. Pratt* (Salt Lake City: Desert Book Company, 1973), 298.

2. Ibid., 297-298.

Chapter 30. Parenting

1. Randy Pausch with Jeffrey Zaslow, *The Last Lecture* (New York: Hyperion, 2008), 37.

2. 1 Nephi 17:19.

3. Ibid., 3:7.

Chapter 32. Narrow Escape

1. The Freedom Writers with Erin Gruwell, *Freedom Writers Diary: Their Story, Their Words* (New York: Broadway Books, 1999), 125-126.

2. *True Women*, Dir. Karen Arthur, with Dana Delany, Annabeth Gish, Angelina Jolie, Michael York, Jeffrey Nordling (Hallmark, 1998).

Agency and Consequences

3. *The Blind Side*, Dir. John Lee Hancock, with Sandra Bullock, Tim McGraw, Quinton Aaron, Kathy Bates (Warner Bros. Pictures, 2009).

Chapter 34. A Most Important and Sacred Subject

1. The Church of Jesus Christ of Latter-day Saints. *The Family: A Proclamation to the World.* (Salt Lake City: Intellectual Reserve, Inc., 1997).

2. Moses 2:28.

3. Ibid., 5:11.

4. G. Kenneth Cardwell, Letter to Joseph F. Cardwell (St. Peters, MO: November 27, 2007).

5. James E. Faust, "First Presidency Message: Fathers, Mothers, Marriage," *Ensign*, August 2004, 4.

Chapter 35. Council and Counsel at Midnight

1. M. Richard Walker and Kathleen H. Walker, *House of Learning: Getting More from Your Temple Experience* (Salt Lake City: Deseret Book Company, 2010), 31-39.

2. Doctrine and Covenants 8:2.

3. Ibid., 9:8.

4. The Church of Jesus Christ of Latter-day Saints. *The Family: A Proclamation to the World.* (Salt Lake City: Intellectual Reserve, Inc., 1997).

5. 2 Nephi 1:13-14, 21-23.

6. Ephesians 5:31.

7. Doctrine and Covenants 42:22.

G. Kenneth Cardwell

8. I Corinthians 6:19.

9. Abraham 4:18.

10. Doctrine and Covenants 93:30.

11. Ibid., 88:25.

12. Helaman 14:31.

13. Alma 41:12-13.

14. Ibid., 41:10.

15. 3 Nephi 27:11.

16. Helaman 13:38.

17. Doctrine and Covenants 137:9

18. 1 Peter 3:5.

19. 3 Nephi 27:27.

20. Alma 30:17

21. The Church of Jesus Christ of Latter-day Saints. *The Family: A Proclamation to the World.* (Salt Lake City: Intellectual Reserve, Inc., 1997).

22. Eliza R. Snow and James McGranahan, "O My Father," *Hymns of The Church of Jesus Christ of Latter-day Saints*, (Salt Lake City: The Church of Jesus Christ of Latter-day Saints, 1985), 292.

23. Clare Middlemiss.

24. Mathew 7:6.

Agency and Consequences

25. *Coal Minor's Daughter*, Dir. Michael Apted, with Sissy Spacek, Tommy Lee-Jones, Beverly Dangelo, Levon Helm (Universal City Studios, 1980).

26. Pratt, 297.

27. G. Kenneth Packer, "" (BYU Fireside, November 3, 1963).

28. G. Kenneth Cardwell, "Anticipation" (St. Peters, MO: an unpublished poem, October 8, 2007).

29. Stephen R. Covey, *The 7 Habits of Highly Effective People: Powerful Lessons in Personal Change* (New York: Simon & Schuster, 1989), 235-260.

30. Doctrine and Covenants 25:14, 16.

31. I Corinthians 13:12.

32. Pratt, 289.

33. Doctrine and Covenants 121:41-44.

Chapter 36. Braiding the Whip

1. Charles H. Gabriel, "I Stand All Amazed," *Hymns of The Church of Jesus Christ of Latter-day Saints*, (Salt Lake City: The Church of Jesus Christ of Latter-day Saints, 1985), 193.

2. G. Kenneth Cardwell, "Weekly Healing" (St. Peters, MO: an unpublished poem, June 13, 2004).

3. http://Community.webshots.com/photo/fullsize/2757946130052762935FpWcme. November 7, 2008. (Note: Because of the size of a Caterpillar D9 bulldozer, this author was not sure it could be transported by truck. This photo verified that it can be.)

4. Herbert L. Nichols Jr. and David A. Day, P.E., *Moving the Earth: The Workbook of Excavation*. 5th. Ed. (New York: McGraw-Hill, 2005), 2.20-2.37, 2.49-2.50, 3.7, 15.1, A.7. (Note: All the calculations of material moved in this story were based on the tables within this reference.)

5. Caterpillar Tractor Corporation Website. http:www.cat.com/cda/layout?m=1636328x=78f=1 51853. June 7, 2008. (Note: All dimensions, weights, capabilities and capacities of the bulldozer, Hidalgo, were taken from the specifications given at this website.)

6. Laura Hillenbrand, *Seabiscuit: An American Champion* (New York: Ballantine Books, 2001), 268.

7. John 2:13-17.

Chapter 37. The Demonstration

1. Caterpillar Tractor Corporation Website.

2. Nichols, 2.20-2.37, 2.49-2.50, 3.7, 15.1, A.7. (Note: All the calculations of material moved in this story were based on the tables within this reference.)

3. Nichols, 15.1.

4. Alan J. Lerner and Fredreck Loewe, *Camelot* (New York: Random House, 1961), 69-70, Act 1, Scene 11.

5. Ibid., 110, Act 2, Scene 8.

6. 1 Nephi 4:13.

Agency and Consequences

7. Nichols, 2.20-2.37, 2.49-2.50, 3.7, 15.1, A.7. (Note: All the calculations of material moved in this story were based on the tables within this reference.)

8. Ibid., 2.20-2.37, 2.49-2.50, 3.7, 15.1, A.7. (Note: All the calculations of material moved in this story were based on the tables within this reference.)

9. Tolkien, 822-824.

10. Jacob 2:7, 10.

Part Four: And The First Shall Be Last

Chapter 42. Tragedy

1. National Resources Conservation Service, Conservation Practice Standard, *Firebreak*, Code 394, May 2005, 1.

2. G. Kenneth Cardwell, "Amazing Grace" (St. Peters, MO: an unpublished poem, October 16, 2002).

Chapter 44. Date in Missouri

1. Doctrine and Covenants 6:12.

2. Ibid.

3. Ibid., 121:43.

4. Gail Langer Karwoski, *Seaman: The Dog Who Explored the West With Lewis & Clark* (Atlanta: Peachtree, 1999), 5, 7-8, 30, 74-77, 79-80, 147. (Note on this reference: while this is a book of historical fiction, only those incidents actually recorded in the official journals of Lewis and Clark are cited.)

G. Kenneth Cardwell

Chapter 45. Prepared for the Extemporaneous

1. Simona Cremante, *Leonardo da Vinci: Artist Scientist Inventor* (Florence, Italy: Giunti Editore S.p.A., 2005), 94.

2. James E. Faust, "10 Ways To Make A Difference," *New Era*, November 2004, 4.

3. Ibid.

4. 1 Nephi 17:17-19.

5. Ibid., 8:33.

6. Moroni 7:12-13.

7. Doctrine and Covenants 8:2-3.

8. Alma 7:11-12.

9. I Nephi 8:9, 11:25.

Chapter 46. Obstacles

1. Doctrine and Covenants 121:43.

2. *Freedom Writers*, Dir. Richard LaGravenese, with Hillary Swank, Scott Glenn, Imelda Staunton, Patrick Dempsey and Mario (Paramount Pictures, 2007).

Chapter 47. Sharing the Load

1. Doctrine and Covenants 6:14-16, 22-24.

2. Lerner and Loewe, *Camelot*, 55, Act 1, Scene 6.

3. Alan J. Lerner and Fredreck Loewe, *My Fair Lady*. (New York: Signet, 1956), 113, Act 2, Scene 4.

4. http://www.advexp.com/high.html.

5. Lerner and Loewe. *My Fair Lady*. 113, Act 2, Scene 4.

Chapter 49. Agency and Consequences

1. Doctrine and Covenants 130:20-21

2. 2 Nephi 2:27

3. Doctrine and Covenants 93:24

Chapter 50. The Fulcrum

1. Holland.

2. Nellie Talbot and E.O. Excell, "Jesus Wants Me For A Sunbeam," *Sing With Me: Songs for Children*, (Salt Lake City: Desert Book Company, 1969), B-67.

3. Lerner and Loewe. *My Fair Lady*. 113, Act 2, Scene 4.

4. David Nevin, *Meriwether: A Novel of Meriwether Lewis and the Lewis and Clark Expedition* (New York: Tom Doherty Associates, LLC, 2004), 33-35.

5. Alma 38:12.

6. Truman G. Madsen, *Four Essays on Love* (Provo, UT: Communications Workshop, 1971), 36-38.

Chapter 51. Ordeal

1. Doctrine and Covenants 122:7-9.

2. Alma 14:11.

3. Mormon 4:5.

G. Kenneth Cardwell

4. Doctrine and Covenants 135:4.

5. Helaman 7:19.

6. Moroni 9:9-10.

Chapter 52. Healing

1. *The Sound of Music*, Dir. Robert Wise, with Julie Andrews, Christopher Plummer, Richard Haydn, Peggy Wood and Eleanor Parker (Twentieth Century Fox, 1965).

2. Doctrine and Covenants 133:61.

3. Ibid., 90:24.

4. Ladinsky, 4.

5. JS-H 1:31-32.

6. Ibid., 43.

About the Author

Gaylen Kenneth Cardwell was born to Daniel Gaylen Cardwell and Vera Hazel Shoell March 4, 1948 in Salt Lake City, Utah. He grew up in Roy, Utah and graduated in 1966 from Roy High School in its first graduating class. He attended Weber State University on a track and cross-county scholarship before serving a mission for The Church of Jesus Christ of Latter-day Saints in England. Since his mission, he has served in many positions within the Church including Gospel Doctrine Instructor, High Counselor, Elders Quorum President, Scout Leader, Ward Clerk and Executive Secretary to three different Bishops. Currently he serves in the Cub Scout program and as a Temple Ordinance Worker.

Professionally, Mr. Cardwell is a 39-year logistics and supply chain professional. Most recently, he was a Senior Consultant with Logistics Management Institute (LMI) assigned to USTRANSCOM at Scott Air Force Base, IL. Previously, he worked in commercial business, as a defense contractor and academia. These included being a contractor through YOH Aviation to the Boeing Company at their Phantom Works Division; eight years with Spectrum Brands, the third ranked manufacturer of chemical products for home and garden use, as Manager, Freight Claims and Inventory; and as an Integrated Logistics Support Manager at ESCO (a former division of Emerson Electric) for the Combat Talon II Radar System. He is the author of four published papers with the International Society of Logistics. For nearly 20 years he was also an adjunct professor and member of the professional advisory boards for the Logistics program at St. Louis University and the Supply Chain Management program at the St. Louis Community College.

Mr. Cardwell holds both an A.A.S. in Transportation Management and a B.S. in Management Logistics from Weber State University in Ogden, UT. He also holds a two-year certificate in Traffic Management from the College of Advanced Traffic Management in Chicago, IL and is a Certified Professional Logistician and a Certified Adjunct Professor.

G. Kenneth Cardwell

Mr. Cardwell enjoys writing poetry, playing the trumpet, singing, camping, hiking, firing his trebuchet, serving in Boy Scouts and his church. He is married to the former Elizabeth Ann Smith. They raised three sons and one daughter and have one grandson. The Cardwell's live in St. Peters, Missouri, a suburb of St. Louis.

Made in the USA
Charleston, SC
21 May 2014